This book

Sandra Howard was one of the leading fashion models of the 1960s, appearing on the cover of *American Vogue* two months running. She worked as a freelance journalist alongside modelling, before turning to novel writing, and she continues to write regularly for the press. Sandra has three adult children and is married to the former Conservative Party leader, Michael Howard. They live in London and Kent.

You can discover more about the author at www.sandrahoward.co.uk

TELL THE GIRL

Married four times, Susannah Forbes once had an enviably starry career as a top model, mixing with luminaries and legends like Frank Sinatra, Marilyn Monroe and JFK. Her last marriage left her extremely well-off, and she is discovering that life as a rich, sought-after, still-beautiful widow has its compensations. Now, with an instinctive eye for colour and design, she finds herself in constant demand as an interior decorator. Offered a commission by a recently divorced American to make over his lavish Long Island home, Susannah accepts, bringing as her assistant a young divorcée, Daisy Mitchell. But below the surface, insecurity and infidelity are rife . . .

SANDRA HOWARD

TELL THE GIRL

Complete and Unabridged

CHARNWOOD
Leicester

First published in Great Britain in 2014 by
Simon & Schuster UK Ltd
London

First Charnwood Edition
published 2015
by arrangement with
Simon & Schuster UK Ltd
London

This book is a work of fiction. Names, characters, places and incidents are either a product of the author's imagination or are used fictitiously.

A catalogue record for this book is available from the British Library.

ISBN 978–1–4448–2632–6

Published by
F. A. Thorpe (Publishing)
Anstey, Leicestershire

Set by Words & Graphics Ltd.
Anstey, Leicestershire
Printed and bound in Great Britain by
T. J. International Ltd., Padstow, Cornwall

This book is printed on acid-free paper

For Michael — always

For what is knowledge duly weighed?
Knowledge is strong, but love is sweet;
Yea, all the progress he had made
Was but to learn that all is small
Save love, for love is all in all.
Christina Rossetti

But only this:
No reason ask of Love.
John Marston

Prologue

Susannah Forbes had kept up a long vigil. She'd brought reading matter, newspapers, a biography of Harper Lee written by a close friend, but had hardly turned a page. Most of the time her eyes had been on the still shape under the hospital sheets, the blue lips, the slack, slipped jaw. There was no visible rise and fall of the chest, no restless turning. When she had touched the back of Clive's hand, the extreme chill had transmitted itself. The intensive care unit had felt cold enough to be a morgue.

The pauses in his breathing had become longer. He'd been in a semi-coma, but even so tried at times to speak. Susannah had leaned closer, listening hard, murmuring encouragement, hollow words about pulling through. She'd willed him to say more than faint unintelligible mumbles, something to hold onto, some last thread of connection, if not hope.

The mass of beeping high-tech equipment had made the cubicle look like the cockpit of a plane. But all the dials and graphs on the screens had been plain to read, with every jiggering, jittery line undeniably on a nosedive.

The hospital team had explained that Mr Barfield's severely increased respiratory congestion, the thirty-point drop from normal blood pressure and his inability to swallow were all signs, but they couldn't tell exactly when death

1

would occur. It was a time to be realistic and compassionate, they said; time to let go. Her presence at the bedside would be reaching him, helping and giving him peace.

'Talk to me, darling,' Susannah had whispered, bending over the bed once more, staring steadily into his ashen sagging face. 'Hold on, find the strength. You can do it.'

Clive had opened his eyes. His lips moved. 'These last . . . months . . . such joy, more than I could . . . You must . . . be . . . ' His breathing paused again and that was it, nothing more. No more words.

★ ★ ★

It was three years since Clive had died; hectic, stimulating years in a terrific new career, which at Susannah's age was against any yardstick and the longest odds. She'd had the same amazing luck in her first career as a photographic model. That had soared too, with bewildering speed in the high-drama times of her twenties; instant success at both ends of her working life and a rainbow arc of love, emotion and disillusionment in between. Not bad going.

She was going to a dinner party. She'd had a busy, productive day and stepping into a black silk dress, fastening a plaited gold chain around her neck, Susannah was mystified by her edgy, unsettled mood. She wandered into the living-room where the window of her penthouse flat spanned the longest wall.

Susannah stood gazing out, listening to the

2

filtered sounds: a faint murmur of traffic, the whipping and whistling of a fierce wind. The flat overlooked the playing fields and tennis courts of Burton Court, a great open space in front of the splendid Royal Hospital, designed by Wren and home to the Chelsea Pensioners. Darkness had fallen, but a familiar line of tall lime trees was just visible, their leafless branches weaving and swaying as though to music. In the street-lit distance were the elegant Georgian houses of St Leonard's Terrace, tall and sought-after. It was London at its most beautiful.

The dinner was in Chester Square, a mile away at most, and Susannah decided to walk. It felt contrary, being buffeted by a fearsome wind on the way to a formal do, but it suited her mood. Her black velvet evening shoes were lowish-heeled and she had a pale ivory leather coat, snugly warm and satin-soft with a delicate sheen like mother-of-pearl that shouldn't look too out of place.

She wished she hadn't accepted the invitation, something she felt too often these days, as the evening stood little chance of being fun. The hosts, Maynard and Ginny Wilson, who weren't close friends, clung to the formalities of Maynard's past career. He was an ex-ambassador, his last posting in the Balkans. A physically insubstantial man, he looked as though a punch would leave a hollow, and he wouldn't have fared well at a rugby-playing school. He was likeable enough, mild-mannered and amenable, while Ginny was ingratiating, adept at exploiting people's kindnesses; any return of favours seemed an entirely alien concept to her. She had slightly protruding, staring eyes, yet had perfected the kind of helpless looks of entreaty guaranteed to bring out the protective instinct in any male. Ginny had money of her own and Maynard was in business now too — making a packet, it would seem.

Susannah shrugged on her leather coat, faintly imbued with her Chanel scent and as softly supple as luxury car seating. Posh, her skinny little Siamese cat, was rubbing round her ankles. 'Lucky Posh puss,' she muttered, bending to stroke her. Leaving the flat, she tried to think more positively; the Wilsons spread their net wide — you never knew.

The chill April wind tugged viciously at her hair and took her breath away. She skirted round the south side of Burton Court with her mind on penthouses; wistfully on her own, the cosy evening in she was missing, but also on Jimmy Rose's. It had been his luxury apartment, after all, with its fabulous views up and down the Thames that had managed to turn her life on its head. Susannah still found it hard to believe.

Jimmy was a delightful, sprightly man with expensive tastes in property, cigars and champagne. He was a wine dealer and Conservative Party treasurer, and a few years ago had asked her round for a drink, saying he wanted a quiet word, just the two of them. He'd pressed on her a glass of his best vintage champagne and joked about the latest political mess-up before bouncing her with a proposition. He wanted her to redecorate his pad.

'And I'm talking a proper business deal here,

Susannah. I love your style, a whole lot more than many a top designer I could name. I won't take no for an answer.'

She'd protested. Jimmy was a wonderful friend and she knew he admired her own home, but she was no decorator and couldn't possibly take it on. 'I'd only do it as a loss leader,' she said finally, weakening, flattered and tempted, secretly longing to give it a go.

That conversation had taken place before her marriage to Clive. Although comfortably off at the time, Susannah had never been in the penthouse league. Her parents had struggled, she'd had a childhood of making do. Becoming a successful photographic model had been head-spinning, yet her first husband's debts had left their finances strained. She'd remarried, twice, and lost her third husband, Edward, to a brain tumour. It had been a wretched, desolate time, but life moved on and she needed a fresh challenge, like trying her hand at interior design.

A couple of years later, at one of Jimmy's drinks parties for his rich cosmopolitan friends, everyone had cooed and raved about the new décor. They'd been wowed by its recent makeover, the glass cubes and lightness, touches of vivid colour; high praise from a roomful of blasé sophisticates. Jimmy had bowed theatrically and held out a hand to Susannah. It was all down to her, he said, basking in the glow. The credit was entirely hers.

By then, Susannah had done up another penthouse and a lavish apartment in Eaton Square. She'd formed her own company, Susannah Forbes

Design, and had other commissions in the pipeline, new clients dangling plans.

The apartment in Eaton Square had been testing. She'd felt doomed, done for, as though her parachute had stuck fast and on only her second jump. The client, a statuesque Texan heiress, had known exactly what she wanted, thank you very much. No fresh, innovative designs, clean lines and Italian modernity; her eye was in for rich, heavy silks and brocades. She'd dug in her bejewelled heels and refused to budge. Susannah had despaired. Yet realism about who was pay-mistress soon kicked in and, swallowing her pride, she had walled the Texan's entire dining room in sumptuous gold-threaded brocade. With a set of fourteen high-backed chairs upholstered to match, the room had certainly made a statement.

The Texan blonde giantess had been ecstatic. It was precisely the French-château, Marie-Antoinette feel she was after, she'd enthused, promising to spread the word from Louisiana to Long Island, London to the South of France.

Magazines and newspapers had begun to do features and interviews. Susannah was a much-married top model, often in the gossip columns, and with her sudden success as a designer, the spanking richness of her clients, the media had gone to town.

⋆ ⋆ ⋆

She was almost at the Wilsons', walking up Chester Row, a graceful narrow slip of a street

6

that led to the Square. Recalling Jimmy's drinks party had made her feel sorrowful, even a little fearful, and she strained to think why. It was a culmination, she decided — a warning signal perhaps, that the more soaring of life's highs were over and its winding down had begun. Depressing. Susannah bridled at the thought.

She'd been seeing a bit of Clive Barfield in the months before Jimmy's party, bald-headed Clive, a seventy-year-old businessman, a captain of industry with cheeks as saggy as a Beagle's and a trad, timid taste in clothes. He'd first asked her out a year after the death of her third husband, Edward. Clive had made no demands, he'd understood and known her fragile state. Kind, unexciting Clive had been about the only person whose company she could have borne.

Edward had died suddenly, struck down as though by the force of God's mighty hand, leaving Susannah adrift, unable ever to imagine normal life again. Edward had been her foreground, her horizon, and now she was in a wasteland, alone. He'd come into her life when she was twice divorced and still only thirty. Her unflinching certainty about the wisdom of marrying him had amazed no one more than herself.

It had been quite as brave of Edward. He'd ignored all the guarded comments, warnings from friends, and taken her on, along with her eight-year-old daughter, five-year-old dog and two cats of considerable age. Edward hadn't been especially beautiful, with thinning hay-coloured hair that was soft to stroke and touch; a

7

strong straight nose and deep, chestnut-brown eyes that invariably reflected his moods. They'd radiated love and responsiveness, glittered with his impossibly quick temper. Thirty feisty, passionate, sparring, loving years: more than her fair share.

Edward had been an economist, moving in political and business circles. He and Susannah had often had friends to kitchen supper, and when he'd happened to meet and like Clive Barfield he'd suggested asking him along. He'd be good balance for some of the shouters amongst their friends. Clive had become quite a regular after that.

Clive had never married. He was a workaholic, gripped by the need to succeed and perhaps lacking the active libido that might have seen him paired off at an early stage of life. But whatever the married joys and woes he'd missed out on, Clive had struck gold with his non-stick kitchenware business. He'd broken the French stranglehold on that market with solid, well-designed and sensibly priced goods. Pots and pans had made him a very rich man.

He was a dry seventy-year-old and Susannah was no girl. Clive wasn't without a humorous side, yet his expression was so naturally solemn, he was always so thoughtful and slow that any flashes of wit came as something of a surprise. He'd taken her to theatres and films during the year before Jimmy's drinks party, they'd had dinner together, lunch or a drink in the garden of his duplex flat in Little Venice, that quietly posh corner of London. They'd nattered about plants, paintings, Susannah's children; Clive always seemed genuinely interested in their doings, despite having no family of his own. He'd never put her under any pressure, a squeeze of the hand, a kissed cheek — a peck on the lips once or twice.

She hadn't talked to Clive at Jimmy's party, being keen to have useful conversations and make eye-contact with potential clients; she was being feted and praised and loving it. The champagne was Dom Perignon, the canapés, dainty morsels: quail's eggs, mini rolls of rare beef, blinis with a mere scraping of caviar. No more healthy, hefty scoops of the stuff. Even Jimmy was feeling the national pinch, it seemed.

An American, Warren Lindsay, had discussed the décor with Susannah while showing a flattering, more personal interest as well. He then began to pour out his personal woes. Warren was mid-divorce and wearyingly bitter, the scars of battle uncomfortably exposed.

'She's a vulture, that woman, but she's not going to win. I can be pushed just so far . . . ' Warren's honey-bronze eyes had hardened under the jut of a broad brow.

Was he trying to convince himself, Susannah wondered, or was he simply a man of ruthless, unflinching determination? He was her sort of age, possibly a bit younger, with a good head of dark hair, flecked all over with grey-white specks like rocks by the sea. He hadn't mentioned dinner and hadn't really been seeing her, Susannah felt, hard as he'd stared. It had been a slight anti-climax since people were drifting off and it was a natural time to have suggested coming out for a meal. She'd moved away, feeling a mild sense of failure and also that she should really catch up with good-natured Clive.

Susannah remembered thinking he looked even more sombre and lugubrious than usual that evening. He had inclined his head to a quiet spot where the view up and down the Thames was truly spectacular with the lights of London spangling the dark. 'Can we go over there?' he asked her. 'I'd like to propose something, if you wouldn't mind.'

'I've been propositioned in this flat before,' she laughed, walking with him.

'Why? Has Jimmy . . . ?' The air around them was suddenly electric and she saw a previously unknown side of Clive — the steely, formidable force in the boardroom side.

'God no, that's hardly Jimmy's thing! I just meant the decorating job.'

'I wanted to mention this idea in advance,' Clive said gravely, 'to give you plenty of room for manoeuvre. If you don't hate the very thought of it, though, perhaps we could have dinner and, well, talk about it.' He gave one of his rare grins. 'But this little gift,' he said, pressing a small pouch into her palm, 'is quite unconnected. It's for you to keep, whatever you decide.' He smiled more gently, and she did too, amazed beyond belief. He took her arm and they went together to say their goodbyes.

The gift had been a sumptuous single diamond. Converted into a ring, its scintillations were like flames of white fire. It was staggering.

Susannah wore it on evenings out and, walking now to Chester Square, kept her hand in her coat pocket. She glanced down at it wistfully, arriving at the Wilsons' doorstep, thinking how much she owed to Clive. Not least the six wonderfully contented months of marriage before he'd caught pneumonia three years ago, suffered the complications of diabetes, and died.

She put her lips to the ring with a fond heart then banged down the doorknocker. Chester Square was Georgian splendour, magnificent houses, but — probably because of her feelings about Ginny — the Wilsons' house somehow gave off a reek of superior exclusiveness that got up Susannah's nose. The buffed-up brasswork on its sleek, black-painted front door could have been on military parade.

The door was opened silently and the Filipino waiter behind it took her coat. Another waiter escorted her upstairs. Susannah could hear the clink and chatter coming from the first-floor drawing room. She braced herself and prepared to greet her hosts.

1

'Sorry, I didn't quite catch your name when we were being introduced upstairs.' My neighbour at the dinner table gave a thin, bored smile.

'Susannah Forbes,' I said, slightly annoyed. Our hosts, Ginny and Maynard Wilson, had sent a guest list very properly, for the avoidance of any festering vendettas, and it seemed reasonable to expect him to have slotted me in. I turned my place-card his way for emphasis and leaned to peer unnecessarily at his. 'And you're Godfrey Croft, I see.'

I'd absorbed from the list that Mr Croft was married — to Hilary — and a senior player in a private equity firm. He had the comfortable girth of good-restaurant living, close-cropped grey hair, disinterested eyes; he fitted my idea of the City stereotype. Not so surprising then that my name with the tag of 'interior designer' hadn't made it onto his radar when international banker might have registered.

'Do you have . . . is your husband here?' He looked vaguely up and down the table.

'No, the last two died on me.'

'Oh.' Godfrey sat up a bit. 'So your name . . . '

'Is my own, not my last husband's.'

'And is that Forbes, as in the Rich List?' He smiled, showing a little more interest, sneaking a glance at my diamond ring.

'Yes, and some might say I'm rich, but I'm not

on the List and no relation,' I twinkled at him with more warmth. That must have sounded very arch. An almost reverential gleam had come into his eye with the mention of the Forbes List, but I wasn't on it and he wearily offered me the butter dish with a muttered whinge about olive oil being a healthier option. 'Butter has lots of vitamins,' I said cheerfully, digging into the pat. 'A, D and E.'

Some people could be boring in an interesting way but not, on present evidence, Mr Croft. It was too soon to write him off, though. He could be an impressive academic sort of banker, a recovering alcoholic, a demon in the sack; no one was irredeemably dull.

'Did you think of the Forbes List as a way to log in my name like the Americans do?' I asked. 'Like thinking of belly to summon up Kelly, say, with someone overweight?'

'Oh, no, not at all. I'd be very bad at anything like that.' He gave his thin smile.

'Me, too,' I agreed sympathetically, 'and I'd probably only remember the prompt!'

We relapsed into silence. The wine and the first course, a salad with warm smoked duck, were being served. Godfrey was certainly making me feel my age.

His wife, Hilary, was opposite, friendly-faced, countrified-looking; conventionally dressed in a turquoise silk dress and jacket. She was studying her plate rather forlornly, stuck between a Brazilian businessman and a rascally, acerbic theatre critic called Bertrand Joseph, whom I knew. Bertie looked despairing, trapped, his

14

mouth in a downward droop. It wasn't the wittiest of seating plans. Maynard and Ginny Wilson were seasoned diplomats, after all: whatever had they been thinking of?

They were at each end of the Tonelli, black-glass table. Maynard was next to the voluble Greek wife of a government minister who was speaking fast, waving her arms about, and he had the frozen smile on his face of someone who'd lost the thread and was trying to avoid being found out. Ginny, on the other hand, was busily turning it on for the French Ambassador, overdoing the flutter-eyed charm.

Bertie made no effort to entertain poor Hilary Croft; I watched him trying to attract the attention of Ruth Travers, a much-loved actor, quick-tongued and idiosyncratic, seated further down the table on my side. Ruth's face was as wizened as a lizard's, yet it had the sort of strong-nosed ugliness that has its own attraction. She dressed with great style and was wearing a ruby-red crushed velvet number tonight, with a dramatically upstanding collar.

'Hey, Ruthie,' Bertie called across. 'I saw that talentless old ex of yours finally kicked it the other day. Did you go to the poor bugger's funeral?'

'No,' she drawled, eyeing him lazily from under hooded lids. 'In fact, I rather regret going to the wedding.'

It had been said before, but her delivery was perfect. Half the table had smiles.

'But it can't, in fact, be very easy, can it — going to an ex's funeral?' Hilary Croft said, taking it seriously. 'Embarrassing for the grieving relatives, I imagine, especially if they'd taken sides. Awkward for any new partner, too . . . ' She tailed off as her remarks fell leadenly and everyone nearby stayed silent. She looked agonised.

'Susannah went to one of her exes's funerals,' Ginny piped up with her usual bitchiness. 'Max's, wasn't it, Susannah? I remember the pictures in the newspapers.'

'So, not one of your weddings you'd regretted then?' Bertie threw in waspishly. 'And did that air-head new little wife of his look daggers at you through her tears?'

The Brazilian's wife on my neighbour Godfrey's other side peered round him with a fascinated stare, hanging on my answer, but Maynard benignly came to my aid.

'I go to so many funerals and memorials these days,' he said. 'More of my friends seem to die than give dinner parties!' A few awkward titters rippled round, though I felt the joke had a slightly callous ring. 'And I'm surprised how often they've minutely planned their own,' Maynard continued. 'An elevated friend of mine, who shall be nameless, made it his express wish that a man he'd loathed all his life be asked to give the address — to savour the thought of him squirming with embarrassment, I suppose, feeling unable to refuse.'

Plates were being cleared, claret poured. Godfrey was discreetly picking at a back tooth with his little finger, the chewy smoked duck giving problems. I eyed the young woman on my other side, Daisy Mitchell, who had an appealing profile. She wasn't a beauty, but had a lively mobile face with a generous mouth and clear light skin. Her striking sea-green eyes would hold anyone captive, and she had an enjoyable way of bubbling-over; I'd seen her talking to Maynard before dinner, tossing back her light-brown hair. She was in a flame-red dress with criss-cross straps, short and sassy.

Daisy was wearing a wedding ring, and the absent husband, if she wasn't divorced, must be a diplomat or business friend of the Wilsons', I presumed. It was a bit of a raw deal for her tonight, stuck between an older woman and the overweight fogey on her other side. An opera singer, a single man who would have evened up the sexes, had cried off apparently with a sore throat.

Godfrey was sipping the claret with a dubious expression and I said, trying to be friendly, 'You look like a serious connoisseur.'

'I don't know about that,' he replied with unconscious immodesty, swilling the wine in his glass with calculated care, 'although strictly entre nous, I do find this Pichon Lalande a touch insubstantial.' He smiled. 'But then I'm more of a burgundy man.'

'Oh dear, that shows how little I know! I'd thought it rather smooth and good. Only because of having it with a friend, though, I expect, whose son's in the wine trade. He loves the job, has finally found his niche, to his mother's relief. He'd tried to get into insurance, but when asked at interview what appealed to him about the business, he said he felt it had a rather romantic side. They didn't take him on! Still, top marks for originality, don't you think?'

'Not really,' Godfrey said, speaking as patiently as he would to a child, instead of a neighbour at dinner who'd been weakly attempting a bit of levity. 'I'd want people who skipped the romantic waffle and saw the appeal of the profit-making side. I mean, don't you rather enjoy having money?'

I smiled but didn't reply, with no desire to start arguing about creativity, job satisfaction and community spirit. His lip would have curled.

An elderly waiter was patiently holding out a vast oval dish of small pink lamb cutlets. His hands had a tremble and I hurriedly took a couple of cutlets and watercress. It was a natural break, time to swap sides, which I did with a relieved parting smile. Godfrey had smugly enjoyed having the last word, while I thought he was a chauvinist prat.

★ ★ ★

'I've been dying to meet you,' Daisy Mitchell said. 'I'm such a huge fan from all the fabulous pictures I've seen of your interiors, the spreads and features. There's so much I'd love to ask, about your past amazing career as well, but I'm sure it's the last thing you need.'

'Of course not, ask away. I'm only sorry you're stuck with me and not next to some dishy attentive young man.' I let my eyes roam the table. 'Though where you'd go for that sort of

18

honey tonight . . . ' Daisy gave a little giggle. She inclined her head towards the person on her other side. 'Not there,' she whispered. 'He's pickled in aspic. I didn't know guys like that still existed. He thinks the glass ceiling is made of cellophane and we 'gels' don't cut it. He's such a throwback.'

'Not to me, I know a few.' I knew her neighbour for a start, a pompous twerp who headed a family packaging business. 'Tell me about yourself, Daisy. Are you working?'

She grimaced. 'Kind of. Not enough. I write a cookery column and occasional stories for magazines. I need to do more, but I've just got divorced, all very messy and tacky, and it's impossibly hard to focus. I'm so in awe and envious of your fantastic new career. It's brilliant!'

'Pure luck, more like — a friend who had a few clients with bottomless bank balances giving me a break. But you could change course, too. Any interests aside from cooking?'

'I love art and design, but I'm not trained and doing a course would cost money, which is a bit tight right now. My ex-husband had a good lawyer.'

'Children?'

'Twin boys of nineteen; they're non-identical, different in every way.'

'But you can't be out of your thirties yet,' I said, with genuine surprise.

'Almost,' Daisy said, looking pleased. 'I'm nearly thirty-nine. The boys are from a very brief early marriage — this is my second divorce, I'm afraid. You married young too, didn't you, the first time?'

'Yes, I was eighteen. My daughter from that marriage is older than you. Things were bad, but I hung on. Divorcing in those days took serious legal perseverance.'

'You were a top model so it must have been extra hard, being in the public eye. You worked in New York as well, didn't you? Did you take your daughter with you?'

'Sure, she was only a year old. I'd had a nanny in London and took her, too. She was a cantankerous old bird, never out of her brown Norland Nanny uniform and neurotic about her age; she refused ever to let me see her passport. Manhattan wasn't her natural habitat; she wheeled a stately second-hand Silver Cross pram around town, looking suspicious and disapproving like a grumpy old Mary Poppins, yet I grew very fond of her over time. But how do you know so much about my past? It's prehistoric!'

'There's been a lot written. And my mother kind of followed you and kept articles from magazines.' Daisy blushed sweetly, reddening the more as she dug in deeper, trying to flatter me. 'She was a bit older than you, of course. She'd have been seventy this year.'

'Your mother died young?'

'Twenty years ago, of breast cancer. My father's remarried and I'm good with my stepmother. I like her — she's French and grew up in a château. My dad runs a health farm in Sussex.'

The dessert was served, a medley of mini-puds: a pink mush in a thimble-thin glass, a split strawberry, a blob of green ice cream and a teeny chocolate tart.

'Too catered-looking,' Daisy murmured. 'I think the food for dinners at home should look as if there's a nice comfortable cook downstairs, a Mrs Patmore of *Downton Abbey.*'

Daisy was fun with her green-eyed sparkiness. She went into raptures about the dining-room décor; she must have known I'd had a hand in it. Ginny had wanted help with a wall-colour, but soon had me doing the whole room — for love, which I didn't feel. The walls were now deep crimson; shiny black bowls of white tulips stretched all down the table, and two life-sized statues, elegant armless ladies, stood at the window end of the room. They'd been unseen, gathering moss in the unused, paved back garden and I'd persuaded Ginny to bring them indoors. Along with Maynard's abstract paintings, his Wendy Lehmans, they added a touch of class.

Ginny rose to her feet and tinkled a glass. 'Coffee upstairs,' she said bossily, smiling then, as if to convey it was all about consideration for the staff. 'Let's go on up.'

With much scraping of chairs — Godfrey radiating pique — we did as we were told. In the sitting room, where trays of coffee and herbal tea were circulating, Hilary Croft sought me out, to my surprise. She seemed nervous and took sips of black coffee before speaking, as though internally phrasing her words.

'I, um, wanted to apologise for that silly, unfortunate remark about funerals,' she said. 'I'd been feeling so out of my depth and was trying

21

to appear a little less than inadequate, I suppose, though it had the opposite effect. Do forgive me.'

It was warm and generous and I assured her that nothing could matter less.

'I had a very enjoyable time with Godfrey,' I said, being shamelessly disingenuous, 'though I suspect he was humouring me a little when we talked about money.'

'He thinks of nothing else. I despair.' Hilary sighed bitterly, revealing the stresses of her marriage. She gave a wan smile. 'Better go. We're driving back to Hampshire and I can see Godfrey's impatient to be off. Bye, then — and thanks for being so understanding.'

'Time I was off too,' I said, grabbing my chance. 'I'll leave with you.'

We started a stampede. Everyone took their cue, milling round to say goodbye, and I had to wait to thank Ginny, mentally drumming my fingertips as the French Ambassador bade her a flowery farewell. The Crofts were already out of the door.

Daisy came alongside. 'I've so loved meeting you, had such a cool time,' she said. Then, hesitating: 'I don't suppose — I mean, could you ever bear to come and have lunch one day? I'm just over the bridge in Battersea, not very far.'

'Love to,' I said, fishing in my bag for a card. 'Thanks, that sounds great.'

She gave me a quick hug like one of my children, and darted off, bouncy and breezy as ever. 'Bye, Ginny,' she called out blithely, over the smooth dark head of the diminutive French Ambassador. 'Lovely party!'

There were a couple of messages on my voicemail. I played the first while kicking off my shoes. It was from Charles Palmer, one of my oldest and dearest friends, a biographer who lived in rural North Norfolk and was writing a book on the zoo owner, John Aspinall. Charles hadn't been to London in weeks. It was partly the cause of my edginess. What was the point of having a friend and long-time occasional lover if he never showed? He could get in his car . . .

I listened to his message resentfully. Charles sounded miffed, too. 'Where are you? Why don't you ever pick up? Call me, late as you like. I'll have to open another bottle of whisky.'

I loaded up my face with another useless miracle cream. In the past Charles had asked me to live with him, to move into his sub-zero, rambling Queen Anne home that was a rat-run for every gusting gale. Climbing into bed, I visualised the house with its symmetry and distant view of the sea, the wind howling like a demon possessed, windows rattling in their sashes, draughts extinguishing the flame on the ancient boiler, hardly in functioning order on a good day. As regularly as Charles had asked, I'd refused.

I shifted up in bed to lean against the headboard and dialled his number, stretching pleasurably in anticipation, always ready to hear his resonant voice. 'Hi,' I said. 'I was only at a Wilsons' dinner party — for want of anything better to do. How's the writing going?'

'Don't ask. I've had a stream of callers, no chance of an uninterrupted flow. The postman's dusting off his caravan, but his wife thinks the weather has to turn. Mrs Selling came about a good cause and talked about her tits — the garden variety; I kept remembering a line in a play, about a woman getting her tits stuck in the letter box. Then my neighbour Mr Hetherington turned up, very full of a clue in yesterday's crossword.'

'Which was?'

''Primate'. He'd thought of 'chimpanzee' which fitted and been chuffed with himself, but discovered today the correct answer was 'archbishop'! So how was it at the Wilsons', as balls-aching as can be expected? I'd go a long way *not* to have dinner with Ginny.'

'All the way to Norfolk?'

'Don't be sarky.'

'It could have been worse. I had an invitation to lunch.'

'Oh. Don't tell me you've found another Clive.'

'Why always assume it's a man? It was from a girl, almost half my age. She must want something, which isn't rocket science since she's broke, done over in a recent divorce. I think I'll go, though; she was refreshing and fun, plenty of chutzpah. She writes a cookery column too, so the food shouldn't be bad.'

'Don't be in a grump,' Charles said. 'I miss you all the same, though.'

Why didn't he do something about it then?

I said a chilly goodbye while feeling a warm

24

burn of contact. Charles was like a sip of the finest brandy, in many ways.

I played the second message.

'It's Warren Lindsay. You may not remember, but we met at Jimmy Rose's, quite a while ago now. I loved what you'd done to his penthouse and took your card. I'm just passing through, on an early plane tomorrow, but I'm anxious to talk to you about doing up my house on Long Island. I'd be grateful if you could call; any time up until about one tonight is fine. I'm on a different time clock.'

It was twelve-thirty. I debated it for a moment, but decided to call.

Warren described the house in detail: eight bedrooms, large reception rooms, pool, sundeck and more. Some house . . . Warren explained that he was finally divorced and wanted a clean break. 'No reminders, no stick of furniture, no hammock on the deck, you'd have a complete free hand.'

That was rare.

'It's a big job,' I told him. 'It would take months. And I'd need an assistant, probably. You'd be into substantial costs.'

'That's not a problem. I had in mind your coming for part of the summer and staying in the house as my guest, to make it easier. I'd be in Manhattan during the week. I have a cook and maid to see to all your needs and I hope you'd allow me to entertain you at weekends.'

Did I need that in my life? At my age, being chased round the ex-wife's furniture, even before the new was installed?

25

'I'll need to sleep on it,' I said, wishing I'd chosen another expression. 'Send me an email and I'll get back to you in a couple of days.'

Lying in bed, I considered it long and hard. Only the pinpoint reading light was on and the bedroom looked soft and shadowy, ivory and apricot, with the scent of some lily-of-the-valley in a vase, deliciously intense. A huge pine armoire and hand-painted French dressing screen gave the room height and form. My bed was sumptuously comfortable, but it was the size of a playground, built for a *ménage à trois* or even *à cinq*.

I stretched out a toe and felt the cool barren expanse. I had a clear recollection of Warren Lindsay, the grey-speckled hair, his crinkly, earnest gaze and the meaner frown when speaking of his wife. He'd made quite an impression. I could even remember the sense of anti-climax I'd felt when he hadn't suggested dinner as expected.

Did I want to be away most of the summer, missing the best of my South of France garden? It would mean giving up a few summery weekends in Norfolk, too. I made the journey for those. It was boring and selfish of Charles, fossilizing up there for the rest of the year with his deadline and love of his crumbling creeper-clad home.

Would Stephanie move in, man the office and cat-mind? She was elderly, my PA, and lived alone; she'd probably quite enjoy it. I'd done up a house in Connecticut, an apartment in New York, I knew the American scene. And I should be able to find an assistant, someone to do the legwork, the inevitable running around.

Everything seemed to be pointing to heading out west this summer, but I'd known that right away really, talking to Warren Lindsay on the phone.

2

Daisy stared at the text. She'd been drifting off, but heard it come through and knew it would be Simon. Fuck, what did she do now? Call Susannah Forbes first thing in the morning and say she was ill? That was bound to ring false. It would need to be some pretty high drama; a headache was hardly going to do. Daisy bit on her lip, wide awake now, her heart thumping with indecision. She could always tell the truth, of course — that her married lover was suddenly free and she was incapable of turning him away.

A familiar ache of longing rose like quicksilver and snaked through her body, taking instant hold. She imagined Simon rushing her upstairs as he always did, the fierce silent lovemaking, the heaven of it when he stayed on afterwards, sitting about in the kitchen as though he belonged. Daisy gave a deep sigh. She knew he'd never leave his wife, however much he bitched about her. She was the moneybags. He talked big about doing deals, but was employed by her, in fact, helping with the accessories shops she owned; his children were still very young as well. Daisy was everything to him, he said, but they were empty words.

So what, if she had to ditch Susannah Forbes? It had been a mad impulse, asking her, a vague cockeyed hope of something flowing from it, some miraculous lead into who knew what?

Would Susannah agree to postpone lunch? But it wouldn't happen, not if she cancelled this time, Daisy thought miserably; stuff always got in the way. And now she was going to worry all night and look a shagged-out, bag-eyed wreck for Simon into the bargain.

She texted him back. *Can u make it 3? Old bird to lunch, bit diff to chuck. Need to c u, burning up. xx.* Worth a try, after all. His timing could be elastic — he didn't live by lunch-hours, and sex came before food in Simon's book; her cooking was never a priority. Daisy grimaced. He could have the remains of Susannah's lunch for his tea.

He rang early in the morning while she was still running a gamut of excuses in her head. 'Three o'clock's better, in fact,' he said. 'I was thinking I mightn't be able to make it — someone I need to see. Anyone I know, this bint who's coming to lunch who's so important to you?'

'She's not! You are. I'll tell you about her over tea.' Daisy felt quite light-headed.

It made precautionary sense, she felt, to call Susannah and suggest she came at twelve-thirty. Frustratingly, her phone was on voicemail; Daisy left a message.

She would wear the shell-pink cashmere top that Simon liked, a grey flared skirt and ankle boots, but jeans while she cooked. Wild mushroom risotto, she'd thought. The final stage could be done with Susannah there. They'd be eating at the kitchen table, after all — she could sit with a drink. Daisy prepared a tomato and

29

basil salad, washed a garden lettuce and mixed up a lemony dressing. Its piquant scent tingled her nose and cut into the smell of the onions sautéing in the heavy cast-iron pan. Homemade lemon and lime ice cream, thinly sliced oranges; there was a delicious gorgonzola stinking out the fridge, the reduced-price grapes ... Daisy cooked a batch of gooey brownies while she was at it. Simon could have some later.

She checked round. The sitting room was looking fresh and summery, despite it being a cold windy April. It almost resembled a room set for a Noël Coward play with the baby grand piano that had been her mother's — which took up half the room — and Daisy's extravagance of armfuls of fragrant, creamy-pink Angélique tulips. She felt wired up with tension, fiddling, rearranging the flowers. How would it be with Susannah? Two weeks had passed since the Wilsons' dinner ...

The house, two tiny Battersea cottages knocked through, was still small and a squash when her six-foot sons were home. Daisy had designed a glass extension to the kitchen that showcased her exuberant little back yard. She loved the house, but it had to go; it would be hard on the boys when they weren't yet earning and couldn't have flat-shares, but they'd just have to cut their cloth and bring friends to a grottier home.

It was her own house, bought with money left to her by her mother and a small mortgage. Peter, her ex-husband, had taken over the repayments and his lawyer had made much of that, pleading his client's current straitened circumstances, which was a sick joke. What Peter contributed now barely covered the boys' upkeep. They weren't his children, he said. No matter that he'd lived with them for twelve years, that their father had disappeared untraceably to New Zealand immediately after the divorce.

Daisy seethed. No greater shit than Peter existed. All the women, all he'd done to her . . . She was glad now that he'd set his face against more children, hard as she'd pleaded early on and however much she'd longed for them.

She was still brooding when the doorbell rang. Zipping her boots, she raced downstairs and was breathless, opening the door. Susannah had come by taxi; it was turning round in the small cul-de-sac. 'There's a delicious fight going on over the road,' she said, looking round over her shoulder. 'Those two women have been turning the air blue; they reversed into the same meter space and now they're trying to shunt each other out.'

'And swearing like navvies,' Daisy said. 'Just hark at 'em! There's a warden coming — bet he finds a way to give them both a ticket. Come on in. It's fabulous of you to come slumming it over here. I felt guilty even asking.'

Susannah took off a cuddly-looking grey wool jacket and flung it onto the hall chair. She wandered ahead, peering into the sitting room and down to the large square kitchen and its extension into the garden. 'Is this décor all you?' she asked, turning back to Daisy. 'Those raspberry-painted bookshelves and the steel sculpture and the mirrors? I love the cyan blue wallpaper, too.'

'Thanks, but you're being far too kind.' Daisy was chuffed, terrifically proud of what she'd achieved on a shoestring. 'It is all me, though. What's this!' she exclaimed, as Susannah held out a flocked carrier bag. 'You've brought a whole shop!'

'Just a couple of bottles of wine; there's a jar of preserved black truffles for the store cupboard, since it's too late for fresh, and that funny-shaped bottle is black-truffle vodka, something a bit different, I thought.'

'Gosh, how wild! Let's try the vodka right now with the cheese straws.' She fetched glasses.

Susannah took a cautious sip. 'What do we think? Pretty weird? It's sure to go to our heads.'

She kept looking round, taking everything in, and Daisy eyed her curiously. She had lines, dry-looking lips, but her hazel eyes had gold flecks and a glint, a knowingness — the equivalent, in eye terms, of a suppressed smile. Her hair was fair, just below chin length and in great glossy nick. Was that HRT? Did people stay on it that long? Susannah had the sort of high and lowlights that blended away the grey; her hair was shorter than in old photographs, and she was always flicking it away from an eye. People of her age didn't go in for tossing their hair back, but Susannah didn't act old. That was her thing really, Daisy thought.

Susannah asked after Daisy's twins and questions about the house. Stirring the risotto,

Daisy explained about her days here being numbered, resisting whining about the wrench, the late-night crying into her pillow; she mentioned the inevitability, though, with so many bills outstanding. She said the boys, Will and Sam, were reading Classics and Business Studies respectively.

They had lunch at the farmhouse kitchen table that she'd painted mustard yellow and it was a satisfying moment when the risotto was a big hit, the lemony dressing as well. Susannah drank tapwater, she wasn't faddy, and hardly any wine. Still, they'd had the vodka, and as Daisy cleared the plates Susannah sat back, looking as relaxed as if she was in her own home, lifting her legs onto an opposite chair, idly arranging the folds of her burnt-orange wool dress.

She was very slim. Daisy wondered if she'd ever had to diet, how thin models had had to be in her day, and voiced the thought. Susannah laughed. 'We all dieted madly, though there were no size noughts back then, and we always tried to turn sideways to camera. Protein diets were the thing, I remember a six-foot-tall Australian model once taking a whole cooked chicken out of her tote bag and eating the lot in the studio!'

Daisy was beginning to worry about time and she wasn't especially interested in other people's children, but having talked about her own, felt it only polite to mention Susannah's. 'Does your daughter have university-age children as well?' she asked.

'No, Bella's are younger, girls of twelve and fifteen. She was in her thirties when she married

— wiser than you and me! She's a barrister and her husband, Rory, who's a great tall guy, rangy and athletic, has a company selling bagels. It's a fast-growing market, they say.'

'And your other children?'

'Both boys. Josh is forty, Al's thirty-seven. Al called this morning, sounding nervous as a bird — he's just sent off a first novel to a publisher. He designs theatre sets by day, has a three-year-old son and a smiley, curly-top wife who's a GP. There's another baby on the way. It makes me feel limp with exhaustion!

'I worry most about Josh,' Susannah went on, and smiled. 'You did ask! It's very old-fashioned of me, but I'd love to see him married. He's forty, after all. He's a photographer — tall, fair, passionate about his work — out in East Africa on a fashion shoot right now, hoping for leopards as a backdrop. He's attractive to women, so Bella's friends say, and has girls in his life. I just wish he was in a long-term relationship.'

'Perhaps he's being constantly chased and very wary,' Daisy said, thinking who'd want a guy working with models? 'Single men of forty are rare gems.'

'That's all very well . . . ' Susannah broke off with another smile. 'I was about to say he could at least give it a go, but with my record I'm hardly one to give advice.'

'Your early mistakes were understandable and you got it right, you found love.' Daisy worried that sounded sycophantic and had a moment of bleakness, wondering if she ever would herself.

'You've obviously had a bad time with the

divorce, but that's done now,' Susannah said. 'What happened, what went wrong?' Her eyes above those famous cheekbones weren't letting go and Daisy felt cross-examined, sensitive about her mistakes. She was getting in a panic about Simon, too; the clock was ticking fast.

She rose to bring over the bowl of sliced oranges. 'I'll just decant the ice cream,' she said. 'It's lemon and lime — blends well with the oranges, I think. And you must have one of these brownies.' She busied about, but sitting down again it was hard not to unburden, a release to let it flood out.

'I should have known better, I've only myself to blame. Peter was flash, though, and he did mad extravagant things, like hiring a helicopter to go to country operas, whisking me off to Nice, buying crazily-priced wine in restaurants to impress his friends — well, anyone useful to him. It was glamorous fun, but I began to see through the façade soon enough and to realize how much and how often he lied. People would call and want to be paid. I found a receipt for a £12,000 necklace — not one he ever gave me. And he was tight about the housekeeping! The affairs, the barely covered-up tracks, his manhandling if I ever dared to accuse him. He could win me round, as there was a physical bond, but it only lasted for so long. All the pressures and menace piled up and I couldn't go on.'

'I've been there,' Susannah admitted, 'in very similar circumstances. But you have someone new now? You have that look. Don't make another mistake,' she said, quite fondly. 'Two's enough. Is it serious — do you love this man? I'm actually asking for a reason.'

Daisy's cheeks felt as hot as hellfire. Simon wasn't the way forward, as Susannah would certainly tell her. He was in another-mistake territory — even if he were on offer.

'I am keen,' she mumbled, 'but it's complicated.'

'He's married?'

Daisy nodded dejectedly. 'Yes. Coffee?' she asked, trying not to look at her watch.

'That would be nice, just a quick cup before I go. Don't worry, I've got the message. I wondered why you advanced the time this morning.'

'Oh dear, am I that transparent? Please don't feel I'm rushing you. This is awful.'

'It is a bit! If it's serious, though, I'm sure he'll find a way, but . . . is he a Good Man? It's a vulnerable time for you — and look, I'm the last person to talk, but try not to be too accommodating. Sometimes, with your own deep feelings, it's hard to see that his might be a little less sincere.'

Daisy didn't want to hear that. It didn't help. Simon wasn't a Good Man. He was a friend of Peter's, for a bad start: it was through Peter they'd met. She lived for Simon all the same; she marked time, sometimes for more than a week, even two or three, living for those crumbs of contact that kept her going. She knew she was an utter fool.

Susannah was looking at her watch ostentatiously and Daisy pulled herself together. 'Um, you said just now you were asking about a man in my life for a reason?'

'Yes. I had an idea, you see. I've just taken on a very big new decorating job and I'm going to need an assistant. I wondered if you'd like to learn the ropes. It would be a proper paid job, but hard work as well as interesting, and it involves a trip to America.'

Daisy blushed all over again. 'I can't believe this. There's nothing I'd love to do more! I'd try hard to learn fast. I'd still have my column to do, but could handle that, I'm sure.'

'There is a complication.' Susannah had an uncomfortably firm look in her eye. 'The time factor. I'm not talking a quick flit out to the States and back. This job could take up to three months. I plan to go out end of May, early June, when I'm sure your twins will have summer-vac plans lined up. My client has suggested staying in the house, working from within, which would be good. He's my sort of age, recently divorced and immensely bitter about it. This is all about expunging any last trace of his ex-wife, even down to the furniture. It's rare to have such a free hand, a luxury in itself. He's a beer magnate called Warren Lindsay.'

Daisy's heart was pounding like thundering hooves. Three months . . . She'd lose Simon. He'd forget about her, look elsewhere . . . 'Could I perhaps come back once or twice, just to break it up a bit?'

Susannah had an impatient look on her face. Without knowing how selfish and domineering Simon could be, she seemed to feel Daisy was over-reacting. 'Possibly,' she said coolly. 'Obviously you could if there was a crisis with your

37

sons, but probably not otherwise. It'll be serious work with a lot of running around. I need someone I can rely on. Think it over,' she said. 'Let me know in a day or two. If your guy really cares, he'll find a way to come out, make the trip to New York, or at least he'll understand. And it never hurts to be a little less available. Not exactly as a test of his feelings, but you do have your future to think about, your own life to lead. It sounds to me as if you don't think it likely he'll leave his wife.'

Daisy was silent. Susannah rose. 'Will I find a cab easily? My car's being serviced today, always such a bore. I don't mind walking a bit.'

'Best to call one,' Daisy said. 'You'd be lucky to find one, even on the main road.' She leaped up and scrabbled in a kitchen drawer, hoping to find a card. She never used taxis.

'Don't worry,' Susannah said, hiding any irritation. 'I've got numbers in my phone.' Daisy closed the drawer with an apologetic smile.

The taxi firm said five minutes; it was cutting it fine. Daisy's mind was in a whirl. America, a chance anyone would give their eyeteeth for, but three months . . . Simon would try to stop her going. Would she really lose him? Could she bear to take the risk?

Susannah was looking expectant and Daisy played for time. 'I can't begin to tell you how thrilled and overwhelmed I feel. It's fantastic of you. I just have to think it through a bit — is that all right?'

'Of course, no desperate rush. You must be sure it's what you really want to do. There's the bell now. Thanks, it was good to see you again and a scrummy lunch!'

Daisy saw her out to the taxi. Simon was parking his silver BMW, climbing out, and she couldn't help glancing over to him, aware of Susannah following her gaze. With the narrow cul-de-sac, the taxi doing the usual three-point turn, Susannah would see him coming across from his car. She'd be able to form an impression, take in his looks — which weren't all that prepossessing, Daisy knew. Simon wasn't tall, he had a bullet-shaped head and broad thickset shoulders, but he was all solid sex appeal.

He'd see Susannah as well, of course, and almost certainly recognise her. He never missed a trick, especially where anyone who could be remotely helpful to him was concerned.

He filled the doorway, coming in. He lifted Daisy's chin, kissed her hard, breaking off abruptly to stare at her with sharp, inquisitive eyes. 'Why didn't you say it was Susannah Forbes?' He loosened his tie, glowering suspiciously. 'You went on long enough about her after that dinner you went to at the Wilsons'. You asked her to lunch to touch her heartstrings, did you? She's certainly worth a packet. God, to think of all that Barfield money she walked off with. Surprising she agreed to come really, but I suppose, hard as it is to believe,' he kissed Daisy's lips and gave an affectionate grin, 'she could just be a softie like you and easily conned. Probably not much going on up top, either.'

'I don't see why you would say that.'

'Well, she was a model, after all. Bit of luck for you, wasn't it, meeting her. How do you know Ginny and Maynard Wilson, by the way? I've been meaning to ask.'

'Through Adrienne, my stepmother,' Daisy muttered. She hated the way Simon could sound so nosy and acquisitive, drooling unattractively over other people's money. And anyway, didn't he have more pressing things on his mind? Hadn't he come to see *her*? Also, she'd wanted to keep Susannah private — well away from his prying while she agonised about what to do. Simon was like Ginny Wilson, maximising connections, milking them in any way he could. It was silly to have mentioned Adrienne, as well. Simon would be reminded that her stepmother's father was a château-owning French count, and he would store that piece of information away.

Daisy touched his mouth with her fingers and brought her lips close, smelling his male breath, latching onto his strangely transparent blue eyes. 'A little less talking,' she suggested, reaching down with her other hand, 'feels like it might be a good idea.'

His lovemaking had the power to quash every doubt and thought in her head. Simon could ignite her, set her off like a rocket, high up to some other place. She had to gather herself in the chaos of duvet and tangled sheet before being able to turn to him, weak with the exhilaration and knowledge that he was hers, if only for a brief afternoon. He was there in her small brass bed, commandeering every inch of it with his strong, hairy limbs spread wide, there

40

with her, making her feel wanted and whole again, not browbeaten and bitter, a used, rejected and now ex-wife.

He linked hands under his head, elbows wide, and stared up at the uneven ceiling. 'I've got to go, Green Eyes,' he said, turning to meet her gaze. 'Sorry it's a rush, but I've lots on today — one or two potential deals.'

'Are you opening another shop or something?' She tried to hide her acute disappointment, wishing she knew more, how tightly chained he was to his wife's financial ankles, always vainly hoping he'd break free.

'No, not that,' Simon said. 'It's a bad time for the high street. Sarah's really quite depressed. Sorry, Angel, must love you and leave you — much as I'd like to stay. I'll text, work something out soon.'

Daisy felt in a wretched cold place after the heat of her elation. If he could worry about that bitch, Sarah, being depressed, he could at least show a bit of concern for how she, Daisy, might feel. She suspected Simon of talking up his business meetings, even using them as excuses for a quick getaway at times. She felt incidental, taken for granted. Was she just a quick poke on a busy day, slotted in between these phantom deals?

'I'd hoped you'd stay on a bit,' she mumbled, swinging her legs off the bed and standing naked in front of him. 'I'd made brownies for tea.'

He laughed and sprang up — not, as she hoped, to take her in his arms and smother her with loving last kisses and smiles, but to dress briskly, buttoning his shirt with practised fingers, yanking on his trousers with a couple of jerks. 'You're wonderful,' he said, in an automatic, preoccupied way, 'as irresistible as your brownies. But I can't stay, babe, I really have to get a shift-on now.'

He could have said it with more warmth and fervour, hugged her and made her feel he meant what he said; he'd hardly looked up from his ruddy shirt-buttoning.

'I'm going away,' Daisy said abruptly, 'a trip to America. I'll be gone quite a while.'

Simon finished tying his tie. Grabbing his jacket, he kissed her lightly on the nose and lips. 'Not for long, I hope. I won't let you! Fill me in later,' he said, making for the door. 'I'll call. And we will have a bit more time together soon, promise. I'll find a way. Must rush — sorry about the brownies.'

3

'I'm so thrilled and grateful to be coming,' Daisy said, with the sort of determined zeal that masked a degree of uncertainty, as though she had yet to completely persuade herself as well as me. 'If, of course, that is, you still seriously want me along. I'll work my socks off, I promise, but can you, I mean, be a little patient if I need things explained?'

'No chance. I'll be as ratty as a frayed wife, rant and expect instant miracles. You'll need to keep your cool and work it out for yourself — but you'll do fine.'

Daisy stared at me with a mixture of relief and horror on her face. 'And I'm worried about not looking the part, letting the side down. I'm sure design assistants in New York are always the ultimate in manicured chic.'

'You'll leave them all standing. But you can have an advance when we're there, if you like, and do a bit of shopping.' I felt sympathetic and would have loved to buy her something new to wear, but it seemed best to keep things on a business footing.

We were in my office, having a coffee break, surrounded by swatches, samples and wallpaper books, bouncing ideas and feeling our way. I'd asked Warren Lindsay to email a spread of photographs, which Daisy had gawped at in wonder. She'd asked all the right questions, though, and I was impressed. Who'd have thought a Wilsons' dinner party with all its formality could have led to such serendipity?

Warren had responded with Daisy-like zeal; the photographs gave a very full picture. The house was a little way from the ocean, just off Gin Lane, the perimeter road, he'd said, and it looked pure Beverly Hills, with pillared grandeur, white-painted stucco and a wide sweeping drive. The interior shots showed a grand hall, formal reception rooms, fussily decorated bedrooms. A balustraded outdoor walkway linked the house to a clapboard extension, the pool house, which had a wall of sliding glass and an excessively large sunbathing area. The swimming pool itself was the size of Wembley Stadium.

Double doors from the main house opened onto a traditional part-covered American deck with a couple of steps down to the garden and pool. The deck was the place to be, although conventionally decorated with floral prints on the sunchairs and bench seating along the house wall.

'Those fabrics are grim,' Daisy said. 'I'd have practical navy bench seating, plenty of big ticking cushions, and paint the floorboards a nice flat beach-house grey. And a casually-placed easel with a colourful painting would look good, I think.'

We shared ideas. Stephanie, my PA, who was freckly with thin ginger hair turning to white, took notes. She produced printouts with annotations, and organised lunch — thick fish chowder from a local bistro and a *tarte aux pommes*. Stephie loved to mother. She loved cats too, and Posh, resenting her divided attentions, sniffed the aroma of chowder with her nose out of joint. She rejected the prawn Daisy offered her with disdain.

'Can cats be anorexic?' Daisy asked. 'She's very thin.'

'Posh likes Felix pouches and fillet steak,' Stephie said firmly. 'I'll try to fatten her up while you're away.'

When Stephanie clocked off I opened a bottle of Chablis and encouraged Daisy to stay. I'd disliked her lover on sight and worried about him, not only for the type of selfish, boorish man I thought him to be, but for the problems he could cause me with this trip. I needed to rely on Daisy. She had talent and we had the makings of being quite a good team, but hearing her talk about her ex-husband I could see history repeating itself. She'd run to Simon if he snapped his fingers, bend under pressure, and I didn't want that. I could almost smell her making just the sort of mistakes I'd made in the past. It was an uncomfortable feeling, one that was waking my own, sleeping ghosts.

I'd been lurching from one unsettled mood to another. Impatience with Charles for being elsewhere; I missed him, his wit and humour, and while he might be seventy-two he didn't seem it. I could imagine all North Norfolk's horsey, brogue-wearing widows and divorcées, women who'd revel in his cold old house, panting along in his wake.

My nerviness extended to Long Island, too.

Warren Lindsay's image of me was out of date. He'd interested me at Jimmy's party and could well have his own reasons for seeking me out for this job. I wasn't sure that I wanted him to make elderly advances, but — just in case — it seemed worth taking a bit of cosmetic action, anything that could be done in the time that wasn't too radical. Eyeing Daisy's smooth supple skin made me feel the frustrations of aging all the more. It would help to know I'd done what I could.

I sat back, glass in hand, and studied Daisy, who was looking distant and sad-eyed, worries obviously preying on her. She needed America, new excitements — but would she make the most of such an experience? It would be a brave new world where anything could happen, as I well remembered.

We were in my kitchen, Italian and streamlined with steel-grey units and granite worktops. It had a living area up one end where we were sitting: bookcases, armchairs, a flat-screen television, a small round dining table, a low coffee table too, sloppily piled with books and conveniently foot-rest high.

I reached for the wine bottle and topped up Daisy's glass. 'Have you told Simon yet how long you'll be gone?'

'I told him straightaway, that day you saw him, but he hardly took it in. I think he chose not to. I've seen him a couple of times since, and if I raise the subject he refuses to listen — quite deliberately, I'm sure.' She gave a small half-smile, looking embarrassed and torn. Daisy had striking eyes, softness, warmth; she could look

46

entrancing, but without her bubbly liveliness, was almost plain. She'd been full of bounce all day, throwing herself into the discussions and plans enthusiastically, yet now her whole body seemed frail and wilted. Simon was going to be trouble.

'You won't let me down last minute, I hope,' I said.

Daisy seemed shocked that I could think it of her, which was encouraging. 'No, of course not. I'd never do that. And I'm sure you must think I'm being extreme, since we're not really away for that long. I just wish . . . I didn't care so much. Simon is typically selfish and inconsiderate, but he sort of means everything to me. I even know it's a physical thing and I'm not truly in love, but I still can't help myself.'

I thought of men I'd known in the past just like Simon, and how I'd cared so much and been blindly naïve. I'd had enough practical experience to see the hurt he could do to Daisy; his callousness and failings had flowed out like a banner trailing a plane. Trying to warn her was bound to be counter-productive, but I felt a need to try.

'Daisy, just suppose, for argument's sake, you discovered that you weren't the only girl Simon was seeing: could you walk away? I'm sure I'm doing him an injustice, but it's a vulnerable time for you, the aftermath of a difficult divorce. You've had a bad experience and nothing does more to sap one's morale. But that need to feel wanted makes us blind. I keep saying I've been there, but I have! Hang onto your pride, keep faith in yourself, and let Simon make the running. He'll soon come chasing after you, all the way to New York. I'd have a bet with you on that.'

From Daisy's face she clearly felt she had no pride to hang onto where Simon was concerned, his to take no matter how little he gave in return. I battled on. 'And he doesn't, as I understand it, look like he'd leave his wife. These are your best years, Daisy. Think of the future. You have a terrific eye, an exciting potential new career, so much to offer the right man.'

'It's hard to look at other men right now,' she said. 'I mostly feel like a half-alive mouse that the cat's brought in, taunted and powerless. Simon has me under his thumb.'

'When my first marriage broke up I was in just that sort of place. I'd been through a bitter publicised divorce, my private life laid bare. I felt unattractive and unwanted; married men tried it on. It was depressing how many of them thought I was fair game, and it did nothing for my sense of self. I'd felt belittled all through my marriage, completely unconfident. No one talked about self-worth all those decades ago; the concept hadn't been invented. There was no propping-up support system, no armbands to keep you afloat. You just got on with it!'

Daisy eyed me warily over her wine glass, as though she felt on trial, unsure where this was headed. I was a bit uncertain of that myself.

'I can understand how bad you felt after a dreadful divorce,' she said, 'but you were a sought-after top model. How could you have had no confidence?'

'I never believed a word of any of the compliments. But what I'm trying to say now is that, with the benefit of all this distance, I can see how easy it was to fall for the same sort of character as the one I'd just divorced. My defences were down, I'd been made to feel a sexless wimp; I craved any red-blooded male attention, the reassurance of feeling wanted, which led to easy mistakes.'

'You had looks, a fantastic career, and still felt that insecure? Men have a lot to answer for! Was your first husband jealous-natured? Men can be, after all, even when in the thick of an affair of their own. Is it hard to talk about him? I'd love to hear a little of how things were.'

I looked at the soft vulnerable girl leaning forward in her chair, whose genuine interest in my own ancient troubles had brought back her glow. It was mid-May, the days drawing out; evening sun streaming in from the bright sitting room was burnishing Daisy's light brown hair, tinting it pinkish-bronze. I wanted to be young again, making mistakes.

It was getting late and I was due to have supper with a friend, hoping for advice on cosmetic pick-me-ups, since she'd had everything done to her face at least twice. Yet I still felt in a mood to talk on a bit. The memories of Joe felt strangely recent — jogged by Daisy, probably — and still with the capacity to hurt. I hadn't really thought much about my first husband since hearing he'd died, ten years ago now, in California where he'd been living, doing a little acting and getting by. Bella, our daughter, had

49

kept in touch. He'd married again at a late stage and his new wife had been good for him. He'd been drinking less with her encouragement. She'd almost weaned him off alcohol completely, although cirrhosis of the liver had done for him in the end.

'I should go really,' I said, 'and I can't believe you really want to hear about Joe.'

'I'm interested, if you don't mind,' Daisy said. 'According to a theatrical friend of my father's, Joe Bryant was a hot ticket, a class actor and a charmer, too. I remember Dad's friend describing him in that slightly bitchy way of someone in the same business — feeling old jealousies and diluting the praise — as a great self-publicist, but still a good actor all the same. He had a huge following of women fans, didn't he, which seem to have riled this friend of Dad's. He could really do it for them on stage.'

'And not only on the boards. He could have charmed the pants off Mary Whitehouse — probably did! She was a famous defender of all things prudish,' I explained, seeing Daisy's slight fog. 'Joe could win over men, too; he thrived on making highflying friends — it was his motivation. And the great and the good loved having a glamorous, sharp-witted actor around; he had plenty of success. I was the shy, opinion-less foil for his grandstanding and witticisms. He was a clever mimic as well, and we were asked to every party going. Joe's address book read like the guest list for a Royal celebration.

'His working-class background was seen as a plus in the sixties; very of the moment, yet it had

50

been pretty bleak. He'd lived in a council flat on an estate near Tilbury Docks, very barren and windswept. I went there once or twice.' My mind swung back. I remembered how saddened I'd felt for Joe's mother on those occasions, for the estate could have featured in one of today's grim reality TV series, with all the squalor and debris, rubbish whirling up the communal stairs. Joe's was a two-parent family, but his father was either away or drunk, and his lonely mother slept around.

'The amazing thing was the way he completely re-invented himself.' I smiled at Daisy. 'Perhaps it was his natural ability to act or he'd come back to earth as a chameleon, but he instinctively adapted. He used to call me his little bourgeois hausfrau, too dreadfully middle-class. He'd say it in front of his society chums — and that wasn't from the point of view of his working-class background. He was imagining what *they'd* think of me, seeing me through their eyes.'

Conscious of exposing rather too much of a long-buried hurt, I said it was time I was off. We made a plan to meet and talk flights, dates, and I saw Daisy to the door. We were an unlikely couple, I felt — thirty years between us, but linked by our love of design and soft furnishings . . . and our very fallible taste in men.

4

August 1961

'Hello, hello, bye bye-ee,' Frankie screeched, with monotonous regularity.

'Hello, bye bye-ee,' Joe mimicked, dropping his head from side to side with birdy jerks. 'Frankie, you squawker, you middle-class mynah, that's the pits! Fart, fuck, titties, turnips — gonads, jockstrap — anything but bye bye-ee! Okay? Got it?'

Joe swung round and told me, 'It's your fault, wifey. I've heard you. 'Bye bye-ee'!' He pushed back his chair and went over to the cage. 'Fart, fart, Frankie, tits, gonads — got it? God, you do pong! Your cage is a smelly old cesspit. Frankie Wanky was a bird, Frankie Wanky laid a turd. He stinks like a Sudanese sewer.'

Cleaning out the cage was on my to-do list. I'd just come in, dumped down my heavy tote bag and kicked off my yellow summer sling-backs; after a long day on a shoot for *Harper's Bazaar* I was knackered, very glad it was Friday. Working under lights in a heatwave, modelling winter clothes — a Hardy Amies fur coat, a John Cavanagh tailored tweed suit — wasn't much fun.

Frankie, the mynah bird, named after Frank Sinatra whom Joe idolised, lived in the dining room. It was a gloomy room linking the hall and kitchen, which was brighter but tired-looking with chipped, scratched units that I longed to replace. Our ground-floor flat in a redbrick block was rented, though, and between the household bills and having spent too much on it already, I was feeling the pinch. Joe, for whatever reason — booze, horses or Alicia — was always broke and borrowing from me.

He'd sat down again, stretching out his legs under the dining-room table that was late Georgian and one of his many hopelessly extravagant buys. 'How've you been?' I asked, worrying about him at home all day in a stuffy Kensington flat, drinking, playing LPs, running up stratospheric phone bills — if not out seeing Alicia.

He wasn't bothering with an answer so I went through to the kitchen, taking a couple of plates, the breadboard that had left a mess of crumbs and a dish of sweating butter. 'The photographer was Richard Dormer,' I called. 'He's such a nice man. He'd seen the play and loved it; thinks you're in the genius class.'

'Well, I'm off now,' Joe said, staying put, as I returned to brush up the crumbs. 'Two more nights of kissing that snot-nosed halitosis redhead, ninety-seven to date, and all the matinées; I'll be celebrating when we get to Rory's bash on Sunday night, I can tell you.'

I gave him an anxious look. 'Coming home for supper? Be nice if you did,' I said, rubbing the back of my heel, sore from a day in the stiff new chisel-toe shoes. 'Richard Dormer's a class cook and he's told me how to make a delicious-sounding cold soup out of whirred-up left-over salad.'

'Is he queer or something? Anyway, it sounds more like stagnant pond-water to me. I'll settle for breakfast — I'll be home for that.' Joe was in one of his most maddening moods. It didn't mean he wouldn't turn up, just that I wouldn't know. I eyed the empty glass and tonic water bottle beside him. No vodka on show. Where'd he keep it?

'Cy Grant's a mate of Rory's and he'll be at the party with his guitar.' Joe held up his hands, spreading out his fingers. 'Should be good.'

Joe's fingers were quite stubby, considering his lean elegant build. His looks had an intensity that was hard to ignore; a long gaunt face with sunken cheeks, periwinkle-blue eyes, dandyish flowing brown hair that reached his collar. He was a natural for Noël Coward or Oscar Wilde parts, but with the electricity in his every movement and sharpness of his wit, he tended to play more cutting roles than the foppish aesthete.

'Oh, and I talked to Henrietta,' he said, still studying his hands. 'According to her friend Gloria Romanoff, Sinatra's due in London any day now, coming with Dean Martin on a private visit — aside from a day at Shepperton with Bob Hope and Bing Crosby. They're filming *Road to Hong Kong*, and Frank and Dean have cameo parts — astronauts in space suits. I told Henrietta she had to get me to meet Frank or else!'

Henrietta was warm and good sparky fun, which couldn't be said of all Joe's aristocratic chums. He'd nagged her to bits ever since discovering she knew Frank Sinatra — Elizabeth Taylor as well, through Gloria Romanoff, Joe thought, who was apparently a great confidante of Frank's. Gloria and her husband, Mike, who'd chosen to be the last in a great line of Russian aristocrats, owned Romanoff's Restaurant in Beverly Hills where all the big-name stars hung out. Henrietta had been out to stay once and had a fabulous time.

'I should go,' Joe said, still not making a move. He yawned. 'It's so bloody hot.'

'Aren't you quite late?'

He looked at his watch and leaped to his feet. 'Bugger! Shit! Why didn't you say?'

'Bye bye-ee, bye bye-ee!' Frankie screeched on cue, as Joe reached the door.

He stopped and turned. 'No, no, old sport,' he said, wagging a stubby finger. 'Fart, fart, fartee-tartee. Bye, wifey,' he called, a choice of word that gave me cause for a weary smile. 'See you.'

I followed him out into the hall. 'Hope it's a good audience. Make it home if you can.'

* * *

On Sunday morning I woke feeling low, headachy and dreading the day ahead. Nothing was planned. Joe would be at his worst, morose and uncommunicative. He needed invitations to large country houses, lunch with rowdy friends, anything to avoid a quiet day at home. He'd drink heavily and secretly, play records non-stop, nodding and tapping his fingers in time to the music. There was Rory's party, but Joe still had to get through the hours before then. He couldn't handle his own company, let alone mine.

He was beside me in bed, dead to the world; he'd flung off the sheet and was lying on his back, naked, sweaty, smelling of stale smoke and booze. I'd gone to the last night of *Old Love*, but failed to stop Joe getting extremely drunk at the party afterwards. He'd insisted on driving home; it had been a very erratic car ride.

I shifted in bed and felt a slight stickiness, an unexpected trickle between my legs, and had to fight tears; the irregularity of my periods was cruel. If only I could get pregnant, Joe would feel proud and it would bring us closer, I felt sure.

It was unbearably humid. Through a gap in the curtains the sky looked black and ominous, almost as if there was an eclipse; a storm was about to erupt. I eased out of bed, washed, took a couple of painkillers, put on a blue-spotted sundress, loose-fitting and cool, and left Joe to sleep on.

The *Sunday Dispatch* was on the doormat. I took it to read at the dining-room table with a cup of tea and toast. I needed comfort food, not the boiled eggs and black coffee I lived on all week. It was the latest diet craze, protein, oranges and nothing else. Some of the models went to a guy in Harley Street for an injection in the bum to speed up the weight loss, but I was too squeamish for that. I sipped the tea slowly, gratefully, and spread a scraping of butter on the toast.

The first crack of thunder came without warning, as shocking as gunfire; my pulse raced. Frankie cowered in his cage, hunched deep into his silky blue-black feathers. I opened the door, cooing and trying to soothe him. 'There, there, Frankie; there, there.' He wouldn't even step onto my finger and I finally gave into the tears.

Alicia would be at Rory's party. Alicia, whose glossy auburn hair hung straight and lusciously down her back, hair that Joe fondled on dance floors. Alicia, whose thigh his hand caressed under dinner tables. Alicia, whose bikinied body had been such a lure. She'd spiked the workings of the marital clock, possibly irreparably; it could never be wound back to a time of happily-married-ever-after. I burned to know when the affair had started, whether it was before the Capri holiday, whether it still went on, but it was the memories of Capri that caused the most acute pain.

Joe and I had been invited to stay with Alicia's cousin, Sophia, at her holiday home on the island. We'd met her through Alicia and she was an older age group, her husband a land-owning peer. Well connected, as Alicia was herself. They were keen theatre-goers and lovers of the arts, and had taken Joe under their wing.

The first sight of the cliff-top villa perched high above a startlingly blue sea, an extended and sensitively modernised old farmhouse in mature gardens, had been a magical moment. I'd felt rapturous, that mellow evening, and gazed back at Joe guilelessly, lovingly, babbling about being the luckiest nineteen year old alive.

Now, in retrospect, a couple of months on and a year older, I shuddered to think of such naivety. It had all been so obvious. To Sophia our host, whisking me off on hot pointless trips to Capri's super-chic boutiques. To Hughie, the flabby, pink-skinned MP also staying, trying in his kind earnest way to distract me — suggesting cliff-top walks or going for a spin in the speedboat. Alicia's husband, Toby, rich, remote, heavily built and balding, had been detached from it all, absorbed in his books and interminable games of chess with an Italian neighbour.

I swam and sunbathed when left to my own devices, and just before lunch one blistering day had gone into the poolside changing room to dump my wet towel in the basket. Backing out again, heart pounding, hands clammy, sick to my stomach, I'd wanted only to be on the first plane home. Joe had come running out seconds later, chasing after me, trying to hug me, saying it was all in the heat of the moment and meant nothing, nothing at all. But something was lost in that moment, my blind innocent trust. Our marriage was holed, salt water seeping in.

I sighed and washed up my cup and plate, starting when a violent streak of lightning suddenly lit up the window, a brilliant vertical flash, as jagged as broken glass. The thunder that followed was deafening, I almost missed the ringing phone.

It was Henrietta, giggling with glee. 'It's all fixed. My friend Gloria is coming for drinks at six — and guess who she's bringing? Frank

Sinatra and his valet, George! Can you and Joe come at, let's say, ten past? Tell Joe that timing matters. He'd better not be as late as always, as they may not stay long and it's probably his one and only chance.'

'I can't believe this! You're fantastic to have fixed it. Joe will love you forever more.'

He'd be uncontainable. I stayed by the phone in the hall feeling a sense of the unreal, spiralling off with excitement and relief. I had to ring my parents, couldn't wait to tell them whom I just happened to be having a drink with at ten past six that night.

My father was a doctor with a country practice, much depended on locally; he worked all hours of day and night and many of his patients felt they owed Henry Forbes their all. He was a great film buff and as a child I'd gone to the pictures with him almost every weekend. His favourite actor was Edward G Robinson; I must have seen every film Edward G had ever made.

'And isn't it tonight that you're going to be meeting Cy Grant as well?' said my mother Betty, who had a huge crush on him. 'I told you the bad patch would pass, darling,' she murmured, not wanting my father to hear.

'It hasn't and it won't,' I snapped. 'Why do you always have to be so *accommodating* and trying to make wrong things right?' It was mean of me. I was beastly far too often; self-centred, heaping the smallest panic onto those thin uncomplaining shoulders and expecting sage sympathy and support. I got it unfailingly, but how could she mend a torn heart? What could she say about Alicia other than that life had to go on?

The bedroom door crashed open and Joe stood framed in it, looking like an overgrown schoolboy with his thin bare chest and a pale blue towel tucked round his middle. He groaned. 'Christ, I feel poisonous, mouth like a furred-up kettle. I'm going to die. Who was on the phone?'

'Henrietta. We're on. Six o'clock tonight, drinks with Sinatra at her place.'

Joe forgot all about his hangover and Sunday decline. He transmogrified into a comparative saint; loveable, hugging me like a child in his excitement, full of how he longed to write a book about Sinatra and how determined he was to pull it off.

'I'd have time to work on a book, too,' he said later on, as we drove to Henrietta's flat in Chelsea. 'We don't go into rehearsal for *Cakes and Kindness* till mid-Jan. It would be perfect timing. I loathe having to fill in with voice-overs and all the grot.'

'Better not tell Sinatra you named your mynah bird after him — he might take umbrage!'

We rang the bell at nine minutes past six to find Henrietta's guests already arrived. When introduced, I stared shyly at Frank Sinatra, only dimly aware of Henrietta saying my name. He was immaculate in a tailored charcoal suit, double-cuff white shirt; an orange silk hankie was neatly evident in the jacket top pocket. His dark hair was receding slightly, he was tanned, had extremely white teeth, but it was his eyes that impelled me to stare so openly. They were as bright and deep blue as the Aegean Sea, a medium for his extraordinary dynamic talent — and they were staring right back at me.

'Well, get you! They said you were some chick,' Frank's grin spread from ear to ear, 'and they had it in one. The studios would be after you for a screen-test, no question.'

That floored me. I blushed pillar-box red, at a loss to know how to answer. I wittered on, painfully shy, 'I can't tell you what a thrill this is, how I'm pinching myself.'

Joe wittered too, while cleverly letting slip his encyclopaedic knowledge of all things Sinatra, his every record, every film — and he soon enough cut to the chase with practised self-deprecatory charm. 'I act a bit,' he said, 'but I write too, and more than anything else I'd love to write your biography.'

'Gee, hell, great idea, but I might want to write my autobiography one day. Say, how's about you do a slim little book, just about my music, since you seem so well informed? I can see it now: black cover, yours truly on a spotlit stool . . . Why don't you kids come on out? You can tag along to a coupla recording sessions; dig the scene. No skin off my back. You're great, full of enthusiasm. Hey, Gloria, whaddya think? Can they stay with you?'

Gloria, who was sitting with Henrietta on the sofa, beamed, and said, 'They'd be most welcome,' in a pleasingly soft Californian accent. She wore her dark brown hair back from her face, clear of a smooth high forehead. She was probably late thirties; she looked tidy and

61

groomed in a plum print cocktail dress, gold necklace and earrings, an unmistakably American look. 'When were you thinking of, Frank?' she asked. 'October maybe?'

'You got El Dago's inaugural flight late that month, Mr S,' George, the valet, chipped in. He was tall and immensely elegant, terrific-looking. 'That's taking in Vegas, your two-week show at the Sands. You got recording sessions for Reprise goin' on around there as well.'

'Hey, they should come on that trip,' Frank said. 'See the sights and the show.' He turned to Joe. 'El Dago's my new jet, a Martin 404 — they call me El Dago, hence the name. It's a den in the sky — that flight's gonna be a swell party! San Francisco, Vegas for the coupla weeks of the show. We'll catch the end of Sammy D's show, too — hijack it for a gas, maybe! We'll chill out at my home in Palm Springs. Great place, I love the desert. You guys ever been out?'

'Not even to America,' Joe said. 'I've never dreamed of seeing Palm Springs.'

★　★　★

Joe was very full of his new best mate at Rory's party. I dreaded the anti-climax when, as with so many other too-good-to-be-true ideas, it faded like a mirage the nearer it came. But no one else was quite as fascinated with Joe's Sinatra news as he was; they were a sophisticated bunch, well up in celebrities, hobnobbing with film stars themselves, and they failed to swoon with fascination at his every word.

62

I hung about; Joe did the talking. I was glad of the dimmed lights and party fug. The dust and cigarette smoke were as visible on the air as a rain shower. People were talking in groups, downing wine, vodka gimlets; a few couples shuffled round dancing where the rugs had been cleared. A small coterie was gathered where Cy Grant strummed his guitar, sitting at his feet. He was in a green and gold aloha shirt, looking wholesome and approachable, television's man of the moment and it was easy to see why.

The ballet dancer, Moira Shearer, was there, beautiful and delicate. Her red hair seemed almost backlit, the way it gleamed with gold lights. Her husband was beside her, the writer and broadcaster, Ludo Kennedy, whom I'd met before. He had an impressive head of hair of his own, thick and bushy, brushed up and back from his brow. Square-jawed with an intelligent gaze, he was an attractive man, I thought, accidentally catching his eye.

He came to talk to me. 'Let's grab that space while it's free,' he said, as a couple vacated a squashy sofa, a threadbare subsided old thing against the wall.

Ludo flattered me politely and I praised his new book, *Ten Rillington Place*. I hadn't read it, but the reviews had been great, describing the forensic dissecting of the trial of Timothy Evans whom Ludo believed had suffered a terrible miscarriage of justice, hanged for murders he didn't commit. We had a serious conversation then, about East Germany closing its borders and the first concrete blocks of a new wall being laid. Ludo talking of the grim spectre of fresh conflict it raised was hardly party chat, but it was refreshing not to be treated as a frivolous model.

The artist Dominic Elwes was on Ludo's other side; he began firing provocative questions at him, mainly about Jomo Kenyatta who was also in the news, released from prison that week. With Ludo distracted, arguing fiercely on Jomo's behalf, I fastened on Alicia and Joe. They weren't dancing, but just to see them talking together clawed and chewed at my gut. Alicia was in shocking-pink silk, a strapless dress, elasticated at the top, hanging like a sack, yet depressingly sexy and eye-catching all the same.

My view of them was briefly blocked as Tony Lambton came to sit beside me, squeezing in and forcing Ludo to shift along a bit, which didn't go down well. 'There's not enough room,' Ludo complained peevishly. 'And *I* was talking to Susannah.'

'You weren't,' Tony said, which was true enough. 'Anyway, I am now.'

It was a little morale boost, two influential older men sniping over me, though I felt slightly terrified of Tony, an aristocrat and an MP. He had a strong angular face and slicked-down curling black hair, but it was the hypnotic effect of his perennial dark glasses that gave him such Svengali-esque appeal. I felt caught in the glare dancing off those glasses and could well understand why a number of women were said to find him irresistible.

He'd turned his back to Ludo and was studying me. I felt nervous, unable to withstand the scrutiny. 'I want to talk about infidelity, Susannah,' he said, taking a sip of his drink and keeping his shaded eyes trained.

'I'm not very up in that,' I laughed, while thinking inevitably of someone close to me who was. 'Couldn't contribute anything useful, I'm afraid.'

'You need to be up in it,' he said. 'It goes on, it's universal and I want to give you some advice. There are things you should know.' I was kneading my hands in my lap and he covered them with one of his own. 'Within a year your husband will have been unfaithful to you. That's the way it is, a fact that you have to accept and understand.' His hand moved to rest in an unthreatening way on my thigh. 'You should rise above it; maintain your dignity. Carve out a life for yourself, do things that interest you; have some adventures and experiences of your own. A little variety is no bad thing.'

He'd left me feeling stranded, floundering like a gaping fish. I wanted to say with cool control that in my view, fidelity and trust were the essence of marriage and such sophisticated cynicism was beyond me. But Joe *had* been unfaithful to me and it *had* been within a year, since I felt sure the affair had begun some months before. As Tony probably knew — as had the people staying at the Capri villa. But I wasn't capable of high-minded comebacks and could only manage a lightly raised eyebrow.

'You've left me speechless,' I said. 'I think we'd better change the subject, don't you?'

Just then, our host, Rory, came to sit on the

sofa arm, to my huge relief. 'I'm sure you're being an insidious corrupting influence, Tony,' he said. 'And anyway, my aunt wants to talk to you — probably has a bone to pick, she always does. You haven't got a drink, Susannah. Don't go away, I'll be right back. White wine okay?'

Ludo had moved on. Dominic Elwes, at the other end of the sofa, was being morosely uncommunicative. I re-crossed my legs, smoothed the skirt of my short white dress with its silver-banded middle and tried to contain a fiercely beating heart. Alicia was always at the front of my mind, but Tony Lambton had just lit her up like a thousand light bulbs. And now she was approaching, coming to sit down. It was too much.

'Hello, Susannah, how are you? How's the work — hard at it as ever?' Alicia perched on the sofa beside me. 'I was just talking to Joe. He's completely one-track about this fabulous-sounding trip, couldn't get him off the subject. But I'm dying to hear, is Sinatra as sexy and drop-dead gorgeous as you'd expect? Did you absolutely melt?'

'I did a bit, especially when the eyes were full on! But I'm sure this trip's a pipe-dream. It was a spur-of-the-moment, friendly remark that he'll forget in a flash.'

'No, it really seems to be on. Joe said, when he phoned Henrietta afterwards she told him her friend Gloria had confirmed it, saying she was invited, too. And you've got dinner with Frank and Dean Martin at the Mirabelle tomorrow. I mean, wow!'

'Well, let's wait and see, shall we?' I said tightly, seething. Joe hadn't told *me* any of that, only that he'd phoned Henrietta to thank her. No word about dinner at the Mirabelle . . . What shitty right had Alicia to know first? 'And anyway,' I continued, deciding to bluff it out, 'I don't see much hope of tying up plans in a restaurant with Frank and Dino hamming it up. Frank calls him Dag.' I slipped out this newfound knowledge defiantly. 'They'll be planning their nightlife and how to dodge the fans. It's all so academic. We couldn't afford the fares, and I'm sure they dress like it's the Oscars every night out in Beverly Hills, sequins and slinky fishtail ballgowns. No way have I got the clothes.'

'I've got cupboards-full,' Alicia said, 'which I certainly won't be wearing. I'm pregnant actually, nearly five months. You can borrow anything you like. You must!'

I stared, desperate not to let slip any emotion. Whose baby? Joe's? Toby's? 'That's wonderful!' I exclaimed, struggling to force out a semblance of a smile. 'Terrific news.' My mind was feverishly trying to imagine what it might mean. Alicia taken up with the baby — even possibly showing more interest in her husband? Some hope. 'Toby must be over the moon,' I said, fishing.

'He'd better be. He hasn't totally tuned into it yet, though, all the ramifications . . . '

And what were those? I gazed tensely at the smiling, blooming, two-faced woman beside me on the sofa; full-lipped, rich chestnut hair tumbling onto her smooth, bare shoulders. The band at the top of her silky strapless dress was tight, but her thrusting melon-shaped tits were still on show; no one could miss them under the pink-silk folds.

'I'm serious about the clothes,' Alicia said. 'I'd love to think they were being used.'

'Thanks, that's amazing of you, but let's see if this trip's really on.' I shut up after that, unable to take any more. How could she come and plonk herself down next to me so brazenly? How did she have the gall? Even Alicia couldn't keep up the phony smiles and chumminess for long; she soon drifted off, back into the smoky body of the room, leaving me shaking like a reed.

I stayed on the sofa listening to Cy and his Calypso rhythms. My stomach ached with period pains; my eyes smarted from the fug and the effort not to cry. It was after midnight. I had an early booking, a full day's modelling ahead of me and Joe would want to stay for hours. Did I have to take off home alone and leave him to Alicia's charms? But staying or going made little difference, I had scant hope of sleep either way.

Tony Lambton's advice was in my mind, which brought a bitter smile to my lips. It wasn't much use to me — I was hardly going to put it into practice. I was Joe's little bourgeois wifey, after all, far too middle-class to rise above his unfaithfulness and shape up to the ways of the world.

5

Simon's expression was unreadable. They were standing close in the bedroom and Daisy held her breath. It felt like being stranded on a precipice and praying he'd throw a rope; her heart was beating fiercely enough to fracture her ribcage.

He'd appeared unexpectedly an hour ago, at lunchtime. Daisy had been baking bread; the house smelled and looked like a French boulangerie, stacked with still-warm baguettes and loaves. She was late with her cookery column and had planned to write up the recipe then pop over to Chelsea with some loaves for Susannah and Stephanie.

Simon hadn't wasted any time. He'd had her quickly and selfishly as soon as he was in the door, right there in the hall, overwhelming and thrilling her for the short-lived moment. He'd immediately immersed himself in his iPad afterwards, preoccupied, sending emails. Daisy made him his favourite ham and pickle sandwich, poured wine, brewed coffee. When he'd eventually come behind her at the sink, nuzzling her neck and feeling her up again, she'd led him upstairs, knowing she had to tackle him over America and lay it on the line. She couldn't keep putting it off.

She ached for him to understand, to be ungrudging and a little less selfish for once.

'You must see what an incredible chance this is, darling,' she urged, trying as well to please with her eyes, 'I'm otherwise going to have to sell the house, which I really love, and move to a grotty flat somewhere miles out, which would be much harder for you to get to. It's my one chance to avoid that, and it's the boys' home, after all — they've only just started at university. And I can't let Susannah Forbes down, not now.'

'Don't make so effing heavy of it,' Simon said. 'It sounds a very flaky, one-off job to me. Go for a couple of weeks, even a month, get your first pay-cheque, show willing then have some unavoidable crisis or other, and beat it. I need you here, Daisy; you're everything to me, lover girl. And I had thought I meant something to you, too — more than soft furnishings at least.' They were standing facing each other and his eyes didn't stray. 'Does all that really come before me — before us? She's using you, babe, can't you see?'

He brought her face close, holding her jaw, and Daisy parted her lips quivering with hurt and desire. The cruelty in Simon was a sexual force. She couldn't escape.

She'd once heard a heroin addict describe the power of dependent need. It could put you beyond sanity, beyond humanity, unhinge you to the point of raising a hammer to a child or slashing out with a blade; you'd do whatever it took to feed your need.

Simon was still staring, wanting an answer. 'You could come over,' Daisy said helplessly. 'We could meet in New York . . . '

'No, too risky and I have things on here. I'm on the edge of one or two useful deals. Listen, darling, Sarah takes the kids up to her mother in Northumberland at the start of the holidays; she'll be away at least two nights at the end of June. We can have that time together. Don't let me down, Green Eyes. I've got one cold hard woman in my life, don't be another. But if you bugger off for months on end . . . where's the caring in that?'

He kissed her gently and took her to bed. His lovemaking was slow and sultry; Daisy felt enveloped, as if she really meant something to him, after all. And she still felt it later, sitting in her leafy back patch in the evening sun, sharing a chilled bottle of Sancerre and a sweet hour together. Her tiny garden felt like a hidden bower. She went back after he'd left. The wisteria was in scented flower, saxifrage plants filling every crack in the paving; her solanum was in bud, the tree peony had its first shaggy shell-pink bloom . . .

Taking the glasses and bottle indoors, she stood still for a moment, looking round, staring at the mess and clutter from their sandwich lunch. The kitchen was full of rich aromas, piquant basil and geranium plants, the newly baked bread. She had her writing to do, planning, packing. Where was the joy in any of it? Daisy sank down onto a kitchen chair. The plane tickets were bought and she was going — at least for three or four weeks.

★ ★ ★

71

Stephanie was on the phone, dealing with a small flurry of late calls from America, suppliers and contacts mainly, but she was never in a hurry to go home. She looked over enquiringly with the phone pressed to her chest. 'It's Daisy, Susannah. She's been baking bread and wants to pop over with some loaves for us, if that's okay.'

I took the phone. 'Of course, Daisy, thanks — a treat — only can you come right away? My friend Charles is here and we can all have a quick drink before we must be off to the theatre.'

Charles was taking me to a Pinter revival and staying the night. He was occupying himself upstairs while Stephanie and I finished off in the office, mussing up the flat with his newspapers and earthy home-grown vegetables. He'd left them on a kitchen worktop looking like a still-life painting; white-based asparagus spears, baby carrots, plump peapods and a bunch of rhubarb with vast dark-veined leaves.

He hadn't chosen an ideal night. I had an appointment early the next morning with *Cosmetic Solutions* in the slim hope that they had some miracle solution for my faded old face.

I turned, hearing Charles descend the spiral staircase. 'Can I get you two a drink?' he said, coming over, 'Steph, what'll it be?'

'A wee gin and tonic,' she said, her eyes lighting up. 'Then I must be off.'

'And you, Susannah?' He touched my bare arm with his chunky ice-filmed glass. His face could crease and collapse as much as it liked, I thought with frustration, and lose none of its aged appeal. He had a high forehead, eyebrows that were thick and bushy enough to comb — unlike what was left of his hair — deep-set eyes, walnut brown. Eyes that often gleamed with private amusement as if he had some witty diversionary plan up his sleeve that was keeping him entertained. He was rangy without being particularly tall, yet having caught the last year of National Service, good at standing up straight.

'That's a very large whisky,' I said primly, eyeing his glass. 'You'll go to sleep in the play. I'll have the other half of Stephie's tonic, thanks.'

'How boring. They drink like cowboys out on Long Island, you'll have to keep up.'

'Isn't it sailors? Will you come and see me? You know your way round those parts — you even like ice in your whisky.'

Charles shook his head. 'No, I'd queer your pitch. You've set your sights on this maturely perfect American,' he kissed my cheek, 'that's clear to see. And I have to get on with the book; my deadline was last month. Cowboys drink buckets, think of the saloon bars in Westerns.' He gave me a cryptic look. 'You could come to Norfolk instead, bring your Mr Warren over for a long weekend. He might enjoy a spot of squelchy rurality for a change.' I knew Charles too well to bother to correct his nonsense mixing up of the name. At least it meant he cared a bit about me going, which was a comfort.

It would be easy to see Charles in the context of his ancestors, a great-great-grandfather who'd fought for the repeal of the Corn Laws; a family that stretched back to George Villiers, after whom half of Covent Garden was named. And he was, after all, an estate-owning, Labrador-loving countryman. But to pigeonhole him would be to miss his flip side. Charles was a thinker, a dreamer, given to travelling to remote uncomfortable corners of the globe simply to reflect on life. He'd spent a year breaking in horses on a Colorado ranch, another year learning Chinese when he'd taken risks to help dissidents. Even with his biographies, he chose offbeat characters for his subjects, loners and individualists; he liked to explore their lives minutely, yet always allow them their own voice.

He'd reappeared with our drinks and was perched on the edge of Stephanie's desk, smiling and looking expectant. 'Now tell me,' he said, 'do either of you know what I mean by Dinkies?'

'Weren't they those little cars?' Stephanie said. 'Like matchboxes?'

'Quite right, but when I asked the salesgirl in a toyshop if I could see her Dinkies I was nearly arrested! She went all set-mouthed and called over the supervisor. 'Watch it, mate,' he said. 'Any more of that lip and you're outta here'.'

The buzzer sounded and I let in Daisy, who looked bemused at the sight of the three of us, grinning like fools. I introduced Charles. 'We were talking about Dinkies,' he said, beaming. 'Ever heard of them?'

'Not again, Charles! It's not that funny and I'm sure Daisy would have you arrested too.' Daisy shook her head in smiling confusion and took her carrier of crusty loaves into the office kitchenette. She looked almost as if she'd been crying, which was worrying, and was much less

74

exuberant than usual.

'The boys okay?' I asked, as she returned. 'All set for the holidays in your absence?'

'They're trying not to show too great a thrill at the prospect of having the house to themselves. They're at university,' she said to Charles, brightening up and meeting his eyes, as though warming to him and feeling more able to contribute. 'One of them, Sam, has a serious girlfriend already and he even asked, last holidays, if she could move in with us.'

'And did you let her?' Charles gave a teasing smile, ready to be amused.

'No. I told him it wasn't on, that we'd be just too much on top of each other, only Sam was a bit quick for me. 'But that's what it's all about, Mum,' he said. 'That's the whole idea!'' Stephanie took a moment to get there, then, given a rather strong gin, went into gales of laughter.

'I must be going,' she said, a little pink in the face and steadying herself. 'Thanks for the bread, Daisy. With the smell of it, I'll get envious looks on the tube.'

'Time we were off too,' I said. 'Call you tomorrow, Daisy. Oh, and Warren phoned. He's sending a car to the airport and talked of arranging soirées, visits to the Beach Club. I had to remind him we were there to work.'

★ ★ ★

My beauty appointment was probably a lost cause since we were flying out in days, which left too little time to have anything very worthwhile done. I told Charles I was having a medical MOT and kissed him goodbye, feeling guilty about it. He'd be gone before I was home. He had a local lunchtime commitment, his grand-children for the weekend, a cataract operation next week, yet he'd made the time to see me and even shown a little jealous pique.

We got on, got it together in bed in a comfortably familiar way, but there was always the same old impasse. Moving to Norfolk would, I knew, bring a sense of dread. It would make me feel like an old nag being put out to grass, marking out my days.

At *Cosmetic Solutions* I was given a form to fill in by a pretty young assistant with a black bob, and shown into an elegant first-floor Harley Street consulting room. My appointment was with Angelica Kavouni and I was admiring the décor as she came in. 'It's very soothing,' I said, appreciating her positive handshake and eye-contact. 'I love the willow-tree silk panel on the wall, calm and delicate, just right.'

'That's one expert praising another! A client of mine is an interior designer and she helped me with the room. Now, what can I do for you? I see you're a friend of Mrs Beamish.' Angelica was attractive, slim and dark, and she had an intelligent look, intellect and competence. Nothing about her suggested she went in for flannelling.

I explained the shortage of time and that I didn't want any Botox or pouting lips. 'Just something to make me look a bit fresher, brightened up, a little less faded and slumped.'

'You've narrowed the field right away. I would normally offer a range of non-invasive options, fillers and low-dose Botox, which does keep the main expression lines, just reduces their intensity. However, I think Fractora would be ideal for your face. You might consider the other suggestions later on, combination treatments are very much in vogue, but this is a light radio-frequency treatment that will refresh your skin beautifully.'

'What are the after-effects? What's the downside?'

'Have you anything much on this weekend? You will be quite red in the face for a couple of days, but you can cover it with make-up.'

It was Friday. I had no plans apart from supper on Saturday with my photographer son, Josh, who was arriving back from his Kenyan fashion shoot today. Angelica was waiting for a response. 'It's a good time for me,' I said, feeling twitchy all the same, 'if you can fit me in.' Josh could handle his mum with a bright red face, I felt sure.

After the half-hour treatment, which involved a trawl over my face with a small machine that made popping noises, I asked about the safety of breast implants. Not something I'd ever seriously contemplated, though I'd never got over the painful feelings of inadequacy all those years ago, the fear of comparisons with Alicia.

Her affair with Joe when I was hardly out of my teens and blithely naïve, had been shattering. I'd worn my misery like a dead bird round my neck, and even now there were times when I could still feel its weight. Alicia had a lot to answer for. She'd remarried a couple of times and had died very recently, I'd been told.

'Are people put off having breast implants now, after all the scares?' I asked, curious.

'No, not at all. The latest trend is fat recycling from the thighs to the breast. It was proposed at least ten years ago and extensive research has concluded that it's quite safe. It is very popular, because the patient gets body sculpting and the breasts are very soft, none of that unnatural rigidity, and provided your weight remains steady there is a forty to sixty per cent long-term increase in breast size. It is done with special needles too, so there is no scar, and only twilight sedation is needed.'

'It sounds too good to be true,' I said, wondering if I was really too old and squeamish ever to contemplate it.

'No, it is true — and good! It costs a few thousand, though. Well, I'm always here,' she smiled, shaking my hand and seeing me to the door, 'if you ever decide to take the plunge.'

'You mean as in plunging bras and cleavage?' I queried and she laughed.

Taxiing home, I eyed my tingling face in a tiny handbag mirror, peering close for any dramatic reddening, but there was nothing yet to see. I tried to talk some sense to myself: all this effort to restore a little bloom, hung on a five-minute chat with Warren Lindsay at a party. A man to whom the idea of taking me to dinner hadn't even crossed his mind.

His interest had been all about my designing skills, nothing to do with the smoothness of my skin. He'd been in the throes of a bitter divorce, tediously so, and however maturely attractive, who knew how deeply, genuinely dull he could turn out to be? A couple of months on Long Island was all good and fine, but to go out there expecting romance and excitement? Let's get real. My phone was pinging, texts coming in. One was from my daughter, Bella — and Josh was back, he'd just landed. I read his text first. *Off into Vogue, Mum, re pics and shoot, but we're on for tomorrow night? C U then, can't wait!*

I texted back feeling, as always, an emotional rush and tinge of concern. I worried about Josh, never entirely sure how happy he was, how fulfilled. He was at the top of his game, artistic, successful; he had sensitivity, good looks — he could make people laugh. Yet despite all that he seemed vulnerable somehow, even at forty.

Bella's text was warming, too. She wanted to do a family Sunday meal.

Josh home, you zooming off — can you make lunch here, Mum? I'll do easy food. Al and co. can come, too.'

I texted to say that was great, nothing better and I'd bring the wine and a pud. The bonds of family were what mattered and I pulled the ties tight. My three children were loving and thoughtful, never grasping. And close — they got on. Bella was a mother to us all.

* * *

By the morning I had a bright red face. I looked like a tomato. Whatever would Josh think? Out came the make-up and I piled it on thick. I warned him about it on the phone, which caused some laughter and later, when he walked in the door — looking deliciously tanned in an open-neck white shirt, his hair lifted by the sun — he didn't let up.

'What's this all about, Mum, all this beautifying? This American must have really caught your eye. Husband number five, by any chance?' Josh handed over a pair of carved wooden elephant bookends, heavy and polished to a golden sheen. 'These are for the lav or somewhere,' he said. 'I had to buy things, they're all so desperately poor in that beautiful country.'

I had a vivid image of a hollow-cheeked youth in oil-stained rags, squatting in the red Kenyan dust, toiling for hours to turn out something so accurately and elegantly carved. Seeing Josh, feeling emotional, the tears began to prick at my eyes.

I set him straight about 'this American.'

'Don't hold your breath, Josh. I'm not about to marry a client — and after only meeting this guy for minutes I suspected an underlying dullness.'

'Bet you he falls for you, though. He couldn't fail to — you look bright pink and gorgeous,' Josh said, and hugged me close.

We talked about his intrepid models, quite prepared to rough it on the trip, and the obliging leopards who'd almost, Josh said, seemed to pose. We argued about the Republican contender for American President. Josh was for him, surprisingly, while I was against. Over spinach soup and steaks, his favourites, I told him all about Daisy and her ghastly lover. It was a rare delight of an evening and I hugged it to myself, rising to make the coffee.

'Does a trip like this one to Long Island revive memories, Mum?' Josh asked, bringing the plates over to the dishwasher. 'You're an old hand at the States now, but it must have been wild, arriving in California with Bella's dad, modelling in New York, all that glam stuff when you were still so young.'

'Sure, it was amazing, my first time in America and plunged straight into a Hollywood whirl. The flight took over thirteen hours and no films on board, of course. I have been thinking back actually, more than I've done in years. It's partly because of this girl, Daisy, I was telling you about. The mistakes she's making are very similar to the ones I made. It seems we women never learn!'

6

September 1961

We were coming in to land. It was hard to believe. I was glued to the window, gazing down at the sprawl of Los Angeles, low square blocks of buildings spreading as far as the eye could see. We'd flown under clear skies, but it was evening now, dusky and hazy, and the city had a spattering of lights. I felt aflame, burning with anticipation and thrill. Nervous, too: my heart was spinning, the blood speeding in my veins.

Somehow we'd found the fares, the lowest class but still a whopping £239 10s return. Joe had sold a pair of antique Chinese Canton vases, one of his sillier extravagances bought after seeing something similar, staying with one of his smart-set friends.

He nudged me with his elbow. 'We may have to get a cab. I'm not sure if we'll be met.' He sounded surprisingly unsure of himself. It must be even more unnerving for him, I realised, the thought of the recording sessions, being neither too pushy nor fawning; properly respectful while needing to sound in the know. Quizzing a legend like Frank must seem more daunting than a whole row of first nights.

'You'll do great,' I said warmly, and he squeezed my hand, giving me hope.

'I'd bloody better! I've never written a book

before.' It was rare for Joe to show any vulnerability and to need a moment of togetherness. As we stepped down onto the tarmac, the start of a unique shared adventure on the other side of the globe, I carried on daring to hope that it could bring us a little closer and help to heal scars.

We joined a wearyingly long line of tired travellers, shuffling forward, passports clutched. 'It's a bit of a dump, this place,' Joe said, looking round. 'I expected LA's airport to be state-of-the-art; instead it's like a load of old Nissan huts.'

'It's temporary,' a man in front of us said, swinging round with a look of affront. He had on a black motorcycle cap with a *Triumph* winged logo. 'The airport's being rebuilt.'

'It's our first time in America,' I explained, trying to make up for 'old Nissan huts', 'Terribly exciting.'

Joe dug me in the ribs. 'For God's sake!' he hissed. 'Think he gives a damn?'

A woman edged up beside me and stared. 'My, just look at you . . . you an actress? You must be a famous lady.' Joe looked irritated. He was the famous one, not me.

The beefy-armed guy who stamped our passports chatted about his aunt in Liverpool and wished us a great vacation. Through customs, though, and uncertain what to do, the airport felt a colder place. People pushed and jostled, no one seemed approachable.

A youngish man wearing a natty, sharp-pressed dark suit came towards us. 'Mr Joe Bryant?' he enquired. 'I'm here to meet you, the limo's right outside. I have a note from Mrs Romanoff.'

Keeping hold of a pair of black leather gloves, he felt in a pocket and handed over a heavy cream envelope, blue-edged and crested. 'I'm Arthur, by the way,' he said. 'You folks stay close and the porter will follow.'

The limo was vast, long and black, luxuriously carpeted. Splits of champagne in a bucket, along with two flute glasses, were wedged on a ledge. 'Wayho!' Joe exclaimed, grabbing one, popping the cork and catching the spills with puppy-like licks of his tongue.

We read Gloria's note. *Welcome friends! We want you to hurry and come to a party! Arthur will take you directly to the house — the maid is there to look after you — and he'll bring you on to the restaurant just as soon as you've freshened up. We're hosting the party in the ballroom and it's a black-tie affair. Longing to see you, make it as soon as you can!*

We'd been on the go for eighteen hours. We were on borrowed time, though, and riding high. Joe was grinning like a hyena.

The Romanoffs' guest cottage was thoughtfully furnished with curtains and loose covers in matching chintz. It was an English look, yet with little differences, another way of folding towels, an abundance of cushions; jelly beans in a bowl, spare toothbrushes . . .

'Stop gawping, can't you?' Joe yelled from the bathroom. 'Let's get there.' I dived into my suitcase, settling on a dropped-shoulder white silk top and a long taffeta skirt; my own clothes, not Alicia's, the skirt full and a jewel-coloured tartan, ruby, emerald and amethyst.

84

I had brought one or two of her outfits with me. I'd fought with my pride, but in the end felt a grim masochistic need to make Alicia very well aware of me, to plant myself squarely in her path to Joe and try to touch her conscience. I was Joe's wife and he was signed up to me, not her, and we were off to California. Alicia would be far away, out of sight — if not out of his thoughts or mine.

She'd pressed me about the clothes as well, calling after Rory's party, suggesting a time to come, but in the event it had been ghastly. Being in her bedroom, stiffly polite, choosing a couple of outfits — any two, I didn't care, didn't want to take them — a print dress, a heathery wool suit with strips of black braid on the front like a devil's fork. I'd left her large silent house in Belgravia with the clothes in a transparent, zipped moth-protector over my arm, feeling mangled and trampled, wretched, humiliated.

Whether or not she'd intended to hurt and shock was hard to know, but Alicia had managed it triumphantly — simply by telling me the story of the run of cupboards along her bedroom wall. 'A hidden door was left in at the back when they were built,' she said. 'It doesn't show at all from the landing side with the patterned wallpaper, and I've always thought what a typically French little touch. We'd bought the house from a Parisian couple, in fact. I mean, a lover hearing a returning husband on the stairs would only have to dart in there, behind all the clothes, and make good his escape!'

How could she have said that? Had she no shred of sensitivity in her soul? It slowed me up, sitting on a padded chintz stool in Beverly Hills, putting on false eyelashes, the bile rising inside me all over again. Alicia might be thousands of miles away, yet I could never escape like the lover in the cupboard. She was constantly in my mind.

It was tiredness, I told myself, making me turn up that particular stone. And I'd been feeling so elated, on such a high.

Joe was staring at me in a vacant way. He looked coolly glamorous in his dinner jacket, slim and sinuous, very British. 'Will I do?' I asked, needing reassurance. 'They're sure to be dressed up as if it's a Royal banquet. Do you think Sinatra will be there?'

'Dunno. Come on, if you don't stop wittering, we'll never find out.'

★　★　★

Sharp-suited Arthur was waiting and we drove in style the short distance to Romanoff's. He shook his head vehemently when Joe felt in his pocket. 'Oh no, you put that back, Mr Sinatra's orders. You go on in and have yourselves a grand time.'

Shown to the ballroom, we stayed by the door, adjusting to the low lighting, the buzz of chatter rising above the band, the red-plush luxury. The crisp starched linen on the tables looked almost fluorescent, brilliant white squares dotted around the floor, which was packed with couples dancing. Many of the faces seemed uncannily familiar. I had the weirdest feeling, staring round at a roomful of strangers, of knowing half the people there.

Gloria saw us. She hurried over with enthusiastic greetings, and as we joined her husband Mike at the table, he rose, grinning from ear to ear. 'Gorgeous girl,' he said, giving me a squeeze.

'Frank's just talking to Tuesday Weld,' Gloria said. 'He'll be with us in a minute. He's on our table, and Bob Hope and Dolores are, too. Oh, do look at Bob on the dance floor, showing off those fancy steps of his!'

Bob Hope was twizzling and pointing his toes, laughing with his partner as they swirled around, looking for all the world like someone I knew of old. It was surreal.

'And isn't that Bing Crosby as well?' I asked, staring gormlessly. 'And Edward G Robinson! I've seen so many of his films. My father used to take me as a child.'

'We'll get Eddie over,' Mike said. 'You must meet him. He'd love meeting you too, you can be sure.'

'Hey, you're here, you made it, that's a gas!' Frank joined us, flashing his familiar white-teeth smile. He immediately took charge, summoning a waiter, seeing to people's drinks and the wine. He ordered a Mouton Rothschild '49.

Joe looked astounded. 'And I'm still reeling from that monumental Margaux '47 we had at the Mirabelle,' he said. 'It'll be hard landings back home!'

Frank grinned. 'You're coming along to Monday night's recording session, right? Just roll on over, eight o'clock at the studios. I never record before evening time, the voice is more relaxed, no broken mirrors in the throat. You should talk to Nelson

Riddle too, while you're here, set up an interview. He's the best, the greatest arranger in the world. He's like a tranquilliser — calm, slightly aloof, never gets ruffled. One of the true greats,' Frank said, 'and they have their ways. With Billy May it's like having a cold shower. He's all pressure, but I don't mind that. Too much time available equals not enough stimulus.'

He turned and pinned me with his dazzlingly blue gaze. 'Joe's gonna be busy; how'd you like to go on the sets of *Manchurian Candidate?* It's a helluva film. I'm real excited about my Major Ben Marco character. I've been living that part, I can tell you, more than any other. I'm through filming now, just one scene left to do in New York, but Larry Harvey's still on set. He'll see you right.' Frank tipped back his chair and called over his shoulder. 'Hey, Larry, come meet these kids from London, Joe and Susannah Bryant. He's a young stage actor and she's one helluva chick, a real barn burner! I'm telling her she should look in on *Manchurian*, see what it's all about.'

It was fixed up in no time. 'It'll be my pleasure,' Laurence Harvey assured me. 'I'll send the Rolls to pick you up.' He had a thin elegant face, high cheekbones; a voice that was like nectar, honeyed and liquidly mellow. He was immensely smooth, super-sophisticated — utterly, compellingly charming.

Mike Romanoff nudged my arm. 'It's a lilac Rolls,' he whispered. 'A gift from Larry's friend, Joan.'

'What's a barn burner, Mike?' I whispered

back when I had a chance.

'A broad who's all polish and class,' he replied, with his pitted, beat-up face creased in a grin. It cheered me up; I wasn't so bourgeois out here, I thought, wishing Joe had heard.

I danced with Bob Hope, who held me very tight and swung me round the floor. I practically flew! Back at the table, baseball ruled. The New York Yankees were zapping the Boston Red Sox in the World Series. Bob, who had a stake in the Cleveland Indians, seemed resigned.

'I'm a loyal son of a bitch,' he sighed. He was never at a loss for a quip. Someone blew a kiss to Gloria and he said solemnly, gazing deep into my eyes, 'People who blow kisses are just hopelessly lazy.'

When his wife tutted at that, wagged a finger and took herself off to the loo, Frank wagged a finger at Bob and tutted in a mimicking way. 'That's one of Bob's standard lines,' Frank said, with a great big grin on his face. 'You watch out for him, he's a player, famous for it. And he thinks he can get away with anything. When Dolores caught him in bed with a broad once, he sat up and said, 'It's not me!''

Bob kissed my hand. 'Not true, don't you believe a word of it. I just like making friends.'

Frank drank bourbon, Jack Daniel's; he pressed others to have vodka stingers and jiggers of brandy, but stuck to his 'Jack's'. 'Not too much water,' he stressed. 'Water rusts you.' He smoked Lucky Strikes, courteously offered cigarettes, which he lit with his gold Dunhill lighter. He watched for empty glasses like a hawk and sprang forward with an ashtray the moment ash was about to fall. His manners were impeccable. There was more to him than an arresting directness and the incontestable blue of his eyes.

★   ★   ★

Laurence Harvey sent his Rolls for me as promised; it was as lilac as the blooms in spring. 'You won't see another like it,' the elderly uniformed chauffeur assured me with pride, holding open the door. 'It's unique.'

By the time he returned me from a day on the sets of *The Manchurian Candidate* I'd watched Larry doing one of his terrifying scenes with Angela Lansbury. I'd mingled with dirt-smeared, sweaty, tin-hatted soldiers who chatted me up on a set that was a squalor of frying pans, bowls of eggs and fold-up chairs. I'd spied other sets littered with oriental lanterns and white wicker chairs, Korean extras lolling around. Press photographers had taken pictures, even of me. It was quite a day.

Next evening we were included in an invitation from Ella Fitzgerald, dinner at her home, just Sinatra, the Romanoffs and ourselves. Frank was coming alone; he'd been on his own at the star-studded party the night we arrived as well. Gloria said the Juliet Prowse phase of his life was over and he was travelling light — albeit dating Marilyn Monroe on and off, in a friendly way. She'd been in a low patch, having treatment, and he thought she needed looking after.

Driving to Ella Fitzgerald's house on a balmy

evening in Beverly Hills, everything seemed beyond dreams. The streets were wide and quiet — no one ever out walking, not a soul — and lined with lushly tree-screened properties that reeked of wealth and seclusion. I felt in a place as remote from everyday life as the Galapagos Islands. World news, events beyond California, hardly rated a mention in the local press. I thought of home for a minute, of my parents nervously minding Frankie, the cracked lino in my kitchen, the modelling jobs I was missing. Alicia too, as always, and whether Joe had called her, long-distance. He'd gone to the post, but was in touch with his agent, other people, and she had a husband, after all. Wouldn't letters be on the risky side?

'Nearly there,' Gloria said, snapping me out of my momentary gloom. She'd told us that when Ella bought the house recently, on North Whittier Drive, an exclusive corner of swanky Beverly Hills, local residents had muttered their disapproval. I'd felt shocked and saddened that even stardom couldn't transcend the boundaries, that discrimination and prejudice was ingrained. Frank, Gloria added, hadn't held back in his disgust of local opinion.

I knew the strength of his feelings. Joe had just interviewed Jimmy Van Heusen, a favourite song-writer of Sinatra's and great buddy. Jimmy had described Frank's loathing of the segregationists, his wild fury at the slightest hint of racial intolerance. Respect for minority groups mattered to him, and he wasn't afraid to challenge convention.

We were at Ella's front gates. The house,

which was like a Spanish hacienda, was floodlit, with a central fountain in a circular drive and exotic palm trees in a richly planted border. Arthur purred the car away and we went inside. The hall with its hexagonal floor tiles, curving staircase and splendid chandelier, had a feeling of space and friendliness. There was an open-plan living room and I loved the bright dining room too, with its blue hydrangeas in a handsome plantier and sliding glass doors that were wide open onto a walled patio with massed groups of pot-plants.

Ella was surprisingly shy and gentle, far from the image I'd formed from hearing her belt out 'Mack the Knife'. Her hair was beautifully coiffed, curling upwards from her face and she was in a navy lace, sleeveless dress with long strings of pearls. She was big with smooth chunky arms, and her maid, who was dressed in black with a frilled white apron, was the same build; darker-skinned than Ella and with a similarly lovely shy smile.

The maid served the first course, seafood on a platter, then took off her apron and joined us at the oval mahogany table. She did the same during the other courses too, slipping her apron on and off with unhurried calm. Ella clearly wasn't having her maid eating alone in the kitchen. It was original and endearing, although the small interruptions and general atmosphere of polite shyness, to which I certainly contributed, left Frank and the Romanoffs to make the running. Prompted by Joe they talked of Hollywood characters and moviemaking.

Henrietta, Joe's society friend who'd introduced us to Frank and vouched for us, had arrived. We'd moved out of the Romanoffs' guest room to make way for her and into a mini-apartment, more of a bedsit, on Sunset Strip. Funds were tight, but somehow we'd paid a month's rental up front. The Strip was a bit of a disappointment. It bordered on the tacky, no longer oozing the gangster glamour of a Raymond Chandler thriller, nor was it quite as in favour with movie people as of old. We were halfway into the month, though, and off to San Francisco, Vegas and Palm Springs in a couple of weeks, whisked away on the magic carpet of El Dago's inaugural flight — just as Frank had promised, with his typical spontaneity, within minutes of our meeting him at Henrietta's flat. It still seemed unbelievable. I was learning fast, though, that he always followed through.

The first week on our own in the apartment had been almost like old times, Joe busy, being by his standards sweetness and light; taken over and stimulated by his brave unexpected project. A book on Sinatra and his music was quite a challenge. I was helping where I could, making notes, jogging Joe's memory. We'd had a bit of sex too, at last, which had been a comfort, feeding into my cautious hopes of finding our wavelength once again.

But it hadn't happened. Instead, we seemed now, after a second week, to have slipped into reverse. There were no more jokes and communication, no more lovemaking; any hope of building on a few precious days of closeness seemed dashed. Joe was in a bad place.

Was it the sex, my coy, naïve ineptitude? I found it hard to let go. I didn't know what to do and the sense that anything we did was very basic and perfunctory, unlike what Joe and Alicia got up to, made me all the more uptight. I'd only had a single exploratory relationship before Joe, a shy tender lover whom he'd swatted away with ease. Joe had swept me up and proposed in weeks; he was all glamour and panache. An impresario fan of his had even insisted on giving us a full-scale society wedding at his home in Holland Park, the guests spilling out onto a huge balcony overlooking leafy communal gardens.

I longed for Joe to cover me with tingly kisses, arouse and gently educate me, but he didn't think that way. He'd told me of one or two early involvements with older actresses, laughing about how predictable that had been, experienced women, though, obviously who'd known it all. I didn't. I'd married at eighteen with no real clue, no more than one embarrassing sex lecture at school, but I'd absorbed enough from books and films to know I had a lot to learn. The theory was all very well, what I needed was the practical. I needed an expert, a man to give me orgasms at the least, teach me variations, how to enjoy finding ways and wiles of turning him on. Joe had never even tried.

And always Alicia loomed, inhibiting me still more with the fear of comparisons, relentless visions of that tangle of naked limbs in the pool changing-house, visions of Joe's head where it never was with me . . .

'Tell me what I should do, what excites you,' I'd whispered one time.

'Well, not that thing with your nails. Can't you . . . Oh, forget it. What's the point? Keep thinking of England,' he'd muttered sarcastically, flinging himself off me and hunching his back.

He'd been drunk, tensed-up himself, but how long could I go on making excuses?

Yet Joe had been different on our first week in the apartment, fun, affectionate, amusing, charming. Why had he travelled backwards? He'd been awash with excitement and wonder, talking about the recording session, how the Sinatra magnetism had affected the entire orchestra. He'd explained in detail, painted pictures: Frank's total involvement with a song, how he'd shudder, his face contorted into a snarl, his whole frame rocked, quivering, as he sang a key note or lingered on words like 'November' or 'summer breeze'. Watching that sinewy body wrapped round the microphone had been an overwhelming experience, Joe said; it had left him as physically drained and exhausted as he imagined Frank must have been.

'He was mesmeric, wifey. It was an experience I'll never forget, the power of him, the assault on all my senses, standing there, somehow so forlorn and alone, gripping that mike with his chunky gold signet ring glinting in the spotlight.'

Bill Miller, Sinatra's pianist, was called Suntan Charlie because his face was sombre and parchment pale. Joe recounted how he'd cracked up, along with them all, when Frank had said to the lady harpist, 'Make like you're killin' time, baby. Like you're likin' it and want it to last longer.'

Yet even in the telling, even in those cheering, involving moments, I'd sensed Joe killing time himself. He was a restless spirit, not cut out for normal family life. He couldn't handle it. I knew that at heart. Not for him a few hours of togetherness, snug in a cosy marital chrysalis; he couldn't wait to break out and flex new wings. Joe needed lights, action, adulation — and booze.

We were seeing Henrietta that night, at Romanoff's where a flow of fascinating people invariably gravitated to Gloria and Mike's table.

'You don't say!' they'd exclaim open-mouthed, as Joe regaled them with his quick wit and Englishisms. 'No kidding?'

Joe had no business being bored and frustrated, I thought bitterly, no business being so vile to me. Plenty was happening — dinners, parties; Frank was giving a little supper party for Marilyn Monroe the following week and had told Joe we must come. It would be very casual, he'd said, just a few good mates. I was wild with excitement.

It was eleven in the morning. Joe hadn't been up long, but the atmosphere was heavy already. He had his glass of vodka and tonic. He'd given up hiding the bottle.

I debated going out, leaving him to it, but where — to sit in a deli with a book?

'Coffee?' I asked, doggedly persevering. 'I'll nip out soon and get something for lunch. Then why don't we go to see a flick? Quite sexy on a rainy day.'

Joe had his back to me; he was hunched over a rickety, spindly table, his makeshift desk, and stayed facing away. 'Sexy? That's a laugh. You go if you like. I'm busy elsewhere.' He rose abruptly and felt under the blotter, pocketing an envelope hidden there, then strode out of the door, slamming it hard behind him.

I stood watching from the window, not bothering to stem the tears. I saw him pause by a mailbox on the sidewalk a moment, stare at the envelope, protecting it from the rain with his hand before he slipped it into the box and hailed a cab.

I was married, I told myself yet again. I had to make it work somehow.

* * *

That evening, Joe came back from wherever he'd been, more jokey and even-tempered. I felt picked-up too; the telephone had rung minutes after he'd left, a call from my London agent. If I found myself in New York, Sally, the booker, said, I must go to see the Ford Modeling Agency. Eileen Ford had been on the phone that morning, wanting to get me over, a reciprocal swap with one of her girls. 'Why not stop off on the way home,' Sally suggested, 'and pay the Ford Agency a visit? Crazy not to while you're there.' Perhaps I would.

At dinner, over the filet mignon and strawberries Romanoff, zesty with orange, drenched in Cointreau, Henrietta was bouncy and friendly, taking snaps of everyone with her Box Brownie camera, jollying us all along. I felt better, squashed up in the cosy horseshoe bench seating, more able to cope. Late on in the evening, Frank arrived. He sat with us at the Romanoffs' table, wisecracking as people came to pay court, flattering and sweet-talking his audience and stopping every female heart. He held the men's attention, too. Those spellbinding blue eyes did it every time.

'Hey, it's David O!' he said, as a well-built man of around sixty strode in.

Joe looked stunned and catching my eye, whispered impatiently, 'You do know who that is, wifey? It's David O. Selznick. He produced *Gone With the Wind*.'

Frank introduced us. David O had a powerful, slightly formidable face, dark crinkly hair, a large nose. He was a legend. Joe asked after his next film in reverential tones.

'I'm out of it, young man. I'll never make another. Hollywood has moved on. Your wife,' he said suddenly, 'is very beautiful. She has the classic look that everyone in the business is after; it's not all Gina Lollobrigida and tits.' Was I hearing right? I tingled with adrenaline, and my insides clenched tight as he carried on, talking directly to me: 'You should have a screen test. I'll fix it up. Call you, Gloria? I'll do that.'

Only that morning I'd been in tears at the window of the hideously functional building on

98

Sunset Strip, Joe dragging me down into a bog. I had a life, too. Was David O serious? Could I conceivably have a shred of acting ability in me — let alone be any good? If he followed through, a huge *if* — I had at least to give it a try. Life was built on dreams.

I said my stumbled thanks, heart sinking as I became conscious of Joe's frozen smile. Only a wife could have picked it up, but I knew that phony beaming crust of old. It was a thick layer of ice, that smile — it needed to be, to contain the seething. Joe was boiling over inside, lethal fumes that would escape the moment we were alone. It was breakpoint. He didn't want me doing any screen test. I felt wretched, wondering how he'd play it, determined to fight for the right to give it a go.

It was late. People were leaving, even Frank who was off to New York to film his last scene for *Manchurian*. Gloria and Mike were going with him, taking a mini-break from the restaurant. I sent signals to Joe, ignoring the hostile vibes, and he finally made a move.

Gloria drew me to one side during the goodbyes. 'About that call you mentioned from your model agent,' she said. 'We have free use of a suite in the St Regis Hotel in New York and I wondered if you'd like to keep us company. It's a reciprocal arrangement, no costs, so don't worry on that score, and we'll travel with Frank. It's only for forty-eight hours, a quick in and out. Do come!'

How a day and a mood could turn; how things spun on a pin. Joe's acid resentment over a screen test that had been restaurant chat, flattering but not remotely likely to happen, was put on hold. We had to pack a bag and be ready to roll by noon the next day.

7

November–December 1961

The suite at the St Regis was stupendous. I'd never seen such luxury: elegant Sheraton furniture, sofas, writing desks, opulent cream and gilt mirrors, sweeping curtains with swags and tails — and we had yet to see the bedrooms. The sumptuous sitting room had stopped us in our tracks.

Gloria smiled at my awe. 'We can have a nice big room-service breakfast here in the morning,' she said. 'They roll in a table with a heated drawer, a rose in a vase — the works. Let's meet then and make plans, but right now I'm pooped! I'm going to grab the chance, since Mike's out with Frank, probably till dawn, to curl up in bed with a book.'

Manhattan was giving off a tangible buzz. I could feel its throbbing pulse even up on the seventh floor and hear, far below, the blaring horns and metallic sound of screeching brakes and slamming car doors. The city was a temptress, beckoning, luring us out to explore.

'You two should go see the lights,' Gloria urged. 'Stroll the streets and eat out. Frank has plans for tomorrow night, I think, and then we're off again. It's your one chance.'

'George told me about Patsy's, near Broadway,' Joe said. '"Mr S's favourite place", he called it, which sounds a pretty good recommendation.'

101

'Yes, true, Patsy cooks all the traditional Italian stuff that Frank adores. Patsy's a man, his name's really Pasquale — his surname — but back in the forties some immigration wonk wrote down Patsy and it stuck.'

The last thing Joe wanted in his present hostile mood was to be saddled with me, on his very first night in New York. But we were Gloria's guests and she was beaming in that firmly encouraging way of hers, so he had no out.

We went to our bedroom, the smaller of the pair of suites, but still palatial. Our scuffed overnight bag looked lost and sad on the large tapestry-lined luggage rack. Joe flung himself down on the vast bed, scattering the heaped decorative silk cushions, the chocolate and cream of a bowl of profiteroles. 'This bed would sleep an orgy,' he said, but with a scathing edge and he wasn't holding out his arms. His bitter resentment clung as tight as a wetsuit. There was no way to reach him, no way in — and all over a stupid film test.

The concierge said the lights of Broadway stretched from 50th to 41st Street, which was just a few blocks west and down from the hotel. We set off in silence, soaking up the city in our separate ways, the drugstores and tattier shops of the West Side, the harshly lit diners that reeked of onions and fried chicken. There were red-plush establishments too, with a uniformed maitre d' on the door, and an apartment block or two whose entrances looked inauspicious, but probably, being so central, housed grandiose living space inside.

102

The streets steamed. Backed-up yellow cabs, frustrated drivers in Hudsons and Cadillacs, rusting trucks, they all leaned on their horns. People pushed past, unseeing, pressing ahead while never jaywalking; they waited dutifully at every crossing for the lights to change.

Broadway was a familiar sight from postcards and films, yet to be here, right at the hub, gazing up at all the sparkling winking neon, gave me the sort of spring in my step, the bouncy pizzazz that often kicks in after seeing a catchy warm-hearted show. The huge ads and hoardings were as brazen and colourful as peacocks or birds of paradise, all vying to be the brashest and best. I'd made a decision too, and had a sense of release to add to my urge to skip and dance on the pavements.

We seemed to be expected at Patsy's. A table was booked in our name. It was probably George's or Gloria's doing; they'd have known, with the theatre crowds, that the place would be heaving. The tables were tight-packed and it was impossible to talk or even shout over the din, but Joe's look of relief at not having to communicate with me hurt deeply; he could at least have smiled, if only for appearance's sake.

He was ridiculously wound-up and jealous, but was it understandable? He was used to topping the bill, not sharing it, and the movie crowd had made quite a fuss of me, taking fair English looks and shyness as a sign of class and treating me almost like royalty; I'd been having a head-swelling time. And Joe, less in the limelight than usual, had chosen to take that personally. It was pointless and petty, and he knew it — but that only made matters worse.

We ordered fusilli pomodoro for Joe, veal piccata for me — I was still on the protein kick, hung-up on weight loss — and Joe asked for a carafe of red wine and a double vodka and tonic as well to keep him going. 'That'll be Patsy, don't you think?' I gestured towards a long-faced elderly man in a grey busboy's jacket who looked to be in charge. Joe shrugged. He continued to studiously avoid eye-contact so I stared at the walls that were littered with wood-framed photographs, probably of famous people, but no one familiar to me. I watched waiters carrying plates aloft, eyed noisy groups waiting at a small mahogany bar, hoping for tables. I hated us being so conspicuously sour and silent; nearby diners would be whispering, saying that if we were out on a date it was going nowhere, or if married then we'd certainly had the mother of a row.

'The man I think is Patsy is coming our way,' I muttered, leaning forward to be heard. Joe instantly rearranged his features and began to spark. He knew how to play the part.

'Mr and Mrs Bryant? It's a pleasure to welcome you here. I hope you're being well looked after.' He nodded to a waiter arriving who set down glasses of champagne, and Joe was excessive in his thanks. 'My pleasure,' Patsy assured him, wreathed in smiles. 'Now I'll leave you to enjoy your meal.' I wondered, staring after him, what chance we had of that.

Joe downed his champagne and I pushed my glass towards him. The bloom was off my decision, but it was made and I'd stick with it. I sighed. Where was the rosy, copybook marriage of my naive teenage imaginings? Why hadn't I had the baby I yearned for? Was it stress? Something wrong? Should I see a doctor? I had to keep giving our marriage my all; separation or divorce seemed unthinkable. Alicia, the victor . . . She was pregnant. Didn't she want what I wanted, a loving loyal husband and a happy home for her child? A fulfilling relationship, the faithful version that I'd dreamed of?

'Joe, it's not easy in here, I know, with the noise, but can we talk?' He stared impatiently, bristling with suspicion. 'Look, love,' I said, sitting forward, leaning over the table, 'I'm sure nothing will come of the film test and neither David O nor anyone else will follow up on that offhand mention, but just for the record and in the unlikely event, I'd say thanks, but I'd be wasting their time. You're the actor in the family, not me.'

Joe looked too patently relieved, almost triumphant. 'You're tops at modelling, hon, you know that. Do what you do best — the devil you know and all that cock. Acting's a tricky old game. It really isn't your bag, old darling,' he said, trying but failing to sound warm and conciliatory. 'Wouldn't do to have the wifey falling splat, after all. You've made a good decision there, it's just not your scene.'

Why shouldn't it be? Why couldn't he be encouraging, pleased for me to have the chance to find out at least, and even, just possibly, to shine?

I felt a deep, quiet anger, rising tension and bitterness, a reversal of roles. Joe's putdown was cruel. I'd given in, done what he wanted, put him first, hadn't I? Didn't I deserve a scrap of credit for that? Couldn't he, just once, make me feel properly appreciated and loved?

He squeezed one of my knees under the small table, a patronising token gesture that only swelled my rage. Then he poured the last of the carafe into his glass and ordered another, joking and chatty with the waiter, oblivious, it seemed, to my uptight reaction.

But whether innocently or deliberately, he'd shaken my confidence — fragile enough at the best of times — and I began to feel almost relieved. It would have been a disaster for sure. I couldn't act to save my life — I wasn't the type. I'd have felt ill with embarrassment and never able to live it down. Better never to have known what might have been, than suffer the pain of humiliating failure.

Joe was drinking steadily, but he was back on form, making caustic witticisms that had people at nearby tables smothering smiles. He'd finished a second carafe and was onto a third brandy, but meeting my anxious eyes, accepted it was time to go. 'I know, you need your beauty sleep, wifey old bean, off seeing Eileen Ford tomorrow. Can you be on the books of two model agencies at the same time, though?' he asked, showing unexpected curiosity. 'Would you come out to work here for a few weeks or what?'

'Reciprocal arrangements,' I said. 'An American model would probably go to London and I'd come out here some time for a bit, I suppose.'

'When? Where would you stay? Have you thought it through?'

'No, I'm just going to see Eileen Ford since I'm here, that's all.' I had a hazy idea that she occasionally put up models in her home, but I wasn't going to elaborate. Joe needn't think he could have a clear run with Alicia. His questions had seemed a bit keen.

He summoned a waiter and I imagined the bill would be steep, though Joe, in his relief at my decision, looked as if he thought it was worth the doubling of his overdraft.

The waiter returned with a big grin. 'No check, nothing to pay, all seen to.'

I felt uncomfortable. Who'd taken care of it with all that drink? George? Gloria? But as Joe left a decent tip and stood up to go he looked rather more humbly relieved and pleased. He took it as a sign of having made his mark with Frank.

Frank was certainly very good to us, always including us, ever considerate of our needs — as he was with everyone he gathered up into his circle. He travelled with a pack. Sinatra had many names — the Chairman, the Pope, King of the World — and he wasn't called *Il Padrone* for nothing; he suited that Sicilian role of lordly father and protector and had adopted the mantle. He expected loyalty and adulation while in return tucked all his friends under the widespread wing of his generosity.

Joe was up for sex the moment we were back in our hotel room. He was hard and horny,

107

leaning me backwards onto the bed, tossing my shoes, light little pumps, over his shoulders; pulling off my pants and pinging the suspenders on my stockings. He felt around a bit, a two-finger attempt to work up an orgasm, but it was a bit half-hearted and heavy-handed and I was too bottled-up and brooding. I wanted Joe sober, making genuine love to me, not randy sex that felt too much like payback time. I was his wife, not just an available bit of pussy to poke when he was up for it. I was his bloody wife.

★   ★   ★

A white-haired waiter wheeled in the breakfast table and prepared it carefully; smoothing down the pristine tablecloth, arranging gleaming cutlery, glasses of fresh-squeezed orange juice and positioning a slim vase with a single yellow rose. Yellow for jealousy, I thought morosely, as he indicated the warmer drawer with the bacon and eggs.

Joe gave Gloria a run-down on Patsy's. 'You're going again tonight,' she said. 'Patsy's is the one place where Frank can dodge the press. It has a secret door with stairs up to the first-floor restaurant, and Ava Gardner's coming; she's in town. She'll see Frank, but only with others around, never on his own. I feel for him. It must be painful — he does still love her so.'

'Will it be a big party?' I asked, overawed by the evening in store.

'Not very, our lot plus George and Joan Axelrod and the Rubirosas; Rubi is Frank's polo-playing, playboy friend. His wife, Odile, is miles younger and very flirty — especially with Frank! Wear your last night's dress, you looked gorgeous, or you could pop into Bloomingdale's and treat yourself. It's near Eileen Ford's. How about you, Joe?' Gloria turned to him. 'Any plans?'

I glanced at him, anxious to know as well.

'Oh, I'm fine, plenty to do, people to look up. Shall we meet back here around six?'

* * *

The Ford Modeling Agency was on 51st and 2nd Avenue. I walked, leaving acres of time — sensibly as it turned out, since there were steep steps up to the office on the first floor, and it hadn't been easy to find. Pushing open the door, I saw three girls manning a whole row of black telephones, lined up like London cabs. No one looked up; they were too busy thumbing at folders and diaries, holding one phone and speaking into another.

'Who are you?' the nearest girl snapped, noticing me at last. 'Got a book?'

I shook my head, feeling tongue-tied, but a woman at a desk on the far side of the room immediately yelled across to me: 'You're Susannah Forbes.' It was a statement, not a question. 'You're early. Come right here and sit down. I'm Eileen Ford.'

She was a slight, gimlet-eyed woman in a sleeveless charcoal-wool dress who exuded such raw boundless energy that I felt helpless, a limp ineffectual rag. She stood up and shook my hand briskly, throwing back a loose wedge of wavy brown hair as she did and indicating a chair. Her every gesture seemed electrically wired.

'Welcome,' she said. 'Glad you made it. Hey, Rusty!' she barked out, giving me a fright. 'Come take a look. She's perfect.'

The middle girl of the three returned her phone to its cradle and came over. She was tall with strong features, thick eyebrows, deep-set eyes and a mane of reddish hair. She must be the chief booker, I decided, warming to her and grateful for her friendly mother-hen manner.

'Hi, great to meet — ' she said, breaking off with a smile as Eileen cut in.

'Well, whaddya think?'

'She's got it made,' Rusty answered. 'She should go see Penn, of course, and Gil Foreman, he'll love her to death. So will Lillian Bassman, Dale Kane, Bert Stern — they all will! Shall I hit the phones?'

Before I knew it, I was being packed off on a couple of go-sees, without even my book. Eileen said she'd sort that, get onto my London agent for pulls of my head sheet and follow up on the calls. She pushed me to stay in New York, offering a bed and to arrange for a three-week work permit. It was tempting. I was smarting, chewed-up about Joe . . .

But there was Frank's inaugural flight, Marilyn Monroe, and a small sombre voice warning like a priest through the confessional box, of fresh lures and excitements in the Big Apple. I had a marriage to try to keep afloat. As

110

I said my goodbyes and left, the other two bookers looked at me with new eyes. That cheered me up at least.

Gil Foreman's studio was ten blocks downtown, also on 2nd Avenue. I was saving dollars and kept walking. It was a crisp bright day. Sunlight glanced off grimy junkshop windows, refractions of light gilding the leaves on trees, patterning the uneven sidewalk. The wide avenue with its small shops and seediness felt quintessentially New York, energising, from its steaming manholes to its skyscraper skyline. It was alive, different and enriching.

Few people were striding along the sidewalk. A man in a smart suit and brown felt hat gave me the eye. Two bored kids larking about by a roadside news-stand were making faces at passers-by. 'Hey, miss,' one of the kids called after me. 'Wanna be my date?'

Life felt good. But whenever my mood bubbled up, the shadow of Joe was always there like a wisp of cloud over the golden orb in my lit-up sky. I never felt completely light-hearted. But it was a thin sliver of cloud today. I enjoyed the sight of a typical deli with a colourful fruit and veg stall extending onto the sidewalk. A large green and blotchy-white fruit, like a marrow only rounder, caught my eye. 'What's that?' I asked a Mexican-looking youth in a lumber shirt, idling, leaning against the doorpost behind the stall.

'Watermelon. Want one? You from England?'

'No, sorry — just curious.' I'd never seen the whole fruit before.

I reached Gil Foreman's warehouse of a

building. His studio was on the fourth floor. The elevator creaked and shuddered its way up and I stepped straight out into the studio. Facing me was a sort of partitioned-off reception area where a curly-haired girl at an L-shaped desktop was on the phone. I waited, gazing at all the model charts pinned up behind her: no shortage of competition. I could see above the partition into the studio, a vast all-white space. Huge pipes swooped and dived along the ceiling like the inside of a submarine. Loud music was playing, Ray Charles thumping out 'Hit the Road, Jack', and I could hear the click of a camera shutter, voices, a shoot going on.

She finished a call and looked up. 'Hello? Ah, you're the English girl Rusty called about. Gil's shooting, not sure how long he'll be. Can I see your book?'

'I'm afraid it's in London. I hadn't expected to be here.'

She gave me an impatient look as if to say what the hell was I doing there then, but was conveniently distracted by a man coming out of the studio.

'Gil, this is the girl — ' she began, before he overtook any need for her to go on.

'Hey, you're Susannah Forbes!' He came closer and grinned. 'Don't go away, I'm nearly done in there. Hang about — talk to Dee. I want to take a proper look.'

I opened my mouth, but didn't speak, didn't even properly close it again. He was giving me a double-take look that reached into me somehow, this shortish man with a wide full mouth who

112

was holding his arms, slightly apelike, well away from his body. Some quiver travelled through me: that hadn't been a professional look. He swung back behind the partition only to immediately stick his head round it again. 'Don't go away! I want to photograph you.'

He was taking forever. Dee had long given up on small talk, was busy making calls and I'd studied the charts on the wall till I knew every face; studied my diary, my nails. A striking black-haired model finally appeared. She sloped cat-like up to Dee's desk with her tote bag, signed a release form, gave me a cold curious stare and left.

Gil didn't give me a cold stare. He stuck me on a stool in front of a white backdrop and began clicking away. I felt him studying me through his lens. He hadn't much hair — what remained was thin and wispy, but his body shimmered with agility. 'I want you for a bourbon ad,' he said, looking up. 'I want to show these to the client.'

'But I'm flying out tonight, with my husband. Eileen Ford wants me to come back and I'm longing to, but . . . Well, it may have to be after Christmas.'

'Stay just like that — looking at me like that. That's the picture! We'll get you here. Or I'll come to London.'

'I really have to go now.'

'Who else are you seeing?'

'Irving Penn — and I'm due there, sort of now. I, um, must go.'

My head was in a whirl by the time I got back to the hotel. 'It was all amazing!' I confided to Gloria. 'I saw Penn, who's just the best. Everyone at his studio treated him like God. He was delightful, friendly, very calm, measured; he had a sort of solid quiet dignity — and pointy ears! He said we'd definitely work together if I came out — it sounded wonderfully positive. There's masses to tell, but I'd better change quickly if we're expected down in the bar. Oh, and I made it to Bloomingdale's. I've got a new frock.'

I'd bought a low-cut cinnamon dress with a wide matching belt and slim skirt. It showed off my waist and I felt good, but all eyes tonight would be on Ava Gardner.

Frank and the people whom Gloria had mentioned were established in a quiet dark corner of the King Cole Bar, attracting stares, but being left alone. I liked the look of Joan Axelrod, with her short waved blonde hair; she said a warm hello. Odile Rubirosa's greeting was less warm. As her husband Rubi bent to kiss my hand, she turned pointedly to Frank.

He was commanding attention, taking charge and encompassing us all. 'You gotta have Bloody Marys here,' he asserted, as a waiter brought a trayload of them to the table. 'It's the House special, invented right here in this bar. Fernand Petiot, the barman, called it a Red Snapper, and I dunno how the name got changed, but it sure tastes as good! Great bar. Salvador Dali comes in, lives in this hotel when he's in town. Bill and Babe Paley do too, and Marlene Dietrich in her day.'

'That's some Bloody Mary,' Joe said, tasting it. 'Perfection!'

Joe sipped his drinks slowly, but they still disappeared fast and Frank never allowed a glass to remain empty. It worried me no end as refill after refill arrived.

Mike was relating some lewd catchphrase of Frank's, that a hard dick had no conscience. I was more involved in trying to catch Joe's eye to slow him up on his fourth Bloody Mary. 'We'll be going soon,' Gloria whispered, catching the look. 'We're meeting Ava there, and Frank will want to be ahead of her for sure.'

The secret door with steps up to Patsy's first floor was down a skinny little alley that smelled a bit pissy and beery. A solid metal door opened onto a single flight of stairs up to the restaurant where Patsy was on welcoming hand. He ushered us into a screened-off area where a large round table awaited us, white-covered and laid with an artillery of cutlery and glass. Frank settled himself on a plush bench, leaving a space beside him, and gestured to us to sit where we fell. He called for drinks, 'Like now!' and a flurry of bustling waiters saw that bottles of champagne, wine, Jack Daniel's — which made me think of Gil and the bourbon ad — and vodka arrived. We'd been drinking for hours already; the long mural on the wall behind Frank, a sepia-coloured Bacchanalia, seemed a fitting backdrop.

I was seated between Mike and Rubi, Joe was next to Odile on Mike's other side. The clock ticked on — and no Ava. Joe was on his eighth vodka, including the Bloody Marys; I was counting. Hors d'oeuvres were spread over the table to keep us going, and spirits unsurprisingly, were high. *Breakfast at Tiffany's* was just about to open. I was dying to see it, and Frank showered George Axelrod with praise. 'You're gonna win the Oscar, no question. And *Manchurian*'s gonna make it bigtime, too — I feel it in my bones. My best role, your best screenplay . . . '

Joe was up in Axelrod's films and raved about *The Seven Year Itch*. 'An iconic, uncappable masterpiece — and yet you're about to cap it! Adapting Truman Capote can't have been easy either, for sure.'

'*Breakfast at Tiffany's* wrote itself,' George shrugged. 'I could see it all.'

Frank was watching the door. The tension in him was reaching across the table, seeping everywhere, like the glass of red wine that Rubi had spilled.

I had tensions of my own. I'd edged my chair back, about to go to the loo, and had seen Joe's hand on Odile's thigh, rubbing rhythmically. My heart throbbed to a chill beat, I felt wretched through and through. She hadn't brushed his hand away . . . It was the drink, I told myself. She'd know that and was probably just avoiding a scene. Oh, shit.

I stood up abruptly and walked past Joe's chair, close enough to cause him to lift his hand.

116

He wasn't quite as drunk as to be unaware of me.

I calmed down in the ladies' and returned to see Patsy murmuring in Frank's ear. Ava must be arriving. She came in, undoing a headscarf, taking it off and shaking out her lustrous jet-black hair to dramatic effect. Frank was on his feet, we all were, and he settled her next to him with such a look on his face: pride, elation, love and concern.

His emotions were worn on the outside like clothes, but they needed to fit more comfortably. His and Ava's marriage had been doomed, their personalities just too huge to be cut to size. They would stay friends, I thought, come what may. Neither wanted closure. I saw Frank's arm was along the bench behind Ava, his laughter was responsively loud as she took centre stage, swearing cheerfully, downing a Jack Daniel's in one; he adored her.

Gloria was a long-time trusted confidante of Frank's and an objective friend. She'd told us that Ava had gone to live in Spain after the divorce and set up with Ernest Hemingway. They'd had a passionate year together and he'd taught her to love bullfighting, although perhaps too well, since she'd left him for one of its stars, Luis Miguel Dominguin.

Ava herself was a star like no other. I could only stare with open-mouthed fascination at her wondrously arched eyebrows, vermillion lips and the alluring cleft to her chin that exquisitely defined her individuality. She was in a black dress with lacy, unlined sleeves, drinking neat bourbon and easily keeping pace with Frank.

'Are we making a night of it, honey?' she drawled, holding his eyes. 'Doin' the town?'

'Painting it as red as your lips,' he said, bending to light her cigarette. She threw back her head and exhaled. No one could take their eyes off her. 'How's the bullfighter?' Frank grinned; he was all flashing white teeth and tension.

'Fighting, how else? Luis is a toreador in the sack. It's been fucking madness, crazy stuff, but it's winding down. Had to, I guess. I needed a big fat slug of the city.' She touched Frank's cheek. 'So tell me, I hear plenty going on with you and Marilyn?'

'That dame needs looking after,' he said, 'no kidding. Hey, what's with these empty glasses? Patsy, sack the staff!' He needed the tableful of people, friends, but it was quite a strain to be party to his stressed-out emotion. Ava was above showing it; she couldn't care how rude she was, how wild, how pissed. She was uncontainable, a Colossus of a personality. We were little timid mice looking on.

Waiters surrounded us. The booze flowed. Food arrived. Succulent prawns, meatballs in a rich appetising sauce, spicy and thick with tomatoes, crispy zucchini, buttery spinach speckled with garlic. A frothy creamy chocolate pudding followed, Tiramisu. It was new to me and I had to taste it. I'd been eating little, sticking as virtuously close to the protein diet as possible, and gooey puddings were taboo, a real fall from grace. Plunging in my spoon I felt as

118

guilty as a schoolboy dipping into a porn magazine. The Tiramisu, heavily laced with alcohol, was sinfully, deliciously exotic.

It was well after one when we left. Sinatra and his party rolling into Peppermint Lounge caused a stir. The place was packed with everyone Twisting, crushed up together closer than sardines. No one took much notice for long; there wasn't room.

'The Twist has really caught on,' Gloria shouted into my ear. 'Peppermint Lounge was just a sweaty little den and now it's the buzziest place in town. All the city's ravers keep pouring in; it's amazing how they're completely hooked on this new dance.'

They were certainly Twisting like crazy. Someone quipped that we should be drinking screwdrivers. But the Jack Daniel's kept coming, chinking with ice . . .

I was still focused on Joe's straying hand. Did he have other women as well as Alicia? Was that better or worse? Equally bad, but either way I felt sure Alicia was more to him than a casual affair. And if he did play around, did she actually know — or even care? She was a sophisticated, heartless bitch. Somehow I didn't feel tearful; cut-up and bitter, yes, but Gil Foreman was softening the fall. That look had caused more than a momentary frisson. It lived on in my mind. I wanted to see him again.

A kind of defiance was building up in me. A dangerous feeling, but there must be more to life than being walked over. Was I falling out of love with Joe? The thought sobered me into a state of grim determination. I tried hard to concentrate on Joe's specialness. I remembered our wedding day when my father had trodden on my full-length veil. The tiara I'd worn, borrowed from one of Joe's friends, had been askew in every photograph.

Joe had made it a positive highlight. So much better, he said, it stopped the pictures looking all cornball and sugar candy. At his best Joe was compellingly loveable and fun to be with — but was that side of him a thing of the past, gone forever more?

8

'Miss Forbes? I'm Jackson, ma'am, Mr Lindsay's driver. You had a nice flight? Let me take those. The car's right across in the parking lot.'

'Thanks. Good to meet you, Jackson,' I said, giving him my best smile as he slung Daisy's heavily filled laptop bag onto his shoulder and wheeled my small carry-on case. 'It's great to be here.' A porter followed with the main luggage. I'd grown used to the perks of wealth, thanks to poor dear Clive, but porters were new to Daisy.

'I'd been dreading lugging those hefty cases ourselves,' she said, looking back. 'Such luxury!'

'Stick around.' I fixed her with a loaded look. Would porters be enough to keep Daisy from doing a flit home? On the plane she'd swung between a buzzy thrill at the Club Class, New World adventure and looking physically ill from her private angst. Simon was sexually dominating and an unpleasant bully, but he had her in a pincer hold.

Warren Lindsay's black Mercedes purred along the highways. I'd taken to Jackson on sight; he had a distinguished air about him, a natural courtesy. And albeit elderly, he drove confidently and fast, which was cheering; I'd always found the speed limit in the States frustratingly low. I leaned closer behind his solid grizzled head to speak to him. 'About an hour from here, would you say?'

'Maybe a little less, ma'am. We should be there just on six, I reckon.'

The Mercedes sped on, eating up the miles, and I dropped off. Opening an eye, I saw Daisy was bent low over her mobile, but she looked up with an exhilarated shine. 'I'm terribly excited and nervous,' she said. I felt quite nervous, too.

I knew Long Island and its smart village resorts, called the Hamptons, of old, and reaching Southampton enjoyed the feeling of familiarity. We crossed Main Street, the heart of the place that had a sort of square, slightly self-conscious chic about it, a sense of belonging to its summer regulars, and drove on down residential streets that led to the coast.

Jackson slowed in front of a pair of immense wrought-iron gates, curved at the top and incorporating a central scrolled design of Warren's initials. They opened silently as the car approached. The house name was painted on one of a pair of supporting square white pillars: *Great Maples* — our new home from home.

Warren Lindsay was on the doorstep to greet us, casually dressed in mimosa-yellow Bermudas and a short-sleeved white linen shirt. His legs were tanned, his hair more uniformly grey; I felt a small snaking of adrenaline. He pumped my hand, smiling from me to Daisy, pumped hers, welcomed us and asked after the flight.

'It's an honour to have you as my house guests,' he said, with the sort of grave, old-fashioned formality, characteristic of some Americans of his kind. 'My luck was in when you accepted the commission and I'm very grateful. I

122

hope you'll both manage to relax as well, though, while you're here and feel right at home — even as you pull this tired old place apart.' He gave me a long look before turning to Daisy, as though anxious not to exclude her. 'Susannah has told me how pleased she is to have you along — and I get to be lucky twice over!'

His eyes rested long on Daisy as well, which made her blush and become even more effusive.

'You have the most magnificent, sensational house, and seeing it for real after all those brilliant photographs — I mean, actually to be here . . . ' She burbled on while Warren looked flattered and pleased.

'Now I'm sure you both want to rest and freshen up,' he said smoothly. 'I was about to go change myself, but you made such good time. First, come meet Martha who does the cooking, and Luisa, my maid, who will show you to your rooms. She'll help with anything you need, never minds staying late, and Martha lives in so there's always someone right on hand. Martha's an absolute pearl, an excellent cook; you'll enjoy her repertoire, I know — but tell her any of your special requests, of course. Now what shall we say? Meet around eight for a little light supper?'

'Perfect,' I said, 'but really just a snack before the time change catches up with us.'

★ ★ ★

The Hamptons had their own personalities and I'd filled Daisy in, coming over. Easthampton attracted the celebrities, Bridgehampton was new money and Southampton was old — and in more ways than money; some of the immense houses of the famously exclusive, ocean-hugging Gin Lane dated back to the 1880s. They were seriously gigantic properties, called 'cottages' locally — though not euphemistically. It was more just a case of quaint American phraseology.

The sweep of Gin Lane encompassed a peaceful lake, opposite which was the staid and respectable Beach Club. Its members were a select band, proudly aware of belonging to a group to whom life had been kind. People had to wait years and go through endless hoops — mainly the dislikes and foibles of oldstagers — even to be considered, let alone deemed appropriate and allowed to join. Warren was a member, not surprisingly, and since *Great Maples* was just off Gin Lane, walking distance from the Beach Club, we would potter up there often, I was sure.

Luisa, the maid, settled me into a spacious, richly carpeted bedroom. It had a desk, a round table with potted orchids and a piled fruit bowl, walk-in hanging cupboards. It looked out over the neat lawns, tennis court and lavish patio of the photographs, and standing at the bay window, absorbing it all, my modernising urges were to the fore. The house, whose architecture hinted at Lutyens, had square bays and sloping roofs that presided over a basement and two floors. It needed to shake off its shackles of convention, the intercommunicating reception rooms, safe chintzes and European landscape paintings, the high surround of drear box hedging, immaculately clipped. I wanted to lift ceilings, add fanlights, do away with walls; cover the remaining ones with contemporary paintings by the American artists I most admired. Daisy was going to be kept busy.

My ideas for *Great Maples* had begun as a jumble, a shaken kaleidoscope, but now I could see the final pattern. It would be a revolutionary makeover, lighten Warren's bank balance and be too innovative for some of Southampton's stuffiest notables, yet a talking point at the dinner tables, I felt sure.

A rest made all the difference. Showered, dressed in a pair of tight white jeans and sapphire silk top, I went downstairs feeling good, pleased with my smoother-looking face, thanks to Angelica, and more confident, ready for a little flirt or whatever was Warren's game.

He was alone in the sitting room, leaning against a sepia marble fireplace. A huge vase of flowers, stiffly arranged with spikes of delphiniums, filled the grate. He was wearing pink summer trousers now and a loose linen shirt that looked fittingly expensive. Coming forward to greet me, he held aloft a tall misted glass topped with a slice of lemon. 'Join me in a gin fizz? Or would you like champagne? There's anything else as well, of course.'

'I don't often drink spirits, but that gin fizz looks great. Luisa's whisked away armfuls of creased clothes, she's been a marvellous help.'

'That's good; you're in charge now here, remember. I'll come and go, but I promise to make myself scarce and not interfere. It really is a delight to see you again, Susannah, and looking even more lovely than I recall.' Warren brought over my drink and his smile had a provocative glint. 'And after all the travelling too . . . I can't thank you enough for taking this on, I'm impressed with my powers of persuasion!' He held my eyes, only letting go and turning to the door as we heard Daisy's heels tapping across the polished hall.

She came in looking shy and uncertain, arresting in a short white dress with a dizzy print of red poppies. Warren beamed. 'All well, Daisy? Beats me how you can both look so fresh and well after that flight.' He glanced back to include me. 'We're drinking gin fizz. It's mostly soda and crushed ice: can I tempt you?'

'Easily,' Daisy laughed, looking more relaxed and assured. 'And everything's fabulous, thanks. I feel as if I've stepped into the pages of a Scott Fitzgerald novel.'

'Well, you have the name and look the part . . . ' Warren knew how to flatter.

We chatted on — a little formally at first, though the drinks soon burnished our conversation with a sparkier sheen. Martha brought in canapés — roulades of asparagus and skewered prawns with a dip that she said was mango and basil. She was a tall, thin, studious-looking woman, more like a historian or lecturer, yet from her obvious pride and involvement, I felt she must have found her niche and be a natural cook. She soon murmured to Warren that dinner was ready, and we wandered through into the dining room.

It was a depressingly elaborate room, too formal even for city living. A long mahogany table laden with silver, a pair of ornamental pheasants, curly-handled sauceboats, huge candelabra; three silver placemats as well that looked lost, set miles apart.

'May we move up closer together?' I suggested. 'It'll be easier to talk, and I need more of a feel for your lifestyle, Warren. There is so much I'd like to ask. For instance, this is a rather formal dining room and it would help to know if you give many large dinner parties, that sort of thing.'

'God no, none of that now. Willa — that's my ex-wife, Daisy — was the one for entertaining. She never stopped — lavish parties, people for drinks, and we often sat down twelve to dinner at weekends. Martha says she's under-employed these days.'

I'd begun to shift the place mats down to one end of the table, but Martha melted into the room and took over. From her body language she seemed not to mind my interference; it was a good sign. We needed to be able to rub along well together while Warren was away in the city during the week.

Martha had made a supper dish of ravioli filled with lightly spiced crab in a piquant tomato sauce. It was all delectably good.

'So back to my lifestyle,' Warren said, once we'd exhausted our compliments. 'It couldn't be quieter. I lead a hermit's life now, it's a hell of a lot more peaceful.' He gave a curt laugh, more of a dragged-out snarl, as if control of his resentment had snagged and unravelled like a pulled thread. The bitterness over Willa was well dug in.

'Willa had the Long Island crowd in her palm,' he continued. 'She was queen bee, high priestess of the bitching and partying set, which is all the wives do out here all summer while their poor-sod hardworking husbands swelter in Manhattan earning a crust to pay the checks.'

'Hmmm,' I said, thinking how similarly bitter Willa must feel, 'I had an August in the city once when I was modelling, and those same 'poor-sod' husbands spent all their time chasing after any female in sight.'

'Well, can you blame them in your case?' Warren looked pleased with himself, as though feeling that was one up to him. 'Now I have a favour to ask. Southampton has a grand Benefit ball in a couple of weeks; it's the event of the summer, always well supported, and it would give me great pleasure if you'd both come as my guests. My stock would go through the roof, of course, escorting two beautiful women — not that the gossip won't have got started way before then. Your arrival is going to cause quite a stir.'

'I'm sure we'd love to come, wouldn't we, Daisy?' She nodded energetically. 'Can you fill us in a bit more, though?' I asked. 'Explain what it's in aid of and whether it's a dinner, a full-blown dance — the form?'

'And what people will be wearing,' Daisy added, looking alarmed — worrying, I suspected, about keeping her end up with the very rich.

'Oh, it's a dance, the Red Tide Benefit Ball, and called that because there's a sort of red tide that sweeps into the bays every so often, discolouring the waters and killing the fish in their thousands. It's a rampant form of algae, phytoplanktons, that creates terrible problems. The fish are washed ashore, no one can swim, the beaches stink; waterfront properties are unrentable and popular bays like the Peconic, Shinnecock and Gardiner's really suffer. It's a generic problem with no real solution. It goes as mysteriously as it comes,' Warren said, 'but strangles the clam and bay scallop industry, and the fishermen really struggle. So the Benefit's in aid of the Baymen's Association and we locals dig in deep.

'And as for what to wear, Daisy,' he gave her a saucy look, 'it's all about outdoing everyone else: big, big rocks, the full gold lamé, everything you can throw at it — and not only the women. I'll be among the restrained few. Probably wear a blazer and light trousers; no one wears black tie out here any more.'

'Do people know you're redoing the house?' Daisy asked, looking more alarmed than ever. 'The reason we're here?'

'No, I haven't talked about it, in case of a change of plan. I'd explain when introducing you, of course, but as I said, the gossip will already be well under way. Someone will have seen the car returning with you both in it, and Tom Horne will have made sure word gets round.'

'He's the village grapevine?'

'You can say that again!'

Martha came in with seconds of ravioli and a chicory, cherry tomato and rocket salad. She returned with a platter of Italian and French cheeses in perfect squidgy condition, with huge amber Muscat grapes. We were in for a summer of good living.

'So fill us in on Tom, the local gossip,' I said, when she'd left, 'and some of the more colourful characters who'll be at the Benefit.'

'Tom's a long, tall beanpole of a man; he folds himself over like a paperclip when he's dishing the dirt, muttering into any interested ears. He's one sharp cookie, I can tell you; started with a small café on Main Street, opened another one up the road and has since acquired a couple of chic boutiques as well. Any whisper of an owner in trouble and he's in there. People shop with Tom simply to keep up with the scandal, I think, and hear who's the latest to go under the knife. Tom's boyfriend, Oscar, keeps the books. He's a canny operator too — short and carries a bit of weight. They're quite a pair.'

'Easy to spot at the Benefit then,' I said. 'I guess they'll be there?'

'Tom wouldn't miss it if he had to be stretchered in. The same goes for Maisie Stockton who loves the big occasion and she sure knows how to flaunt it — and some! She'll outdo the lot of 'em,' Warren said. 'Have on the biggest rocks, be wearing the barest frock — the last time I saw her, she had on a dress with a print of bare buttocks on the back. She's the sixth wife of Art Stockton, a little snail of a man

130

who's made a packet in oysters. Maisie's no airhead, though, she's a fun-loving Southerner who loves to shock — not difficult in Southampton — and she doesn't give a damn. Knows she's a match for any of 'em.

'There's a bunch of grand dames, regulars at all the charity dos; they defer to a hideous old alligator called Gertrude Whelp who's thought to look quite like Diana Vreeland.'

'Diana Vreeland was in my life in the sixties,' I said, 'and terrifying! I shivered in my boots when summoned to her inner sanctuary at *Vogue*, but she was one of the greats.'

'You wouldn't say that of Gertrude,' Warren laughed, 'with her dreadful halitosis. She stands real close, too, to make it worse, peering over her pince-nez and breathing out evil fumes.'

'I did ask for local colour, Daisy,' I said, smiling. 'There'll be normal, conventional types as well, and a few pampered young tennis players staying the weekend.'

'Southampton's into tennis,' Warren explained. 'We have our famous Meadow Club that's been going since the 1880s. It's strictly run and very social, with a good bar.'

'American women always have such good legs,' Daisy said. 'Is it all the sport, or do they do the sport to show them off?'

'Bit of both, I guess — assuming you accept the original premise, of course. However, from where I'm sitting there's no arguing about British women's complexions, so petal-soft.' Warren smiled from me to Daisy, evenly distributing the flowery compliment.

131

'On with the house,' I said, drawing his eyes back. 'I know you've promised me a complete free hand, but there are limits which I may be stretching and we should talk it over. This isn't just a redo of décor. I want to take out walls, raise ceilings; open up the hall with a high wide arch ... It would be spectacular, looking through into here with the ceiling lifted, the added height and brightness, but you need to be prepared.'

'I have complete faith,' Warren said, 'and I want a total transformation, no single reminder of Willa — not a footstool nor a flower vase; it matters to me. After three long years of wrangling, this divorce is a hard-won victory which I mean to enjoy.'

I'd heard that ruthless edge on our first meeting at Jimmy's party, but Daisy looked shocked. She swallowed uncomfortably, as if reminded of lawyers and bitterness, the nasty taste left by her own divorce.

We talked on. I mentioned a handsome refectory table in place of Warren's mahogany one with its extending leaves; banishing some of the curlier pieces of silver to his Manhattan apartment, replacing them with resplendent pottery bowls. 'You need a breakfast room,' I said, 'to make for easier summer living, the indoors and outdoors more naturally connected, everything flowing out to the deck, the chairs and pool.'

Warren had heard of the top architect I wanted to employ, which was helpful, and he accepted the need for a project manager to

132

oversee the construction work. 'All of that would begin after the summer,' I said, 'to architect's plans. Daisy and I would have done our stuff by then, ordered everything in, and you'd be back in the city, fulltime.'

'It will be finished by Christmas?' Warren queried, looking concerned, making clear how important that was to him. 'My son and daughter are holidaying in Europe this summer, showing their children the sights, but we always have Christmas here together.' It was the first mention of family and I felt pleased that he so obviously cared.

I touched his tanned arm reassuringly. 'Don't worry, I'm good at keeping people to deadlines. I'll come out in the autumn and crack the whip, make sure we're on track.'

The time difference was catching up — partly the fault of the gloomy unflattering lighting, which failed to create a mood of soft intimacy; as comparative strangers, we needed that. Martha came in with coffee and fresh mint tea. She pulled closed the heavy cream and burgundy curtains, which killed off the room entirely, then left as silently as she came.

Daisy was silent too. Had my hand on Warren's arm made her feel in the way and taken her mind to Simon? I'd grown to care about her and was also anxious how things would pan out; her mobile face mapped her emotions all too clearly. 'My bedtime, I think,' she said, brightening with conscious effort. 'It is sort of three in the morning.'

Warren smiled in sympathy. 'You must be

done in, both of you, though you'd never begin to know it.' He kept smiling from one to the other. Did he always smile so much or was it newness and nerves? 'Try to think yourself onto American time in the morning, though, Daisy dear,' he said, causing her to lower her lashes rather coyly. 'I want you to feel really settled in properly here. And tomorrow, as it's Sunday and the weather's so good, I thought maybe we'd have lunch at the Beach Club. How would that be?'

'Sounds great,' I said. 'It's a while since I was in Southampton, but I'm sure all the old regulars are still around. It'll be fun to catch up — with most of them, at least.'

'Nothing's changed; same old faces, same muddle of sandals on the steps to the beach. Henry Koehler's painted them, you know, and it's become an iconic work. It's a bonus having him as a local; he's very involved, sure to give a painting to the Benefit auction.'

We said our goodnights. Warren held my hand in both of his and repeated his fulsome words of welcome. He was a lucky man, he couldn't feel more proud and pleased that I'd taken on the job — just a summer pad, after all . . . He talked on, over-egging it, flattering me excessively. I felt momentarily bored, unsure as yet how to read Warren, but recognising that this was a little overture, his calling card; first steps on the road to developing a relationship.

Daisy had slipped past us on her way upstairs to bed, and I soon followed.

I closed the bedroom door and leaned against

134

it, thinking about Warren's gushing praise and the summer ahead. The bedroom curtains were drawn, a curving sweep of chintz that was pretty in its way with sprigs of violets on a white ground. The bed was neatly turned down, my nightdress laid out on the coverlet, pinched in at the waist in a dainty, decorative way. Bottled water in a cooler was placed beside the bed, the lights switched on, glowing softly; towelling slippers were carefully positioned for ease of stepping into, a monogrammed towelling dressing gown within reach on a chair. So much pampered privilege. I felt an arrow of discomfort. Had Luisa felt the weight of life's inequalities while prettily arranging my nightdress? She was a doe-eyed Latino, charming, smiling, spruce and tidy in her strawberry pinstriped maid's dress that had a faint look of my old school summer uniform about it.

Whatever lay ahead, the stage beyond Warren's smiling flattery, I felt able to cope. If only I'd had the confidence I felt now, though, when I was younger, the same ability to hold my own and promote the very small amount of talent that I had. It was a miracle of happenstance, this second career, an extraordinary late blossoming and moment in the sun. It was far easier as well, nowadays, to soak up the limelight and go with the flow, swim happily in the waters of overdone praise.

I was sure enough of myself now, at this age, to make the most of it and not dwell on feeling undeserving of such an accidental career. Success softened the hard undeniable truths of growing old and also somehow recalled for me the whirling highs and heady passions of my first career long ago, as a young model. I'd suffered from acute feelings of inadequacy in those days, despite being in demand and wanted by men. I'd had time on my side then, decades of passion, enticements and living ahead of me.

Not any more. This second career had all the gossamer fragility of a late-autumn rose; it was fleeting, weak-stemmed, a few frail petals opened up to the rays of a fading sun before the battering storms swept in to rust them and the winter cold finally laid them to rest.

I would enjoy the commission, Long Island, the summer here with its promising possibilities. Warren was interesting and enigmatic, an attractive man, but I wasn't a young beauty any longer with the world in her palm and time to repair mistakes. It would be precautionary and wise to limit any emotional investment, yet however much older and more self-assured, when it came to emotions was the ground ever any easier, was there ever a more solid footing? Did common sense and reason ever really prevail?

9

Daisy woke in the night and reached blindly for her bedside light. She fumbled about, not finding the switch, disorientated for a moment before everything came flooding back: the flight, Long Island, Warren and her challenging new job. It was a fantastic experience being here, terrifically exciting, but the chances of screwing up, Daisy felt, were overwhelming. She'd just about managed at home, tossing ideas around with Susannah, absorbing all she could, but now, out here, not really knowing a thing, not even her way round New York properly . . .

The room was in complete darkness. She had turned off the air-conditioning and lay in bed listening to the heavy silence of a sleeping house. Beams didn't creak in Warren's huge mansion; the only sound she could hear was the thudding of her heart. No whisper of noise from outside, no returning car, no tapping branch at the window. Daisy felt from the absolute quiet that it must be about three in the morning.

She eventually found a light switch low on the electric flex. The bedside clock was obscured by the phone, its luminous face would have helped. It was four o'clock, not three, harder still to get back to sleep. Daisy switched off the light, determined to try, which meant steering clear of Simon and all her spin-off worries and fears. She tried to concentrate on Warren's house, which was more depressingly staid and formal than expected, and so deeply stamped with his ex-wife's taste that he'd hardly needed to describe her. Willa stalked the place: she was in the furniture, the fabrics; reflected in the silverware. It was understandable on the whole, his obsessive need to remove every trace. Daisy pictured Willa as tall, imperious, big-boned, with thick-fingered hands; her jewellery, she imagined, would be unstylish while unquestionably real. Willa was one of life's takers, by the sound of it, with a lump of ice for a heart. She'd clearly had more interest in silver salvers than in poor old Warren. Who'd forced the issue on the divorce? Had she walked out? Had he just had enough? Either way, Willa wouldn't have gone quietly. Daisy felt intrigued to know more — and about Warren.

The flight had been great, the Club Class seat unfurling like a cat unballing itself, stretching out into an almost full-length bed. It made it easier to understand how business people could go straight into a full day's wheeler-dealing after a long overnight flight.

Simon flew long-distance occasionally. Surely he could find a reason to come to New York; if they could just have a night or two together it would ease the pressure and make all things possible. Susannah had given the okay to that, she'd even suggested it. Daisy let out a quavery doleful sigh. She knew in her heart Simon wouldn't come. And the knowledge of that blighted her thrill, sullied the uniqueness of the adventure just begun.

She wondered if Warren was seriously interested in Susannah. They were of an age, after all, and with so many top interior designers in New York, why else bring her all the way out here? Yet he had quite a roving eye. Daisy had sensed his interest, the sweep of his gaze, his warm attempts to make connection. She smiled to herself. He was likeable, handsome in a mature, good-taste-in-clothes sort of a way and he had bonfires of money to burn. Had he had a facelift? More and more men did these days, it seemed.

She settled on her side, longing to feel drowsy, when the sound of a text arriving put her on red alert. She clambered out of bed and back in again with her mobile. Her heart was fluttering madly. It was from Simon. He was texting, thinking of her . . .

How goes it, Green Eyes? Missing me enough to come home? I need U here, hate no chance to call by. Cut it short whatever. Don't you want me any more?

Daisy wanted him desperately. His text was contact, making her wet with need, but why couldn't he sign off with more warmth and make her feel loved? He was passionate enough in bed, shouting out his love loud and clear when he came, pouring out his feelings then. Would Simon find another soft welcome, another place to call by? Oh hell. Tears weren't going to help. She knew the harsh realities of life. Simon's feelings were of the sexual moment; he was never going to put himself out or give much of a damn.

Susannah had said play hard to get and he'd come running. But his wife, the vindictive Sarah, was that sort of woman and Daisy knew her own attraction for Simon was not being a mean tough bitch like his wife. That mattered to her as well for her self-esteem.

She texted back, sitting bolt upright in bed, thumbs flying. *Loved hearing, love u! All okay here. Scary job but will get me to NY and can overnight there. Can't u come out and c me? Please, please try! Miss u.* xxxxxxxxxxx

* * *

Daisy opened the curtains onto a beautiful morning; she must have gone back to sleep. It was seven o'clock. The lawn was glistening with dew, low rays of sunlight were finding routes into the garden and in patches of heavy shade the thick lush foliage looked as dense and dark as to be sinister. She felt a shaft of loneliness.

She opened a window, refusing to give into feelings of gloom, and breathed in fresh scented air. It gave her an urge to set about preparing for the day, fake-tanning her legs to try to keep up with the members of the Beach Club, re-varnishing her toenails and washing her hair.

As the sun rose and the light streamed in she began to feel almost exuberant. She dressed in shocking-pink cropped pants and a tee of a lighter-shade, worrying, as she went downstairs to breakfast, about being under-dressed. Perhaps her high canvas wedges would add a bit of glam.

They had soundless rope soles and Warren didn't raise his head as she entered the dining room. He was deep into the *New York Times*.

140

'Hi, isn't it a fabulous day!' Daisy exclaimed, a bit over-loudly, anxious to let him know she was there. She gave Warren such a start that he dropped his bulky Sunday paper onto the table and sent an army of cutlery flying. They were both on their knees then, retrieving skittering spoons — which must have surprised Martha as she came in to see the cause of the clatter.

Martha offered bacon and eggs, which was tempting, but since Warren seemed not to be having any, Daisy weedily declined. There was fresh-squeezed orange juice, fresh fruit, muesli, muffins, dainty triangles of toast; she wasn't going to starve.

Sipping juice and staying politely silent to let Warren return to his newspaper, it came as no surprise when he set it aside and studied her. Daisy smiled and lowered her eyes, busying herself with sprinkling blueberries onto a plateful of muesli.

'I can't tell you the joy of this beautiful British invasion,' Warren remarked, smiling she looked up. 'I only wish I was half my age! But seriously, Southampton's not such a bad place and it will give me a great deal of pleasure to show you round my favourite haunts. You'll be the talk of the Hamptons, I can tell you.'

'We are here to work,' Daisy laughed, glancing to the door as she heard footsteps. 'And with Susannah's plans it sounds like we'll be at it twenty-four seven.'

'Morning all,' Susannah said with a yawn, coming into the room.

Warren leaped up and pulled out a chair. 'Hey,

141

how are you? Sleep okay, I hope?'

'Blissfully. It's such perfect quiet here, the sort of silence that sings. How are you doing, Daisy? Make the most of today. It'll be all go from then on, I can tell you.'

Daisy gave Warren a what-did-I-tell-you glance, yet she felt overshadowed by Susannah and more subdued. Susannah was the star making an entrance, the diva coming on stage, Warren's attention instantly distracted. And she wasn't even dressed and made up, simply wearing a loosely tied silk kimono dressing gown. Still looking incredible, getting away with the no-makeup look, but then she had that sort of high-boned face that was kinder to aging.

The money must help. Daisy tried not to let spiky jealousy take hold; she hated to feel covetous, never allowed herself to do so for long. Susannah had had her own financial struggles, after all, and a hurtful, difficult love-life. Losing the one husband she'd truly loved must have been devastating, even if everything had come good in its way in the end. Would it ever do that for her? Daisy knew she couldn't look for parallels; she had none of Susannah's looks or talent, and her own life was such sad small beer.

The aroma of Susannah's crispy bacon was making her jealous, if nothing else. Daisy averted her eyes and caught another of Warren's surreptitiously friendly glances. It was cheering and diverting. Was he flirting, or simply trying to put her at her ease? His small attentions were gratifying all the same, balm for the ache of physical need.

They left at noon for the Beach Club. Susannah was wearing mandarin cut-offs, not unlike Daisy's bright pink ones, and a floaty white shirt, fine soft muslin and fastened low enough to draw the eye. The slim gold chain round her neck glinted so lustrously, any thieving jay or magpie would have swiped it for their nests; it reflected the sunlight sheen of a glorious day.

A plump girl manning the entry-point was chatty and annoyingly repetitive. 'Hi, how you doin', Mr Lindsay. And these are your summer guests ... And they're here for the whole summer, are they, the whole summer?' She was snacking on a plate of chips, pausing to wipe her fingers — doing anything but signing in Warren's guests. Daisy felt impatient and turned her attention to the bronzed, fit parents with small children, teenagers and elderly singles arriving, clustering and calling out to each other in East Coast American speak.

They were wearing shorts, kaftans or maxi beach dresses, depending on bulk and age. The ancients had on the full warpaint, dangly earrings and wide statement hats. Could they have come straight here from church — or want people to think they had? Daisy was pleased about the shorts, that it was okay to wear them; they looked good on her, suited her legs.

Signed in eventually, Warren took them past an Olympic-sized swimming pool that looked temptingly people-free; rows of wooden changing rooms stirred childhood memories of the

dated old beach huts at Frinton-on-Sea. He led
them on to the clubhouse, where a huge open-air
deck overlooking the beach seemed to be the
hub of club-life, scene of the action; the slatted
round tables, bright with sheltering royal-blue
sunshades, were filling up fast.

Daisy's first glimpse of the ocean freaked her
out, the sight of the giant thundering breakers
remorselessly powering to shore, unravelling like
scrolls as they crashed onto the sands. The sea
was pewter-grey, at times it looked navy, and the
vast arcing waves were topped with showers of
silvered spray. The beach stretched for miles in
either direction, sun-bleached white and virtually
deserted. The call of the gulls was haunting, and
a strong breeze, pricked with sand, carried the
smells of sea and salt on the air.

'Wow!' she exclaimed feebly. 'That's a
breathtaking view.'

Warren gave a proprietary smile while
Susannah seemed to understand Daisy's inability
to find the right words. 'It does that to me too,'
she said, 'and it lives on. I used to come here
quite regularly, to stay with a good friend from
my modelling days before she became overrun
with grandchildren and I had my new career. I
often think of this beach, though, back home on
bleak rainy days.'

'First thing to do is grab a table,' Warren said,
looking gratified, 'which isn't that easy. There's
an unwritten code about who sits where; woe
betide you if you bag the favoured spot of a
board member, or some fat slob's chosen piece
of shade. The gossips have their pet tables, too,

where they can keep watch on the entrances and exits like bodyguards.'

He secured them a table and they settled in. 'Now drinks,' he said. 'You got to have a Rum South Side, it's the Club special — rum, ice and fresh mint leaves whirled up in a blender; cool and frothy. I'll join you in one. I usually save my booze calories for evening, but this is a red-letter day.'

'Drinking at lunchtime?' Daisy grinned. 'I'm not sure my new boss will approve.'

'Dead right,' Susannah said, 'but since I'm having one . . . though that's my lot. I don't want to turn into a South Sider — which is what they call the over-fifties round here, all the afternoon boozers who never budge from their chairs.'

'No chance of you ever doing that,' Warren snorted. He summoned a waiter, gave the order and sat back with his customary smile.

A constant stream began to flow past their table, people reuniting with Susannah or angling to be introduced. Warren's guests were indeed hot news. Daisy met an aging Paula, a prying Abigail. She felt the eyes of the men at nearby tables on her; it was fun.

Elderly couples, cosmetically enhanced women of an uncertain age and their paunchy husbands, invited them to their houses, for lunches, cocktails or just to visit — with or without Warren. Susannah deflected them with masterly ease. 'Goodness, how long is it? So good to see you! We'll certainly try, but we have a punishing schedule.'

The rum drinks that looked mostly ice and mint leaves packed a hidden kick; Daisy felt an internal glow as well as the sun on her outstretched legs. She'd pushed her chair clear of the sunshade's arc, loving the heat and brilliance; she felt in a good place.

'Ready for lunch?' Warren queried. 'It's self-service; we can bring it out here.' Daisy stood up a bit over-keenly; she was hungry. They went indoors to a heartening sight: hot and cold lobster and meat dishes, salads, slices of gateaux and apple tart. Sturdy capable women in white waisted aprons doled out mammoth portions, huge dollops of a chopped lobster, celery and mayo mix that Warren promised was 'chunky and good'. The devilled eggs were a Club special, he said, and they must try the various salads. Daisy was less coy than at breakfast, she didn't hold back.

After the meal she said she'd love a swim. 'But in the pool if that's okay? Those breakers would toss me up like a beach ball, and I have had quite a large lunch!'

'I'll stay and soak up the sun, I think,' Susannah said, smothering a yawn.

Warren said he'd keep her company, but he went with Daisy to show her the towels and lockers and explain the form.

She was glad to swim alone. It was thinking time. Other swimmers were sociable and curious, but soon left her in peace to potter up and down the pool. She revelled in the sunny day, the chance to swim, and couldn't help imagining where working for Susannah could lead, the freedom of no more red reminders, all the unpaid bills. No more depending on an ex-husband who'd truly shocked her with his brute meanness. Peter would deeply resent any success of hers — a tempting goal and incentive if ever there was one. Having met Simon through Peter still bothered her, yet with the force of the attraction her discomfort had dimmed.

Daisy swam idly on with her mind on both sides of the Atlantic — Simon, Warren, the compelling roar of the ocean. She spared a thought for her tiny back garden, where the Felicia rose would be in its prime and made a mental note to text the boys about deadheading. She marvelled at the way her life seemed to be pointing in a whole new direction — and all on a pinhead of chance.

She came out of the water, sunbathed a little then tied round a beach wrap, a soft lime and yellow kanga bought on a holiday in Kenya years ago.

Returning to the terrace, she found Warren alone. 'Susannah's been nobbled,' he said, clicking off his phone. 'She's over with Denise, doing her decorating thing. I didn't know she was such a softie.'

Daisy saw that Susannah was poring over some photographs that Denise whoever must have had in her bag; her forehead was knitted wearily, she looked a picture of resignation. Seeing Susannah's forbearance made Daisy feel a rush of affection, a kind of daughterly empathy. She loved her for not being able to say no.

She felt Warren's eyes on her and he rested a hand on her arm. 'Come for a walk on the beach. I can point out some of the Gin Lane houses that are such a feature of Southampton. I'll text Susannah and suggest she catches us up.'

They went down some steps onto the beach, stepping over a great jumble of flip-flops, sandals and mules. 'Everyone leaves them on the top steps,' he said, slipping off his navy Docksiders. 'It's a little tradition.'

'This beach,' Daisy said, feeling curiously at home with Warren, 'gives me shivers with its drama and kind of rugged muscularity. And it's free of people! There are more pairs of gulls than sunbathers — look at them, strutting along the sand.' She sighed. 'It must be a constant pull, I don't know how you can bear to head back into the city after the weekend.'

'It's why I fought so hard to hang onto the house. It cost me. Willa has a new Manhattan apartment on Park, worth a ton, and she's landed a tidy sum to have some other summer place. She fancies Martha's Vineyard, I believe, as the place to be seen.'

'And your children,' Daisy asked, feeling miles out of her depth, 'where do they live?'

'Connecticut, Manhattan. I see them, but they're busy with their own lives.'

He didn't want to talk about his children; that was obvious. Was he lonely? She thought it was possible. He had his obsession with Willa, the bitter satisfaction of winning out to keep him going, and he was productively busy with his billion-dollar business as well; people who had his sort of money always seemed determined to make more.

Daisy smiled to herself. He wasn't so

one-track minded, had been distracted by their arrival and he even seemed to be playing a two-handed game. Harmless enough. She was enjoying his quiet flirting ways, the boost it was giving her morale.

Warren broke into her thoughts. 'Susannah mentioned you were newly divorced,' he said. 'Still smarting, like me?'

'A bit. It's been a torrid time. But since it brought out the very worst of my husband's characteristics, I feel mightily relieved to be free of him.'

'You didn't have any children, no problems there?'

'No, but I have twin boys from a brief early marriage who've only really known my second husband. He's seen them grow up and I'd have hoped he'd feel a little more responsibility towards them. They're nineteen and at university now — except that it's the vacation and they have the run of the house. God knows what they're up to!'

Warren made polite disbelieving noises about their age. 'So you're a free woman now, Daisy.' He smiled and kept up his gaze. 'With a line of guys beating a path to your door, I'm quite sure. Anyone special? Someone not pleased you're out here?'

'Certainly no line of suitors. I am a bit involved, but I'm afraid he's married.'

'Divorce on the cards?'

'I think not. His wife calls the shots. She has him pretty much locked in.'

'Oh. But that could change. You never know.'

Warren eyed her. 'Will he come over?'

'Probably not.' Daisy changed the subject. 'Tell me about these extraordinary properties we're passing. Fancy fronting onto the ocean like this. Are the houses really in single ownership, though? It's hard to believe.'

'Most are. They hardly ever come onto the market and don't hang about if they do. A few are still owned by descendants of the original families, but ever since the Depression it's been down to who has the serious bucks, mainly punters in the financial world these days. The cottages date back to the 1880s; hurricanes have taken their toll, but I think about nineteen of the original thirty-four still survive, at least in part.'

Daisy said, 'I love the grey shingle, it looks weathered and right. It seems to belong, but I can't say the same about the name. Gin Lane!'

'A lot of fun is made of the name. Residents have endlessly tried to change it, but the Gin part is really an Old English term meaning common grazing area. This whole stretch was once just a feeding ground for farm animals — and to think of the land values today!'

They started back, slightly surprised to discover how far they'd walked, and Warren slipped a guiding hand under Daisy's arm. She looked out for Susannah as the clubhouse came into view, but could see no sign of her approaching.

'Do you know New York?' Warren asked. 'Will you manage okay, rushing round all those fabric showrooms, antique shops and whatever?'

'I'm going to have to. Susannah can be very

crisp . . . ' Daisy stopped herself saying she didn't even know her way round the job, far less Manhattan. Susannah had probably built her up as an experienced assistant. Warren was, after all, paying the bills.

'I'll give you my card,' he said, 'when you have somewhere to put it.' Daisy had been conscious of being in a bathing wrap while he was in shorts and shirt. 'My office is central and I'm on the end of a phone. Don't hesitate to call — in fact, I'd positively enjoy giving directions and help. We could combine it with a bite of lunch.'

'Thanks,' she said cautiously, feeling that could be tricky waters, a delicate situation. Susannah, for all she knew, might have serious designs on Warren and a jealous nature, despite the jolly Charles whom Daisy had enjoyed meeting the time she'd popped round with home-baked bread. He'd been staying over; he and Susannah seemed like old friends and to gel well. 'It's a comfort to know I could call,' Daisy added, not wanting to sound too abrupt. 'I'm sure to get lost at first.'

Warren was good company after all and seemed decent enough; she doubted he'd try anything much. He'd told Susannah he was almost seventy — which probably meant seventy-one or two.

Arriving back, they found Susannah ensconced at another table. She was surrounded, being feted by a group of old codgers, whose South Side-drinking wives or whoever were gassing too much to notice the glint in their husbands' eyes.

Warren did. His face clouded slightly and his lips were pressed together in an irritated line. He

151

seemed instinctively watchful of the men round Susannah like a tiger warding off any chancers with an eye to its territory. He was a business giant, of course, a man with a steel core who wouldn't allow anything or anyone to stand in his way. Complicated, Daisy could see, and accustomed to winning his wars.

10

Warren and Daisy were back from their walk and I joined up with them again. Daisy was being boringly gushy about the beach and now bloody Margo Foster was coming over, looking freshly Botoxed and dieted to the bone. I wasn't getting much of a look-in with Warren. I'd met Margo once before, fended off her husband, and could have done without her fixing on Warren now with a staring-eyed, predatory look. 'Quite a little harem you've come with today, Warren dear,' she smirked, arriving at the table. 'What summer fun — can I be squaw number three?'

'That wouldn't suit you at all, Margo, honey. Mrs Bronson Foster-Barlow not number one? That would never do!'

Warren had jumped up to peck her cheek and now, introducing us, explaining our design credentials, he began to pull out a chair. 'No, I won't stay,' Margo said, with a glacial edge, knowing when she was beat. 'Mustn't interrupt your little housing session. You're busy with that, I can see.' She was another pampered, bored, married-for-the-money Southampton regular and making a play that Warren had dealt with quite deftly on the whole. I was pleased, liking him more, and amused.

He smiled ruefully between Daisy and me by way of an apology for the invasion. 'Tea here — or shall we meander back? Martha will give us some at home, I'm sure.'

'Let's get back,' I said. 'It's been great, seeing the Club again, a lovely day, but I'm ready to go now.'

Daisy looked sorry to leave. She'd obviously had a high old time, especially with Warren, to go by the body language. 'I just have to get changed,' she said, pushing back her heavy wooden chair and fixing her wrap more securely. 'Won't be a mo.'

'Such a sweet girl.' He gazed after her. 'A little troubled about the man in her life, I thought. She wouldn't discuss him apart from admitting he was married. Is there a problem, the wife kicking up or something?'

'No, I don't think so, but he's a dreadful shit. The wife's the meal-ticket, I gather, and he's just taking advantage of Daisy, making unreasonable demands with no intention of getting a divorce.'

'Is there any way to warn her off?'

'I've tried, but however selfish and overbearing, he's a sexy ram and she's in thrall to him. She knows it's hopeless and going nowhere, she doesn't need me to tell her.'

'Perhaps being over here might help, well away and having new experiences.'

It was an unsettling conversation. I felt tense and piqued, suspicious of his interest. Surely I didn't need to worry about Warren and Daisy? I'd become fond of her already, my new young soft-natured friend, and to imagine her being competition hadn't entered my mind. Yet now, thinking of those compelling green eyes . . . She wasn't an obvious beauty, but Daisy had warmth

154

and spontaneity, an eagerness to please, youth on her side and Warren was at a susceptible age.

'She seems to have that fatal knack of falling for the wrong guy,' I said, breaking into the small silence that had fallen. 'I had it too, and had to live with the consequences.'

'But you don't make those mistakes any more?'

'I take better care.'

Daisy returned, all smiles, and we strolled the short distance back to *Great Maples*. Could she seriously fall for a man of Warren's age? He was too civilised and well behaved, I thought, to jump on her uninvited. And Simon was a high bar.

The shadows were lengthening, and away from the beach there wasn't a breath of wind. We passed houses with impenetrable hedges, formidable gates, alarm systems that clung to the walls like leeches, the owners' privacy secure. Staid homes, grandee living. I didn't hold out much hope that my plans for Warren's house would be his immediate neighbours' glass of iced tea.

We had our tea out on the patio, warm and in a pot. It was a lapsang souchong blend, Martha said, and it had a lilting flavour, fragile, fragrant. I was reminded of a modelling trip to Malaysia, the tea-plantations, the romance of that part of the world. Martha had baked almond cookies, too, that were irresistible.

The fabric on the wicker chairs was floral, the teacups as well. There were plenty of flowers in the garden . . . I couldn't wait to strip Warren's house from teacup to bathroom tiling. The architect I wanted to employ was a New Yorker, Grace Mansfield, whose sassy original achievements I much admired; architecture was still such a male-dominated world. She was also young, vivacious and stylish, as I'd told Warren in the interests of pressing her case.

Daisy coughed politely and rose. 'I'm just off to chat to Martha,' she said. 'I've talked my editor into an American slant for my column, a Stars and Stripes banner, top of page, and Martha has promised to share some traditional recipes. Clam chowder, Southern fried chicken, pumpkin pie, that sort of thing.'

Warren smiled absently, probably too used to gourmet white-tablecloth restaurants or the Martha equivalent to be madly interested in culinary cogs and wheels. I couldn't picture him in the kitchen, donning an apron and propping his favourite recipe book on a stand.

With Daisy gone I asked after his working week and the family beer business, and he opened up with enthusiasm. 'My father built up the company — the brewery's upstate, of course, while our head office is usefully in New York. The business jogged along, The Lindsay Beer Company, it was called, but it was only when we changed the name from Lindsay to Lippy that sales really soared. They hit the roof. It was like one of those fairground hammers sending the ball shooting up. Changing the shape of the bottle-top to a pair of lips was the clincher, as it made it big with the boozy young and fun-lovers. Lippy Lager is a huge seller. It's a good feeling, to travel the world and see our beer in places like

Mongolia, Zanzibar or Mozambique — I've never gotten over it. Don't drink the stuff myself, too many calories, but the sight of a few hefty beer bellies around the place sure does my heart good!'

'Fascinating how simply changing a name can make such a difference.'

'Yes, I'm a complete convert to branding now. The firm we employed was ace.'

'Is your son in the business too, working with you?'

'Anything but, very sniffy about it; he's an international lawyer. My daughter married the boss of the branding agency, though, so she's kind of on board.'

'Were they all right about the divorce? You'd been married what, thirty-five years?'

'Oh no, not nearly that long.' It seemed an odd thing to say without elaborating and I wondered about it as Warren talked on. 'The kids were quite upset. They said we were a great team, that sort of scene, but how can you live with a woman who makes you feel lower than a worm in a hole?' He gave a small, strangulated sigh.

I asked more questions about his lifestyle — for my own curiosity while using the cover of the job. His glances were provocative, his answers, too. 'I've been living a lonesome hermit's life out here, these last couple of summers . . .'

'I find that hard to believe.'

'No, it's true. Though now, this summer, you're certainly bringing me out of my shell, making me feel like putty with that smile.'

157

I left him soon after and went to my room. Warren's flattery had been overdone from the start. I was determined not to read too much into it. I liked the protective undergrowth of ambiguity; it felt too early to be clearing a path and knowing the score.

A little rest would make me brighter-eyed and more on the ball over supper, with any luck, and I had emails to see to, texts to read: my mobile had been vibrating away at the Beach Club. I decided to shower first; they could wait.

Reaching for the dressing gown that Luisa had left ready on a nearby chair, I belted it loosely and stretched out on the bed with my phone. Bella had texted to say that Sapphire, my granddaughter, had won Silver in the life-saving class. I sent congratulations. I read a text from Josh, my unmarried son, who seemed convinced I wouldn't be behaving myself. There was an excitable voicemail from Stephanie, my secretary, assuring me that all was fine. She'd moved into the office and Posh was well and happy, purring for Britain. Cats were fickle creatures, I thought.

Charles had left a voicemail too, that I listened to with irritated affection.

'Just had an urge to call, but since it's lunchtime with you I'm sure you'll be at the Beach Club with your Mr Warren and that lovely girl, Daisy. I hope you're having fun, Rum Sours and a riotous welcome from all those old-school WASPs. If you happen on that weird CNN man we stayed with once — the one with the heavy-going wife, remember? — say hello from

158

me, will you? I quite liked him. Pity about her, doubt they're still married.' They weren't, I'd heard so already. 'It's pissing with rain here in rural North Norfolk, but not there, I guess. Missing you, but then I have been for decades. Enjoy your American.'

It was midnight, a bit late to call, and I'd have sounded cross, impatient about *Mr Warren* and *your American*. Charles was only reversing the names for his own silly entertainment. And it wasn't funny at that.

I texted him, resisting a whinge. *Thanks for the call. Hope you rested up after cataract op, all went well and you have sharper vision now. No more bloodshot eyes, walking into doors . . .*

Yes, lunch at the Beach Club, v sunny, usual crowd; lazy day before getting stuck into the house. Definitely needs a revamp, could double up as company boardroom. Ex-wife's abominable taste. Lavish mod cons tho and charming, superb cook. Warren Lindsay is charming as well, by the way, and an excellent host. Speak soon, wrap up warm in those inhospitable climes

Miss you, too. Loads o love. xx

PS. The Taylors (CNN guy) have split up, you were right!

Charles came on the phone and we had a little bantering chat. I cut the call short, keen for my few minutes' kip, which inevitably made him a bit prickly.

'Sounds as if you want to rest up and shine,' he said. 'Lindsay Warren must have plenty going for him, more than his hosting skills. I hope he's good fun as well.'

'It's all good fun out here,' I snapped, 'and not pissing with rain.'

'Call if the mood takes you,' Charles replied, unperturbed, 'if you have a free moment one day.'

'Will do,' I said, feeling contrite. 'Best go now — and you should be asleep anyway. You'll call, too? Any time.'

★　★　★

Going down to dinner I could hear Warren and Daisy laughing, Warren being 'good fun'. He was falling over himself to entertain her, they were getting on rather well. I shouldn't mind, it would be taking her mind off Simon at least and Daisy was in her own world half the time, white-faced with downcast eyes. I did genuinely care about her.

Warren was enjoyably attentive as I joined them, and we rehashed the Beach Club for a few minutes before Martha summoned us for supper. He kept up the warm glances, pulling out my chair and sitting beside me, though he immediately pinged a cosy look across the table to Daisy as well. The table was laid with crystal glasses and enough silver to fill the London vaults. And all for Sunday supper. I was in my skinny white jeans with a black T-shirt, Daisy in a button-through denim dress. Warren had on a cream sweatshirt; we hardly did the gleaming silverware on the table a good turn.

'So, Daisy, have you got your marching orders for tomorrow?' Warren beamed.

'We're hanging out here, I think, working on new floor and furniture plans,' she said cautiously, eyebrows raised in my direction. 'There's plenty to keep us busy, elevation drawings and the like, I think, with all Susannah's dramatic new ideas.'

She pattered on, rather sweetly trying to sound like a seasoned assistant while I slid into a small brood about Charles. I knew his silly reversal of Warren's names was his way of transmitting feelings; he'd chosen to presume that Warren was suspect and wanted me to know his thoughts. Charles would never say he didn't like what I was doing. Ours was a good solid relationship: sensitive or emotional feelings were never aired, never allowed to show, they were kept in check or occasionally relayed in code. He'd succeeded this time, however, in making me feel testy and on the defensive. He'd not met Warren, after all, and had no business making assumptions and being such a tremendous transatlantic snob. Surely, if I liked 'my American', as Charles insisted on calling him, that should be credentials enough?

All the same, it made me keener to peel away some of Warren's layers. It might take a few closer encounters, I suspected, which tweaked my adrenaline. I felt my face glow. Warren was discreet, personable, appropriate, and at my age such opportunities were as rare as black pearls. I didn't feel much guilt, just a twinge. The physical side of my relationship with Charles had always been contained, only indulged in between our respective marriages — his single one and my

161

spread — a natural extension of a continuing friendship that had always survived.

I glanced sideways. Warren was looking slightly bored by Daisy's earnest decorating download. 'How you doing, Susannah?' he said vaguely.

We talked art for a while, restaurants in the Hamptons and New York shows while being served with perfect pink roast lamb. Warren praised an exhibition of Brazilian sculpture that seemed to have made quite an impression — more for the flaming beauty of the sculptor, I felt, than her exhibits. From her photographs she was a fiery stunner.

'I have a couple of powerful American artists in mind,' I said, feeling a need to remind Warren of my not inconsiderable spending plans, 'whose paintings have terrific zing.'

'Who like? Need they be American?'

'No, not at all, but a Josef Albers or Ronald Davis would look splashy and great in here when the room is transformed. And a de Kooning would really set the tone.'

Warren didn't flinch even though he must have known the cost of a de Kooning, who was a Long Island painter, after all. Yet I sensed he was less willing, when it came to art, to allow me a complete free hand. He changed the subject, talked of the excellent reviews for Chekhov's *Three Sisters*, newly opened on Broadway, and seemed about to suggest seeing it, but held back. Was that because bringing it up with Daisy there inevitably meant going as a threesome, which possibly wasn't ideal?

Daisy would enjoy it hugely, of course. I could

162

still remember the thrill of exploring New York years ago.

She was looking at me. 'Does Manhattan always trigger memories for you, Susannah? Take you back? I mean, it must have been wild, modelling out here in the sixties.'

'I never knew you'd modelled in New York,' Warren said. 'I'd assumed only London.'

'I worked mostly there, sure, but I was on Eileen Ford's books as well — if that name means anything to you? She was the great doyenne of the time, and the agency still thrives today.'

'I'm well up in Ford models, I can assure you! Back in the sixties, they were the girls to know. I've lived in New York all my life, but the sixties was the best time by far, escaping my parents and having an apartment of my own. And to think we could have met then!'

We were still sitting round the table, drinking camomile tea. Daisy looked ready for bed, but she stayed when Warren carried on.

'So reveal all, Susannah. Let's hear more about Fords and the lofty life you led.'

'Lowly, more like. The modelling could be a very hard slog.' I didn't elaborate. I wanted some time with Warren. Daisy's chaperoning had its moments, but they could be overdone.

'So downplaying it,' she said, smiling, and smothered a yawn. 'Forgive me, jetlag is catching up, and it is a working week.'

'And for me too,' Warren said, returning her smile, too warmly, as she stood up to go. 'I dread that long commuter crawl on a Monday. Jackson and I leave at five but it's never early enough.'

That sounded a bit overkeen. Warren had made his billions, he could afford to relax; he must be more hands-on and in love with the business than I'd thought.

'Have a great first week, Daisy,' he called after her, his eyes at the level of her short denim dress. He immediately trained them back onto me, ready to turn on the charm.

'You must need your beauty sleep too,' I said primly, rising from my high-backed tapestry chair.

'Don't go. Let's chat for a while, talk over plans and have a little downtime. How about we walk to the village for a drink? It's a beautiful night.'

I went, on a slight high, to collect my handbag and we set off.

The evening air felt as soft and soothing to the skin as fine silk. We ambled past the towering, immaculately clipped box hedges that were such a feature of Southampton. 'Whoever has the clipping concession,' Warren said, seeing me staring up at their great height, 'is onto a real money-spinner.'

The sidewalk had a thin strip of paving bordered by neat grass verges, and he walked on the grass to stay alongside. The occasional shade-providing trees, sycamores, maples, had to be negotiated. Street lamps, spherical and harmonious, threw out circles of gentle yellow light. 'If I ever managed to get back on a Thursday evening,' Warren said, looking ahead, 'would I be in the way?' He slowed and turned for a reaction.

'We'd be delighted to welcome you in your own home,' I said. 'But we might not always be there. We might be up in the city, staying overnight with a friend of mine, antique hunting in Connecticut, looking at paintings in Washington.'

'Ah, I can see it'll need pre-arranging,' he replied.

That had sounded encouragingly provocative, I thought, as we reached the village. Warren eyed a brightly lit café-bar on Main Street. 'Too rowdy, taken over by kids.' We walked on, rounding a corner, rejecting another café until he settled on a small restaurant with a long, near-deserted bar. A single customer, a heavy man in a grimy sky-blue tee, was seated at the far end, nursing a tankard of beer. We climbed onto high stools topped in forest-green leather and I cast an eye round. The place had a vaguely Tyrolean feel, with bench seating, booths up the sides; it was dimly lit with pairs of green-glass lamps that hung low over the middle tables. 'The owner's German, I believe,' Warren said.

He ordered our drinks, scotch and a glass of white wine for me. The gaunt middle-aged woman serving us had short spiky black hair and a wiry tension about her; she didn't seem inclined to chat. The gloom and lack of customers were depressing. I thought rather longingly of the noisy café we'd passed.

Warren touched glasses. 'I'm excited about your plans for the house,' he said, 'and being shaken out of my rut. Willa never let up about that, she went on and on about how she

165

despaired of me ever doing anything original and new.'

I was surprised. I'd held Willa entirely responsible for the dreary pomposity of *Great Maples*. I hadn't marked Warren down as a particular conformist, though he could, with that remark, simply be pointing up his ex-wife's nagging in a slightly sympathy-seeking, self-deprecating way. But would he really paint himself as henpecked if it wasn't the case?

'To go back to Thursdays,' he said, 'it's Martha's day off. I hope you won't mind, but she'll be gone overnight, back by lunchtime next day. Also, she does occasional lunches or dinner parties for locals when I'm in the city, to make a little extra — but I've told her you come first and she won't let you down.'

'You needn't have said that. We'll be fine — please tell her to carry on as before. Does she have family she stays with or her own place?' I was interested to know more about her.

Warren hesitated before answering. 'Martha has a few problems,' he said finally. 'Her son's in a federal prison in New Jersey, you see. She visits weekly and stays somewhere nearby. I feel sorry for her. She had him real young: a night or two out with some guy who didn't stick around. And it seems her very religious parents didn't want to know either. She gave up studying, brought the boy up alone, but only found out about the drugs when the police became involved and he was put on probation. He'd been stealing to feed a coke habit. He couldn't get clean, kept re-offending, wrote fraudulent cheques and now, at just twenty, he's behind bars.'

I felt desperately sad for Martha, sure that she lived for her son, while also feeling heartened by Warren's sympathetic attitude. It showed a decent side. I felt more reassured about my judgement and reasons for being out here. In some ways it had seemed madness, taking on a huge job when I didn't need the money. I liked to think I'd be attracted to a man who had a little more going for him than grey-sprinkled hair, good facial grooves and vast riches. Enormous wealth could give a misleading veneer of glamour; pleasing at times, to see oneself reflected in the smooth polished sheen — although it was so often only surface deep.

I asked about the chances of Martha's son receiving treatment in prison, but Warren didn't seem to have much faith in that. 'I went to visit him once,' he said. 'The boy, Daniel, is in a correctional institution, Fort Dix in Burlington County. God, the place, the doors clanging behind me . . . ' Warren sighed. 'But Daniel seemed bright enough. His mother says he's artistic. I'll see what I can do for him when he comes out.'

Warren asked for the check and we wandered out. Back onto the residential side streets, the grassy pathway, he gave me a sideways, almost coquettish look, and reached for my hand. He entwined fingers, his thumb gently rubbing my palm. 'I'm not sure whether this is transgressing some designer-client decorum,' he said, 'but strolling home on a balmy summer's evening . . . perhaps it's not such a terrible sin?'

167

'I've known worse.' I smiled and he squeezed my fingers a little more tightly.

* * *

We were nearing the house. I could see the gates slowly widening, opened by a buzzer in Warren's pocket or some unseen payroll hand. They closed silently behind us and as we approached the front door, a sensor lit up; we coyly avoided glances. Inside, the hall seemed to echo with quiet. Large bulbous lampstands on side tables gave out puddles of sharp light. I thanked Warren and wished him a good week. He kissed my cheek lightly, wished me a productive time in his absence, and I took myself off upstairs.

I knew he was staring up after me. I'd enjoyed his company, very much, but was I being ridiculous? Shouldn't I simply be grateful for an exceptionally full life, a lot of happiness, and act my age? Oh, fuck it, if a man could still look at me, if the urge was there . . . It was summer on Long Island and I had a stimulating challenging contract. Closing my bedroom door, my face bore a very wide smile.

11

November 1961

We were about to go to Frank's small supper party for Marilyn Monroe. Joe was humming in the bath, high on anticipation, and I could have cried with relief. We'd got by in New York, staying at the St Regis and with all the excitements, but his mood graph had been on a disastrous dive ever since, pointing down as sharply as a stalactite. He couldn't handle being back in our apartment on Sunset Strip, and had done nothing but drink and curse the place. 'Sodding utilitarian dog-kennel.' He'd kicked a cupboard and shattered the plywood door, yanked out an ill-fitting drawer, hurled it to the floor. If he'd spoken to me at all it was to bitch and abuse. I was pathetic, holding him back, no stimulation . . . 'God, what a hellhole, boring, boring!' Joe had poured himself another vodka, and another.

Just a few close friends, Frank had said. Amazing to think we were being included. Marilyn was still low, she'd been having treatment for the cocktail of pills she popped, Gloria had explained, and Frank was anxiously trying to look after her.

Joe appeared out of the steamy box bathroom tucking a voluminous bath towel around himself. It was one he'd bought out here with our

169

precious funds, saying that the apartment's towels were 'smaller than sanitary towels'. He shuffled close and gave me a kiss, thrusting his tongue deep. He hadn't been near me since New York. The towel slipped as his hands groped my buttocks and he pressed against me, hot, damp and aroused. I was dressed already, showing off my Californian tan in a white shift, which was going to look in a sorry limp state. It had a wide black lace-up belt; Joe fumbled with the laces ineffectually then gave up and poked me fully clothed, pinned to the wall, finding a way round my pants and coming in seconds. It was the night ahead, the stimulation — it had nothing much to do with me. Joe hadn't looked at me with any meaningful connection — unlike Gil Foreman. I couldn't think about that look without feeling fresh shivers.

The Romanoffs had arranged a car for us. A white Cadillac was waiting, parked alongside the Air Force blue US post box where Joe posted letters that he kept private from me. The driver took his time, chatting about the TV games show *What's My Line?* to Joe's evident frustration. He was wired up, champing to be part of the action. He couldn't wait to talk to Marilyn Monroe.

We arrived at 2666 Bowmont Drive where a policeman and a St Bernard were keeping guard. A sign on the Sinatra gatepost read: *If you haven't been invited you'd better have a damn good reason for ringing this bell.* We had and did. It was hugely satisfying. The house was on a hilltop with fantastic views over Hollywood and the San Fernando Valley. It was quintessentially

Beverly Hills, a sweep of drive, steps cut into the rock that led down to an illuminated kidney-shaped swimming pool and a private cinema apparently, beyond. Frank greeted us and when Joe raved about the sound quality of the music — it was Oscar Peterson playing, I thought — Frank said he'd had the house built round the hi-fi system. Special gravel had been packed into the walls of the main room and two huge loudspeakers were installed just under the ceiling.

The room was a mix of Japanese-Italian in its décor, I decided, while looking for familiar faces among the scattering of people already arrived, some standing talking, others sprawled on an L-shaped white sofa. The Romanoffs were there, Frank's secretary, another Gloria, Gloria Lovell, and his great bachelor buddy, Jimmy Van Heusen; blonde Dorothy Provine too, who I'd been told was a close friend of Frank's.

No sign of Marilyn. Joe began talking to Dorothy, waving his hands, and from the lissom, animated sways of his body he was clearly out to impress.

I was still with Frank and a man came up, demanding to be introduced to me.

'This is Leo Durocher, Leo the Lip, the Dodgers' new coach,' Frank grinned. 'He's a legend. There's no ball-player to touch him — Leo has to win. So be warned!'

'At baseball,' Leo said, winking. 'What are we out at the park for, except to win?'

He and Frank talked baseball for a bit and I gathered that Leo would be on the El Dago trip

171

as well. I liked him. He had a square jaw, a big face-creasing grin; he seemed unthreatening and fun. 'You play gin? Gin rummy?' he asked me suddenly, turning.

'Yes, but I'm not very good . . . '

'But I am! We'll play together in Palm Springs.'

'And you can teach him all about cricket,' Frank quipped, but automatically. He was restless and distracted, I could see; his eyes were darting around. They were as startlingly blue as ever, the cobalt of a Vermeer painting, the standout blue of seventeenth-century art. 'Marilyn's always late,' he said, explaining his looks of concern. 'George should have got her here by now. That chick needs protecting from herself, she messes up easy; it's not like it's a heavy night.'

It was an hour more before Marilyn appeared. She came into the room with George, Frank's valet, who gave his boss a tiny acknowledging shrug.

'Hi, guys!' she said, gloriously breathily, looking shyly self-conscious at the same time. She was in black open-toed high heels, raspberry Capri pants and a silky, tight-fitting cream sweater that showcased the famous pointy tits to perfection. I could see how she needed the ripples of adulation, the tangible awe and sexual adoration that filled the air; they were her survival pack. Marilyn had to feel loved by all and wanted by every man in the room.

'Hey, babe,' Frank drawled, hugging her protectively close as she sidled up with a little

172

wiggle. 'How goes? Hey, liquor for the lady,' he shouted, snapping his fingers. 'And fast!'

Earlier and more sober, we'd talked politics: China's warning to America not to send troops to Vietnam, U Thant just elected UN Secretary General. Frank's conversation was informed and wide-ranging and, except when talking passionately about music, always peppered with jokes and cracks — even when having one of his regular bitches at the press. No matter that he'd been as tense as fuse wire about Marilyn, he'd seemed to feel it was expected of him, even in his own home with no need to put on a show, to be the entertainer and not let people down.

We'd got on to films, plays — *A Man for all Seasons* opening on Broadway, hard on the heels of Harold Pinter's *The Caretaker*, so enthusiastically reviewed. And writers, too. Frank reminisced about James Thurber, who'd died that very day. 'Sad. He was a big-leaguer, a real funny guy and a true perfectionist; he minded to hell about the scripting of his *Walter Mitty*. He thought the Danny Kaye film was bombsville.'

Now, though, with all the waiting, people were loosened up, telling raunchy jokes, and the tempo had changed. I watched Joe home in on Marilyn, as charming and witty with his flattery as only he could be, but she seemed unsure, nervous of him, curiously. She edged away to talk to Jimmy Van Heusen and I knew Joe wouldn't take that well.

'We're having telly dinners, individual trays,' Frank said, as waitresses in white aprons separated nests of tables and spread them about.

They brought in the food on trays, each with a red rose in a thimble glass; lobster cocktail, followed by an Italian chicken dish.

I found myself next to Marilyn. It just fell that way. Jimmy, attractively bald with roguish eyes, had walked us both to the sofa, gossiping, making crude quips — like wanting to rename the Bowmont of Frank's address, Blowmont, which Marilyn enjoyed — and we'd settled down. Jimmy was beside me while Frank came to sit next to Marilyn.

He was the perfect host, up and down, ever observant, constantly topping up wine glasses, refilling them more like, and Jimmy on my other side was concentrating on his food. Marilyn was momentarily alone.

'I'm sorry you're stuck with me,' I smiled nervously, floundering, 'and you must get sick of hearing this, but it is the most incredible thrill to have the chance to meet you. I mean, the whole world would give their eyeteeth to swap places with me right now — which is quite hard to get my head round!' I was sounding more naïve than a hick schoolgirl. Good thing Joe was out of earshot.

Marilyn turned and took me in; she had a gentle smile. 'Gee, that's nice. You're a lovely girl. You could be in films too, no kidding, but it's tough, a bitch. And you English have so much — all that history and education . . . ' She petered out with suddenly sad eyes and gulped down her red wine like water.

'And think what *you* have!' I exclaimed, feeling awash with my own inadequacies. 'What

174

you've achieved with your beauty and talent and guts.' Frank was back beside her by then and she lightly touched my arm before turning, smiling and brushing my hair away from my face. It was always half over one eye, a sort of comfort blanket, I suppose. I felt moved; it had seemed such a warm gesture of Marilyn's and it gave me a glow.

She began talking to Frank and I picked at my chicken, listening curiously.

'The President's gonna be in town on the nineteenth, lunch in Santa Monica. Pete called, he just wanted to let me know.'

'Look chick, so TP's visiting the Lawfords, seeing his sister, but — '

'You're just jealous,' Marilyn interrupted, snuggling up and giggling, sounding as though she wanted him to be. 'Sure TP's hornier than Casanova, but he can have real feelings too, you know. I'm telling you . . . '

'Who's hornier than Casanova?' Jimmy demanded, leaning across and putting his arm round me. 'Not talking about yours truly, are you, by any chance?'

It was three in the morning before people began thanking Frank and saying goodbye. I plucked at Joe's sleeve one more time and finally got him away. He was silent in the car, then swaying and stumbling on the harshly lit stairs up to our characterless apartment. Inside, he slammed the door shut violently with a thrust-out foot. And coming out of the bathroom minutes later, he took a swipe at me and knocked me down. It wasn't quite the first time.

I'd have a bruise on the side of my face in the morning, which was one thing while I wasn't working . . .

The drink was to blame. Was I as well, though, just a little? I'd been dwelling so much and so often on a single look from a short, weird American photographer. My marriage was disintegrating and I didn't know what to think, what I should do.

★ ★ ★

El Dago's inaugural flight was a whirlwind of excitements. The trip of a lifetime, as Joe kept saying. He was in his element again, starry-eyed. El Dago had its own stars too, tiny sparkly lights set into the dark blue of the ceiling over the bar area. The press had made a bit of a stink about the plane — a twin-engined Martin — though, as Frank said, there were people with private planes all over the country. It was quite a plane, a unique airborne den-away-from-home. It had an electric piano and a tape machine, low stools fixed to the floor beside the bar, armchairs, banquette seating, a separate little conference-cum-card room, and the rest room even had a sofa and telephone.

We flew to Las Vegas via San Francisco, where we had a night atop Nob Hill, staying at the Fairmont Hotel as Frank's guests. It was sheer luxury. Henrietta was with us; she'd been back home in England, but had come out again for the El Dago trip. I was glad to see her; we'd become mates and I thought she understood about Joe's moods. The Rubirosas, whom we'd met in New York, were also part of the group. Dorothy Provine was too, along with the Romanoffs and a woman called Mary, who took the very rich on tiger shoots; she had a sleek, cat-like elegance, quite like a tiger herself. Bill Miller, Frank's pianist, and George, his valet, were with us, of course, and Frank's daughter, Nancy, who was coming as far as Vegas to be at her father's opening night at the Sands Hotel. Her mother, Big Nancy, would probably be there too, Gloria said. Frank was on good terms with his ex-wife, he called her up almost daily. Joe and I were going to be in Vegas for the whole two weeks of Frank's engagement, then it was onward in El Dago to his home in Palm Springs.

We ate Chinese on our one night in San Francisco, at Kan's, a regular haunt of Frank's in the city's great Chinatown. He'd lived with the problem of being mobbed and had booked the private dining room, which was called Gum Shan — Gold Mountain. Exquisite watercolours lined the walls — images of early Chinese history — and the food, the shrimp with cashew, crispy Peking duck, ginger beef, was sublime.

Earlier, Frank had taken us to Saks where he insisted we all choose a gift. 'Anything, just whatever hits the spot.' I felt uncomfortable about it, shy to accept a present at all, and picked out a small silk scarf, wine-red, not my colour, but the least pricy item I could find. Others were less reticent. Mary, the tiger lady, chose a shimmering sequinned black sheath, Leo Durocher, a pricy Mexican bowl, and Joe

177

became the proud owner of a pair of authentic cowboy boots complete with shiny spurs. He didn't ride. When would he ever wear them?

I'd hate to have got through life without seeing San Francisco; the streets as steep as ski runs, the trams that felt like riding a Big Dipper, the fabulous Golden Gate Bridge — all the crackle and buzz of that living, breathing city. We'd packed in plenty, but it was time to move on to Las Vegas.

★ ★ ★

The Sands Hotel sign was a tall neon light box that stood proud of the building and hit you in the eye like a tabloid newspaper strapline. The hotel too, with its space and scale, the low spread of pink-painted walls, rich vegetation and vast car park, made an instant impact; it felt at the very heart of the action, a giant of Vegas. Other establishments, however gimmicky and lit up in neon, seemed tackier, almost Lilliputian in comparison.

Las Vegas was unreal, like a one-horse, Wild West town gone crazy. It was hardly more than a single street, an incongruous slash of glitter and gaudiness in an unending monochrome desert. My eyes had been out on stalks, driving into town, having a first glimpse: winking lights, screeching automobiles, back streets and residential sprawl, but all the splashiest clubs and saloons, the Pioneer Club with its vast neon cowboy (Vegas Vic who had a movable arm), The Golden Nugget Gambling Hall, The Horseshoe

Gambling Saloon were all contained, tight-packed into the famously flashing and uniquely exhilarating strip.

We'd arrived at the Sands in time to see Sammy Davis perform. It was the final night of his act. Frank would be taking over and starting to rehearse in the wee small hours, he told us, when the last stragglers from Sammy's audience, which was hundreds strong, had dispersed.

I watched the show at a table with Joe and the Romanoffs. Frank was nowhere to be seen — resting, I presumed, relaxing his voice. Sammy sang, danced, delighted the diners and drinkers in the packed room, but the whole place erupted when, near the end of the act, Frank strode out onto the stage. The audience yelled and roared as he and Sammy camped it up, harmonising, singing in turn, wisecracking; everyone went wild. Sammy, small, sleek, one-eyed, immaculate in his tuxedo, did cartwheels with abandon until he was finally raised on high by a couple of waiters and transported bodily off stage — for going on too long, Frank quipped, and keeping the punters from gambling.

Joe stayed to watch Frank rehearse. I went to our low-lit room where the curtains, which were three thicknesses deep and with a blackout blind, had been tightly drawn. Punters who slept in, had a late lunch by the pool, and an afternoon zizzing in the sun, were popular with the management; they'd be fit and eager to stay the course and gamble the night away.

I had no idea how late Joe was back from the

179

rehearsal session, but in the morning he described it with wonder. How Frank had sung lyrical ballads, cradling the microphone while waiters crashed about turning up tables, clearing detritus, and men had been up wobbling step-ladders painting a new backdrop. Even as electricians shifted equipment in their midst, Sinatra, and the orchestra too, had carried on, oblivious to all.

Joe was back on me in Vegas. He looked quite proud when Jack Entratter, who ran the hotel — a big man whose smile was both fearsome and avuncular — paid me lavish over-the-top compliments. Joe was back up high, way high. He loved Vegas, from the blackjack tables to the one-arm bandits, from Dinah Washington singing late-night in a bar, to the hours he could keep, the unlimited booze he could consume.

I played the fruit machines, since it let me off the hook when I couldn't keep pace with Joe and the other drinkers. The punters pulling down the handles alongside me were a motley bunch: rheumy, paunchy old men, young men, mostly obese, with hideous crew cuts, shrivelled aged women jangling their bracelets, fleshy peroxide black-root blondes with blood-red nails and caked-on make-up . . . but they all had one thing in common: their concentration was total.

By day I swam, read books by the pool and thought about the future, wondering yet again why it was that I hadn't got pregnant. I'd cried less about it recently; my intense jealousy of Alicia, the pain and final insult of her own pregnancy, was a lessening hurt. Not my instinctive suspicion about the father, though, which still burned like a pot of acid chucked in my face. A maggot had burrowed into my marriage; it was lodged there, a canker at its core, and I didn't know whether or for how long Joe and I could go on.

Frank was king in Vegas. We saw little of him by day. He occasionally toured the bars and gambling rooms by night — he was part-owner of the Sands — which always caused a small stampede and kept the burly guards, who looked ten foot tall, on their toes. He even took over a blackjack table once or twice and turned dealer — but only to women, five at a time, tittering with excitement in their busty frocks or faded Chanel suits, smelling of cheap drugstore perfume. I felt sad about those tired suits. They spoke of falling on hard times, a deserting husband perhaps, compulsive gambling or a business deal gone wrong. Somehow Frank fiddled things so the women always went away with winnings. Gloria said he bore the cost himself.

Playing the fruit machines, I won the jackpot one night. The three stars lined up and a profusion of coins showered to the floor while a disbelieving crowd quickly gathered, transmitting awed intense envy. I'd swear Frank had fixed it, but I'll never know.

He gave a dinner party at the hotel the night before Henrietta flew home. She'd holidayed with a friend in LA, come with us on El Dago as far as Vegas, but had to get back. Henrietta had money, but a job in publishing that she loved.

181

Frank ordered some incredible French vintage as usual and Joe leaned forward. 'Never in my dreams ... that's the vino of the Gods, generosity gone mad.' He was flushed, he'd fallen asleep in the sun; it gave him a glow and with his staginess, his wiry, nervy magnetism, he was an arresting presence.

Frank had a fatherly smile. 'Look, kid, I've been rich twice, poor twice, I like to give.'

Henrietta was in high spirits, making the most of her last hours and, as before, taking pictures of everyone at the table with her Box Brownie camera. It was a prized possession of hers, I knew, and since I was seated between Frank and a short bald man called Johnny Formosa — smooth-faced and cuddly, but who still looked straight out of one of the tough-guy films I used to see with my father — I became party to a fascinating little scene. It was over the photograph Henrietta had just taken of Johnny Formosa and me. On a nod and a whisper from Mr Formosa, a hotel heavy had gone round the table, leaned over Henrietta and removed the camera from her lap. 'May I borrow that?' I heard him murmur, taking it anyway, to her shocked surprise.

Frank had absorbed what was going on, just as I had. He had an urgent word with Johnny Formosa, across me, muttering that he shouldn't worry: she was on her way back to England and the film was safe in her hands. Chubby-faced Johnny frowned dubiously, having some sort of anxious private debate with himself, but he finally stood up, took the camera from the heavy and walked round with it to Henrietta. His expression when returning it was contorted, like a man badly stubbing his toe, but intended, I felt, to approximate to a smile. 'Just taking a look,' he said. 'Nice piece a kit.'

Henrietta caught my eye, and as we went to the ladies' we fell about, indulging in wild giggly speculation about the nature of Mr Formosa's particular line of business. We decided it might be for the best if we never knew.

*　*　*

Flying on to Frank's house in Rancho Mirage, Palm Springs was another high spot, but it was the last hurrah before going home. Joe had rehearsals, his new play opened in the West End in late January, and Christmas wasn't far off. I wanted to see my parents. I also had modelling jobs lining up fast. The agency had telephoned the Romanoff residence, keen to know the exact date of my return.

Frank's house, known locally as The Compound, was on the seventeenth fairway of the Tamarisk Country Club. But for all my sense of gearing up for London and imminent change, staying at it was bliss. It was a lazy, way-out, desert weekend, days to treasure, an experience to be packed away carefully between layers of tissue paper, preserved for years to come.

It was unforgettable, the times spent poolside, gazing up while Frank joked and entertained us with his mimicry; he could do Bogart, Jimmy Cagney, Louella Parsons, to perfection. The times at the card table, partnering Leo

Durocher, the gin rummy duke, who joked, as Frank refilled his bourbon glass, 'God watches over drunks and third basemen.' The times I watched Odile flirting sexily, catching her host's eye — although Gloria said Frank was too fond of Rubi to make any clandestine assignations. He'd made one and broken it apparently, which couldn't have been too popular.

The time we went out to eat on a hot, hot night with not a whisper of breeze, at the restaurant called Don the Beachcomber, which was part open-air, with sweeping palm fronds, slatted screens and peacock-back chairs, just like exotic film-shots of Hawaii I'd seen. I was encouraged to try a Mai Tai. It was fruity and thirst-quenching. I downed it and had another. The room began spinning, swimming, I tried to focus . . . When we came to leave, I felt Joe take my arm. He steered me, supported me: he knew, understood, and I had never felt more grateful. 'My saviour,' I muttered, slurring the words as he laid me down and undressed me in the cool dark of our room. He lay down next to me and made gentle love. It felt beautiful, was beautiful — a Joe I had known once, long ago.

The times when George, who was friend and father to Frank, as well as valet, told me stories. About Marilyn who, for all her warmth and sexiness had untidy, grubby habits and that wouldn't do for Frank. He was a neat freak and shacking up with Marilyn, as she wanted, would never have done. George told of how Frank wanted him to keep watch over Marilyn whenever schedules allowed, all day and all night, too.

'Mr S is worried silly about that chick, but hell, looking after her sure takes some self-control. I mean, fuck it, I'm no fag — she has me walking up the walls! Never bothers with clothes, wandering in and out of her bedroom asking for reassurance about her body, her sex appeal — threatening to go test it out on guys in local bars . . . Marilyn's so goddamn insecure.'

George talked about Joe Kennedy, patriarch, founder of the Kennedy dynasty and one-time Ambassador to Britain, coming to stay at the Palm Springs house — very keen to persuade Frank to raise funds for the Presidential push.

Not George's favourite guest, it seemed. 'That guy! He hated blacks like me, wanted an all-white staff. He was rude and crude, the creep — just a great big anti-Semitic hood under that fancy Ambassador façade.'

The times over those few days that I just absorbed; took in the house that was filled with books — Keats, Shelley, Henry Miller, biographies of politicians, hefty books on astronomy, a book on cacti: there were splendidly architectural spiky cacti plants in the grounds. Striped awnings too, orange and white; orange was a colour Frank loved. 'It's cheerful, like the sun,' he said more than once. He wore orange sports shirts, orange silk handkerchiefs in jacket pockets. The paintings round the house were vivid, modern. The background music — on another incredible sound system — was usually jazz, Count Basie, Benny Goodman, or singers like Ray Charles.

Only very late at night would Frank ever play

one of his own albums, murmuring the words or
pointing out favourite pieces of orchestration. It
was never a fast, fun album. He would put on
something sad and moving like *Only the Lonely*
and often grow distant.

I thought he seemed nervous as well, on
occasion. President Kennedy was soon to visit
Palm Springs and coming to stay at The
Compound. The amount of preparation had
been prodigious, with the building of a heliport
and a special new Presidential Suite; Frank
needed things perfect in every detail. I hoped for
his sake that all would go well. I hoped too, that
the gentleness Joe had shown me when the rum
had gone to my head had been a sign and, home
again, back in real-time living, we would find a
new path, wide enough to travel together.

12

December–February 1962

'So tell all,' Sally said, when I phoned into the agency for my bookings. 'Was it truly unbelievable?'

'You can say that again. I haven't landed back yet, I'm still way up in the clouds.' I kept it short, keen to know what I had on in the next days, wanting to unpack and get sorted.

'Duffy tomorrow and Wednesday, two full days for *Elle*. *Vogue* on Friday with Norman Parkinson, that's on location, Camber Sands, leaving at six o'clock from his house in Twickenham. It's summer evening dresses on the beach, I'm afraid, but he says he'll have flasks of coffee and rum.'

'God, I hope not rum, can't do rum. I'm freezing in my winter woollies after Palm Springs, and *Vogue* pay such peanuts, too.'

'We're trying to push them, Susannah.'

'I'll be a shrivelled prune, hypothermia at the very least.'

I took down my immediate bookings. Another day with *Vogue* on Monday, the photographer was David Bailey. Sally reeled off future jobs. It was all go till Christmas. Great to have work, to be in demand, but editorial jobs — whole days with *Vogue* and *Elle* — didn't pay the bills. Joe and I hadn't earned a farthing in three months.

'I'd better get some rest now, Sal, after the overnight flight. This is my only free day.'

'Before you go, we've had a call from Gil Foreman's studio in New York. They want you for an ad — Jim Beam bourbon — and are prepared to come here to shoot it. I told them you're fully booked till Christmas, but they asked if you'd ever work nights. It'd be well paid at least, Susannah — you should do it. The account exec's coming as well, even a stylist. It's a big campaign, a big deal.'

Sally couldn't imagine the fluttering butterflies she was causing. 'It's provisionally booked in for next Tuesday evening,' she went on. 'Eight o'clock. Gil Foreman can't do weekends apparently and his studio's done a lot of rearranging. He really seems to want you.'

'He took a few test pics in New York for Jim Beam. Of course I'll do it, Sal, how could I refuse?'

He was crossing the Atlantic, following up . . . but what of it? No good getting carried away, he obviously just felt I was right for the job. Coming to London didn't mean much with a money-no-object account like Jim Beam. And yet . . .

I began the depressing business of unpacking cases full of creased, dirty clothes. The pile grew. Perhaps our smiling Spanish cleaner, Palmira, wouldn't mind a day on laundry. She was into washing, even made her own soap and had once shown me how, boiling up great lumps of fat for hours. I'd tried to tell her, in my non-existent Spanish, that I'd be better off sticking to Daz.

Joe was out seeing his agent. His new play was opening on 31 January, exactly when Eileen Ford wanted me to come to New York. It all got going again in February, she said. If I came a couple of days early and did some go-sees, I'd be booked right up.

The phone rang. It was Alicia and, far from fluttering butterflies, my stomach froze to a block. She couldn't have assumed Joe would answer. Was it me she wanted? Did she know he was out? I felt on red alert, but having just unpacked the outfits she'd loaned me that I longed not to have taken, I was at least able to thank her and get it over with.

She wanted to probe. The questions kept coming. Yes, we'd had a sensational time, I said. Yes, it had been extraordinary. Was she trying to gauge how things had been between me and Joe, how much he'd missed her? 'Isn't the baby almost due?' I asked. 'How are you feeling?'

'Vast,' she laughed. 'I'm an elephant. Come and see for yourself, if you're bringing back the clothes. Tomorrow any good?'

'I'm booked all day. I could drop them in at the weekend?'

It was too much to hope that I could just hand the clothes to the housekeeper and scarper; Alicia and Toby wouldn't risk weekending at their Gloucestershire home with the birth so close.

'Joe could bring them,' Alicia said, turning me to ice. 'He's looking in later today. He wants Toby to up the ante and be an entrepreneurial angel for the play. But Tobs is such a mean old

189

bugger at heart, he'll never cough up. Joe's on a loser there!'

I shivered some more. She must have talked to Joe already that morning — he must have called her even as we landed — and she wanted me to know it. All my quiet hopes dashed, just delusions, Alicia was right back on the scene. Joe's play was financially sound. It had to be, with rehearsals about to start. The Toby-as-an-investor line was just what had come into her head, the bitch, the cow. How could she?

I heard myself give a false little titter. 'I wouldn't trust Joe with your clothes for a minute. No, I must see them safely delivered. I hardly wore them, by the way, so don't think I've done too much damage.' Unlike Alicia . . .

'Absolutely no rush with the size I am! The baby's due any day now, but the betting's on late — a Christmas baby, we think.' Who was the 'we'? Joe? Toby?

Alicia had even taken my mind off Gil Foreman. I went back into the bedroom and stuffed a pillowcase full of Joe's dirty laundry. Could she really have a clue whether the baby was his or Toby's? It got to me. I grabbed the pillowcase in hysterical rage and hurled it across the room. Shirts, pants, socks, flew out, airborne like paper planes, hanging suspended for seconds before landing in a sorry mess. Then I fell on the bed, crying uncontrollably, exhausted and over-reacting, but the bitterness was rife.

Yet the bile in my bloodstream soon drained, the tears were shortlived. Gil Foreman was coming to London. A sort of disbelieving elation was taking root; who cared if it was for purely professional reasons? He was coming to London and I was seeing him the following week.

★ ★ ★

It felt best to wise Joe up to my evening booking well in advance. 'You'll never guess,' I said, having asked after his agent, where he'd just been, and not mentioned Alicia's call, 'but one of the photographers I saw in New York is in London next week and he's booked me. It's for an ad for Jim Beam bourbon, but it has to be after-hours so I'll be working late next Tuesday.'

'Why can't this jerk Yank snap you in daytime? What's wrong with nine to five?' Joe sounded testy and suspicious, which I hadn't expected. 'You're not going to start working nights as well now, are you, wifey, like some squint-eyed office cleaner or tart?'

'I'm fully booked, Joe, there is no other time. And the money's good, I really should do it.'

'God, you're such a tedious bloody slave to your modelling, so typically bourgeois. I'm home and around for once, you could have thought of that. About the only time for ages too, with the play coming up — which with any luck should have a decent run.'

When I'd be home and around, I thought sarcastically, but that would never have occurred to Joe. 'He's a top American photographer, love,' I said instead. 'It's quite a coup.'

Joe sniffed. He was resentful of any success of mine, bad-tempered, sensitive about my paying the bills, although that never seemed to stop him spending like a gambler's moll. It was a vicious circle. The more Joe ran up debts, the greater my need to work.

He always made me feel guilty about it, though, dreary and over-cautious, convinced that I was quite as boring and bourgeois as he made out. Joe's sneers always hit home. So what, if we had a few outstanding bills? Alicia, no doubt, would have had a far more cavalier approach. Vanity came into it, I knew. I was busy and in demand, didn't believe in the compliments, they just went with the job, but the small success of my career taking off was a secret source of pride.

Alicia's clothes burned a hole in my cupboard. I felt guilty about not taking them to be cleaned. Tough titty, it was bad enough having to return them and face her. I decided to drop them in on Monday morning, on my way to *Vogue*, so I'd have every excuse not to stay.

Over the weekend, Joe's mood yoyo-ed between ebullience and surliness. He'd asked some actor friends for Sunday lunch, and the cooking gave me space, time for private thoughts. And on Monday morning, when Alicia's tired-looking elderly housekeeper came to the door, I could have kissed her. I felt released.

I sat in the railway-carriage dressing room at *Vogue*, putting on make-up. Slate-grey clouds over Hanover Square, a mug of tepid instant coffee on the go, my thoughts were one way and obsessive: how was I going to handle seeing Gil Foreman tomorrow night? With fortitude and resolve? Feeling the way I did?

Jean Shrimpton wandered in. She hadn't been modelling long, but we'd worked together once or twice before California. I remembered her as a willowy girl, all legs and shaggy brown hair, yet now, seeing her afresh, I couldn't stop staring; she had a lightness and grace crossed with sexy gawkiness, and her eyes, under a wispy fringe, were arrestingly wide apart. I thought of sleek sophisticated older models, flame-haired Fiona Campbell-Walter, beautiful Bronwen Pugh. Jean was gorgeously, irreverently different.

'Hi,' she smiled. 'I'm not here really. I just stopped by with Bailey to see the pictures we did for Young Idea.' She leaned close into the mirror, applying an ice-pink lipstick, 'They're in the January issue and he said I could pick one up.'

Clare Rendlesham, *Vogue*'s most fearsome fashion editor, came in carrying a bright yellow suit over her arm. She gave Jean an icy, we-need-to-get-on-now sort of look, which I tried to balance by saying to Jean I couldn't wait to see the January *Vogue*.

'Not for my pics.' She laughed and chucked the lipstick into her handbag that she slung over her shoulder, meandering to the door then in her own time. She was relaxed and easygoing, completely unfazed by Clare. There was nothing bourgeois about Jean Shrimpton, I thought wistfully.

For the first shot Clare put me in the short-skirted marigold-yellow suit she'd brought in, which seemed garish and dressy with too many buttons. It didn't win any Brownie points with Bailey either. 'Looks like a slab of margarine,' he said, 'and stiff as a Willie with it. 'Aven't you got any less crappy gear, a frock with a bit of fucking movement?'

'It's the suit I want, it's very new season,' Clare retaliated, flashing her eyes all the more angrily when Bailey said it would get by on an Easter card with a load of fluffy chicks.

While I stood waiting, positioned on a pearl-grey backdrop in *Vogue*'s small studio, wondering who'd win, Bailey aimed the wind machine at the suit's neat skirt. It sagged sadly into my legs, and Bailey had his way.

He was brilliant at playing the fashion editors, artfully, wittily rude with his East End cheek and cunning, and he knew how to have fun. Yet they all loved him, even Clare. He flicked through the rail in the dressing room and chose a dress that was flatteringly figure-hugging to the hips while floaty-skirted. Then with Elvis on disc, 'Blue Suede Shoes' blasting out, we were on a roll.

Bailey said I had a faraway look in my eyes, just right for the mood. He didn't know where and how far from the job my eyes were straying. He wouldn't have minded, probably quite approved of looks that shouldn't be there. It was dreadful being this obsessed, feeling so driven and disorientated, living for tomorrow night. It was all imagined, anyway. There'd be no passionate coming together, only the hollowness and ache of the let-down.

Joe ignored me when I got home. He was learning his script, which seemed little excuse for not even looking up. He'd either forgotten or lost

194

interest in my booking the following night and I wondered about it. Joe hammered away at things, he never once let up. I sighed and cooked a favourite paprika ragout of his for him to have when I was out working.

In the morning I packed deodorant and scent in my tote bag, as well as the usual shoes, gloves, bras and make-up, in case the day overran. But I hoped to get home before my booking with Gil. I hurried off to a casting for a commercial, for a new soap called *Care*. I hated castings. It was the one time in the job when I could be made to feel like a piece of meat. I felt it at times too, when some berkish account executive hanging around on set, chose to speak to the photographer as if I wasn't there. 'Tell the girl the shampoo bottle needs to be closer.' Or, 'Tell the girl we need lots of lovely smiles!' I had a name, why couldn't these people use it? I hated to lose my identity.

The casting was at J. Walter Thompson, a very grand and reputable agency, most of whose executives were old-school, chummy and plummy; they knew a bit about good manners. They spoke to me directly, unlike the 'tell the girl' twerps.

Three men and a woman sitting round a table in a fuggy room perused my book, my portfolio of photographs and pulls from magazines. They showed me script boards and asked questions. Did I use the product, like the product? Was I free on the appointed day? I left JWT feeling reasonably treated at least, whether or not I got the job.

Berkeley Square was snarled up with traffic and vibrating; all the blaring, honking horns were a mechanical cacophony. Angry drivers inched forward, leaned out of their windows yelling obscenities, no nightingales to be heard ever again. I felt emotional, rooted for a moment. It was a soft beautiful day, the sunlight, ethereally pale, bleeding into thin cloud and lifting the sky.

I suddenly realised that Alicia's husband, Toby, was right in front of me, scanning the traffic for a cab. He turned and saw me, too. 'Well, hello, beautiful Susannah, good to see you.'

'Can I give you a lift anywhere, Toby? I'm parked round the corner, on my way to Chelsea.'

'Thanks, but I must get straight to the airport, I'm in danger of missing my plane.'

'How's Alicia? All okay?' I wondered at Toby, flying off when the baby was due.

'All fine — though this sprog's bound to pop today or tomorrow, just when I'm in Milan. Still, Alicia thinks I'm better off out of the way. Ah, at last. *Taxi!* See you, Susannah, must rush.' He blew a kiss and leaped into the cab, solidly built, an enigma.

I drove my Mini across London, absorbing the bit of intelligence. I was due at Keith Ewart's studio in Glebe Place off King's Road. We were doing a commercial for Black Magic chocolates. I loved working with Keith. Enthusiasm radiated out of him like soundwaves. The downside was the chocolates. Even with a bucket beside me, and spitting out every one, I still felt yuckishly sick by the end of the day. But we didn't overrun. I had time to go home to clean up.

Joe was just leaving. 'I'm out tonight, wifey,' he said, giving me a rather edgy glance, 'since you can't be buggered to be around. Tomorrow night too, as it happens.'

I found some fight. 'Funny thing, I bumped into Toby today, in Berkeley Square. He was rushing to the airport, flying out to Milan, just when Alicia's baby is due.'

Joe was nothing if not a good actor. 'Well, there's no point in him hanging around, is there?' he said, without a flicker. 'He'd only be in the way. I'm off, going to hear some new guys playing at that joint in Soho, the Blue Gardenia. A group called The Beatles — useless name, but I'm told they might take off.' I was almost amused. Joe never usually told me a thing about what he was doing, but being caught out had made him slip up. Did our sins always find us out? Was I about to go down the same road?

★ ★ ★

The Grosvenor House Hotel at eight o'clock, Sally had told me: the stylist would have all the clothes. That made a change. I usually had to take half my own wardrobe for ads.

'Fancy bringing a stylist all this way,' she'd said. 'What it must all be costing! They're doing the photography at a restaurant round the corner, I believe.'

I asked at Reception for Gil Foreman and the aged uniformed man on the desk, who looked a permanent fixture, picked up the phone. I rested my heavy tote bag and eyed my reflection in a

197

smoky mirrored pillar. I was wearing a new coat, white leather with a curly Mongolian lamb lining. The cold had been reaching in ever since being home. And underneath, the wide-belted cinnamon dress bought on the day of meeting Gil.

I looked expectantly at the receptionist, but my smile quickly faded; he was still on the phone, arguing heatedly, and it seemed to be all about me.

'I'm sorry, I'm sure, as you say, you're not alone, but this young lady isn't staying at the hotel and she cannot come up to your room.' I stared at the ground, agonised; did he think I was a prostitute? He carefully replaced the phone and cleared his throat, I had to look up and face him. 'Mr Foreman is on his way down,' he said complacently.

The lift doors opened and Gil appeared, spitting with rage. I could feel the heat of his fury. A curly-haired, slightly raddled — looking girl, carrying armfuls of black dresses, came out with him as well as a fleshy, florid man, heavy on the Brylcreem, who must be the account executive.

Gil came up to me. 'Hi! How goes?' He squeezed my hand. 'We'll have to get straight to the restaurant, do the styling there,' he said, looking daggers at the old boy on the desk.

The stylist introduced herself. 'I'm Kitty. Love the coat!'

The account executive held out his hand. 'Marvin Parker, Cole and Dempsey Agency.' I shook his hand, feeling an instant dislike. He had slack wet lips, mousy hair slicked flat, and the way he was eyeing me made me wary. I knew the type.

'My assistant's round at the restaurant, setting up,' Gil said. 'Let's go.' He had one last snipe at the man on the desk before we left. 'Isn't it time this hotel moved up a gear?'

Gil walked beside me; he was about my height, five eight or nine. He leaned close and I felt his breath, warm at my ear. 'Bad start!' I smiled back at him, feeling shivery. It was a cold night.

The restaurant, Portofino, was in Mount Street, down a flight of stairs, dark and plush: small lamps with deep-red shades, soft dim lighting. The tables were arranged in semi-circles, enclosing and intimate. They were empty apart from two couples in evening dress, settled in at the rear. 'Your backdrop,' Gil said, following my glance. 'A male model's on his way, too. And that's Jack, Mr Muscles, my assistant, making with the lights.' Jack grinned back in response. His black T-shirt was stretched tight over well-developed pectorals and bulging upper arms.

Kitty and I went to the ladies' where she hung the dresses on cubicle doors. Gil came in and held each dress against me, looking up from them into my eyes. I stared back. He chose a simple black shift, low-cut and sleeveless.

'Any booze going?' Kitty said, as he turned to leave.

'Work first.' He flicked at her corkscrew curls. 'And tease that hair away from Susannah's face, Kitty. I want to see both eyes.'

199

She made me up, which I wasn't used to, putting gold eye shadow on my lids, a speck under the brows. 'Gil wants minimum jewellery,' she drawled. 'No distractions.'

I felt good in the dress and ventured out shyly, to get started.

The male model had arrived, a handsome medical student called Gordon, whom I knew. 'We're old friends,' I said to Gil. 'We've gazed across tables before.'

'No gazing tonight, your eyes are on me. And Gordon fella, sorry mate, you're just a buck with a back in this shot, a dark silhouette. No catching Susannah's eye.'

'Hey-ho,' Gordon sighed, 'so it's not my night after all. But I'm not proud and who's complaining?' he said with a wink. 'We students need the loot.'

Marvin, the executive, grunted — he wrote the cheques. I tried to contain my dislike. He was drinking champagne and eating canapés, creamy vol-au-vents and smoked-salmon rolls, cramming them into his mouth. I didn't give it long before he made a pass.

We got on with the shoot. Gordon's back and the bourbon bottle formed the frame while I fingered my glass of rich amber liquid, looking straight into the unflinching eye of Gil's Hasselblad lens. It was no filter. He was reaching into me through that lens, speaking a translatable language.

He shot a few reels of film then went over to the couples behind me. I turned, watching him arrange glasses and bottles with care. Then he

200

came to sit beside me on the plush bench and played with my hair, tucking it behind my ears. My skin pricked all over. 'The background's a blur,' he said under his breath. 'Anything to keep Marvin happy.'

I shivered as Gil held my hair tightly back from my face. I looked into his eyes, very aware of his wide mobile mouth, bottling powerful feelings that weren't legal. I dreaded the inevitable problems with Marvin, whose beady eyes on me couldn't be more overt.

'Kitty!' Gil called, still holding my hair. 'I want it scraped back. Come, see.'

She darted over. 'Perfect. Wow! Back to the ladies', Susannah, up it goes.'

It gave me a nice long neck, but I felt more naked. My hair was protection. We carried on.

'Look at me,' Gil said, 'keep looking.' Other photographers would have said, 'Look straight to camera.' We worked well together, though; the professional rapport was there — as well as communicating in other ways.

I could feel the tugging need in me and had a sense of being trapped, my skirt caught up in brambles, held back from where I wanted to be. The frustration was unbearable, yet breaking free would lead to other pitfalls and prickly situations, that much I knew.

'All done,' Gil said, straightening up and stretching. 'We had it in the first shot.' He turned to Marvin. 'You have your picture, a hundred times over. You'll be spoilt for choice.'

'The restaurant has laid on food,' Kitty said, pouring a brimming glass of champagne for herself. 'Smells great, like fritto misto — fries as well, I hope.'

Jack was dismantling lights, labelling film and packing up. Gil was telling Gordon how well he'd do in the States. 'Don't tempt me,' he sighed. 'The scalpel calls, and years of poverty!'

Marvin sidled up and took my arm, his fleshy fingers pressing in deep. 'Sexy dress, that,' he said with a lascivious smile. 'Keep it on, we're going on the town, painting it all shades of red.'

'Sorry, but I must get straight home. I've an early start tomorrow. And I must go and change right away.' I struggled free of his hold. 'I'd hate to splatter this very elegant dress.'

'I'll talk you round,' Marvin said, drawing a nail down my arm. 'Here, have some champagne.' I took the glass and escaped to the ladies; shaking him off more permanently wasn't going to be an easy or pleasant task. He'd turn nasty, I knew. And he'd keep me from Gil.

Kitty took down my hair, taking swigs of her drink all the while. 'Gil will sort that creep,' she said. 'Get him pissed, tell him where to go for skirt — tell him you're married!'

'I am.' I held up my ring finger and she clapped a hand to her mouth and laughed. We both did.

The food was served quickly, crispy fried fish and chips. I wasn't hungry, which was just as well; I picked away the batter to reach a bit of unadulterated, uncalorific fish. Gordon told gruesomely funny medical jokes, enough to put anyone off their food; he had a warm heart and his priorities in the right place, I felt.

He and the two couples didn't linger; it was nearly midnight. Marvin, having demolished a heaped plateful, was moving in for the kill.

My coat was on a nearby chair, tote bag beside it. 'All set to go, Susannah?' Gil said. 'Shall I walk you to your car?'

'She's not going yet.' Marvin shifted his weight closer, crushing me into his side. 'I've got a date with this chick. I'm gonna show her a good time, aren't I, babe?'

'Susannah's husband wouldn't be pleased,' Gil observed, shrugging on a cord jacket over the worn blue sweatshirt he was wearing. 'We did well to get her here tonight at all. The client will love this ad, Marvin. The campaign will do great — one up for Cole and Dempsey! Order up some more booze, have a smoke, I'll be right back. Just must see Susannah to her car.'

He held out my white coat, but Marvin wasn't giving up or letting go. He hung on, keeping me in his tight sweaty grasp. He smelled of stale cigar and his breath stank, too.

'I'm game for a good time,' Kitty said, downing her glass with a sexy smack of the lips. 'Les A's a swish joint, I've heard, and the Four Hundred — all on expenses, Marv!'

'Sorry to be boring,' I smiled, trying to sound sadly resigned as I wriggled free. 'I'll really be in the doghouse, though, if I don't hurry home. London's swinging, it's a hot ticket, you'll have a ball.' I slung on my coat; Gil had my tote bag. He was halfway to the door.

'Kitty was a brick,' I said, climbing the stairs and out into the cold night air.

'She's a boozer and not too choosy. They'll have sore heads on the plane.' He slowed down a little. 'I suppose you do have a car?' He grinned and kissed my cheek.

We sat in my Mini with the engine on. 'I thought I'd outgrown cars,' Gil said, 'but since there's no chance of my hotel after that little scene with the old creep on the desk . . . '

He traced round my face with gentle fingers and brushed over my lips. I held my breath.

'There's a lot I want to ask.' His eyes were searching, his mouth unfairly close. 'You're not happy, are you, Susannah? Is your husband treating you rough?'

'He can be very gentle.' I needed Gil to kiss me, more than I could stand.

'But not always — that was a gentle answer! Does he drink?'

'There's that . . . '

'And women? One in particular?'

I nodded. 'For over a year now, I think. I don't know about others.'

'I'm married, too. My wife — this sounds comically typical, just happens to be true — but ever since the second child, she hasn't let me near her. We get by all the same, quite companionably. I look after her; love my kids to death. I could never leave.'

I felt an acute sense of let-down, a cold demoralizing and moralizing hand, but what did I expect? 'You'd better get back, hadn't you?' I forced a smile. 'Marvin's waiting.'

Gil took me in his arms, those long, bandy arms that hung away from his body. He wasn't beautiful, but as I lost myself in his big wide hungry mouth I was somewhere beyond my experience. It was more than kissing: I believed in it, believed in Gil. My heart was in a panic as his hand went to the car door.

He didn't open it; he turned and sat back. 'There's no rushing this, Susannah,' he said. 'We can't anyway. I know the problems, but it'll happen, it will.' He took my hand and kissed each of my fingers. 'You're definitely coming to New York? You won't stop working — mostly for me. I spoke to Fords and Eileen said the end of January, that's seven weeks.' Gil fished in his jacket pocket and scribbled on a scrap of paper. 'Call collect on this number — early, one o'clock your time — and let me know when's best to phone.'

I drove home with tears streaming down my face. Was I in love? Was I going to go to New York and start an affair? Was that what my marriage had come to? How could I last through the next seven weeks?

* * *

It was almost Christmas and I couldn't wait to see my parents. Joe had nagged me to go down to Dorset and bring back Frankie — he loved his mynah bird, really missed the squawker — but I was madly busy and we'd be there so soon. The urge to unburden on my mother was strong, but what could she do, poor Mum, except fret?

I worried about a present for Joe's mother. We were seeing her on Saturday, the day before

Christmas Eve when we were driving to Dorset, and I wanted to choose something she'd really like. She was alone in her flat in the wastelands of Tilbury. Joe's father hadn't shown his face in months.

I came home from doing an ad for Yardley, wanting Joe's help on what to give. He was buried in his script, uncommunicative, so I went through to the kitchen and got on with cooking lamb chops.

'Would your mum like perfume?' I called. 'Or a new blouse, perhaps?'

'Get her gin, or beers for her 'friends'.'

'You can if you want,' I yelled back, irritated. 'I'd rather give her something feminine.'

Joe looked up finally when I came in with the supper. 'Alicia's had her baby,' he said, 'a couple of days ago. I saw it in *The Times*. Shouldn't you send some flowers?'

My insides turned. Joe knew how to punch low. 'That's your department,' I muttered. 'You've got more time on your hands. What did she have?'

'A boy. Good chops these, nice and tender.'

* * *

My parents' cottage was near Bridport, thatched and in an acre of waterlogged garden. It was lit up, we had a warm welcome, but Dad looked worryingly ashen. Night call-outs, everyone's winter ills — a country practice was hard for a doctor and he was worn out. I was, too, after a long, not very friendly journey, and seeing Joe's mother the previous day had been a strain. She'd looked a mess: bleached hair, black roots, empty bottles . . . Joe talked about her lovers, but I felt sure she was wretchedly lonely. I'd suggested as we left that he ask her to his first night. We had the back bedroom for her to stay in; we could stand her a new dress and a trip to the hairdressers. 'She'd be so proud and pleased to be there,' I said.

I could see Joe mulling it over. He wasn't shy of his working-class roots, he played up to them, and I was hopeful — about that if nothing else.

The tree in the hall twinkled with the baubles and ancient, multi-coloured lights that had done all the Christmases I could remember. It was only the four of us. My brother, James, who was in the Army serving out in Kuwait, since Iraq had threatened to invade, was briefly home, but staying with his in-laws in Yorkshire. I prayed Joe wouldn't be too obviously bored, drunk and maudlin. He hated festive family-holiday times and being contained. A regular drinks party with locals on Boxing Day was a danger area; I could see him being belittling and manipulative and turning conversational screws in a destructive Pinteresque way. He'd done it subtly before.

He proved me wrong. Joe was as charming as only he could be. Apart from going overboard about Frankie's cage being on a rather distant worktop. 'Out in the scullery, is it, Frankie my bird, you old wanker? Give us a 'bye byeee' then, you old fart. Let's hear your vocals, see you're not pining away.'

Frankie obliged and Joe beamed. My mother advanced shyly that Frankie could now say 'time

207

for bed', which made Joe even more all over her than before. He flattered her extravagantly, chatted companionably with my father — about recent events, the first man in space, the death of the farthing. He asked Dad's advice.

'How should I act a doctor, Henry?' They were seated on either side of the fireplace, Joe's long legs stretched out on the fireside rug. 'The stereotype bedside-manner smoothie feels very old hat.'

'We're tired-out smokers and drinkers these days,' Dad laughed, accepting a cigarette as Joe immediately leaned forward with his silver case. Dad's colour was back, Mum smiling. They were definitely signed up members of Joe's fan club that Christmas Day.

I had to tell Mum something of the worsening situation with Joe, even now while he'd calmed the seas; I couldn't bottle it up when I'd always told her everything. She knew anyway, more or less. She was no fool yet could always only repeat her mantra about nothing to do but soldier on.

She looked frightened, if not horrified, when I tentatively mentioned Gil, and begged me not to do anything *silly*. The deep furrows on her face eased slightly when I assured her that he was never going to leave his wife. It was nothing like that, just . . . a sort of momentary attraction. Three weeks in New York, I added soothingly, might actually help. Joe took me for granted. It could be a turning point, a way back.

But would it be, I wondered, hurrying between London studios on dark January days. Mum had looked dubious. It was unseasonably mild, a sunny month, but I was in shivery turmoil and seeing my problems as insurmountable. I shut my mind to them, relived kissing Gil, the sensation of his fondling hands holding back my hair; outwardly professional, but I extracted every drop of meaning and emotion, more than had been there.

Telephoning him without reversing the charges, I'd suggested times to call, yet the light, joking conversations that followed only heightened the pain. I thought of his energy and ability, his obvious passion for his job. I saw him photographing beautiful models, finding the angle, the look; I imagined his hands fondling and holding back other girls' hair. But flashes of violent jealousy evaporated whenever he called. He made me feel I was his all.

I was almost grateful for the weeks of waiting. A state of yearning was a staying of time, an unbroken spell. It was a covering filter over infidelity. I was demented with impatience at the same time, desperate to reach where we were going. But where was that? And how would it end?

Joe was madly rehearsing. His part in *Cakes and Kindness* was a fresh challenge; he was playing a near-suicidal introvert who has been written off, considered a work-shy dropout. A young English teacher befriends him, with unhappy results.

Joe was bursting with energy, enthusiastic, focused, like an irrepressible puppy, winsome and wicked, commanding forgiveness for every sin. I could see in him the Joe who'd swept me off my feet, whom I'd married with shining eyes trained on the happily-ever-after. The Joe I'd watched nightly, gazing adoringly up at the stage. He wasn't seeing me, though, in any meaningful way.

My trip to New York was all arranged. Eileen Ford had spoken to the agency and offered a bed if I couldn't get fixed up.

I was fixed up, surprisingly. Gloria Romanoff had been in touch, thrilled I was coming to New York, feeling she'd helped it to happen and been involved from the start. She had a friend, Joan Ferrone, she said, whose husband advised Jackie Kennedy on paintings; Joan and her husband would be delighted to have me to stay. They had a spare cot — as Gloria called it, which I took to mean a small single — in their New York apartment and were often in Washington. I wouldn't be in their hair.

Eileen was insistent that I arrive on Monday 29 January. 'You're gonna need those few days, get in the go-sees before the February rush.'

Go-sees were hell, appointments with studios and ad agencies to show myself and my book, photographs and pulls from magazines, but they were essential, the only way to ensure being booked. I couldn't, though, when it came to it, miss Joe's first night. It was probably for the wrong reasons, feelings of guilt, but I still cared and felt the tug of the ties. 'Sorry, Eileen,' I said, 'I just can't make that day. My husband's play opens on the thirty-first and I must be there. I hate to let you down.'

There was a silence. 'Okay,' Eileen snapped finally, 'husbands first, but you're on the first plane next day. And get some sleep! Your feet aren't going to touch the ground.'

13

Daisy was doing her make-up at the dressing table, getting ready for the Red Tide Benefit on behalf of the Baymen's Association. She was looking forward to it, albeit rather sheepishly, having said often enough to friends that charity dances with loud corporate tables and interminable auctions weren't for her, and also because she knew her anticipation was all about having a dance with Warren. It wasn't that she seriously fancied him, but he made her feel good about herself. He was softening the separation from Simon, and there was no doubting his covert interest in her.

The Benefit was Southampton's splashiest, most social summer event, he'd said, and she worried about her understated dress. It was emerald satin and backless, but looked very plain, laid out on the bed. Still, it did its best for her — it showed up her eyes.

Susannah had offered the loan of some jewellery, but Daisy felt that was too great a responsibility and, given the competition — the combined value of the rocks on show would clean out the Federal Reserve, according to Warren — it seemed better and slightly wittier to wear none at all. At least no one could accuse her of one-upmanship.

It was time to get a move on. She applied another coat of long-lash mascara, leaning in close to the mirror; she was more used to the well-lit one over her Battersea bathroom basin than a dressing table with small useless shaded lights and a sprigged muslin skirt. The bedroom décor, blue silk curtains with swags and tails, a velvet chaise-longue and curvy buttoned bedhead, was very dated and English country house.

The room smelled potently fragrant, since her hand had slipped, pouring stephanotis bath oil into the tub. It was lingering on her skin and Daisy lifted her arm to drink in the perfume. It made her feel a physical longing. Simon wasn't the type, though, like some romantically inclined Italian or Frenchman, to bestow rapturous kisses the length of her arm, and she wondered, with a private giggle, what Warren's inclinations might be.

It was mad of her to think of flirting with him on the dance floor. Did she want to risk souring her warm relationship with Susannah and so much else — all that could lie ahead? She and Susannah had good fun as well, amazingly; they really got on.

Daisy felt bemused that a man of seventy, sixty-nine if you believed him, and however presentable, could make her even whimsically fancy a little fling. Perhaps she had a wayward gene, a sort of inbuilt self-destruct button that determined her being lured into fraught situations with unsuitable men.

There had been no excuse for calling Warren in Manhattan. True, he'd told her to phone any time and had been keen to help, but to act on it on the flimsy pretext of confusion over an address — and it was her second week, she knew the city a little better — was to give him a green light. He'd been upstate at the brewery, mortified to be out of town, and had quickly suggested lunch the following week; quite funny, how frustrated he'd been. He'd kept saying so, couldn't stop.

They had a date for Tuesday — not one written into the diary — yet there was no real harm in it, surely? It was no more than a touch of spice to cheer up the working week. She'd felt a bit lonely, staying overnight with Susannah's friend in Manhattan to avoid the long slog back to Southampton on the Jitney bus. Not that the friend, Janet, another sixties model and one of Eileen Ford's 'girls', hadn't been welcoming, but two days trailing the city, the fabric showrooms, Bruschwig & Fils, Clarence House, Lee Jofa, collecting samples, placing orders, had been very solitary. Daisy had scoured the antique shops around East 60th Street, 1st Dibs, Kentshire, Newel — names on Susannah's list, as well as Sotheby's and Christie's. She'd read up on renowned American designers, people like Albert Hadley and Sister Parish, Mark Hampton, Peter Marino. She'd had lone lunches, boringly healthy pastas and salads — couldn't she be forgiven a single call to Warren?

Daisy gave her lips a last lick of gloss and stepped into her dress. She hoped the high strappy evening sandals weren't over the top. They were mock snakeskin with slender straps that travelled up her ankles — quite sexily, she thought.

Susannah knocked. 'How are you doing, Daisy? Need any bits and bobs?'

'Thanks, but I think I'm okay going without,' Daisy smiled, opening the door. 'Wow, Susannah, you look completely gorgeous — and get that dazzling necklace! It's like seeing stars from a bump on the head!' It was a circle of diamonds, sparking brilliantly in the dark of the hallway, with a dangling ruby pendant, magnificent against the white chiffon of her slim-fitting dress with its cut-away shoulders and a low flounce.

'That's a bit over the top,' Susannah laughed. 'You're right, though, Daisy, no jewels needed. The dress and your eyes do all the talking you could want.'

Warren was waiting downstairs, looking presentably dashing in cream trousers, blazer and a Liberty-print tie: a very American look with the black tasselled loafers. He took both their arms as they went to the car. 'I call this having my cake and eating it,' he said, 'I won't be short of envious glances, walking in.'

'Is it usual, having a big Benefit like this in the grounds of a private house?' Susannah asked as they set off, Jackson driving, the three of them snug on the back seat.

'It's catching on. People sometimes offer if they want to join one of the clubs, or they're strong-armed into it, or else they've just traded up and plan to have work done. They get all the kudos and a tax break as well. And who cares if the lawns get churned up when the construction trucks are about to roll in anyway. It's win-win for the owners.'

'And I suppose the social climbers pay up for the chance to snoop round some lavish estate they'd never get to see otherwise — the homes of fashion moguls and hedge-funders.'

'Too right. The last thing on many people's minds is supporting a good cause.'

They'd chosen to arrive late and the reception was in full swing. Tom Horne, the beanpole village gossip of Warren's description, was easy to spot. Gertrude Whelp too, whose leathery, violently made-up face and weighty jewels made her unmissable. She was surrounded by a small coterie of face-lifted and heavily lacquered hangers-on. It was a largely older crowd, but the spattering of fit ultra-chic younger women, probably the tennis players Susannah had talked about, made Daisy feel her age. She would be thirty-nine in October.

The extensive grounds were floodlit; mainly all lawn and with a too-formal rose garden, but silver-leaved plants tumbled out of tremendous urns and an herbaceous border had speckle-throated foxgloves, spikes of ocean-blue delphiniums and a coppery pink oleander bush. The bar was under a cream-and-white striped awning where a harpist was playing stalwartly, completely drowned out by the chatter.

Daisy declined the circulating canapés on straw platters lined with glossy leaves, asparagus wrapped in prosciutto, pigs in blankets — a sort of frankfurter sausage roll — and crudités; she hadn't come to eat. She felt spare, low and anticlimactic, eyeing Susannah, who looked relaxed and elegant, cornered by the gossiping

Tom Horne. Warren was cornered too, accosted by a mature woman in a sweeping metallic-blue silk gown. He was listening to her attentively with an easy interested smile, but Daisy perked up when he looked over with steady eyes and soon made his excuses.

'Let's go over to the tent and start a move,' he said, taking her arm. It was open on one side, and Daisy could see white balloons bobbing against the ceiling. The tables had been given names — *Georgica, Cupsogue, Shinnecock.* 'They're beaches,' Warren explained. 'We're on *Coopers*, Southampton's best. My neighbours, Elmer and Jan Harvey, are on our table, also the Stocktons, Maisie — the sexy Southerner I told you about — and her husband, Art — and the auctioneer. He's unmarried so you're not next to him. I'm not losing you that fast!'

Warren didn't exactly have her to lose, Daisy thought, pleased. People were following their lead, drifting in, but they were first at the table. It looked pretty: white roses tinged with mother-of-pearl, white tablecloths and napkins, scattered white seashells. 'Those are in honour of the Baymen,' Warren said, 'and the flowers will have been donated, I'm sure. The committee does its best.'

'I like the simplicity, the all-white theme. It's fresh and cool-looking on a muggy night like tonight. What's the unmarried auctioneer's name?'

'Gerald Carter. He's a smoothie from Christie's, but likable enough. You're between Elmer Harvey and Art; I'll just have to be patient

216

till I can ask you to dance.' Warren's hand was on Daisy's bare back, and the slight, light movement of his fingers was giving her shivers, her body responding involuntarily. He leaned close. 'You don't know what you're doing to me, Daisy — you looked exquisite, out there in the garden. I . . . Ah, here's Maisie and Art on their way. Hi, guys!' he called out. 'Come meet Daisy, my beautiful house guest. She's one half of the design team who are about to pull me apart.'

'That's some dress,' Daisy whispered, as the Stocktons neared. 'And some! At least she's wearing a thong.' It took more than guts, chutzpah and a sense of fun to wear a completely transparent dress. Maisie's huge rising-moon boobs and a scintillating collar of amethysts and diamonds held the eye, but the diaphanous dress won the day. The top, a vast mauve-satin bow that cried out 'untie me', gave way to sheer full folds of a paler mauve that billowed away from a shapely body, well worthy of being on view.

Warren complimented Maisie on her dress with a deadpan sort of smile, then peered out to the garden. 'I'll just go look for Susannah, see if she needs rescuing from Tom.'

'Ah hope she spills some of that theyre gossip,' Maisie drawled, in a sultry southern accent. Art was a tiny snail-like man who came just up to her boobs. Daisy struggled to contain a giggle with her private thoughts, which bubbled up even more as she saw a couple at the next table gazing over at Maisie in absolute horror. Maisie grinned back confidently, beaming as well at other Southampton worthies as they filtered in, all clearly muttering darkly about 'that dress'. Their faces were set. Maisie didn't care; she was having fun. Warren came back with Susannah, and last to arrive at the table were his neighbours, Elmer and Jan Harvey.

At dinner Elmer asked Daisy if it was her first trip to Long Island. She must visit the wineries, he said. Art, on her left, prodded her thigh and was less predictable; he told her she had class, that breeding showed — pity he couldn't afford a seventh wife. She tried to catch Warren's eye, but he was laughing, concentrating exclusively on Susannah. Gerald, the auctioneer, was late, an empty place across the table from her. Daisy felt miffed and short-changed.

Gerald made it in time for the first course, which was caramelised baby beetroot, chèvre, crisp chicory and coriander. He had a cultured face, with a high forehead, thick brown hair, neatly parted, and a very long nose. Daisy had often wondered about kissing someone with a long nose; did the nose have to be consciously circumvented? Was it a case of trial and error, heads cocked sideways, embarrassing accidental bumps?

Gerald talked to her across the table. 'I've been doing a bit of pairing off and I'd say you're my date for tonight — what a bonus!'

'But you're spoken for,' Daisy replied, 'I couldn't possibly come between a man and his gavel.'

The food was good, Szechuan beef and bok choy, spicy with soy sauce and ginger. Art gave Daisy's elbow an enormous nudge, making her drop her fork onto the plate with a clang; he was flicking through the programme. 'Get these auction prizes!' He stabbed at a page. 'Mrs Bronson Foster-Barlow will host and cook dinner for ten . . . I'd pay good bucks *not* to be cooked for by Margo, scrawny goddamn bitch.' Daisy remembered her from the Beach Club, advancing on Warren with drawn claws. 'Two tickets for the Open,' Art carried on. 'Don't want those. Hey, Maisie,' he yelled, making everyone leap out of their skins. 'Seen the Carolina Herrera frock?' He gave Daisy another prod. 'Suit you too, girl, I'll say. Star Prize, along with the Henry Koehler; good punchy oil with the hunting coats. Think I'll bid for that.'

'Yes, you bid, Art,' Gerald said. 'And bid 'em up for me, won't you, real high?'

Elmer Harvey was clearly a staunch Republican and Daisy, more into American politics since Obama, argued with him in a desultory way. She leaped up over-keenly when Warren came to ask her to dance.

The band was playing catchy salsa music, but it was slow progress to the dance floor. Daisy was a new face, people asked to be introduced. She felt ridiculously impatient, hardly able to hide it and be calmly polite. She wanted to dance with Warren, feel his hand on her back, the thrilling undercurrents of his fingers light on her skin. It was disturbing, weird; a little flirt was one thing, but to feel this turned on? Simon did it for her; he only had to walk in the door . . . but Warren? He was an old man.

He held her firmly as they danced, moving

219

easily, his hand pressing and directing. She quivered inside. She thought of dates with men other than Simon in the months since the divorce, when there hadn't been the slightest spark.

Warren avoided resting his cheek on hers, but it was close, he could speak into her ear. 'Will I even last till Tuesday,' he whispered, pulling away with a smile then, as though to make light of his words. Susannah, dancing with Elmer Harvey, came alongside and Warren tossed out gaily, repetitively, 'I'm a lucky man tonight, twice over!' Susannah threw him a glowing smile and danced on.

He squeezed Daisy's hand. 'Perhaps we should get back. I can see the dessert has arrived.' She smiled, falling into him slightly as they left the floor. He put his arm round her, a steadying arm. 'Thanks for the dance. I want another one soon.'

A compote of mixed berries awaited them with a brownie on the side. 'The brownies are from Tate's Bake Shop,' Warren said. 'It's like your village post office, the place where everyone meets their neighbours and has a chat.'

'Delicious,' Gerald said, rising. 'Always are. Must go, be sure and do your stuff for me, you guys!'

The auction dragged on. The bidding went high, but slowly. Gerald earned his donated keep. 'A day for four on a fishing boat out of Montauk.' There was dinner for two at some local restaurant. A man in a Chinese-yellow jacket bid a phenomenal sum and everyone clapped. Gerald finally reached the two Star Prizes. The Carolina Herrara designer dress was first up. 'An elegant resort dress in a flowered and striped print.'

'Ah couldn't squeeze mah boobs into that,' Maisie chuckled. 'Jest imagine. It's the size of a Band-Aid!'

'Like it?' Warren asked Susannah in an undertone. Daisy stiffened. She couldn't hear Susannah's response, but minded her hand on Warren's blazer sleeve and the warm smile, which he returned. And when he began to bid, Susannah looked delighted.

Daisy sat rigidly upright, trying to maintain an expression of light innocent interest. Hands went up and she willed Warren to drop his down. At three thousand dollars, he and a kitten-faced woman with a pink bow in her hair were the only remaining bidders. At five thousand, Gerald pressed Kitten Face to an extra two hundred, but she shook her head with a face as black as an old boot — unbecoming with the little pink bow. Daisy smiled tightly. It was a ridiculous amount to pay, she thought piously, hugely inflated. It was for charity, she knew, but even so . . .

Gerald banged down his gavel to further loud clapping and Susannah looked over to Daisy. 'It's yours,' she said beaming. 'We thought it was just your dress.'

'I'll say,' Elmer Harvey heartily agreed, and Art gave Daisy's thigh another thumping prod. 'There you are, girl! Didn't I say that 'ud suit you? Wasn't I right?'

Having a last dance with Warren before going home, Daisy was floundering, awash with embarrassment. She'd been overcome, blushing to her roots, feeling it was almost immoral to accept the dress. And she wasn't used to being so much the centre of attention — unlike Susannah, she thought, giving into a bitch. Then as well, however generous of Warren, he'd first thought of the dress for Susannah. It had been all her doing, her urging . . . Still, he'd looked pleased with the idea, Daisy had to admit. And wouldn't he have felt it right to put Susannah first? He was sitting next to her, after all, and she was his design consultant, not Daisy. She was a mere assistant, a minion — *and* one who was chancing her luck.

'You're thinking hard, I can tell.' Warren's hand on her back, with just a little extra pressure, drew her close. He smelled good, ferny and countrified, out of a bottle, but still pleasing. His cheek rested against hers. 'I must have a drink with Susannah when we're back,' he murmured. 'I'd like to feel she's relaxed about everything. I hope you understand.' His body was moving with Daisy's, touching, pressing. 'Will you come to the restaurant on Tuesday? I've booked at San Pietro. It's always packed, great Italian food, and extremely central. You'll find it easily. I eat there often, it's a natural place for me to take you to lunch.'

'It sounds a perfect treat,' Daisy said, acutely sensitive to his touching body, her urge to yield and press closer. She knew, with that last remark, he was colluding with her, making her aware of the delicacies. He was a free man, but he'd invited Susannah out to his home for a whole summer; he must have had his reasons. There'd been plenty of unspoken understandings, Daisy felt sure. Susannah had said as much before they left, joking about it, telling how she'd been mildly attracted to Warren at some drinks party yonks ago. Attracted enough to take the job, she'd said, and explore the possibilities.

Daisy couldn't help wondering about other women in his life. It was quite a time since the start of his divorce and there was no doubting his need for female company. It was on her mind as they said their goodbyes. It seemed unlikely she'd pick up any clues, though, simply by having lunch with him in New York.

Jackson brought in the rustling, tissue-lined carrier containing the dress and Daisy took charge of it, blushing again. 'What a night it's been, and last couple of weeks,' she said. 'How can I ever say a quarter of the thanks that are due?'

'I enjoyed the bidding,' Warren said, 'and it was all in a good cause — *two* good causes. It's time I gave a small drinks party, I think. I'll ask our table — Gerald too, I suppose, and a few others as well. And you, Daisy, must wear the dress. You'll be the star of the show.'

14

'Daisy isn't used to being on the receiving end, is she?' Warren said. 'She was so damn embarrassed about the auction prize, as if she couldn't accept it. It was a resort dress, not a diamond-encrusted ballgown, after all — no big deal. I guess that boyfriend of hers must be a tight-fisted sod, not one to take her shopping and shower her with gifts.'

'He doesn't part with a dime. She's tight on funds, too, and very relieved to have this job, I think. He's a selfish, testosterone bully, but that seems to be half the attraction.' I turned to smile at Warren and the poolside swing seat we were sharing rocked gently to and fro. We were lingering in the garden after the Benefit ball. It was two in the morning, his hand resting lightly across my thighs. I drank in the beauty of a quarter moon, platinum in the violet sky; the underwater pool lighting was a distraction, yet it was a magical night, the air as soft and warm as loving arms, and the cicadas making their own particular music.

'Daisy assumed you were buying the dress for me, of course. She was a touch uptight about that and took a little time to adjust.' Uptight wasn't in it, I thought irritably. During the auction Daisy had looked like a wife watching a scene of brazen extra-marital flirtation.

'She's a sweet thing,' Warren said, 'very

unspoilt and unsophisticated. She can be forgiven for being a tad jealous when you were the most beautiful woman there by miles. I had a kind of reflected celebrity status as the bringer of such beauty and glamour to the party. There were plenty of swivel-eyed stares!'

It was a flowery compliment and I felt mollified. Warren was pleasing company and attentive in all the right ways. 'It's late,' I said, leaning companionably against him, 'and such perfect weather, I want to make the most of tomorrow, another lazy Beach Club day. It's definitely my bedtime, I think.'

'Am I coming with?' He turned my face to him, holding my jaw. His mouth was close, his eyes searching.

Daisy was upstairs, probably not asleep, and I didn't feel ready for the subterfuge yet, of creeping past her door. 'It feels a bit soon,' I said, reaching for Warren's other hand and stroking it. 'But didn't you once speak about getting back on a Thursday? I'm driving to Providence this Thursday, to see a Ronnie Landfield painting; it's a garish abstract, just right, but perhaps you should see it first. I was going to try to do the trip in a day.'

'You couldn't possibly — with the ferry crossings as well? You'd have to stay over, it's the only way. I'll have Jackson take you in the Mercedes. Would I be able to see the Landfield in the evening? I could get away mid-afternoon on Thursday, come by chopper and drive back with you next day. We could stay in Newport,' Warren said, taking all that as read, 'at the

225

Vanderbilt. Nice hotel. Jackson can sort his own accommodation.'

'No need for Jackson, I'd enjoy the drive. I can meet you, too, if you let me know where to be.'

'That's an offer,' Warren's mouth was on mine, 'that I'd be a fool to refuse. Step by step then,' he murmured. 'Newport's very atmospheric, wonderful food.'

It was an anticipatory kiss, hungry, but lingering, too. His mouth felt good. Charles kissed me in a similarly leisurely way, an enjoyable preamble that suited our years; we knew where we were at, which was a soothing security. With Warren I felt a less comfortable sort of adrenaline flow; he was still a stranger, but we were on an exploratory journey and that was about to change.

★ ★ ★

On Monday, Daisy and I spent the morning with the project manager, Jeremy Dean. He'd come on board rather cautiously, and the more I detailed the plans, the more his arched dark eyebrows knitted anxiously under a pronounced widow's peak. He had a pair of shades stuck down the front of a tangerine shirt, rather naff-looking, but I'd done my research and he seemed to be thorough.

'Don't look so worried, we're doing all the legwork,' I assured him. 'Everything will be ordered, measurements double-checked, the architect on the end of her phone. I'll come out, too.'

226

'I think the plans are awesome,' he said. 'I just hope my guys are up to the job.'

'It's *your* job to see they are,' I said firmly. 'We must have schedules for each individual trade hired, a clear timeline, rigidly adhered to. Watch over the electrician for the floor outlets, clear cord too, please; and take particular care with the ribbon pattern on the marble floor.' He made notes in a hardcover exercise book, which was a good sign, writing steadily in a tidy hand. Daisy made a few on-the-ball contributions, but she was on a learning curve, absorbing, desperate to gain experience, fizzing with enthusiasm for the job in hand. She already had a good grasp. I felt we were on track, as long as she stuck to it. If she did that, and shook off Simon, she'd go far.

After lunch, one of Martha's lusciously light salads, chicken and minted cucumber, Daisy and I set off for East Northport, towards Long Island Sound. We were going to look at top-of-the-range pool tables. Warren's basement was about to be transformed.

Later, over a welcome cup of tea on the terrace, I talked Daisy through the week, all her city chores. It was a huge project we were embarked on. 'Have a look for silk screens,' I said, 'and I'm after one of Joseph Albers's *Homage to the Square* paintings. I haven't located one online. See what the galleries come up with. And check out the contemporary rug scene — think spot paintings, zigzags. I know people who'll make to our own design, but I'd like to see samples, the best you can find of what's out there. You're clear on it all, you know where to go?'

227

'Sure thing,' Daisy said. 'I'll get the first Jitney bus tomorrow. Shall I stay over?'

'No, Wednesday here on paperwork then you can be off again on Thursday with a new list. Have that night with Janet; you'll need the time. I'm going to Rhode Island to see a painting and staying the night there.' I smiled. 'You've got it, Daisy, you're doing fine. How are the boys, things back home? Is Simon weakening yet and coming over?'

'You know, it's funny, but he is threatening to! I've been so busy and preoccupied, and I had a sense on the phone last night that it's actually made him a bit keener. I was convinced that if I were away for any length of time he'd give up on me and look elsewhere, but now he's talking about a possible business trip to New York.'

'What did I tell you,' I said, feeling relief. Some good hard sex with Simon might shake her up a bit; take her eyes off Warren. 'And the boys, all good there?'

'Well, here's another funny thing.' Daisy turned to me with a soft, helpless look on her open face. 'Their father's turned up! He went to New Zealand after we divorced. We were both still so young and he had no job, couldn't handle being a father, especially of a bawling pair of twins. He said it was best if he stayed away, and he did. We never heard a word. He worked as a waiter in Auckland, the boys say, and has his own bistro on a marina there now. He's over on holiday and tracked us down through the solicitor.'

'How have the boys reacted?'

'They were fascinated to meet him, of course, and say he's got a ponytail, an earring and a boyfriend! He cooked them dinner in my kitchen, seems he's the chef at his outfit, gave them each twenty pounds — big deal — and said any time they felt like sampling the joys of Auckland . . . '

'So if it's only a holiday and he's returning, isn't that a happy tying-up of loose ends?'

'As long as they're not fired up to go there and want to emigrate.' Daisy's eyes were misting; she was feeling emotional. 'They're all I've got.'

'They're almost adults, they've got their lives to lead,' I said. 'Think about yours now, Daisy. You've found your niche and you have independence within your grasp, which would make your sons proud, I'm sure. I can't see them taking off for New Zealand. You're obviously close — I'd love to meet them sometime when we're home.'

Talk of being home focused my mind, for a moment, on Charles. I should give him a call, tell him I was going to Newport, somewhere he'd talked about and said I'd enjoy. It would be slightly more politic, I decided, to leave Warren out of the equation.

I was going on a jaunt to Newport with him, but where else? Could I imagine sharing his New York apartment, having summers on Long Island — as well as, or in place of, my London life? That, I told myself sternly, was jumping a whole battery of guns.

* * *

229

On Thursday I dropped Daisy at the Jitney bus stop and continued on, enjoying the car that Warren had hired for our use. It was a Thunderbird, sporty and good to drive. I took the Hampton Bays Road towards Riverhead, following Jackson's directions faithfully, and reached Orient Point and the Cross Sound Ferry in good time. I had a booking, and waited patiently in a long line of cars, glad to be on my own. I felt younger, freer, a sort of blowin'-in-the-breeze feeling — literally, once on board and on the upper deck where the wind off the Sound was tugging powerfully enough to pull me overboard.

The crossing took an hour and twenty minutes. I had a flapjack and coffee and was chatted up by a weird man in light fittings who gave me his card. Americans swapped enough cards to save a forest. I often wondered if they ever put them to practical use.

I lost my way on the Connecticut side, even with a satnav, but I had time to spare. I was meeting Warren at six and taking him straight to see the Landfield, which was a private sale. The painting had pizzazz and wasn't vastly expensive, but I feared Warren might take fright, since it was as unlike any painting in his house as Paris, France was from Paris, Texas.

Having eventually found the highway I made good progress, exiting onto a country road that weaved quietly through forested land. Sunlight slanted through silent trees and the road was almost deserted. I felt high on exhilaration like a girl in love, but I was neither a girl nor in love, and the night ahead came with a health warning.

Sex pumped up the volume, mood music was dangerous, however old I was and inured by experience; I didn't want to be left with emotional knots to unpick.

That evening, standing well back from the immense blast of wind, I watched the helicopter drop tidily into its chalk circle. Warren leaped out and as the deafening whir of propellers subsided, he had a quick word with the pilot, who handed him his bag.

'Good flight?' I asked.

'Sure thing! The East River chopper service is just down the road at 34th Street and I had Hank, my favourite pilot.' Warren turned to wave to him. 'A bit of late lunch on board and,' he said, taking my arm, 'a chilled demi-bouteille of white wine.'

He kissed my cheek, asked after my journey and took over the wheel. We drove into a residential street and drew up outside a house that looked Dutch colonial, built of white-painted clapboard and with a small, bright green, much-watered lawn. Warren squeezed my hand, hanging onto it as we climbed the front steps and rang the bell.

The seller had erratic taste in art and his lesser works showed up the quality of the Landfield. I sensed Warren adjusting to the loud, glorious splodges of colour and hoped he'd appreciate the fun and energy of the painting. He finally gave me an imperceptible nod and proceeded to bargain. I was riveted. The painting, at 3,200 dollars, was only slightly over-priced, yet Warren drove down the poor man — a dentist probably,

231

or schoolteacher — a full thousand. His wife left the room, throwing him a look of contempt.

'You're a demon businessman,' I said, as we stowed the bubble-wrapped spoils and drove away. I'd had to ask for the wrapping — the seller thought he'd done with us.

'It gets to be a habit,' Warren confessed. 'I mean, it certainly wasn't in the major league, not a pricy painting, but I'd checked it out and reckoned he'd stuck on a thou. He didn't do badly, it was a more realistic deal. Shall we go to the hotel then down to the waterfront? It'll give you the flavour for your first time in Newport. It's always lively and packed round the Wharfs, kind of preppy, good spots to eat, too. How does that sound?'

'Pretty good. A bistro or even a pub would be great, nothing too smart.'

'I've booked a small suite at the hotel, and another separate room; I thought you might like some time to yourself before dinner.'

That was thoughtful, delicately put, and allowed me to keep my options open. My respect for Warren was growing — and I liked the way he kissed.

'Give me half an hour or so,' I said, 'then come and have a drink.'

The hotel, quite recently opened, hadn't lost a sense of its past glories as a Vanderbilt family home in the transformation. My room, which had a well-designed divider to create a small sitting room, was up-to-the minute as well as comfy, clean and fresh with a sort of crisp green apples fragrance. I got going and had a scented bath — jasmine, not green apples — deciding to wear a rather joyous silk print dress, almost as vivid as the painting, with pink espadrilles that had a funky, two-tone chevron design.

'You're determined to get my eye in, aren't you?' Warren said with a grin, coming into the room. 'But it's no test, you'd make a couple of sewn-together dishcloths look like an elegant dress.' Warren didn't do funky; he was in an open-neck striped shirt and cream pants.

He kissed me and accurately guessed my scent was Chanel. 'I feel slightly guilty,' he said, popping the cork on a bottle of champagne, 'after all Willa's attempts to modernise me and the house. But she was so belittling, it made me dig in all the harder.'

'I'd kind of assumed that the décor was all her doing,' I said, curious.

'It was, mostly. She loved the English country-house look and was mad for collecting extravagant pieces of silver, but I was a bit stuck on formality, as I can see now.'

'It's easier for me, sweeping in with a new broom,' I said tritely, trying to be diplomatic. 'I'd better warn you, I'm feeling inquisitive. I want to know all sorts of things, mainly about you, as well as trying to do Newport in twenty-four hours! Do I get to see those vast summer-cottage palaces, before we leave, the images I have from Edith Wharton and *The Age of Innocence?*'

'We'll do the Cliff Walk. It's rocky in places, but runs along the foot of some of the great houses like The Breakers and Rosecliff, right by their rolling lawns.'

We hadn't made inroads into the champagne. Warren had downed a glass or two, and I suggested it would keep for later — casting the die. I showed him how to keep in the fizz with a teaspoon handle down the neck of the bottle, but he had no faith in that, and he was hardly into economising.

It was a deliciously sultry night. I was fascinated to see Newport, but my mind was on sex; thinking of my droopy body measured up against any recent younger women to cross Warren's bedroom threshold. He had adult children and his ex-wife was hardly young, but he must have moved down the age-scale since Willa. My body wasn't bad, still slim, but even if I'd had all the surgical pick-ups going it would be little more pliant or defying of gravity. I thought of lithe bodies like Daisy's, her glowing skin . . .

The waterfront was buzzy, arty, teaming with young tourists. Warren tucked my arm through his. 'Newport has none of its old closed society and eccentricity, gilded balls and bathing parties,' he said. 'It's a very different place today, even from the Kennedys' day — Jackie's cultured, pampered childhood and Jack having his 'Summer White Houses' here. Eisenhower had them here, too. It's still one of the great yachting centres of America, though, and the clam chowder at the Black Pearl Tavern where I'm taking you,' Warren said, giving me a kiss, 'wins every award going.'

The place was heaving. Our table wasn't ready, which wasn't surprising, but a couple vacated two bar seats usefully, right where we were standing. 'The Black Pearl hasn't changed in thirty years,' Warren said. It had glossy black walls, low ceilings, intriguing nautical maps. Space was in short supply, making it feel as snug and cramped as a stable. No question of its popularity — a waiting queue stretched way back outside the door.

Once established at a midget table, wine and cups of the award-winning clam chowder ordered, with oysters on the side, I began my inquisition. 'I know you're Manhattan-born and raised, that you shot the family beer company to world class with the name-change and lips-top bottle; I know Lippy Lager went viral; I know about your long marriage that . . . '

'It wasn't that long. Willa isn't the mother of my children.' I stared and he smiled at my surprise. 'You made that assumption once before, but Daisy was there, I think, and anyway you'd hardly arrived. It didn't seem a time to go into detail.'

'So was Willa your second, third?' I asked, feeling slightly nonplussed.

'Only the second! I'd rushed into the first, very young. Peggy was too, and when the kids were through college we called it a day. She remarried, lives in California, had another last-minute child. She visits, sees the kids and grandchildren, or they go there.'

'And Willa?' I paused as the chowder and oysters arrived and Warren poured the wine, a fine white burgundy. The waitress, who looked no more than twenty, was wearing a lilac bustier with black shorts and purple-laced sneakers. Warren beamed at her — and me.

'Have this while it's hot,' he advised, still grinning and eyeing me over the wine, 'and I've got the drift of this inquisition. We can skip the questions and I'll tell you all I can.' He refilled his glass and topped up mine.

'The chowder gets my vote,' I said. 'I must tell Daisy about the hint of tarragon, a little tip for her column.' I was playing for time, worrying about Willa being younger than I'd thought. 'You must have felt the more responsible for your children,' I suggested conversationally, 'with your first wife over on the West Coast.'

'Sure. Willa was okay with the kids, though — especially early on when things were going well with us. They were still quite young and sorting their futures. It was a help.' He smiled and poured himself more wine. I wasn't keeping pace.

It more easily explained Warren's extreme bitterness if Willa was a younger model; he'd have had particular sensitivities, especially if teased about his prowess and aging looks.

The hip waitress cleared our plates and said she'd be right back with the swordfish mains — Warren's recommendation — which came with chips, veg, side salads, hefty hunks of bread. 'And another bottle of the wine,' he said.

'We'll be staggering out of here with this lot! Go on then, anticipate my questions.'

'Good fries,' Warren said, munching a couple when they arrived, looking me in the eye. 'Well, you want more lowdown on Willa for a start?' I

236

nodded. 'And to know about any other woman in my life since?' I noted the use of the singular, as I was probably meant to. 'Willa was forty when we met, I was fifty-six. She had a party-planning business, basically just knowing a few good caterers and florists, but she gave that up when we married and spent money instead. I didn't care, I was in her clutches, hooked and she could play the line. She could do no wrong.

'She queened it in Southampton and the Fifth Avenue apartment; threw bashes, hired yachts, jets, went in for lavish exotic holidays. She hadn't been married before. She wanted children and when that didn't happen, she took it out on me. I think Willa blamed my age, yet she was in her forties so hers came into it too. The rot had set in, but I still gave it my all, couldn't help it.'

'But there came a point?' There usually did. He was still obsessed, that was clear. Willa hadn't extinguished every spark, although his passion seemed entirely channelled into acrimony and loathing now.

'Yes, sure, something snapped,' Warren said, refilling his glass, 'with all the personal criticism in front of mates of mine, the constant hiring of jets, the holidays taken when I was tied up . . .' His eyes were distant for a moment. He was well into the second bottle of wine and not used, obviously, to unloading emotional feelings.

'And before you ask,' he said, leaning over the table to reach for my hand, which he put to his lips, 'I'm not seeing anyone right now. I have been — someone in the city who was in a marriage that was all society and show. But that's

237

over now, done and dusted. She's stayed married. She'd said often enough — tediously and predictably, to be honest — that she was living a lie, a sham, but as a true conformist, when it came to it she couldn't give up being Mrs J. Edwin Nesbit Junior, sister-in-law to a senator. It meant more to her than upheaving her life for me.'

'More fool her.' I knew Warren better now, I decided. He was more than a dry, driven billionaire, he was a decent, family-orientated guy whose one really passionate relationship had turned sour. And I was more settled and at ease with him; it felt less like a casual summer dalliance. He'd talked freely and openly, here in Newport, and hadn't invited me out while still in a relationship. But was he entirely over Willa? How much acid was still eating away at his system? That was impossible to say.

We had coffee, brandy for Warren, but we were squashed tight into the table, sitting on hard spindle-backed chairs, and I was ready to go.

I felt self-conscious, strolling back up the steep lane to the hotel, flushed with nerves, like making a speech on a sensitive subject to a highly critical audience. I wasn't up to youthful sexiness, but the urge, the need to be kissed and wanted, was very much there. Warren was silent. Neither of us spoke as we walked up two splendid flights of stairs with a thick chestnut carpet-runner and I opened the door to the suite.

We stood looking at each other, slightly out of breath from the climb.

'It feels strange,' Warren said, moving closer and unzipping my dress, gazing at me steadily. His hands were roaming lightly in a way that felt good. 'Even when we met, and it was my most twisted-up time,' he carried on, 'I registered you. I was attracted. Who wouldn't be? You stuck fast in my mind all through that god-awful business. I thought of you — elegant, talented, famous, successful, a timeless beauty — and now,' he said, bending to my mouth, 'here you are.'

★ ★ ★

We lay in a wrapped-limb, not very contorted position. I could smell the brandy, the wine, a whiff of sweat, not unappealing, from the exertion of our uphill return.

'I'm sorry, sorry,' Warren mumbled, burrowed into my neck. 'I don't know what got into me with all that drinking. I'm not a boozer, never have been. Nerves, I guess, talking about me, which doesn't come easy — or some sort of devil's curse.'

I felt like saying that it hadn't been for want of trying, Warren had been doggedly keen, he'd quite worn me out, but in reasonably satisfying ways. 'No saying sorry,' I told him, and he groaned into my neck. 'Can we go to sleep now?' I said. 'I'm very comfy — and who knows what the morning may bring.'

In fact, it brought Warren sleepily rolling into my arms again and well able to make it after his little local difficulty of the night before. We had breakfast in bed — he looked very pleased with himself in a relieved sort of way — then I shooed him off to his other room and enjoyed the chance to dress in privacy. Step by step, he'd said, staying out late in the garden after the Benefit ball. We'd taken quite a big first step, it seemed.

★　★　★

The Cliff Walk past the great mansions of Newport, a sunny morning, the sharp tang of salty air and seaweed . . . I was sad to leave. It seemed no time before we were driving off the ferry from Connecticut and were back on Long Island again.

'I saw Daisy in the week,' Warren said, as we set course for Southampton. 'I'd given her my card that first weekend when you'd just arrived, in case she got lost in the city, and she called up in a panic on Tuesday to say she'd been going round and round in circles, trying to find an address downtown in Soho.'

'Can't think why she'd needed to be right down there,' I said stiffly.

Had she been looking for silk screens? I don't know. Anyway, I told her to take a taxi, simplest — and another one to join me for a bite of lunch at my usual haunt. I go to San Pietro. It's a bit all-male, but excellent food and they make a great Italian fuss of you.

'She's a sweet girl,' Warren carried on. I felt exasperated. If he called her a 'sweet girl' one more time . . . 'And so bright and breezy, she makes me feel quite young again. But I'd hate you to read anything into it. I just wanted to say that. Last night meant a lot, Susannah. I hope it felt as right for you as it did for me. You're fabulous. I can't tell you how much it means, having you here.'

But I'm not a girl, I thought, and didn't make him feel young again, like the one also here and on his doorstep — who wasn't such a girl, as it happened, at not far off forty, for the prospect of anything between them to be a complete joke.

'Did Daisy tell you her boyfriend's coming over?' I queried. 'In the next week or two, I think.' She hadn't, obviously; Warren looked quite jolted. But then Daisy had only heard on Wednesday that it was definite, after all.

We were in Bridgehampton, nearly there. I sighed inwardly. Trust a younger woman to take the edge off what had been a rather special night and day. Still, Warren had felt he needed to own up about Daisy. He wasn't instinctively pro-grammed to deal in cover-ups and lies. I felt comforted by that, half-able to carry on believing in his natural decency.

It was a belief that had let me down badly in the past. The past. Daisy kept bringing it back. The married men chancing their arm, the casual chauvinism, even near-depravity at times, of the sixties. The highs, lows and disillusionments, the buckets of tears wept. How much of that had shaped and toughened me, and taken away my belief in the existence of decent men? It had been blind belief at twenty, before the scales had fallen from my eyes. Did the heartache of

241

rejection harden into cynicism? For all the emotional knocks, though, I'd never given up the quest. The hope was there, and the need. I knew I'd always keep looking.

15

February 1962

I hefted my case onto the check-in stand, holding my breath. I was sure to be over the 44lb limit with all the modelling gear and three weeks of clothes. My pockets were stuffed: a jar of night cream, costume jewellery, a thick-buckled belt, anything heavy I could squeeze in. The young man at the desk studied me, my ticket, the suitcase weight, me again. He had chickenpox scars, a light coating of dandruff, a worried, earnest indoors face.

He cleared his throat. 'It's a full flight, but, um, there's a space in First Class; I'll pop you in there.'

'Oh, but that's wonderful, such a relief. I can't thank you enough, you're my friend for life!' I flashed him my most ravishing smile and began to breathe again. I was blushing, he was blushing; it seemed wise to move on quickly before any of his superiors trawling the desks reversed the kindness of his heart.

In the departure lounge I double-checked my passport, the crisp wad of dollars — fifty pounds' worth, the full allowance — the address of Gloria's friends where I was staying. Telephone numbers, Gil's studio, the Eileen Ford Agency. I tried to calm my pulse.

I hoped Joe's play would be well received. I'd

felt doubtful, eyeing the two reviewers that I recognised in the first-night audience, urbane Kenneth Tynan of the *Observer* and Bernard Levin; they were robot-faced, giving nothing away, but loved to shock, I knew, and it was easy to imagine the razor-edged, damning phrases forming in their minds.

Joe's mother had certainly had no criticisms. She'd adored the play and the party, preened in her new dress; she couldn't stop thanking me as I drove her to the station before leaving for the airport in a rush. Joe had slept in, he'd barely lifted his head from the pillow to say goodbye. Not a good send-off when I was about to see Gil. The BOAC terminal was only up the road from Victoria station and I'd hoped he'd take me there. The cabbie delivering me had been kinder, heaving in my case with a smile.

If only they'd call the flight. My nerves weren't good. Would I really get the work that Eileen Ford had promised? Gil had booked me for ads; they'd cover the fare at least. A cigarette ad and one for Chevrolet, being shot in Boston. Was Boston to be the scene of my infidelity? I should rise above Joe's affair with Alicia, Tony Lambton had advised, laying a sophisticated hand on my thigh, and have a life of my own. But that didn't mean straying down roads with No Entry signs writ large. I had principles; I'd taken vows.

Being in First Class felt like a good omen. I revelled in it all, the caviar and lobster, the pot-bellied old businessmen giving me the eye, the sumptuous reclining seat with space enough for two. The shy ticket-desk man, who'd saved me from a crippling over-weight-charges fate, deserved a place in heaven — or at least first-class travel for himself. I couldn't concentrate on my book, couldn't do justice to all the food. Time seemed to evaporate all the same, but not my nerves.

As the no smoking and seatbelt signs flashed on, a strange sensation — an intense form of panic — came over me. I felt shaky and chilled, my skin cloying damply. It was as though a thick fog was descending and blurring my vision, hemming me in, making me woozy. It must be the downward motion. I needed air, water, had to get to . . .

'Stay still now, head down, you'll be fine. It was just a little faint, that's all.'

I raised my head enough to see an air hostess's smiling face; she was strapped in beside me, turned to me and leaning over to speak.

'I blacked out for a minute,' I said. 'So sorry, so stupid. I've flown before . . . '

'Shush, don't worry, it happens. Take it slowly. We're about to land.'

The wooziness had passed. My legs worked fine, descending the stairs, and the cold air was wonderful. The stewardess stayed with me, looking advertisement smart in her navy suit and cap, and saw me safely into an immigration queue. 'Don't forget to look at the message board,' she said, as we parted, 'in case anyone's called and left word.'

I did look, in the slim hope of a note from Gil, and my pulse raced when there was an envelope on the board with my name. I told myself it was more likely that Joe had called, feeling contrite and not caring about the cost. No good expecting love notes.

It was from neither of them. *Welcome, welcome! A light supper awaits and we're dying to meet you. So glad you're here! Call if any problems. Joan and Walter Ferrone.*

I felt a pang that it wasn't Gil, but it was still cheering, considerate of the Ferrones, and a sudden wave of excitement swept over me. Three weeks in Manhattan, a new world with Gil in it and, thanks to Gloria Romanoff, even a very smart place to stay.

I took a cab from the shuttle-bus station to the Ferrones' apartment block. A uniformed door-man helped with my case and escorted me into the elevator and right to their door. Joan Ferrone, with her fluffy pinkish-blonde hair, and Walter, solid and jowly, greeted me like adoring parents. No welcome could have been warmer. They were a childless couple, Gloria had said. They showed me round their splendid Park Avenue apartment — apologetically when it came to my room. 'It's a box with a cot,' Joan said. 'So wee!' I took in the fresh freesias, lacy pillows, charming patchwork bedcover, checks and stripes, all shades of blue. There was a small elegant desk. I loved it all.

'Come sit,' she said. 'Thaw out and have something to snack on. Is it this cold back in England? You'll need galoshes when the snows come; what size do you have? People have phoned for you. Eileen Ford, who sent these lovely lilies, but we thought they'd take all the oxygen in your tiny room, and Gil Foreman who said you're working with him tomorrow. I think he just wanted to check you'd arrived.' Joan kept up a constant mothering stream.

The eclectic paintings in the apartment, even to my uneducated eye, were astounding — exquisite portraits, pastoral scenes and, if my eyes didn't deceive me, a Dali no less, and a pair of Picassos. I could see why Walter was an adviser to Jackie Kennedy on White House art. I praised the paintings in reverential tones.

'We'll be glued to the television on the four-teenth,' Joan said, as though that naturally followed, 'watching Jackie Kennedy do her tour of the White House. The whole nation will be too; it'll reach millions. Quite a moment for Walter.' For Joan, too, it seemed. 'Now you must tell me about these slippers!' she exclaimed, with another conversational switch that seemed her way. 'Gloria wanted me to say they've arrived and Sinatra loves them. She kept it kinda cryptic.'

I blushed. 'Well, it was just the impossible problem of how to thank Frank, so I thought of tatting him evening slippers with a design of his entwined initials. I did them in orange, his favou-rite colour, on a black background. It got to be a joke at the studios, me tatting away, but finished and with proper leather soles, they looked quite smart.'

'Gee, Walter, isn't that just the cutest thing! Now, Susannah, you need to eat and catch some sleep.'

★ ★ ★

247

First thing next morning, Eileen Ford called. *Vogue* wanted me, *Harper's Bazaar*, too. I had provisional bookings, the Chevrolet booking with Gil in Boston, a string of go-sees. I felt as if I was in someone else's shoes; this couldn't all be happening to me.

I washed my hair and left for Gil's studio in Arctic temperatures, snug in my Mongolian lamb coat and a chestnut baby-soft vicuna scarf, borrowed from Joan at her absolute insistence. I spoke stern words to myself — both about not losing the scarf and holding back a little with Gil, keeping my cool. The hot fast palpitations of my heart were another matter.

We did the cigarette ad. I smiled and touched foreheads with the male model, holding a Lucky Strike cigarette between two forefingers, keeping it casually clear of my face. The model's aftershave was potent, ticklishly redolent of citrus and herbs, and I threw my head back laughing, at one point, trying to avoid a sneeze. Gil said that was the picture.

'Thanks, Hank, you're done,' Gil said. 'Susannah, stay where you are, I want to take few headshots before you go.' He came to fuss round me and muttered, 'Meet for a drink, seven o'clock, 114 MacDougal Street. You have to see the Village, it's a good start.'

I didn't need to write it down. My impatience to be alone with him was almost orgasmic. It was four o'clock; he carried on taking shots, saying photographing me was a drug. I fretted about time, wanting to stay, hating to say I had to rush, but I was embarrassed about what Dee and his

248

assistants might think, and I had go-sees booked in.

I chased across Manhattan, on a high wire of nerves with the photographers and editors who leafed through my book. Everything depended on how they saw my pictures — future jobs, income, being in New York at all, seeing Gil — yet I couldn't concentrate, hardly heard a word they said.

I took a yellow cab downtown. The lights were synchronised, we had a smooth ride; the driver nattered about my accent, while my heart sped up like a clock building up to strike. In MacDougal Street the cab drew up outside a tired brick building with dropped sills and an uneven front step. The bar was called the Kettle of Fish and Gil was there.

He slid off his barstool as I came in, crushing me in his big arms, kissing me hard on the mouth and swallowing me up. I was glad of my New York anonymity, although the raddled barman, couple of Afro drinkers, idling students and a bearded guy with a guitar couldn't have given a sod. Gil smelled of the beer he was drinking and cigarettes while the smoke swilling round the bar was distinctly sweetish. The regulars had moved on from cigarettes.

I asked for coffee, Gil collected his beer and we went to sit in a dark corner at the back. 'Great music here,' he said. 'The big names come. They hang out with the beatniks at the Folklore Centre next door, come to drink and play here between sets, but it all happens at the Gaslight, downstairs on the other side. It's a steamy dive and the only windows are into airshafts to apartments upstairs, so there's no clapping allowed or the residents complain. You just click fingers. There's a guy called Bob Dylan who comes. He's ace. They lock this place down to the public when he's composing and playing. He'll make it big time.'

'You sound very sure,' I said.

'I heard him do 'Cocaine Blues' when he was still Robert Zimmerman and it blew my mind. He's a poet too, big on Dylan Thomas.' I rested my hand on Gil's arm and he grabbed hold of my wrist, stuffing all four of my fingers into his mouth. I couldn't handle it and stared, lips parted, feeling my weakening resolve.

'That's the picture, what we're going back for.' He continued sucking on my fingers, watching me; I felt the blood rising steeply into my face. 'You'll make it big time here too,' he said, releasing me. 'New York'll love you.' He glanced at his watch. 'Shall we go back to the studio? You okay with that?'

I felt panicked; it was crunch time. 'I'm not sure. It's eight already and the people I'm staying with, well, they may have food ready. I just told them I had a long day.'

'Call them. Say you're running late, doing test shots. It's only half a lie.'

★ ★ ★

His studio was in darkness. Dee, the girl on the desk, and his two assistants, Jack and Bob, had gone home. It was Friday night; Gil would be

250

going home later as well, to his family, his two small kids, while I'd be left to lick the wounds if I lost my fragment of resolve. I hid a sigh.

Gil was turning on lights. 'Okay to use the phone?' I asked. 'It's my first night staying with these people, the Ferrones; they're friends of friends and I'd hate them to worry.'

'Don't sound so tense.' Gil came close and blew lightly into my ear, 'I'll get you relaxed yet. Is that Walter Ferrone — Jackie Kennedy and art?'

'Yes. And it's an awesome apartment, you should see the paintings.'

'They're in the columns a lot with those — and with Jackie. How do you know them?'

'Tell you in a minute,' I said, picking up the phone. I needed to get it over with. Would they know from my voice I had something to hide? This was the bad bit, spinning lines.

Joan made it easy, too easy. 'Gee, honey, that's so considerate to call. Walter and I were just popping out, catching friends for dinner. I'd left you a note. The maid's done you a tray, soup to heat up and a bit of cold chicken. Talk in the morning? But I sure hope you're not working late Monday night. We're giving a small party — with a special guest!'

Gil was close beside me and able to hear. 'See?' he said. 'Easy. But there's no soup here, we're on a wine diet. Tell me about the Ferrones while I open a bottle. We'll take it up to my eyrie; there's only a very low bed to sit on, but we can just talk if you want.'

I shut my mind to the eyrie and told him

251

about the Romanoff connection, the serendipity of Gloria being a friend of Joan Ferrone; it brought back coming to New York in Frank's plane, my scary meeting with Eileen Ford, and Rusty, the mother-hen booker. I remembered her saying, 'She should go see Gil Foreman, he'll love her to death.'

'Hold the bottle a sec,' Gil said, having led me across the studio floor, 'while I get the hatch. The glasses are up there.' He unhitched a long pole from a wall-bracket and used the hook on the end to open a trapdoor above our heads. A sturdy stepladder was attached inside, which concertinaed down. Gil reclaimed the bottle and went on up, taking my hand as I climbed out at the top. 'I sleep here sometimes,' he said. 'Working late, early starts . . . you know.'

The loft had space and height; I could stand. A couple of low shaded lights flanked a Japanese-style bed that had a tartan rug throw. A shelf running along behind the bed and round the wall held books, a water carafe, a few glasses, a clock, a record player.

'Are you going to tell me about all the girls who've trodden those stairs?' I said hollowly, looking round, feeling ashamed to be there, one of many.

Gil bent down to the shelf to deposit the bottle and, straightening up, took my hands. I felt the current between us, the strength of its pull, but where was the coastguard's warning? I mustn't give in. I had my pride, my principles. What principles? It was as good as being unfaithful to Joe, feeling this searing need. Joe had let me

252

down, but this had nothing to do with tit for tat. It was a new sensation entirely, new to me at least, raw indescribable longing. But my eyes were more wide open, seeing Gil's loft, the reality of where I fitted in, and I stood rooted, painfully torn.

He knew my particular agonies exactly and didn't try any persuasion. Letting go of my hands he sat down on the low bed and leaned forward to pour the wine. He put on an LP.

'This is Bill Evans, *Sunday at the Village Vanguard*.' It was cool melodic jazz. Gil turned down the volume and patted the space beside him. 'Come down to my level,' he said, which felt a little too apposite for comfort. 'I won't bite!' I fought an impulse to say it was his bite that I craved and sat slowly down on the edge of the bed.

He handed me a glass of hearty-looking red wine and tucked my hair back behind my ear, making no comment when I gave an involuntary shiver. 'I know you hate to think of the girls I'll have brought here,' he said, 'and sure, it's much as it seems, this pad. But you're in my life now, Susannah. I can't get enough of you, I have to keep taking pictures, photographing your face with its haunting delicacy and innocence.' He traced over it, and over my lips. 'I live with it. You'll be my undoing, I know.'

'But should you be mine? I'm married, Gil, I shouldn't be here. Go easy on me.' It was pathetic. I had a mind, a conscience, and I was asking him, a New York photographer, up here in his horny den, to go easy?

'We mean different things by undoing. I'm

253

talking about feelings and getting entangled, and you're meaning infidelity and sex.' He was right about that. 'How were things at home when you left? Husband okay about you coming, being here in New York?'

'Who knows?' I muttered. 'Joe shuts me out; his other relationship holds more thrills.'

'But you still have a sex life?'

'On and off, and very basic, I think — but then I'm not very up in what is and isn't. I've failed to have a baby, though, which might have brought us closer.'

'Still trying?'

'Oh yes, at least when Joe remembers he has a wife. Forget that, it was a needless bitch.'

'So you're here now, sitting on my bed and no protection? You must really want to resist!'

'Well, it hasn't happened in almost two years. I've never had proper periods. I suppose, well, I just didn't think . . . ' I felt so naïve, completely out of my depth, almost in tears.

'Shall I tell you what I think?' Gil kissed my lips. I nodded, straining to be held, the touch of his lips was cruel. 'You want me to make love to you, we both know that, and there's nothing I long to do more, but how would you feel then? Unclean? Guilty? Frightened of where it might lead — or not?' I kept nodding like a car toy. 'I'm very qualified to take you through 'what is and isn't' — there's not much that isn't — and you'd soon get the drift and be a quick learner, I'm sure. But it would change you, Susannah, change your life. I think that's a good idea, but then I would.'

'How changed?' I was fighting an uncontrollable urge to caress his face.

'At worst it could turn you right off your husband, you're close to that now. At best, being more sexually sophisticated should shake him up a bit, make him jealous and he'd certainly see you with new eyes. You'd find it easier to relax too, which would help with that baby.'

I sipped the last of my wine. 'Joe doesn't notice me enough to be jealous.'

The glass was being taken from my hands; my chin lifted up. I looked into Gil's questioning eyes, grateful for his honesty, his going easy. All the heavy pressure was my own. 'Kiss me,' I said.

The impact, the shock of it, the force of his big wide mouth engulfing mine was overwhelming. I closed out the world and let it happen, quivering through and through as his hands stroked my throat, collarbones; unbuttoned my blouse, lifted my breasts clear of my bra. He brushed lightly over the nipples — just enough to drive me demented — and I groaned. The blouse slid from my shoulders and he reached for the clasp of my bra.

'I'm lying you back and you're letting go, leaving it all to me. I won't get you pregnant. Now I know where you're at, we'll find ways.' My nipples were painfully hard, aching to be drawn out further. And when they were, wetly and unrelentingly, I came — just like that; I couldn't help it. Gil lifted up and looked at me with warm, amused, lustful eyes. 'We've got quite an evening ahead,' he said. 'I'll have my work cut out keeping pace. Good thing I've got no

255

neighbours and we have the place to ourselves.'

He came in my mouth, we'd progressed that far. I felt fine with it, not revolted; if I'd had a thought in my head it was that if I was going to be unfaithful there was no point in being half-hearted about it and coy. Gil teased me over my speed of advancement.

'But you were irresistible,' I said, not entirely facetiously, 'and it *was* one-to-one tuition — I could hardly ask for more. Is that clock right? I've got to fly.'

'I'll see you into a cab. Shall I come visit you in Boston?'

'Don't ask questions when you know the answer — three soft taps on my door?'

'You left a scarf here earlier, that you said you mustn't lose . . .'

★ ★ ★

I had breakfast with Joan, relieved to be able to return her scarf. 'What a long day you had,' she said, 'and after that exhausting flight too. You must have a nice quiet weekend, you look just a little tired.'

'It was a long day; I was quite late back. It's all hugely exciting, though. I can't thank you enough for having me. It's wonderful to be here.'

She looked pleased. 'Now,' she said briskly, 'Monday: Jackie Kennedy's coming into town and we're giving a little soirée in her honour — very small, just a few of us who helped with her White House tour. She wants a chance to say thank you.'

256

'Would you like me to make myself scarce?'

'Heavens, no! Everyone's dying to meet our beautiful young house guest! Walter's eyes were popping out of his head when you walked in the door.'

'Popping' seemed to be Joan's favourite word. She was popping out, popping to the florist . . . A stream of people popped in too, all weekend. The apartment was like a busy hotel foyer with all the through-traffic as Joan prepared to receive the First Lady.

I slept for hours, keeping out of the way. Eileen Ford had asked me to Sunday lunch at her upper-eighties brownstone house and it was all action there, too. Eileen seemed to be in three rooms at once, chasing children, cooking, taking calls, yelling at her husband, Jerry. She told me I was much in demand and she wanted me back in the spring.

★   ★   ★

On Monday I worked with Melvin Sokolsky for *Harper's Bazaar*. His stylist who was called Ali MacGraw, was the most beautiful girl I'd ever seen. She had long black hair, silky smooth, and perfect features — an Elizabeth Taylor type of flawless beauty. Walter's eyes would have been popping out of his head six times over if she'd walked in the door.

'Surely we should change places,' I murmured, feeling like the before-picture beside her. The *Harper's* team were organising the clothes and she had little to do.

She was warm and friendly. 'Oh no, I enjoy working for Mel. I'd like to act one day, maybe.'

I just had time at the end of the day, before the shops closed, for a quick dash to buy a new bra and suspender belt. Joan had approved my best dress, a short black silk shift, for the soirée. I wasn't shopping for Jackie. I was far more obsessed about Boston than meeting the wife of the President of the United States. 'Bergdorf Goodman,' I remembered Gloria saying, 'for something special,' and the name had stuck.

The store felt like a furnace after the below-freezing temperatures outside. The lingerie department was on an upper floor and I was directed to the elevator. It was full; I just squeezed in. It went up slowly and I felt as shaky and weird as I had coming into land at Idlewild. The elevator seemed to sway, advance and recede. I was trapped, pressed against a bosomy lady, I felt a cold sheen coat my skin, my legs going weightless . . .

It was a moment before I registered. The elevator door was propped open and powdered faces peered. A large lady with ruby-red lipstick spoke. 'She's coming round!' Ruby Lips leaned closer. 'Now don't you worry, dear. I expect you felt claustrophobic; it was quite a squash. Put your head down again, don't try to stand. You'll be right as rain.'

'So sorry, so sorry,' I said, for the second time in four days. I felt such a twit, sitting on the floor of the elevator, head bent, being clucked over by matronly shoppers in furs.

'Gee, you're from England! Did you just

arrive? Did you miss lunch, dear?'

'She's English,' someone called back to the gathering crowd. 'Fainted.'

I smiled at the faces and said I was fine now, how kind they were, how the store must need to close. I had to get back; Jackie . . . I made to stand, but that caused consternation. A cup of water was procured. My colour was back, they said, finally, at last.

Joan seemed mightily relieved to see me. She was right by the door, beautifully coiffed, wearing a shimmering peacock-blue gown, very soignée, and the entrance hall looked luxuriant with plinth-high urns of flowers that were pure scented extravaganzas. Joan wafted with her own perfume, too. 'Hurry and change, honey,' she said. 'The first guests are here already and Mrs Kennedy is on her way. We've just had a call.'

I blamed *Harper's Bazaar* fulsomely for my lateness and beat it to my room.

* * *

Jackie circulated, shaking hands, smiling and inclining her groomed head regally as she accepted adulation and listened to polite cultural chat. She was wearing a rich rose-coloured silk dress and jacket, which made me feel, in my sleeveless black shift, like a drab little washed-out minnow. Walter introduced me, transforming my surname into Forbes-Bryant, and the First Lady exchanged minimal pleasantries — coolly, I felt, with impatience in her expression.

'Your husband's not here?' she queried.

'You're making this trip alone?'

'He's just opened in a West End play, *Cakes and Kindness*, so he's tied up. This is a good time for me to be here, though, so it sort of fitted.'

'Bryant, is that as in Joe Bryant?' She looked mildly more interested. 'I read a piece in the *New York Times* that held him in high regard. 'A mercurial talent, magnetic on stage'.'

'He's had some lovely reviews. This new play hasn't, unfortunately — but Joe was singled out for praise.' She stared, absorbing that, then continued to talk about the theatre.

'You know, I'm sure the Old Vic is here and opening with *Macbeth* tomorrow,' she said. I kept smiling and neglected to say that it was news to me. 'They were just in Washington and I attended a performance of their Shaw's *Saint Joan*, which I thought was superb.'

An elderly couple nearby, who both looked like bloodhounds, shuffled closer. 'You wouldn't believe the advance bookings,' Mrs Bloodhound said. 'Record sales, and with tickets at over four dollars!' She turned to me. 'Your London stage is wonderful.'

Jackie clearly felt she'd graced us with quite enough of her presence by then and taking Walter's arm, talking of people to thank, she swept off without a parting word.

I'd heard about Joe's reviews from my parents. I'd phoned them, battling with Joan to pay for the call, after failing to reach Joe all weekend. He must have been out of London on Sunday — lunch with Alicia in Gloucestershire? He

260

could have phoned.

I was still with the lugubrious bloodhound couple, still feeling unsettled by Jackie's coolness, but perhaps it was just her way.

A man in a pink bowtie came over to talk and said I had an ethereal beauty. Just the pallor of passing out in an over-heated department store, I thought ruefully. Others came to chat and involve me. I smiled valiantly through all the consciously arty discussions; praise of an exhibition of Gorky drawings, dissection of Saul Bellow's *Seize the Day*.

With Jackie's departure, a few of the guests stayed on for supper and the atmosphere was like kicking off high heels after a long modelling stint. Walter and Joan nattered and hosted, looking tired but proud and distinctly relieved, their job done, responsibility over; they could await all the thanks and flowers.

I debated slipping away from the table and off to bed, but no chance. Their friends were civilised, art-world people, yet still asked me about London hotels, the Queen, Princess Margaret's antics in Antigua; Joe's plays. I was feted, even called the belle of the ball, which was ridiculous. I just happened to be thirty years younger than any of them and with the curiosity value of being an English guest.

'I think Jackie suspected my art-world credentials,' I confided bravely to Walter in a whisper, still smarting from her aloofness. I felt much more relaxed and Walter was certainly mellow.

He threw back his head and laughed, jowls

wobbling. 'She looked daggers at you, didn't she! Don't worry, it was just your looks. She lives with Jack's roving eye and resents anyone half as pretty as you. And we see Jack on occasion. I expect she thinks you're within striking distance, so to speak.' Walter went on chuckling, and since he'd planted an image of the President rearing up like a randy snake, I started giggling, too.

★ ★ ★

I was able to get back to the apartment during the lunch-break next day, to pick up my bag for the flight to Boston, and I tried Joe again then, hoping to catch him before he left for the theatre.

'I wondered if you'd ever ring,' he said grumpily.

He sounded hangdog and sorry for himself, neglected. He'd have taken the play's knocks badly. Joe had loved the script, his starring role; the play had backers, he'd have lulled himself into imagining a long run and continuing glory.

'Where were you all weekend? I tried you endlessly.'

'Out to lunch, out of London — the Cotswolds.'

'With Alicia and Toby then, I guess. Was it fun, a big lunch party?' Joe was silent so I ploughed on. 'Are they coming to see the play?' I hadn't seen Alicia at the first night, which had surprised me. 'Mum said your personal reviews were terrific, darling.'

'She's lying. Fucking play, fucking awful

reviews. They're talking about three weeks. Alicia's been,' Joe said, out to hurt me in his present mood. 'Toby was busy.'

He didn't know he was making it so much easier, undermining my guilt. My capitulation weighed heavily. 'Don't be depressed,' I said, feeling wretched myself. 'Must go, with the cost of this call, but guess who I've just met, who the Ferrones had to drinks?'

'I can imagine. I know what Walter Ferrone does. I suppose you'll be ogling Jack next, hopping on a plane to Washington. Frankie stinks, by the way. What do I do with his turds?'

'The tray slides out. Tip it all onto newspaper and parcel it up. I give the tray a scrub as well.'

I told Joe about work and that I'd paid off the fare already, and said, trying to cheer him up, that Jackie had read a complimentary article about him and had been impressed.

I could almost hear the coin land as his mood flipped. 'Good about your work — you should do another trip. I might come too, with this bitch play folding so soon.'

Joe was so transparent, instantly setting his sights on the chance of meeting Jackie, but who cared?

It was another trip to New York. Another chance to see Gil . . .

★ ★ ★

Much as I worried about Joe and what I'd done, how bad it was, I lived for those chances. I loved Gil, adored him; I wasn't in love, my head told

263

me that, while my body pulled in the other direction and my thoughts were deliciously devoted to ever kinkier sex all day.

In Boston, photographed on a curve of entrance steps to a grandiose hotel, I wore the slinkiest long evening gown I'd ever seen, skin-tight and shiny silver, with a white fox-fur stole. The racy pillar-box red Chevrolet Impala coupe was my accessory, like a clipped, pampered poodle. The ad gained an extra dimension, though, with my new sexuality. I could never have done that dress full justice, wiggled myself into a Monroe pose, without the further progress of Gil's visit to my hotel room. I'd been fastened to the bed, played with myself under guidance, under Gil's watchful eyes; and with our intense sexual connection, doing that ad had felt just like carrying on from the night before. I was still in the beginner's class, he'd said, the nursery slopes. The serious skiing, grown-up stuff, the slalom runs, had yet to come. My imagination boggled.

We all flew back to New York together. Gil had a car at the airport. His assistant, Jack, loaded in the camera kit and I drove with them into town. I was being dropped off first. I'd see Gil soon, as he'd booked me for further jobs — but would I see him after hours as well? A cheery wave goodbye seemed a wretched parting. My mood was sinking, my heart in my boots.

Gil was at the wheel. It was hard being squashed in the back with Jack and the adman, whose leg was hard-pressed against mine; I needed it to be Gil's. I ached for his touch.

264

He held my eyes in the driving mirror, which was a connection at least. 'Take a look at the hoarding over the bridge,' he threw back. 'A little surprise . . . '

It was more than that, a seismic jolt to the system. My face — it was the Jim Beam ad we'd done in London — my eyes staring out, apparently at a male silhouette, but making direct contact with anyone seeing the ad. Even the beautifully lit clearly-labelled bottle had a lesser role.

* * *

I worked with some famous names during the next days and weeks, photographers held in universal awe. Bert Stern, who never said much, but his eyes would fix on me almost like Gil's. Richard Avedon, the golden boy of the moment — with flowing black hair — who was wild, talkative, all sinewy energy and zaniness. And Irving Penn who was a genius, no other word; I arrived one day to find him photographing running water. 'I want to capture it in perfect stillness,' he said. The picture when I saw it, was unique, a vertical flow of clear water, arrested, sharp, gleaming, deeply etched and black-rimmed, hauntingly powerful against a stark white ground.

A few days before going home, I went to a party. One of the Ford models I'd met and liked, a tall gazelle of a girl called Janet, wanted me to come along, saying she needed a chaperone. 'Don't be surprised if Jack Kennedy turns up,' she grinned. 'Liz, our host, tipped me the wink. He was just in Florida and has been known to make detours.'

'Is Liz the attraction?'

'Among others. He can pack in more than one in a night, you know.'

Janet came round for supper beforehand and received the Ferrones' parental treatment, too. We promised earnestly not to stay out late. 'Eileen hates her models partying,' Janet reassured them. 'We'd all be locked up in a boarding house if she had her way.'

Janet's friend, Liz, had an apartment in an old-fashioned block with a tiny elevator that opened straight into her lobby. Her rectangular living room was a squash, yet people were talking and drinking in a quite civilised way. I'd half-expected dancers on tables and leering lechers like the executives at the Madison Avenue ad agency I'd just been to see.

I was chatted up all the same, but thanks to Gil's tutelage, I was more savvy and able to hold my own and, having met Jackie, was quite cool about it when Jack walked in the door.

Liz, the host, introduced me as hot new English blood just arrived, which I minded. Jack grinned and flattered me. He had a staccato, very direct way of talking; no wandering-over-the-shoulder eyes, either — they stayed concentrated. He caught me completely by surprise when he said out of the blue, 'You know the Ormsby-Gores, don't you?'

Why on earth should he think that? I barely even knew David Ormsby-Gore was our

Ambassador to America. Then I remembered. Sylvia, his wife, had been to see one of Joe's plays and come backstage. Joe must have followed up, kept in touch; he did things like that.

'My husband knows them,' I said, taking a punt, 'through the theatre, I think. He's an actor — Joe Bryant.'

I was flirted with a little, almost as a reflex action, I suspected, and as the President moved on, was left wondering how he could possibly have made that connection; I'd even been introduced as Susannah Forbes, not Bryant. It must have been through the Ferrones in some way.

Jack wasn't about for long at the party, at least not in the main room. Liz was nowhere to be seen.

★ ★ ★

I saw Gil, when we worked together and after hours whenever he or I could manage. But there had to be a last time. It was the Monday night before my Wednesday flight home.

I couldn't always read his feelings, and his lifestyle made me over-cautious, but on that last time of togetherness there was no denying that Gil really cared. It was a branch, something to cling to; it stemmed the fall of the parting.

'It's unbearable, this. I wish we had a whole night,' I said, hardly able to swallow.

'We will one day, but it's not going to be soon.' He caressed my hair and let his hand slip to a

267

breast; my tits were painful, taut and swollen, they'd had a lot of attention in the past three weeks. 'I need to say something that I don't think you're quite prepared for,' Gil said, gazing at me with an unreadable look in his eyes. I felt fearful of what was to come. He gathered me into his arms. 'You don't seem to know it, but you're pregnant, Susannah, my beloved. It's clear enough, I know the signs.'

One of the women in the Bergdorf elevator had muttered the possibility; she'd sown a tiny seed, but it hadn't seemed possible. I'd kept the faints to myself — they were perfectly easily explained, as far as I was concerned, with the claustrophobic airlessness — and the eating so little, and I wasn't about to mention them now. I felt stupid enough as it was.

'How can you possibly know?' I demanded, staring up at him while held tight in his arms, this not-the-father lover whom I adored. 'I mean, it can't really be — can it?' I felt my lower lip wobble as emotional enormities and hope-filled satellites spun round in my confused mind.

'It shows, Susannah. You have a glow, blue veins, tautness, size — you've grown in three weeks.' He reached to encase my breasts in his hands.

I knew he was right at heart, as I steadily returned his gaze, frightened, glad of the tenderness I saw. A baby, a son or daughter, a lifelong joy — but what about its happy home?

'I'll miss you bad while you have the baby,' Gil said. 'You'll get by with your Joe, but come out again. We'll do head shots, maternity — and come in the fall for sure. I'll see you here or fly over there. I'll take pictures of mother and baby: they're the most beautiful of all.'

★   ★   ★

I was in tears saying goodbye to the Ferrones, heartfelt ones, which made them happy, I think. I'd shed plenty of tears in private, too. Joan and Walter hugged me like their own daughter, Joan was wet-eyed, too; there was always a bed for me, they said, and they could make room for Joe.

I was dry-eyed on the plane. When I'd called with the time of return Joe had sounded in much better humour, dying to quiz me about Jackie Kennedy, for sure. It was harder to tell, though, how he'd take my news. I knew in my gut I was pregnant, knew Gil was right.

John Glenn had just landed back from space; he'd circled the globe three times at a speed of 17,000 miles per hour. And I was landing back in wintry Britain, an unfaithful wife and mother-to-be.

16

August 1962

My baby was born two weeks early, on 25 August. I'd driven myself to hospital when I couldn't find a cab, stopping once or twice for another tourniquet band of pain, but made it there and parked in the hospital car park. It hadn't been a false alarm, which was my great worry, and the contractions had soon come more regularly. It was a difficult birth, though, about twenty hours in all and had to be a forceps job in the end.

When I'd recovered enough to sit up in bed, the nurse who'd been with me through the worst of it, came to talk to me. She had my baby daughter in her arms. 'Would you like to hold her now?' she said.

I nodded mutely and took the precious little bundle from her very cautiously, studying the tiny screwed-up face, topped with a surprising amount of dark hair. I wasn't given long, soon had to relinquish her, and the nurse laid her gently in the crib beside my bed. Straightening up, she showed me a row of little nicks on the palm of her hand. 'From your nails,' she said with a kindly smile on her face. 'You were holding on very hard.'

'That's awful, I'm dreadfully sorry. You shouldn't have let me!'

'It's nothing; you were having quite a bad time. The oxygen wasn't having much effect, I'm afraid. Do you expect your husband soon?'

I looked at my daughter in the crib beside my bed. 'I want to call her Bella,' I said, 'Isabella. She's beautiful to me — but you don't think Bella's overdoing it?'

'It's a lovely name. Right now you need bed-rest, and plenty of it. You're very drained.' She was about ten years older than me and seemed immensely mature, a mother figure, competent, with thick eyebrows and a steady responsible gaze.

I was grateful she hadn't repeated her question about Joe. I hadn't seen him for three weeks, not since the morning at breakfast when he'd said, yawning, that he was sick of doing voiceovers and that he was shoving off for a bit, having a breather. He'd chosen a moment to tell me when I was hurrying out to do my last modelling job, a make-up ad for Cyclax. I'd worried about what he said, felt edgy and distressed all day while trying to look the opposite, but it was nothing to the shock of arriving home to find Joe — and his suitcase — gone.

I'd called my mother in a sobbing panic and she'd tried her best to soothe me. 'Some men take fright at the thought of all the responsibility. I'm sure he'll be back soon.'

But he hadn't returned in a week. And I'd had the further shock of Marilyn Monroe dying. I grieved for her, pictured her despairing, desolate, with no one there to give her love and support; the cruelties of life bore down on me. I remembered her kindness to me at Frank's supper party, a later time when I'd seen her just before the El Dago flight and she'd whispered to me about a certain very important person, whom she really thought cared. To know she was gone had seemed beyond imagining. Joe had vanished, I'd been in the last, wearying stage of pregnancy. I'd felt morbid and very much alone.

Two more weeks and no Joe. I'd phoned my mother constantly, in an inconsolable state. 'I'll come for the birth,' she promised. 'I'll be there to help. We'll manage.'

Suppose the baby came really early? I thought, but after putting Mum through so much, I kept that fear to myself. 'You haven't told Dad?' I asked, dreading him knowing.

'No, not yet, he's such a fan of Joe's. Let's not worry for a while, shall we? Joe didn't leave you a note, any contact address?'

'Nothing. I can't even see if his passport's there as the drawer's locked. Oh, Mum!' It had been stupid, pathetic, the constant tears; the sense of my world about to implode.

I lay back on the hard hospital pillows. Joe had some filming in September, which was reassurance of a sort. I felt it likely he'd be back for that. It was only a bit part, playing a young schoolteacher in a B-movie, but he'd been excited about it, dying to get into films. Little comfort all the same, while I was lying there, aching and sore, shuddering to remember the indignities of the enema and pubic shaving, hating the look of my flabby stomach and feeling a miserable wreck.

The ward was all bustling activity. I watched the new fathers arriving and peering into cribs, whole families visiting. Mum was still on her way from Dorset.

I gazed at my baby daughter. She was on her side, snugly wrapped, eyes tight shut; she was a part of me, her own person too, but for now she was utterly dependent. Suppose she was ill, not feeding? I didn't even know how to hold her properly. Every protective fibre in me was straining; I was determined to do right by her. A lifetime of love was beginning its course, flowing strongly and devoted to keeping her afloat.

★　★　★

I settled into a routine. I wasn't being allowed home for a week, but rather dreaded going anyway. The maternity ward smelled of Dettol, cabbage and starched sheets, with a pervading whiff of babies and sweaty talcum powder, but a hospital was a comfortingly predictable place and hermetically sealed. The outside world felt cold and draughty in comparison, as teetering and uncertain as a tent in a storm.

I made friends on the ward, despite my notoriety: recognised as a model, no husband in sight and endless lavish flowers arriving. Sally from the agency had turned up with a big bunch of pink roses. She'd known the baby was coming, having called just as I was dashing to hospital — right after I'd phoned my cleaner, Palmira, in a panic about who'd feed Frankie, the poor squawker, with Joe still not around.

Palmira had promised to care for Frankie. She had come to see the baby, too, bringing a sweet bunch of pinks.

I worked out the chain of the flowers. Sally said she'd spoken to Eileen Ford, who must have told Janet, my American model friend — who, I expect, had told the Ferrones. I knew she'd kept in touch with them after the evening of the Jack Kennedy party. The Ferrones must have told the Romanoffs, who'd told Frank ... so many flowers. And Eileen must have told Gil, since he freely called me his favourite model. He'd signed the card *Gil — big kiss, love you both to death.* Joe, with his theatrical friends, certainly wouldn't have read much into that.

Mum had been completely enraptured by her first grandchild. I was quite pleased to have beaten my brother James to it; his wife was also expecting. The Army was out of Kuwait, although James felt Iraq's designs on its neighbour weren't over, but he'd just been sent off to Kenya. Mum said she'd written with my news. She was back in Dorset temporarily, returning to take me home at the end of the week.

Dad promised to come as soon as he could. He knew about Joe now. He'd had to be told. I'd played it down, but couldn't lie and Dad was in a blue funk of disbelief. I felt better, selfishly, for his knowing my problems, thinking it might help if he ever learned about Gil.

It was impossible to sleep at night; the grey, ill-meeting cubicle curtains did little to screen the nocturnal disturbances and sounds, small

274

wails, shuffles, even tears, and I had plenty on my mind. I tried to ration my thoughts about Gil and how very much I missed him, but with little success. He'd changed me, I was under his influence; it kept me going. And during the long hospital nights I thought back endlessly over the past months.

*   *   *

I'd felt more confident, arriving back home that wintry February early-morning after we'd parted. I'd been tired and pregnant, but walking in the door of the flat, Frankie had fluttered his wings like mad and screeched, 'Bye bye-eee,' fit to burst. Even Joe, albeit a bit piqued by Frankie's devotion, had seemed quite pleased to see me.

He'd been flummoxed by my news, genuinely, not knowing what to think, I felt sure. Joe could always extract the maximum drama out of any situation, though, however unexpected or testing, and my pregnancy, his prospective fatherhood, was no exception.

In front of friends, touting for sympathy, he'd put on a sort of back-of-hand-to-the-brow, pity-me performance. 'God, has it come to this, shitty nappies and prams in the hall? I'll be commuting and playing bowls next.' And even at home without an audience he'd acted up. 'It'll have blue eyes, this sprog, you'll see,' he'd said, flashing his own. 'All men of power have blue eyes.' Had Kennedy's been blue? I couldn't remember.

'What about women of power?' I'd protested,

not quick enough to shoot that down. 'Is a daughter allowed brown eyes?' Joe had sniffed and poured himself another vodka.

His play had closed within a month. He had a part in a summer production, quite exciting, a new Festival Theatre opening in Chichester, but April and May looked like being fallow and jobless.

'I think I'll go to America,' he'd announced one morning. 'You probably can't travel, I guess?' Joe, as ever, was transparently focused on a new scalp. He was fascinated by Jackie Kennedy, determined to meet her — all the more so, since I had already done so — and to do it solo, without me around to dilute the fix.

I'd met his eyes coolly. 'I've never felt better, and actually I was planning to go again myself. Eileen wants me back — there's still stuff I can do.'

Joe needn't think he could knock me around verbally any more and tread all over me. I'd felt more immune, better able to hold my own since Gil. He'd shifted the goalposts and made me more confident, yet harder and more cynical, too. Deep down I knew that my infidelity was destructive and could only do long-term harm.

★ ★ ★

I sighed and turned over in the hard hospital bed. It had seemed a seminal moment, that newfound ability to be my own woman, stand up to Joe and feel less bruised. But now I felt set right back again, weedy, tearful and insecure.

And with the nights so disturbed, my thoughts were constantly backward-looking, always on Gil, especially the last time I'd seen him — when Joe had been in the city as well.

* * *

Joe and I had flown to New York in late April. He'd done his homework: he'd made contact with Sylvia Ormsby-Gore, learned when she'd be in Manhattan and timed our arrival to fit. She and her Ambassador husband, David, would be there in the last week of the month, she'd said, when Harold Macmillan was coming to New York for the start of a ten-day Prime Ministerial tour.

I'd met the Ormsby-Gores over supper with the Ferrones, the evening before Macmillan's arrival. I'd really liked them, found David the essence of charming diplomacy and Sylvia a dreamy, offbeat original. When Joe had mentioned artfully that we planned to be back in the States in October, Sylvia had spontaneously suggested a trip to Washington.

'Come and stay!' she exclaimed. 'We'd love to have you both at the Residence.' Joe had practically kissed her across the table. He'd already made himself the toast of the Ferrones' gilded fine-art circle and couldn't wait to be sashaying off to Washington and lapping up the cream of the political elite.

While I'd rushed from studio to studio, Joe had networked and shamelessly sucked up to Joan Ferrone. I couldn't have been further from his mind. I'd felt desperately sad about it; I was having his baby and he was setting the seal on my infidelity. I longed for any sign of affection, I wanted to love him again and feel hope for our marriage.

The first booking of the April trip had been with Gil, for an Avon cosmetics ad. 'He's your greatest fan,' Eileen said. 'Better get on over there and look lively.'

Not easy, an emotional reunion under the gaze of an adman, an Avon representative, Dee, the girl on the desk, Gil's assistants, Jack and Bob . . . Gil had come straight up to me as I walked in, picked up my chin and kissed me on the lips. 'Welcome back, deserter.' He ran a hand over my stomach, slowly, in a circular movement. 'I don't believe there's a bun in there, nothing to show for it at all. It's one great big con.'

'So you're saying I'm just getting fat?' I'd been battling to stay in control. I was there to do a professional job. Pregnancy and illicit passion weren't a combination to make me proud. I had no pride where Gil was concerned, only unbounded need.

We'd found ways to meet without an entourage. He booked me for a shoot on location in Massachusetts, which meant an overnight stay. It had been a strange, surreal experience, a sinful night in a Springfield hotel at five months pregnant; it should have felt sordid, but hadn't — even with Joe just up the road in New York.

'Now here's a question,' Gil said, leaning back against the bed-head in my hotel room; he had me tucked under his wing, his protective encompassing arm, like a helpless needy chick. 'Would you be here if Joe hadn't led the way — if you hadn't seen him in that pool house on your Capri holiday and known what was up?'

'Too apt, that,' I said, playing for time.

It was a question I'd asked myself time and again and struggled to answer. I had such a vivid memory of meeting Gil and the look we'd shared, not quite love at first sight, but with a wealth of communication and gut need. Would I have been less receptive to it if I'd been in a loving, trusting relationship with Joe? It was impossible to know.

I'd leaned up to kiss Gil's face. 'A beam of direct sunlight can do it, can't it — burn through a scrap of paper and start a fire? You were my beam. But as for your hypothetical question . . . I'd have been very close to catching alight, but I think I'd have found the will to resist.'

'Then I owe it all to the other woman.'

★ ★ ★

I'd got back to New York hoping Joe would ask after the job, my night away, anything to make me feel guiltier, but he was busy writing a letter at the small desk in the bedroom and barely said hello. I felt deeply resentful; I even minded him being at the desk, sharing my little room. It had two skinny beds in it now — 'cots' to Joan — squeezed in to form an L.

'Who's that to?' I asked, not expecting an answer.

He turned, unable to hide a look of triumph

and success. 'Jackie Kennedy. I had lunch with her today — and Joan,' whom he clearly wished hadn't had to be there.

'Jackie's very into the London theatre,' I said, childishly keen to remind Joe that I'd met her too. 'She'd been to see the Old Vic on tour in Washington. You must have found plenty to talk about.'

He gave me a cold eye. 'We did, we had a very cosy time.'

★ ★ ★

My week in hospital was up. Mum had returned to help get me home and it was almost time to go. I felt quite weepy clearing my locker, except that with Mum trying to cheer me up and being maddening, irritation held in the tears. She had Bella in her arms and was cooing over her when I saw, out of the corner of my eye, Joe walk into the ward.

I felt a strange numbness, a kind of emotional anaesthesia. He had armfuls of flowers — he must have cleaned out a florist's shop — and smiled winsomely at admiring nurses and the occupants of the other beds on his way to mine before seeing us and fastening on the bundle in my mother's arms.

'Hello, wifey,' he said, kissing my cheek, 'and Betty. Good to see you.' He kissed her cheek too, before dropping his eyes to peer with fascination at what was visible of Bella. 'Let's see the little man then — cheeky little blighter, coming this early. He wasn't due for days.'

'Isn't 'cheeky' just a little rich?' I muttered, glowering, longing for more privacy. All eyes were on us; a pall of rabid curiosity hung over the ward. 'She's a girl, Joe, and a week old now — a week you've missed while you were away getting that tan. She's called Isabella Caroline — Bella.'

If there was a flicker, a small reality check, Joe hid it superbly well. He'd wanted a son and the wish had become a certainty in his mind, yet he could still move seamlessly into delighted burbles. He deposited the ridiculously overdone flowers on the bed, lilies, roses, even orchids, and peeked more closely at the tiny, pointy, screwed-up face, buried deep in a lacy shawl. 'Well, well, little lady, springing surprises on us already, are you? You're going be a wicked little madam, I can tell — and quite as beautiful as your mother . . . '

'Don't come that guff,' I mumbled, mainly to myself, feeling furiously hard done by. Joe could have asked after the birth, asked after me, how I was coping. But Joe didn't think like that. He'd wanted to name a boy Dominic, rejecting outright any suggestions of mine, and hadn't bothered to listen to any ideas for girls' names. I felt now, though, that he knew he'd forfeited the right to challenge me on the choice of Bella. And seeing his look of adoring delight, his face aglow as he studied his baby daughter, I really believed he wasn't acting and was just a very proud father, after all.

My mother seemed struck dumb. It was hardly the place for a grand inquisition, and she was a conciliator by nature, even more timid than I was. 'You were missed, Joe,' she said finally, with a hint of an accusing tone. 'Susannah's had a difficult birth, a hard time of it and she's been dreadfully worried about you. And you're even a little late for a hospital visit. We're just waiting for the final say-so before going home.'

'My car's here, Joe,' I said, chipping in before he could think of some retaliating excuse, 'so if you're in yours, perhaps you should go on ahead. I'll give most of the flowers to the nurses if it's okay with you, when we say our goodbyes. Oh, and I painted Bella's room by the way, and stencilled some elephants. Have you seen?'

I fancied Joe's lip curled. How could I have said that, imagined he'd have the slightest interest in the stencils on his daughter's walls? That was bourgeois, typical wifey twaddle.

*　*　*

'No questions, Mum,' I said, on the way home. 'There's nothing to be gained by quizzing him, I don't want an atmosphere — it could even seep into Bella's psyche, for all we know! Better just get on with life now and draw a veil over the last weeks.'

'That seems very wise,' she said, looking like someone surviving an icy skid, intense relief at not having to be party to painful marital strife. 'I'll stay a few days, of course, till you feel you can manage, but it's hard for Dad without me, and with Joe back you won't be alone in an emergency.'

She was sensitive to the oppressive grimness of a mother-in-law in a poky flat, sharing the new baby's box room. I felt grateful.

'I wonder,' she said nervously, as though broaching a difficult subject, 'whether you can afford to rent somewhere a little bigger? And won't you need to organise some help, if you're going to get back to work?'

'I've been thinking hard about all that, Mum, and I don't want to rent any more. It's a rare chance to buy, with my bit of New York dosh, but every mortgage company I've called just laughs down the line. You try getting a mortgage as a freelance photographic model who's under twenty-five — you'd think I'd asked them for a million-pound loan.'

Mum looked wretched. She and Dad had no money; they couldn't help. We were outside the flat by now: it was our last moment to talk privately. 'Perhaps if you made an appointment,' she said in a small defeated voice, 'and it was face to face . . . '

I kissed her cheek — cool, face-powder dry — and wished she looked less tired. My mother was thin and fair-haired; the grey barely showed, but the lines were etched stressfully deep. I felt determined to grab my chances, do more trips to New York and earn the money to give my parents a decent holiday. There must be a way doctors could take a break.

We set about moving me back in. Mum had restocked the kitchen, and after feeding Bella I made supper; soup and eggs were a banquet after hospital food. The evening stretched ahead.

283

While I unpacked and got sorted, Mum took the crib into the sitting room. Bella was sleeping sweetly and the television news was just coming on.

I went into the bedroom and found Joe sitting on the bed writing a letter. His case was half-unpacked and he seemed to have no dirty laundry that I could see. His clothes, shirts, underwear, were all immaculately washed, ironed, neatly folded, but not in the way of a hotel laundry service. He must have been staying at some extremely grand private home.

My resentment was building as usual. I mustn't let it, mustn't . . . I took a deep breath, left Joe without speaking and went into the sitting room to be with Bella and Mum.

The Kennedys were on the television news, Jack being met off a plane. He'd arrived in Italy where Jackie had been holidaying so that they could fly back to the States together. She'd been in Italy most of the month, staying with friends at a private villa. The camera jumped to a scene of them walking through narrow, picturesque, people-lined streets, smiling, waving and acknowledging the cheers.

Had Joe been there too, staying with Jackie at that private villa? It would explain his tan, the laundry . . . My eyes misted over, which my mother noticed straight away.

'What is it, darling?'

'Just,' I wiped at an eye, 'just that it's been such an emotion-filled month, what with the panic of Joe, not knowing where he was, and nerves about the birth. And I keep thinking of

284

Marilyn Monroe, Mum. It's only three weeks since she died, but it's taken this long for the full horror of it to really sink in.'

'It was wretched, love, a sad self-inflicted death, but you knew her only slightly. You can't let it haunt you, you mustn't brood.'

'But it does haunt me. It has me in tears. I can't bear to think she was only in her thirties — it feels so *unnecessary* and cruel. I mean, I know she popped pills the whole time, and mixed them with booze, but something truly devastating must have happened to bring her to that ultimate low. It wasn't as if I knew her really well, Mum, I know that, but I actually felt quite close to her. She was friendly and warm, interested in me when she had no business to be, good to be with — she'd put on this great sexy extrovert show, yet you could tell she was kind of unconfident underneath, almost fearful of herself.'

I smiled at Mum. 'It's no wonder I'm weepy. I feel so guilty at my own good fortune and happiness, you see.' I looked from Mum to Bella and back again. 'When I think of the good things, a daughter of my own.'

★ ★ ★

Whether or not Joe had been with Jackie in Italy, an instinct for self-preservation told me that he'd do what he wanted, when he wanted, and I had to get on with life: be aware, canny, and not afraid to lead my own. Joe wasn't into routines. Normal everyday life freaked him out, the future wasn't certain, and the sooner I sorted out a bigger flat and a nanny for Bella, the better for us all.

It was hot and sunny, the first week of September. I wheeled Bella in Hyde Park and by chance happened on Norman Parkinson one day, who was just finishing a shoot. Parks was my absolute hero: he'd given me my first job and I'd owed him my start in modelling. We chatted and I talked about the mortgage problem, since it was at the front of my mind.

'Go and see my good man at United Friendly,' he said. 'Call him up, tell him I sent you — but he'll only have to look at you. You'll have your mortgage.'

'I even love the name,' I said, feeling on a laughing high. 'Promise you'll come to the flat-warming party?'

Park's 'good man' became my second absolute hero, though for a moment he'd looked like chasing me round his desk, which would have been a little problematic. When I told Mum the news, she said in that wry, shy way she had, 'I did say, darling, that perhaps if it was face to face . . . '

17

Daisy was clock-watching and in a tizz. She was in a meeting with Susannah and the architect, Grace Mansfield, and was pleased to be included. Grace was sleek and gracious, smartly turned out in a red dress and clunky black necklace. The offices were ultra-modern, all glass, space and light, the plans exciting to see, but the meeting had been squeezed in unexpectedly, which had presented Daisy with a tricky little conundrum.

Susannah had come into the city the night before and Warren had taken them both to the theatre; he'd got last-minute tickets through a contact and insisted Daisy come, too. They'd seen Tom Hanks in *Lucky Guy*, a play by Nora Ephron that she'd been working on when she died. It was about the Pulitzer Prize-winning journalist, Mike McAlary, and Daisy had loved all the witty, whacky anecdotes. She'd loved the whole evening, apart from the continuous buzzing bee in her head — the problem of what to do about lunch with Warren next day.

He'd managed a muttered aside at the theatre. 'Meet as planned? Same place?' Daisy had nodded with a nervous smile, knowing that whatever cavalier attitude Warren might take, how much wiser and better it would be to cry off. But then he knew Susannah's movements ... He'd booked the car from Southampton

Limos to bring her into the city, after all, since Jackson was on a day off; arranged as well for Jackson to drive in today and take her straight back to Southampton. She had a date with the site-manager in the late afternoon. But plans had a habit of changing and the clock was ticking on.

Grace looked at her watch. 'You must want to get off, Susannah. Have you time for a quick bite of lunch? You should have something to see you on your way.'

Daisy held her breath. She could still call, it was no big deal, just . . . a disappointment.

'Thanks,' Susannah said, 'I'd love that, perhaps in the coffee shop downstairs? I mustn't be long. Coming, Daisy? How are you for time?'

'I thought I'd whiz up to Bloomingdale's and catch their summer sale. And I really should get on if I want to make the five o'clock Jitney. I'll see you later, Susannah. And thanks, Grace, I think the plans are amazing — the offices, too!'

She left them finding a date for a meeting on site and dived into the loo, pouting into the mirror while no one was there then staring at her own still-undecided expression. It was mad to take risks, and for a man pushing seventy! The stupid thing was that she liked Warren, really quite a lot — which had nothing to do with how immensely rich he was, she felt sure of that. And he was certainly hot for her, no question.

She knew then that the decision was taken. It was completely weird, being so into him. Daisy glossed her lips and squirted scent onto her bra and pants, feeling a powerful sexual frisson. Going to his apartment would be for real this time, not just another flustered goodbye kiss at the door like last week. Warren had been comically anxious not to push it, but she'd have been fertile ground if he had, easily tilled.

It would be a good test of her feelings for Simon, she persuaded herself, stepping out of the elevator. He was arriving next week and staying Thursday to Sunday, which was hard to believe. Susannah had said a little cooling off would bring him round — and it had. Daisy had missed him less than she'd feared, but perhaps that wasn't so strange with Long Island, the house, Warren, everything she was doing here being such a thrill. Yet it all had a sense of unreality about it and Simon, however hopeless, was a fact of life, grounded in a world to which she had to return.

Passing the coffee-shop window, Daisy saw Susannah and Grace, seated already and reading menus. Jackson was waiting, the car was right outside, and her heart pumped at a happier pace. She waved to Jackson before flagging down a cab. Sixteen blocks uptown felt a respectable distance; she sat back in the cab, tingling with guilty exhilaration and the adrenaline of risk.

It was Daisy's second visit to San Pietro. The front of house staff recognised her instantly and she had an enthusiastic welcome. A waiter escorted her through the busy restaurant — jam-packed with Manhattan's power-lunchers, dark-suited businessmen and a sprinkling of grey-suited women — to Warren's table. In a jazzy sleeveless sheath with red and cream wiggly stripes Daisy felt conspicuous beside all the monochrome clothes, but the ambience, the jovial waiters, the delicious smells of fresh-cooked fish, were a colourful backdrop.

Warren kissed her cheek, gave her hand a discreet squeeze and pulled out a chair for her. The restaurant's owner, Gerardo, came up, greeting them effusively and lovingly rattled off a list of specials — too speedily for Daisy to retain. 'Can I have whatever smells so intoxicatingly fishy?' she said. 'You decide!'

That seemed popular. Fingers were raised to pursed kissing-lips to indicate that what Gerardo intended to bring would be perfection.

'I've been on tenterhooks,' Warren said. 'So glad you're here.' He gave a warm, gentle smile, resting his calf against Daisy's, leaving no doubt of his need for tactility — or his intentions. She didn't ease her leg clear.

'It was slightly tricky, making excuses and slipping away, but it was the only possible day,' she said self-consciously. 'And it lets me say another huge thank you for the theatre. I adored every minute, but you shouldn't have felt you needed to include me. It was a lovely chance for you to have had an evening with Susannah.'

Warren drew a cautious breath as though about to tread delicate waters, only to be interrupted by the arrival of the antipasti.

'You must never,' Warren said, rather abruptly and startlingly once they were alone again, 'think I wouldn't want you there, too. I think Susannah's terrific, as you know. I've been a little in love with her, long distance, ever since a trip to London way back, and we had a great time in

Newport last weekend. She's elegant and still beautiful. I greatly enjoy her company, but you were in my head all the time.'

He reached over the table to cover her hand with his. It was the most elderly bit of him, bony and speckled with a few small liver spots, but she still felt sexy quivers. 'I don't know what's come over me,' he murmured, his fingers lightly stroking. 'I don't listen in meetings, I step out into the street on green lights, I keep seeing your sparkly eyes — emerald eyes — and imagine lying beside you . . . ' He let that drift, looking sheepish, clearly worried about overstepping it, and withdrew his hand.

Daisy felt it was time to talk about Simon's visit. 'You've been really wonderful to me,' she said, giving him her most adoring smile, 'but you know I mentioned about my friend, Simon, possibly coming over? Well, he's arriving a week tomorrow, which makes me feel a little guilty about this lovely cosy lunch.'

It was a slight foot on the brake and she wondered how Warren would react. She didn't want to put him off altogether, just slow up a whisker for dignity's sake.

Warren looked relieved, as a waiter chose that moment to clear the plates, glad of a temporary hiatus — although his face took on a glaze of frustrated irritation when another waiter took his time serving the main course. 'Sea bass in a crust of sea salt for the lady,' he said obsequiously, with a gold-tooth smile, 'and your risotto with asparagus and shrimp, sir.' He hovered around being smarmy, pouring more wine, water, asking if everything was all right more than once.

'Fine, fine,' Warren snapped — impatient now, it seemed, to make clear he was anything but put off. His eyes holding hers had a look of gentle lust. 'Will you come back afterwards and have coffee at the apartment? It would give me a chance to ask about Simon. You look tense whenever you mention him, and we haven't gotten very far.' That could be taken two ways, deliberately so?

'If I could just — ' Warren stopped mid-sentence and stiffened. Having just accused her of being tense, he was a frozen block. He was facing out into the restaurant. Who had he seen? Daisy died inside. Had Susannah known his regular lunch place and come to thank him for the theatre last night? It couldn't get worse.

'What is it, Warren? Someone you've seen?'

'Yes, only my ex-wife, which I could certainly do without. She's with a guy I know, a parboiled old jerk, but she's seen me and is coming over. Shit, shit, this won't be easy. Gee, I'm sorry — steel yourself.'

'I'll try.' Daisy smiled and let out her breath while Warren audibly drew his in and set his face. She was dying to look round even as Warren struggled to his feet with more muttered expletives.

Willa proffered both cheeks with speedy turns of the head in such a way as to dispense with any need for actual kissing. 'No surprise, seeing you here, Warren,' she said. 'Same old haunts, same old groove.' She laughed, harshly and confidently.

Daisy stared open-mouthed. Willa, who looked halfway between her own age and Susannah's, was a siren vision with rich-red lips, lustrous black hair, a sensual body and a voice dripping with sexuality. She was in a slate-grey linen dress with a skinny nude belt, a wide heavy bangle that looked solid gold; it was spangled with diamonds, pure moneyed elegance. She was a typical rich bitch, yet reeking with class.

'So, Warren,' Willa said, 'aren't you going to introduce me to this child?'

'I'm Daisy Mitchell.' It felt best to take over, since Warren seemed silenced, in some kind of a trance.

Willa stared coldly before saying, 'I don't know you. Are you a daughter of some old crony of his?' Did she know every available female in New York?

'I'm more parent than daughter. I have adult sons!' Daisy laughed, little put off by Willa's hostile dark-eyed stare. She was surprised at her ability to hold her own; at home she was often made to feel like a naive country cousin, but not here in the States. The warmth and interested curiosity of Warren's neighbours, the Beach Club crowd, and the reflected glory of being his house guest had given her a new confidence.

'You're English,' Willa asserted, given to talking in statements, it seemed. She spun round a chair from the next-door table without so much as a 'May I?' and motioned to Warren to sit down with an impatient wave of red-painted nails, as though she were drying them.

He found his voice. 'Yes, she is. Daisy's over

from London, one of my house guests staying in Southampton this summer.' He made no mention of the redecoration project, obviously keen to dispatch Willa back to her table and not prolong things. 'I see you're with my old crony, Chuck. He's looking lonely over there,' Warren said, with some bite. 'Give him my best, the old gasser. Solid chap in his way, pity he's riddled with arthritis these days, poor bugger.'

Willa ignored him and continued to fix Daisy with a cold calculated gaze. 'So let me guess: you're a young divorcée, a bit short of money . . .' She was getting her own back, all right. 'A word of warning, if I may, on that score. Warren's a tight-fisted old sod, as I should know,' she gave a rich bark of a laugh, 'but I'm sure you'll enjoy your stay.' And with that stinging little parting shot, she gave a honeyed smile and sauntered back to poor-bugger Chuck, leaving the chair unreturned to its table.

Daisy felt deflated and drained. Warren would think the worst of her now. Willa had known which nerve to touch, all right. She'd made Daisy feel cheap and tarty, money-grubbing and scruple-free. Warren's riches couldn't be ignored. His money shaped him; it gave him an aura of power, steeliness and drive, but she wasn't a gold-digger, not in the business of prospecting and out for all she could get. She just happened to like him. The money was neither here nor there.

Warren was looking distant, crumpled, knocked off his stride; his lips were tight-pressed in a grimace. 'Sorry about that. I can see she's upset you,' he said. 'She was jealous, bitchy as ever, but if it's any consolation, she got to me, too.' That was obvious enough; he still looked quite ashen. He managed a grin and settled his leg back against Daisy's. 'I've a very small present for you, you see — a nothing and only tiny because of all the fuss you made over the auction prize — but now you'll think I'm just being tight-fisted!'

While Daisy protested earnestly, Warren reached under the table and transferred a package from his briefcase into her bucket handbag. 'It's only a little silver chain,' he said, 'really just a token. Now, will you have dessert? Sure? I'll get the check and let's get out of here and have coffee up the road.'

Daisy took the chance to go to the loo and peek at the present. It was from Tiffany's, simple silver links, just the right chunkiness and length. Fantastically wearable, she couldn't refuse it.

Walking the few sunlit blocks up Fifth Avenue with Warren, shyly enthusing and thanking him for the necklace, she imagined Susannah in every car that drove by. Only when the door to his apartment had closed behind them did she stop feeling exposed.

Warren, too, heaved a sigh once they were safely inside. He touched her hair, lifting it lightly away from her face. 'Can I kiss you?' Daisy didn't speak. He wasn't allowing much wriggle-room for coy protesting anyway, taking her in his arms with his body pressing, his mouth inches from hers. She could feel his hard-on and he'd had a quaver in his voice which she sensed was from the effort of self-control. It was the best thing about sex, she thought, as his mouth sought hers, feeling wanted when you wanted it, too.

He kissed her long and passionately, crushing her breasts until she pulled away, touching his lips with her fingers and giving a small smile. It alarmed her, how ready she was to fall into bed. 'We're here to talk about Simon,' she said, trying to get a grip. 'And I really can't stay long. I've got so much to do yet, not to mention a bus to catch.'

'You can't possibly get the bus, I'll put you in a chopper, that's easily fixed.'

'God, no. I couldn't let you do that! I'll be fine, there'll be a later bus if need be, I'm sure.'

'Then it sounds like we'd better get started on talking about Simon,' Warren said dryly, taking Daisy into a vast bright room overlooking Central Park. The light was streaming in, even with protective voile curtains. He ripped off his tie, chucking it onto a chair. 'Shall I make coffee? My maid's off, but I don't make a bad cup.'

'Not for me. I'm wired-up enough already.'

She looked round, absorbing the sumptuous, slightly off-key grandeur. A magnificent Aubusson carpet, a genuine old one, beautifully preserved, set the tone. The furniture had a continental feel, unyielding sofas, heavily fringed, cream-damask drapes with swags and tails. The paintings were mainly English sporting scenes — Herrings and Ferneleys at a guess — that needed a clubbier, more library setting. There were quantities of American silver — Warren must collect the stuff — and more huge candelabra, although they were probably better suited to his lifestyle here, with business entertaining. Daisy felt a small pang of homesickness for Battersea, her cramped house with its friendly clutter and exuberant back patch of garden.

Warren drew her down onto a small Bergère sofa, walnut-framed, hardly suited to lovemaking, and kept his arm round her. 'If I'm honest,' he said, fondling her hair with his other hand 'Simon's the last thing I want to talk about — for reasons which must be clear as day. I guess you'd say I'm biased, but the guy sticks in my craw. He sounds a louse, a loser, and you said yourself, Daisy dearest, that he's not about to leave his wife. You don't need him! Creeps like that are a dime a dozen. He'll go on taking advantage. You gotta stand back and see it's time for going cold turkey.'

'I think that needs translating,' Daisy said, smiling up at Warren, gratified by the intense, burning-up look on his face.

'It's like if you were trying to lick a drugs habit, we'd say going cold turkey. You're a sweet, beautiful girl, Daisy — irresistible. I could kick his ass for treating you like a rug under his feet.'

'I know it's hardly an ideal relationship,' Daisy said, holding her ground. 'He's a married man for a start, not something I'm proud of. And then there's the casual cruelty and put-downs that hurt so much when you care. I'm sure you've been there with Willa. Simon refusing to fly over, telling me he wouldn't stick around if I went away for so long was hard to bear, yet now he's coming after all. The boys more or less knew about Simon in my life anyway, but they certainly do now; he's called our home, asked about my movements in a roundabout way — when they expected me back, that sort of thing. He's changed.'

'Men don't change,' Warren said, with one arm round her, the other resting on her thigh, as if all he wanted to do was get her to bed. 'Simon won't change his spots. Once a jerk, he'll go on being one — and you know it.'

Daisy looked away. It was true. Warren turned her face back, fixing her with another burning gaze. 'You're different from any woman I've ever known. Lovely, that goes without saying,' his light brown eyes were burrowing into her, 'but you're soft, caring, too vulnerable and tender-hearted by half. You need protecting, Daisy. I want to look after you and be there for you. If you'll just let me do that a little, let me try . . . '

Daisy allowed herself to be led into the bedroom. His bed was colossal, heavy and masculine with a scrolled mahogany bedhead. 'Sure it's okay?' Warren murmured. 'You're not just being kind?'

She kissed his cheek. 'Kindness doesn't come into it, I'm not that sort of saint!'

'I've been having these fantasies ever since you arrived, undressing you, doing what you'd most like . . . '

'I'm not wearing much in this summer heat,' she said, quivering with the exquisite lightness of his fingers on her skin. She wasn't used to Warren's kind of gentleness, the delicacy, his tenderly persistent fingers, and succumbed with a sigh as he found his way round her body and its needs. He could hold her, swooning, unbearably close and keep her on the point, but when she tried to reciprocate, he took away her hand. 'I don't trust myself. I'll come too quickly,' he whispered, 'and I'm in my dreams.'

Only when they were lying back in the lee of his cumbersome bedhead, contented, shattered — more relaxed than would have seemed possible an hour ago — did Daisy think about the difference in age. It hadn't been on her mind in the heat of the moment, but it crept in. Still, he wasn't in bad nick for a man over thirty years older — and unselfish too; certainly by comparison, not a bad lover at all.

He was gazing at her, looking irritatingly soppy, which made her wonder how possessive and jealous he might start to be. Gerald, the auctioneer from the Red Tide Benefit, had mentioned having dinner one night and said he'd call. She decided to talk that up to Warren and test the water for his reaction; it wouldn't be a case of tempting providence since she didn't much care either way. Except that, feeling so dreadful about Susannah, hating the sort of quasi-mistress situation that she seemed to be in, Daisy could see it might be helpful if she went out with another man.

The lunches, Warren's gift of the necklace, succumbing so readily that afternoon, she felt racked with guilt. It was hard to be loyally selfless, though, where men were concerned and, Daisy tried to persuade herself, she was hardly pining for Simon. Warren's attentions were serving a useful purpose — in many ways.

She leaned up on an elbow and smiled at him affectionately. 'Guess what. It came as a surprise, but Gerald, that auctioneer, has asked me out. He says he's often in the Hamptons doing viewings during the week and would love to take me to dinner.'

Warren didn't look in the least put out, annoyingly. She felt peeved when he smiled, looking amused. 'You know he's gay, of course? With anyone else I'd be jealous as hell. Let me know if you decide to go, though, and I'll use the time to entertain Susannah.'

Daisy wondered how much to read into that. Was Warren keeping his options open, playing it both ways? She tried to contain an instinctive sense of rivalry. She had her own ideas about Gerald's orientation, which helped: maybe he played it his own sort of both ways, but his looks over the table at the Benefit had been very heterosexual. Simon, she thought wryly, was going to have to stand in line.

'You've got a tantalising little smile twitching at the corners of your lips. What's it about?'

'I was just thinking how much more relaxed I feel,' Daisy said, removing Warren's hand that was beginning to wander. 'But the pity of it is, I really have to race now, sharpen up and do my job.'

She went naked in search of the bathroom, opening the wrong door first, into a walk-in cupboard with acres of sliding shirt-shelves and tweedy-smelling suits on thick brass rails. The bathroom, when she found it, was a palace. She washed in one of two huge handsome basins set into an expanse of rouge marble, grabbed a towel from a daunting monogrammed array, came back and hurriedly dressed.

Warren was sitting on the bed, buttoning his shirt. 'Sorry about this mad rush,' she said, kissing his forehead, 'but I have to get on or you're never going to see *Great Maples* finished.'

He gripped her wrist and put his face to her arm. 'I'd rather it never was. I want you to stay forever.'

18

Martha came out onto the deck. 'Call for you, Daisy. He said to say it's Gerald.'

Daisy looked at me apologetically; we had furniture plans, inspiration boards, a hundred swatches spread out on a glass table and were in mid-discussion.

'It's fine,' I said, 'go and take it. You can't leave him hanging on.'

He was probably asking her out. She'd said he came to the Hamptons to do views and had mentioned having dinner. They'd had a flirty little chat at the Benefit, I recalled, despite Daisy being more focused elsewhere. I smiled to myself. Between Simon arriving and whatever little thing she had going with Warren, Gerald looked like being on slim pickings. My smile faded fast. I could do without the Warren situation, it was galling to say the least. He was too honest to be accomplished at hiding his feelings and I could see the emotions she aroused in him. It didn't help that it was easy to understand.

Daisy was a lovely, warm-hearted, pliable girl and Warren needed a woman in his life — more than one, it seemed. He must feel humiliated by Willa too, which was clouding his judgement, making him flex his muscles and push on the boundaries. I suspected that Willa was still in his system, and knowing him better, could see where they'd come unstuck. He was a traditionalist stay-at-home New Yorker, not built for gadding round hotspot resorts in the biggest yacht of the lot, whereas she'd wanted an exotic backdrop, a forum to display her glittering spendthrift wares.

And what did *I* want? Certainly not to play second fiddle to Daisy; I'd have to rise above that. Yet I was here, enjoying the summer, loving the project and proud of how it was going. The house would look sensationally different, contemporary summer living at its height. The design magazines would want to feature it for sure. Warren would be hailed for his avant-garde zest, which would be one in the eye for Willa. I felt he'd enjoy that — and the accolades, the splash the house made, should help him adjust to the new look.

'Sorry about that,' Daisy said breathlessly, bounding back out. 'It was Gerald, the smarty-pants auctioneer, following through. He's asked me out to dinner next Thursday.'

'Are you going to go?' I asked hopefully.

'I've said yes, with the proviso of things cropping up. He's in the Hamptons anyhow and it's a whole ten days away, so I've got plenty of time to change my mind.'

'Simon this Thursday, Gerald the next, it's all go! You'll stay in New York with Simon? Be sure to have a proper break and see he takes you to some decent clubs and restaurants. It's time you called a few shots.' Daisy grinned cheekily, as though she couldn't wait to show off her new confident self. Simon could be in for a surprise, I thought.

We carried on discussing the new breakfast room, Daisy teaming up swatches with her natural eye. She was being positive, prepared to argue, transformed from the cowed, demoralised girl of a month ago. Sun, and a little sex presumably, had polished and burnished her morale. She was bubbling over and her sparkle was iridescent.

'What time does Simon get in?' I asked.

'Late afternoon. I don't suppose he'll be at the hotel till around eight, though, so I can put in a day's work. Perhaps . . . if I go up Wednesday and stay over?'

'Perhaps,' I repeated a little ironically, picking up on her hesitancy. 'But couldn't you go late, Daisy? There's more than enough to do here and you'll have Thursday, after all.'

'True,' she said, with a slight look of angst.

Had I just scotched a lunch-date with Warren? Evenings would be trickier, I could see, since she overnighted with my old modelling friend, Janet, who'd report back. Well, tough. Daisy couldn't have everything on a plate.

Warren had said he wanted to make the most of me while she was seeing Simon and taking Friday off. He was coming back Thursday night — we had a date. That was all fine, but Daisy was the focus of his sunburst of libido, not me. Still, I felt he'd soon come to see that it wasn't an ideal liaison, and for the moment I could handle his facing both ways, which he did rather adroitly. And as to how things eventually shook out between us, only time would tell.

Thursday was Martha's day for visiting her son and Warren was taking me to dinner at the

Meadow Club. It was a stiff WASPy, members-only tennis club, proud of dating back to the nineteenth century, with sepia postcards and photographs displayed on the walls showing the petticoated players of early days.

The Club had a weekly white-tablecloth lobster night on summer evenings, when members turned out as coiffed and manicured as the rows of immaculately maintained grass tennis courts. I'd been on past occasions and recalled wearing a bib and tackling huge, hunky lobsters, splendid fiery-red specimens, served on suitably sized white platters, with corncobs and paper-cup containers of melted butter.

* * *

On Thursday, with the house and my time my own, I made a bit of an effort and had my hair done by blond, softly spoken Steven, the darling of Southampton's über-elite. He was both extremely informative and discreet, and so valued by his clients that they would even whisk him away on Atlantic crossings. He was charming, filled me in as discreetly as ever and sent me out looking as dolled-up as could be.

I was ready by eight, dressed in shell-pink silk palazzo pants patterned with grey scrolls, and felt slightly maddened when Warren called from the car, still miles away.

'Piss-awful traffic, I'm afraid, the highway's solid. Jackson's doing his nut, but we're an hour off yet, I'd say, and the Meadow Club's kinda stuffy on time.' Stuffy all round, I thought, angry.

305

'I couldn't be sorrier,' Warren said, sounding it. 'Lobster night on hold, but we'll go soon and it's easy to get lobstered out, after all, as the summer wears on. I've called up Parmigiana — they'll still be open, no bookings, but we should be all right. You okay with slumming it up the road? Can you bear to? The mussels are good.'

'Sure, no problem — I'm keen on Parmigiana. Daisy and I are regulars.'

I kept the irritation out of my voice with difficulty. Apart from having to change down, I had my own ideas about why he'd left late enough to hit the rush hour — a rearranged lunch-date with Daisy. No doubt he would have been anxious to shore her up and make his mark before she saw Simon.

It was at least an hour before he made it back, bursting in, still being effusive. 'God, I'm sorry, such a drag for you, all this hanging about. A quick clean-up, then we're off.' Warren kissed me as though he meant it and hurried upstairs to change.

He drove the half-mile to the village with one hand on my thigh. I was far from in the mood though, too suspicious of afternoon activities with Daisy. A quiet evening and separate beds tonight, no question.

All the same we had fun pigging it out at La Parmigiana. It was a deli-restaurant, owned by the Gambino family who knew all about authenticity; they made their own sauces, everything fresh, and bottled it up for sale in the deli, too. Warren and I sat at the back and had mussels marinara in bowls that would have served salad for twelve. Normal portions, in the eyes of the family, were for pygmies in a fantasyland, some alien race at least. It would have offended their Italian big-heartedness to serve anything less than too much. Our veal scallopini came atop a mountain of mushrooms, mozzarella and spinach, resenting the confines of its plate, and the pizzas served to near neighbours overflowed the entire table.

'Do people ask for doggie bags and make all this lot do three meals?'

'No, they eat it up, unlike you,' Warren said, 'and with luck, wash it down with Lippy Lager.' He played footsie with me and had such a warm, comfortable-looking, loving smile that I couldn't be cross for too long. I enjoyed him, even loved him a little, but not with a depth where jealousy became an insanity. I'd lived through those times of feeling bloodied and raw; being older and a little wiser had its compensations.

'I hope you won't mind, but I had a bite of lunch with Daisy again today,' Warren said, without looking too penitent about it. 'I felt she needed a little pep talk before seeing Simon. She's a hopeless case, clinging to an asshole creep who's never going to leave his wife. It's one dumb way to ball up her best years and send them down the garbage shoot, that's for sure. Can't she see through the jerk!' he exclaimed, sounding infuriatingly desperate and plaintive.

His obsession with her was hard to take, and he knew how to kill the mood. 'I don't doubt you bolstered her up this afternoon,' I said, wanting to stick in a few pins. He needn't take me for a total sucker.

He flushed and looked so humiliated that I felt softer. 'What about asking Daisy if she'd like to bring Simon here on Sunday?' I suggested. 'Take him to lunch at the Beach Club? His flight's not till late, I think she said, and it's a quick run from here to the airport. Daisy could take him in the hire car. Perhaps we could manage to show him up a little, even make her feel a bit ashamed of his boorish ways. It's just a thought . . . '

I could see Warren coping with a whole gamut of emotions. Whether he could handle seeing them together, feeling a masochistic need to as well; not trusting himself to be civil.

'She may not want to bring him, of course, but if she likes the idea,' I said, 'and isn't in need of being alone together, perhaps that's a good sign. I'm sure she'd be proud to show Simon this house and Southampton. After all, he never stops putting her down.'

Warren clocked into the fact that since he was the source of the house and the set-up, she'd be showing him off as well. And curiosity as usual won the day. 'Women do think of things in clever, different ways,' he said. 'I'd never have had that idea.'

It crossed my mind, as we drove back, that seeing Daisy in a Gatsby-esque setting might make Simon all the keener, hardly the intended outcome. But it wouldn't last, I decided. Men didn't change — Simon probably least of all.

We went into the house and stood looking at each other in the hall. I'd embarrassed him to hell, been open enough about how wised-up I was, and he was clearly feeling guilty, humbled and distressed. Aside from the guilt, however, I sensed he really wanted to snuggle up companionably and sleep together. He knew better than to dissemble, though, or struggle away, embarrassingly trying to minimise my hurt about Daisy. Whatever his relationship with her, we had one too; we gelled well and understood each other. We'd shed a few layers.

'Better not tonight,' I said, giving him a light good-night kiss on the lips, 'but we'll have a good time tomorrow. It's our day, our weekend. I'll text Daisy, say you have a nice plan to put to her and suggest she calls you.'

I wasn't sleepy and felt like talking to Charles. I only lasted so long before feeling a bit starved of him. It was five o'clock in the morning in Norfolk — the time difference was a bind. I texted. *Feel out of touch. How's the wind/chill? How's you?*

Charles phoned. 'Sorry if the text woke you,' I said. 'Don't you turn off your phone?'

'I wake early in summer, it's the best writing time. And it is summer here, incidentally; there's a cornflower-blue sky, tweeting birds. I'm still in bed at the moment, though, with a sleeping dog at the foot — in lieu of anyone up close.'

'I can't say I'm sorry about that.'

'I'd banish poor old Ollie if you were around. I don't go in for threesomes.'

'I tried one once in the sixties. It was awful, madly self-conscious and comic. Like I mean, who goes first?'

'The one whose bed it is?' Charles suggested. 'I won't tell you what I've tried in my time.'

'Spoilsport.'

'I don't want a threesome with your Mr Warren, by the way,' Charles said.

'No, I see that. He's spoilt for choice out here anyway, very juiced up over Daisy, but not suggesting threesomes as yet.'

'When are you back? I'm missing you, too.'

'You could always come out this way. It's peaceful in the week, good for writing.'

'But I have to be here, for all the usual reasons.'

'Window-seal? Draught-proofing? A new boiler?'

'You haven't answered my question about coming home. Are you staying out there forever? Toying with being Mrs Warren?'

'Unlikely. I'll be finished by mid-August and want to see the grandchildren. Bella's lot will be at my house in France. Shall we catch up in London or there?'

'Let's wait and see, shall we? 'Unlikely' doesn't sound the end of the road.'

★ ★ ★

Warren and I had a good couple of days. We pottered to Sag Harbor, a nearby village that had a whaling history and was more with-it than the Hamptons, where we browsed in its boutiques and strolled the dock. He suggested a glass of wine and a lobster roll on the porch of Ted Conklin's American Hotel. It had a spray-paint of celebrities — Truman Capote and Robert Caro, Billy Joel and Bono — and traded on big-name atmospherics. Warren marched me off to hire bicycles after that and we bought a picnic lunch before taking the ferry hop to Shelter Island.

We pedalled along unmade-up tracks, stopping to pick beach plums, a kind of sweeter blueberry growing wild by the pathway, until we found a secluded beach and pitched picnic. Cheese, fruit and cold white wine — a swim, a languorous hour stretched out in the sun, soaking it up, lifting my face to its rays.

I'd dutifully applied sun cream, but was I undoing all the good work of the treatment I'd had before coming? The sun damage to my skin was done years ago, though. We'd known nothing about the dangers of sunbathing in my teens and twenties. Sunscreens hadn't had protection factors. The oils we'd used had probably actually fried us, the way I'd bubbled up in blisters and peeled. Women's magazines hadn't warned of the consequences and dictated which factor to use. The lines and sunspots had crept up on me, but there was no going back, no point worrying now, and I loved the enveloping warmth of the sun. I lay back feeling cat-like and oblivious to all cares.

Daisy was shelved for the moment, stashed away. Warren and I were easy in each other's company, and climbing into bed with him that night felt like a natural rounding-off of a relaxed and contented day. Any tension-causing sensitivities over aging bodies had been dealt with in Newport. The sex simply felt like the warm glow of a good-vintage nightcap, and after swimming and biking over rough ground, my legs felt as

311

heavy as oak logs. I slept deeply.

Next day we did more of the same. Idling at *Great Maples*, visiting the Parrish Art Museum for an exhibition of Alice Aycock drawings. I enjoyed a Fairfield Porter, a portrait of his wife, and two richly layered paintings by William Merritt Chase.

'When are Daisy and Simon turning up?' I asked next day at breakfast, which we were having out on the deck — Warren at last persuaded to forsake the dining-room table.

'She said between twelve and one. She's going to call Jackson and he'll pick them up from the Jitney stop.' Warren stared at me, looking embarrassed, nervous of revealing his feelings. The mood was changing, our peaceful time together almost done. 'Daisy's not very forthcoming about Simon, is she?' he said. 'What does the guy do exactly?'

'Lives off his wife's earnings, helps a bit with her accessories business. Daisy says he talks about doing deals the whole time, hoping for a cut in whatever, I suppose. Bet he tries it on with you. Any wheeze to get a sniff of your money — he's bound to know a small family beer business that's just ripe to be taken over.'

'I might be tempted to string him along.'

'But you don't want to encourage him too much. He'd be constantly yapping at your ankles, sticking around.'

'God, I don't want that!'

'He'll probably show himself up for the ill-informed twit that he sounds,' I said, wondering how Daisy would manage to handle

312

Warren's jealous tension.

Being civil to Simon was going to be hard for him, and I couldn't help finding this hurtful. In an earlier life I'd have suffered paroxysms of possessive pain. However, I was more in control now and accepted that Warren had separate, different feelings for me. Yet I, too, was going to have to cope with the tension.

We'd spent the night before curled up in bed, watching an old Woody Allen film, and in the morning Warren had left me to sleep in, thoughtfully, yet probably needing adjustment time himself. He was smiling now, over fresh-baked croissants and coffee, watching me attentively, and clearly anxious to keep me sweet. I felt like telling him not to bother. Warren wasn't a natural actor like Joe, whose reinventing skills had taken him far; Joe could have played the double-handed role to perfection, yet he'd never even tried. He simply hadn't cared enough to do so. I lifted a Sunday newspaper to hide a sigh.

'It's hard to believe this weather,' I said, lowering the paper. 'We've had such a run of sunny, sultry days and soft nights. It's heaven!'

'Just as you are,' Warren said, looking sheepish when I made a face.

'Not your best effort,' I said, grinning. 'As corny as they come!'

He kissed me and we moved, plus the Sunday papers, to basket chairs with footrests and settled in for an hour. I heard the faint crunch of tyres on gravel. We were dressed to go, looking the Beach Club part. I was in white cut-offs and an

313

iris-blue shirt, Warren in coral Bermudas and well-aged loafers. He hadn't heard the car, obviously a little deafer than he'd care to admit, and started at the sound of the front door and Daisy's call of hello. He rose swiftly and awkwardly from the basket chair, giving me another quick kiss on the way. 'No more perfect peace,' he murmured and I really thought he meant it.

Watching him size up Simon was an education. Simon looked just wrong in khaki shorts, a blue office shirt with the sleeves rolled-up and trainers. Warren's lip curled in a superior way as introductions were made and enquiries after the journey. Simon certainly didn't cut a prepossessing figure, but the poor guy couldn't have brought much with him for a three-day city weekend; clothes were the least of it.

Coming out onto the deck he stood squatly and his darting eyes held a gleam of avarice as he took in the sheer scale of the real estate, the excessive luxury. With his bullet-shaped head, thick neck, hefty chest and biceps, he looked quite alluringly thuggish. Warren was too stolidly male to have sensed the brute force of Simon's sex appeal. I could feel it, but my dislike was a strong filter, funnelling off the fumes of sexuality like an extractor fan. Daisy could only drink them in and suffer.

'Who's for a vodka gimlet?' Warren enquired, stiffly polite, as Martha brought out a tray of tall green glasses, chinking with ice, filled to the brim and topped with lime and a slice of

314

cucumber. They looked enticingly cool and innocuous.

'Sounds just the job,' Simon said, taking one since she'd rested the tray on a table right beside him. 'Looks and tastes it, too.'

'Susannah? Daisy? Will you have one?' Warren said frigidly, handing us each a glass while casting a black-mark eye at Simon to register open disapproval of his manners.

'Don't you think we should go soon,' I said brightly, 'or we'll never get a table.'

'I've seen to that,' Warren smiled. 'I pulled rank. They're keeping one for us.'

'That's so clever of you,' Daisy enthused. 'I'll just go and grab a bathing suit then, and freshen up a bit. I'll leave you in good hands, Simon. Be quick as I can.'

He'd had a second gimlet before we left, downing it in three gulps.

We drove to the Club. Warren being the polite host sat in front with Jackson, swivelled round permanently, checking on bodily proximity — Simon's chunky thighs and hairy forearms pressed against Daisy's lithe tanned limbs — but with looks of such anguish on his face that I wondered if he'd put his neck out in the process.

'Daisy's filled me in on the Beach Club,' Simon remarked, 'and the South-Sider cocktails.'

'They're worth trying, first on the list,' I said. 'We're here now — just listen to that great ocean roar. Walking in and seeing the breakers is quite something.'

Lunch had its moments. Simon clearly hadn't expected a help-yourself canteen; it showed in his expression like someone anticipating fine claret and being offered a glass of plonk. But he was mellowed by South-Siders that 'did slip down', as he'd said on his third, and gamely piled his plate with lobster, shrimp and beef. Back at the table, nodding vigorously to Warren's suggestion of a bottle of Sauvignon Blanc, he looked ready for the conversational fray.

'You came over on business, Simon?' I said, trying to coat him in a little modesty.

'Your wife has accessories shops, doesn't she?' Warren put in, taking his chance of a well-aimed bitch.

'I have my own consultancy too,' Simon said, hardly hearing the jibe, 'helping people make connections, acquire new companies, that sort of thing. In fact, trundling out here today on that smart bus I thought of a small family beer business in Northumberland, one that's struggling, but basically sound — just in case it's of interest.'

He smiled at his host while I tweaked at Warren's calf with my toe and strove to keep a straight face.

'Oh yes?' Warren gazed at him blandly. 'I have a European division, of course. You can look us up online for a contact.'

Simon was unperturbed. 'Will do,' he said, slapping his hairy thigh, which caused Daisy to cast her eyes down. He went off to the gents', stopping to engage with a leggy young mum, who seemed to size him up and like what she saw. Daisy, with her well-tuned antennae, looked up at just the moment to clock what was going

316

on, the young mum pointing out her table, inviting Simon over. Daisy watched in deep distress. In the bright sunlight she looked tired and I saw small finger bruises on her arms. She was being pulled in two directions, torn and confused, and I felt for her.

None of us was relaxed, unsurprisingly. I minded Warren's inability to hide his feelings, and Daisy's efforts not to catch his eye were counter-productive. I knew she wanted to. Simon, however, was immune to the Warren-Daisy dynamics. Such was his sexual self-confidence he couldn't imagine her shacking up with an aged tycoon, that was clear, yet he had his own small area of tension; he was a married man, as Warren had pointed out with satisfaction, and had to rely on the anonymity of distance.

Warren was a catch, a honeypot for Southampton's queen-belle singles; they sought him out and stayed. Our table grew. Simon flirted drunkenly and told blatantly tall tales.

Taking advantage of a moment's pause in the chat I touched Daisy's arm. 'Come for a little stroll? I need a breather.' She gave me a pleading look as if to say how could I expect her to risk leaving her men to their own devices, but I was the boss and she rose and came with me.

We wandered down the wide, windswept beach, both of us silenced by the force of the breakers thundering to the shore. We walked on past the occasional vast clapboard properties fronting onto the ocean, weatherbeaten to silver grey; faded grasses beyond peeling-paint picket fences adding to the air of majestic desolation. It

317

was a place to think and be alone.

I shook myself free of a longing for solitude and smiled at Daisy. She could hardly meet my eyes. 'I'm probably prying too much, but how's it been, seeing Simon again?'

'It's difficult. Before coming here, Simon was my world. I was nothing; I made time for him, dressed for him, cooked for him and blanked out the non-Simon hours, which was ninety-eight per cent of the week. I was terrified of not lasting out here, losing him or letting you down.'

'But you've lasted.'

'More than that! I was even quite worried that this time of seeing Simon I'd find it hard being with him for three whole days.'

'It hasn't been like that, though, has it? You haven't been able to break it off and send him packing.'

'He's so dominating, Susannah! I do what he asks; I can't help it. The pull is there and despite what my head tells me I just can't cut loose, can't quite bring myself to stand up to him and say no.'

'You're in a better place now, though,' I said. 'You've seen beyond. There'll be others.'

Daisy laughed, surprisingly. 'I need them,' she grinned. 'The more the merrier — a large cast, I think, so that Simon has to take his place in the queue.'

We turned back for the clubhouse, both laughing. I knew why we got on: she was fun to be with, had energy and creative ideas and, aside from her weakness over Simon, she had a gutsy streak.

We calmed down and walked slowly onwards, wrapped in our private worlds. In my head I could hear distant bells; Daisy had set them off. I remembered the slow separation from Joe, my wild search for solace, morals suspended, safety in numbers, experimenting, plunging in — into another marriage as well. Daisy had time on her side, time to make the right decisions. I wanted that for her. I hoped she would sort herself out sooner and more painlessly than I had ever managed.

19

October 1962

Bella was six weeks old and I was back at work. I'd found a nanny for her, after much searching of agencies and soul. I'd been house-hunting as well, and agreed a price of £6,500 on a three-bedroom late-Victorian cottage off Parson's Green — Fulham, but it felt like Chelsea — with a pocket-handkerchief garden and plenty of turn-of-century charm. It was short on floorspace and the front door opened onto the pavement, but it was freehold; and thanks to my saviour at United Friendly, my mortgage was going through.

I had a three-week trip to New York coming up. The flight was booked and I hoped to sign the contract on the house before leaving, the completion taking place on my return, all being well. I should have been high on a sense of achievement, but instead felt wobbly and insecure, like stepping on bracken over a bog. It was a filthy night, rain slap-slapping against the windowpanes of our Kensington flat. I'd had a long day, working for *Woman* magazine, and the thought of leaving Bella for three weeks was a painful wrench and covering me in guilt.

It was time for bed. Joe couldn't still be on the film set, surely, at eleven at night? There was no point in waiting up for him. I felt so out of tune with Joe. As with a violin, so much depended on the hand holding the bow, and we seemed doomed not to make music. I tried to understand. It was a bad time for him, after all. He was in a bitter sulk — about the move, my bid for a little bit of independence, and also deeply frustrated by his first venture into filming, which was over-running and threatening to cut into his time in New York.

But not into mine. I tried not to allow my sense of freedom and release to take flight. To have the city to myself for ten days, staying with the Ferrones, of whom I'd grown really fond, seeing Gil . . . I shivered internally, fighting an attack of nerves. Gil was a huge heavy decision waiting to be taken; somehow I had to find the will and guts to end the relationship. It seemed impossible, knowing in my heart that determination only took me so far. I had to sort out my life, though — and do it soon, before events, exposure or some other cruel comeuppance took over.

I carried my coffee cup through to the kitchen, hoping Frankie's squawks wouldn't wake Bella, feeling multiple agonies, even worrying whether Gil would still book me. That was an irrelevant, petty thought, I reproached myself. I had a marriage to mend — or end. Or did I go on muddling through?

I sighed and turned off lights, leaving one on in the hall for Joe, and called good night softly to Nanny Hadley. She was shuffling about in the little back room that she shared with Bella. We were slowly finding our feet, but I wasn't allowed much of a look-in with my baby daughter. When Bella toddled up a stage, I decided, it might be time to think again. Miss Hadley, as she wanted to be called, was fearsomely prim and snobbish. Matronly with tightly permed hair of an indeterminate colour, trained in the old school, set in her ways, yet she loved Bella like her own already and I felt safely able to leave her in charge.

She resented me slightly — all her mothers, probably; we were an encumbrance, amateurs in the baby business while she, Miss Hadley, was the professional. I was also too middle-class. She'd have felt her standards were slipping but for Joe. He was the apple of her eye. He'd picked up the speech and mannerisms of his upper-crust friends and fitted her image of a proper gent perfectly. She couldn't resist the thickly spread butter of his charm. Joe must have been about the only man ever to make Miss Hadley blush.

I sensed her disapproval of my trip — 'gadding off', she'd call it — but the counterbalance was having Bella to herself for three weeks and, as I'd reminded her, Joe would be on hand for part of the time. He was hopeless at looking after himself, I said with practical guile. If she could just see her way to mollycoddling him a little . . . Miss Hadley had inclined her head with a sort of arms-akimbo look of satisfaction.

By morning, the drumming rain had magically given way to a clear bright day, calm and mild. I dressed in a suede-fabric top and charcoal skirt feeling more cheered, grabbed a fast bit of toast and gave Bella her bottle with Miss Hadley keeping a critical eye.

I was working for another weekly, *Woman's Realm*, and had to run, but I looked in on Joe just to see all was well. He'd been in a leaden sleep earlier, when I slipped out of bed, his stillness and pallor causing a moment's panic, but it was only from an excess of booze, I felt sure.

He was sitting on the side of the bed, trying to come to. 'Heavy night?' I smiled.

'Don't ask.' Joe sounded friendlier at least, in a better place. He yawned. 'I was at a party with a few film wallahs and they were all on about the Bond film, *Dr No*. It's being premièred at the Palladium on Friday. I really want to see it over the weekend. No one wanted to make it, apparently, and I can't think why; bet it breaks records and proves the doom-merchants wrong.' He was hooked on James Bond — the books were up there, along with Sinatra — yet I suspected something more than *Dr No* was lifting Joe's spirits.

'Great idea, be a thrill to see it.' I was keen to sound positive and hang onto the mood, I lived in hope of turning corners. 'If we can get in, that is.'

Joe never considered such practicalities and didn't now. He chatted on about Bond. 'Ian Fleming was at the first-night party for *Old Love*, remember, with his wife, Ann, and he was just like I imagine Bond to be. Handsome in a hard-edged kind of way, refined, big on the languid chat — but I'm not sure about this Sean Connery, playing the part. He's a Scot.'

'Hardly a disqualification, surely.' I looked at my watch; I'd be late.

'Sylvia Ormsby-Gore has been in touch,' Joe said neutrally, getting to the nub of it. 'She's firmed up on the Washington invite, third weekend of October.'

'But you're filming till the twentieth. Couldn't it be the one after?'

'That's the only weekend on offer, which is a stinky bugger. I'll move hell to get out of the last day's filming, but may have to fly direct to Washington.'

'So I'd go alone from New York?'

'You don't have to come,' Joe said, too quickly. 'It's not really your thing, old wifey, diplomats and stuffy dinners, all the political chat.'

He wanted to play it solo and he was putting me down. I fumed inside. 'Of course it's my thing, I really got on with them — *and* with JFK.' I glared at Joe. 'I can easily book out Friday afternoon and get the shuttle.' I looked at my watch again and back at Joe, struck by a thought. 'Shouldn't you be at the studios, love, like about two hours ago?'

'I'm going to phone — go in later. I'm sick as a dog, my tongue feels like an old Brillo pad. I'm sick of this whole farting film business too, all the boring hanging loose. I can sort the tickets for *Dr No*,' he added. 'I'll go in person and try for Saturday night.'

'I'm sure you'll have the ticket girl eating out of your palm,' I said, wishing it didn't take an invitation to the British Embassy Residence in Washington for Joe even to talk to me.

I left for New York the following Tuesday, missing Bella painfully before I'd even arrived. Was it madness to be going? I had bookings to honour, though, bills to pay; it wasn't only for need of Gil and a breather from Joe. He'd certainly perked up. The *Dr No* film had really hit the spot. Joe had drooled over Ursula Andress rising out of the sea like a Botticelli Venus, and he was full of The Beatles, too, whose first disc, 'Love Me Do', was selling fast and causing a stir.

'I heard them live, wifey, remember? A year ago at the Blue Gardenia in Soho. I told you about that guy in the music business, who'd said they were hot. He knew his stuff.'

'You sound like you think they could be up there with Sinatra.'

Joe snorted. 'That's so typically asinine of you. They're a group; Sinatra's a voice, incomparable, irreplaceable. The way he finds the peak of a song like it's a woman he loves . . . Nelson Riddle said when I interviewed him that music was sex, finding the rhythm of the heartbeat, and he'd done his finest work, arranging for Frank; they knew what they were *doing* with a song. The Beatles are very sexy, new and now, but four talents, way different. They've got the tempo though, the rhythm of the heartbeat.'

Joe on a high the last few days had been infectious in his enthusiasm. Could Alicia be a little less central to his life? Or was it just Washington, lifting his mood, the lure of the

325

velvet coat-tails of power? I thought of the missing weeks when I was pregnant, my suspicion that he'd been in a house party with Jackie Kennedy. I didn't really imagine an involvement, but sensed they'd found a rapport. Still, we were staying at the Embassy, not the White House, and I could hardly see the President and First Lady popping in for tea.

★ ★ ★

The Ferrones were as welcoming as ever. 'Gee, aren't you blooming on motherhood!' Joan gave me a big fond hug. 'I hope you've brought a bunch of photographs. How was the flight? Are you done in?'

'Let the poor girl get a word in edgeways, dear,' Walter said, coming forward to give me a kiss on both cheeks.

I said how terrific it was to see them, how incredibly kind they were, but Joan was off again. 'We've a couple of friends calling by, but you crash on out just whenever. You must be whacked. And I guess Eileen has you working right off, first thing?'

'She's given me a real lie-in, an eleven o'clock start!'

I changed and unpacked my very small thank-you gifts — Bendicks mints, Gentleman's Relish, Fortnum's teas, a couple of handcrafted pewter tankards and a paisley silk shirt that I thought might suit Joan.

I gave them to her in the wide hall and she was in raptures over the shirt when the doorbell rang.

The maid, Mary-Lou, hurried out, but Joan rested the gifts on a chair and sprang to answer it. I'd expected fur-clad elderly friends of the Ferrones, not the two interesting-looking men at the door. 'Pierre!' Joan exclaimed. 'Come in, come have a drink — how are you? Mad busy, holding the line as usual? And it's Matt, isn't it?'

'Yes, Mrs Ferrone, Matt Seeley.'

'I'll go find Walter,' Joan said busily, as the maid took their briefcases and the coats over their arms, 'but first you must meet my dear sweet English friend, Susannah Forbes, who's just off a plane from London, though you'd never think it. She has assignments with Eileen Ford, is in hot demand. This is Pierre Salinger, Susannah, the President's Press Secretary. There's nobody more important than Pierre. He keeps all the balls in the air.'

'Quite the opposite,' Pierre grinned. He had an attractively masculine, hands-on sort of look, and a stocky, sturdy build. His face was stocky too, with a broad forehead and forthright jaw, and he had thick eyebrows, black hair slicked straight and neatly parted.

'And I'm Matt Seeley, Pierre's assistant,' the younger man said, stepping forward to shake my hand, which he hung onto for quite a while.

Walter came out into the hall, remonstrating with us for standing there. 'I've made martinis, nicely shaken,' he said. 'But there's anything, just name your choice.'

We followed him into the sitting room with its glorious Impressionist paintings, and it was martinis all round, except that I asked for

Campari and soda. We stood chatting. Matt asked me how long I was over for. His eyes were whisky-coloured and seemed to catch the light.

'Sit, sit!' Joan implored us all, as though we were her puppies.

'So, Pierre,' Walter said, easing his ample body into a chair facing his guest, 'Jackie has a new task for me, I gather?'

'Yes.' He looked a little sheepish. 'I believe you've seen another still life by William Chase, one to pair with his vegetable painting in the White House family dining room. Jackie's very excited to acquire it and wondered if you'd be able to find a donor — the Annenbergs or Henry Ford possibly, who've donated before, or that lady from Chicago.'

'People prefer their donated items to hang in the State Rooms, but I'm sure we can sort something out.' Walter beamed. 'As long as it's still available.'

Pierre turned to me. 'No English donors around, I suppose?' he enquired wryly.

'Sorry, they're in short supply and badly needed for our crumbling old stately homes.'

'Oh, those beautiful buildings of yours,' Joan sighed. 'Now I know you boys said no to food, but it's all ready. Don't hurry away, stay for a quick bite.'

'We have to meet a couple of journalists, I'm afraid.' Pierre looked politely rueful.

'But not till ten,' Matt countered, 'and in a bar. It would be very welcome . . . '

'I can see I'm being overruled.' Pierre smiled, conceding the fact, yet slipping his junior a covertly raised-eyebrow look as if to say, 'I'll indulge you this once.'

Over a supper of shrimps and salmon, while Pierre and Walter discussed Jackie's keenness to acquire more paintings and Joan hung on their words, I talked to Matt.

He was a Bostonian, I discovered, and as well as his passion for politics had a love of the South of France. He urged me to visit Washington. 'I'm there in ten days,' I said, 'staying with the Ormsby-Gores.' They'd insisted I still come, despite Joe, to his fury, being unable to arrive till Sunday afternoon. He'd told me in triumph as I left, though, that Sylvia Ormsby-Gore had pressed him to stay on a couple of days, since there was a dance at the White House on Tuesday for the Maharajah and Maharanee of Jaipur. I felt very cheesed off, but with bookings all week I had to be back in New York.

'That's terrific news!' Matt exclaimed, 'I'll have to talk to the Embassy and try to wangle an invitation. What shuttle are you looking to get? You need to be in good time to avoid being shoved onto the next one, as it's murder on a Friday evening. It's a mixed blessing, the no booking policy.'

'Thanks, that's timely advice. I was hoping to get the five o'clock.'

'I'm in and out of New York. I might even be on that flight myself.'

Mary-Lou brought the dessert, sliced strawberries in Cointreau, while Pierre cast a glance at his watch. 'Time's up, Matt, we should push on.' He sounded brisk and business like while Matt seemed to take that as first bell. He carried on talking, extolling the medieval charms of Saint Paul de Vence and its views, before stopping mid-flow, distracted, listening keenly to a question Walter was asking Pierre.

'That report in today's *Times*, about the Texan far right exploiting fears over Cold War setbacks and especially, hard as it is to believe, a Communist military build-up in Cuba. Is that really happening?'

'Rumour and speculation. We're playing it down.' Pierre held Walter's eye.

'Understood,' he said, but I sensed an undercurrent, something serious going on.

Pierre was on his feet now, anxious to make a move. Matt promised to do his best to make Friday's five o'clock shuttle and travel together. He fastened his gaze. 'I very much hope we can meet up in Washington.'

'Be nice,' I said neutrally, going with him into the hall while they said goodbye. He was tall, well built, with fine straight hair, sandy to mouse, and a scattering of freckles. I'd liked him, and the Washington trip, exciting enough, had gained a little extra frisson. He couldn't be under any illusions. I'd mentioned Joe more than once.

* * *

I had a quiet first weekend. Janet, my American model girlfriend, came round. I saw Eileen and Jerry Ford on Sunday and spoke to Miss Hadley that morning, as well as Joe. Bella was doing fine, skipping the 2 a.m. feed. I'd had four days in the city and had yet to see Gil. I was working with him on Monday, at two o'clock. Would I stay on afterwards? Should I? Could I really cut myself adrift as I was determined to do?

Gil was my immoral compass, setting me on a dubious course in his own unconventional way. He propped me up. I could battle on, navigate Joe, and I knew more about how the world worked now, which was badly, from Jack Kennedy to John Profumo — if you believed the rumours about him sharing a girl called Christine Keeler with a Russian defence attaché and risking national security. I could manage life's knocks, huddled under Gil's wing, but chicks had to learn to fly.

Monday morning was taken up with a stressful shoot for *Glamour* magazine. It was on location, outside Tiffany's on Fifth Avenue, and a crowd had gathered. I was shivering with cold, hyper-tense, and the booking overran, which left only time for a snatched bite or being early at Gil's studio. I couldn't think of food and was at the studio by twenty to two.

He was still photographing, his morning session running late as well. I crept to the dressing room anxious not to distract him, stupidly hurt when he didn't see me. I gradually understood why. The girl in front of the camera, a model called Lynn, was perched on a stool, legs crossed, one loosely dangling; Gil was arranging the dress. He whispered something, leaning in against her thigh. The intimacy was clear, though only to me. I knew his style of flirting in front of clients, ad executives, his way of relaxing models, yet this was different. He and Lynn were on a private wavelength, the way she was touching him with her swinging calf. Her eyes on him were hard to bear.

I turned from the dressing-room door with an aching wound where my guts used to be. What had I expected? Gil was only doing what he said he did. I'd known he wasn't languishing for months at a time, keeping himself pure. He'd been honest and open about that.

'You're looking sad.' I started and looked up. 'Come here, lover, give us a kiss.' Gil was at the dressing-room door; he was staring, compelling me to meet his eyes. Lynn pushed past him into the dressing room, saying with a playful nudge that he'd made her late. She eyed me briefly with mild hatred — the sort that was merely instinctive feline suspicion — threw on her clothes, a tight red sweater and navy skirt, and flung the dress she'd been wearing at Dee, Gil's secretary, who'd come in after her. Lynn pushed past Gil again then with a lot of body contact while Dee hung up the dress and hurried on out — to see to Lynn's release form, I assumed.

Gil hadn't moved from the doorway. 'I meant it about the kiss.' His eyes were on me, liquid, loving, caring, 'It does for me, seeing you,' he said, coming close and touching lips. 'Hits hard.' Dee was soon back with clothes for me and the session was underway.

'Seven o'clock at the Kettle of Fish,' Gil said, as we worked. 'Where we went before?'

'I'll meet you there.'

We had to see each other. The connection was

so strong. I had to explain. It wasn't Lynn and others before her or to come, though her leering eyes haunted me. I felt cold and alone, a ring of ice forming round my heart; it wasn't Lynn, it was my resolve, the wrench of a final parting. Gil was a secret loving sex-master, protection, survival, but a block on rational thought.

★   ★   ★

The Kettle of Fish, smoky and fuggy, wafting with weed, felt a good place to meet, a comfort-blanket cocoon and neutral ground. Gil was there ahead of me, up at the bar alongside a few layabouts with stringy beards. I slid onto the stool next to his. He was smoking a fat cigar. He put it in my mouth, told me to puff and I spluttered.

'Hello,' he said, in a way that hacked through the ice. I felt wobbly, glad to be sitting down, especially when he brushed lips. 'You're going to tell me we're in another place?'

'Yes, kind of.'

'You're mad at me? Sore about Lynn?'

'Jealous!'

'Don't be. She's pretty, pert, but hasn't got your delicacy — she's two-dimensional.'

'I need to be in the sort of place where I don't lean on you so much,' I said, pausing as he ordered me a Coke, realizing how hard it was to explain. 'I cling, Gil, I can't help it, and that's no good, in reality, for you or for me. I was going to say it anyway,' I added miserably. 'It's not to do with Lynn.'

He studied me. He held my jaw in his big hand, his thumb rubbing my lower lip, peeling it down, feeling the wetness inside. Oh God, don't make it so hard. I watched his watching eyes. Struggling.

'I have a solution,' Gil said, reaching for my hand. 'I'll tell it to you in a last lesson.'

'Subject? Area?' My insides were alive with butterflies.

'Casual sex.'

'That sounds vile — and the opposite of a solution.'

'It's not, it's the least worst way. Hear me out? Open mind? We have no painful bust-up, but no regular calls either, no clinging. We just hook up once in a while, see? Like, suppose I come to London — because I have needs too, as it happens — and say you hadn't found the man of your life, The One, we just get it together casually. Happy memories. Refresher course. Same if you were here. I'd book you anyway, for sure.'

'But that's not much different, no solution. It doesn't square with my resolve.'

'It squares fine, if you're being fair-minded. Think of it from my side: you're not leaning on me, I'm leaning on you.'

'Got an answer for everything, haven't you?'

We went back to the studio and made love feverishly. I felt sustained, whole again, and awash with an unbelievable sense of release. We'd have no more comings together this time, I knew that. It was a non-farewell, a tapering off — an un-final goodbye. 'One last coda to this

334

lesson,' Gil said, as I dressed to go, heavy-hearted. 'I want you to make it with other men. It'll help me fit into your life. And don't worry, you'll know when you find the one you want to stick with. Just don't find the creep too soon! It'll give me a kinda backhanded high too, thinking how well you'd learned at my knee.'

'What kind of teaching is that? There'll be no blow-by-blow reports, I can assure you.'

*   *   *

Joan was immensely excited about my weekend in Washington. She monitored my clothes, insisted on loaning me accessories. 'There's a dinner on Saturday night,' I said, 'twenty-two on the guest list. Another lot coming for Sunday lunch . . . '

'You need a glamorous cocktail gown for the dinner, a 'smart day' outfit for Sunday, and two other pretty outfits. You never know in Washington — things crop up.'

Joe was due to arrive around five on Sunday. He was staying on, though, of course. He'd had his way, after all — solo in Washington, hobnobbing with the Kennedys.

At La Guardia airport I paid off the yellow cab, marvelling at the driver's multitude of gold-filled teeth, and humped my bag to join the shuttle check-in queue. Progress was slow and I rested my suitcase between shuffles forward.

Bending to pick it up again, I felt a hand on mine. 'I have it,' Matt said, coming up beside me, panting. He caught his breath and grinned.

'Whew, I'd have hated to miss this flight! I'd even told your Embassy that I'd drop you off, save them sending a car.'

'Goodness, that's surely beyond the call of duty? You must want to get home.'

'It'll be a real pleasure and I'll sit with you too, if that's all right?' He turned then, to make a winsome apology to the middle-aged business-man behind me. 'Really sorry, nipping in like this. I hope you can understand why!'

'Sure, be my guest, buddy,' the man said, giving me an appraising look and a wink.

'Pity it's only an hour's flight,' Matt muttered, as we slowly edged up the queue.

On the plane I learned about his Harvard credentials and a spell on the *Washington Post*. 'But politics,' he said, 'is the red corpuscles for me, working for Pierre, being right at the hub.' He laid his hand on my arm. 'I did wangle an invitation to the Residence by the way, for Sunday lunch. Perhaps I can take you to a gallery afterwards? I'd really love to get to know you better,' he added more honestly.

Matt whipped me through the airport faff with practised speed; I'd have floundered on my own. 'Wait here, don't go away,' he said, 'I'll just bring up the car.'

It was a silver-blue, two-seater coupé, tapering at the rear and as low to the ground as a racing car. It was a wow. He looked enormously proud when I said so. 'It's a Chevrolet Corvette, the new Stingray — next year's model, but available now if you're in the know — and exactly one week old! Come for a spin?' I climbed in, feeling flighty and having fun.

He revved up, whizzing me round the sights of Washington in a speeding silver-blue flash. The Monument, Lincoln Memorial, the Capitol in the distance across the National Mall . . . 'The British Residence is on Massachusetts Avenue, which we call Embassy Row,' he said. 'It's an Edwin Lutyens building — the only one in the States, I believe.'

I loved the symmetry when we arrived, its redbrick Britishness and distinctively Lutyens tall chimneys. Matt rumbled in through a square arch, into a courtyard and up to the main steps. 'Masses of thanks,' I said genuinely, 'for that exhilarating spin, seeing the sights, all the looking after. I hardly know where to begin.'

'By not minding if I give you a parting kiss?' He leaned over the steering shaft and turned my face. 'It's hard not to, you're very beautiful.'

'I'm far from that — and a married woman,' I laughed, accepting a light press of his lips all the same, drawing back smartly as one of the staff came out for my luggage.

Matt escorted me into the main hall where Sylvia came to greet us with a vague smile. 'Here's Susannah, safely delivered,' Matt said, 'and thanks again, Lady Ormbsy-Gore. I greatly look forward to Sunday's lunch.'

The two eldest Ormsby-Gore children were in England; I now met the younger pair, Alice and Francis, who were in jeans with hair overflowing their hanging-out shirts. They had thin fine features and complete disinterest in a naff unknown visitor. Sylvia personally took me up to my room, which was comparatively small but charming, light with yellow and white fabrics, a bowl of roses and a dish of fruit. 'I like this room,' she said. 'The main guest rooms are so dull. I put Hugh Gaitskell in here recently and he called it his favourite room of all the Residences he'd stayed in.'

Friday night and Saturday were free of formalities, although Embassy people and local diplomats joined us for meals. Debo, the Duchess of Devonshire, who was a close family friend of the Ormsby-Gores, was also staying and she drew me into conversations, making me feel completely at home. She told me about the grimy paintings she'd discovered in the basement at Chatsworth whose real worth had passed the death-duty assessors by. They'd served to save that great house from ruin.

Sylvia seemed to live within herself, dreamily, unconnectedly, yet she was an impeccable hostess and lover of the arts, understandably drawn to a seductive talent like Joe's. David Ormsby-Gore was naturally outgoing as well as appropriately diplomatic and ambassadorial. He was extremely sweet to me, walking me through the splendid halls with their slim, honey-grey marble pillars, gilded chandeliers and the statutory photograph of the Queen on a marble-top table. I felt able to be myself with him, enjoyably, while sensing at the same time that he was under pressure. I imagined some burdensome top-secret duties and thought of Walter's question to Pierre Salinger.

David excused himself early from lunch and

was nowhere to be seen till the dinner party. I'd taken myself off to the National Gallery of Art in the afternoon, fired up by Walter, and had stood for a long time in front of two paintings, a Leonardo da Vinci portrait, *Ginevra de' Benci*, and Vermeer's *Woman Holding a Balance*. They'd made me feel suspended, remote from the chaos of modern life, encased in their enduring beauty.

Twenty-two to dinner, we sat at a long table laid with gold-embossed plates and four sparkling glasses at each place setting. The flowers were softly arranged. I'd worn a fitted emerald-lace cocktail dress that Joan said suited my fair hair and I was aglow with adrenaline, pinching myself. David had told me over drinks that we were having supper at the White House the next night. Very informal, he said, just the Kennedys and us.

I was seated at dinner between an elderly Senator and the Secretary of the Interior, Stewart Udall, who was a delight. He had dark, tight-cropped hair, and an elongated face. Fervent about conservation, he was writing a book about the overuse of natural resources and the dangers of pollution, and he spoke as well, with great enthusiasm, about his home state of Arizona. He also told me, rivetingly, about having just been on a tour of the Soviet Union and summoned unexpectedly to a meeting with Khrushchev. 'It was an eye-opener,' Secretary Udall said. 'Khrushchev was hardly God's gift to good manners. He seemed only to want to tell me of their intention to 'swat our ass'. I'd like to see them try!'

The Senator on my left was more uphill company, a crumbly old codger, slow of speech. He began most sentences with 'When I was a boy . . . ' and revealed some unpleasantly prejudiced views on civil rights. I was reminded of Ella Fitzgerald's neighbours in Beverly Hills.

★   ★   ★

Lunch next day was for twenty, much less formal, in a bright panelled room overlooking the garden. It was a balmy sunny day, very warm; I'd worn an apricot halter-neck dress, glad of Joan's weathervane advice, and loved the feel of bare arms. Matt was next to me, a shy Embassy diplomat on my other side whom I talked to during a first course of minty chilled cucumber soup. The audible chink of spoons on fine china was slightly embarrassing till the conversation got going.

Joe's plane wasn't due in till five, and I realised Matt must have known this, since he'd wanted to take me out in the afternoon. I felt childishly resentful about Joe arriving just in time to make the White House supper when he had Tuesday's glamorous formal dance to go to as well. And the thought, as I turned from the polite diplomat to talk to Matt, made me smile more warmly than was possibly wise.

For a Bostonian, Matt had an oddly Southern lilt to his voice and I asked about it.

'My mother was originally from Hot Springs, Arkansas — Al Capone territory. It's where he and his like used to hole up in Prohibition days.

340

It was a very open place.'

'What does that mean?' I asked, conscious of his eyes on my bare arms.

He transferred his gaze. 'They could buy off anyone. They made it what it is, though — the park, all the amenities, with their ill-gotten gains. You look very lovely,' he said. I batted that away and steered the conversation back to American history.

After an amazing hot chocolate soufflé, liquid in the middle, perfect — I couldn't resist a small helping — we had coffee outside on a terrace that presided over a fragrant rose-garden. I mingled a bit, but Matt sought me out. 'I told Lady Ormsby-Gore I was going to ask if you'd like to go to a gallery and she thought it a very good idea. You will come out for a bit?'

'It's terrifically kind, but I think I'd better not. I went to the National Gallery yesterday actually, and I'm sure you're busy, Pierre keeping you at it all hours.'

'He sure does, but it's Sunday! Come for another quick spin — Georgetown perhaps? You'll love it.' He was hard to refuse with his freckles and naughty-boyish grin.

His car was really quite something. And I loved seeing Georgetown's buzzy Main Street and the residential quarter as well, whose small gracious squares and tree-lined streets were home to the political elite.

'Kennedy left for his inauguration from his Georgetown town-house,' Matt said. 'He lived here both as congressman and senator, and Jackie gave parties for everyone who mattered.' I decided not to mention supper at the White House that night; it felt private, somehow. 'Come for a cup of English tea,' Matt smiled. 'My apartment's not far, it's a condo on Thirty-first, just round the corner.'

'I'd love to go to one of those fun cafés on Main Street.'

He looked openly dashed. 'Can't I entertain you at home? I promise to be good.'

'Then you won't mind if it's a café instead.' He had the grace to smile.

We went to a coffee shop and ice-cream parlour with white wrought-iron tables and potted palms. Matt ordered coffee and a black tea for me. 'It's what we call English tea here.' He grinned; his foot touched mine. 'Tell me about the photographers you work for. Don't they all try to get you to bed? You're out here on your own, after all.'

'No more than anyone else. I'm married and they're hard-working professionals.'

'But you're not with your husband much — you weren't in the summer either.'

'Where? What do you mean?' I stared at Matt, feeling knocked off-course. Trembling.

'In August — you weren't with him: you didn't go, too. Sorry, it's just that I'd seen the guest list, felt things must be a bit rocky. I've no business interfering. Forgive me.'

'Go where, though? What guest list?' I was sure Joe had been in Italy, having seen the television footage, but I still needed it spelled out and the salt rubbed in.

Matt looked quite shocked. 'Italy, the villa

— Jackie's holiday. Didn't you know?'

'Not exactly. I was having a baby. I'd rather not talk about it, if you don't mind.'

'Sure. Will you, though, even just think about letting me take you out in New York?'

I hardly heard him. My mind felt bruised. Gil was in it, Joe making it hurt sorely. Thinking back to all the heartache, not knowing where Joe was, the suspicions and now the confirmation — it had all been about dallying with Jackie.

Matt, fun, attractive, in the know, was offering solace — sex on a plate — and Gil wanted me to get over him with other men. But casual sex? Not Gil's best idea, not a good idea at all. I said to Matt, 'I'll think about it — and thanks, I've had a lovely time.'

'That's progress,' he said, 'of a sort.' He paid and slid his arm through mine as we left for his car. When we reached it he kissed me, leaning me back against the passenger door.

* * *

Joe's plane was late and he was in a flying panic; speed shaving, firing questions about the weekend he'd just missed, throwing on a clean shirt, rushing me. I'd changed into a black linen dress with a scooped white collar, 'smart day' to Joan, but not to me. I longed for Bella news but Joe was too mad keen to get on, splashing himself with some classy smell — Hermès, that he'd never have bought for himself. No good thinking like that, I hadn't got a moral leg to stand on. I'd kissed two men in a week.

343

We drove to the White House in the Ambassadorial car, David and Joe on the jump seats. The Ambassador's car helped smooth the security checks and we were soon in the building, via a side entrance. Jackie came to meet us, wearing a cyclamen-pink dress with cap sleeves, very neat and slim-looking. 'I don't suppose,' Joe said, easy and relaxed with her, 'you can whizz us wide-eyed Brits on a whistle-stop tour of the staterooms, just a very quick peek?' She smiled, looking pleased and proud.

We saw the East Room first, huge and formal. It had a vast grand piano whose eagle supports Franklin Roosevelt had designed himself. 'The portrait of George Washington is by Gilbert Stuart,' Jackie said, 'who called Washington a very apathetic sitter, but captured him most famously.' She showed us the Red Room, lined in red silk and with a powerfully atmospheric Civil War painting, followed by the Blue and Green Rooms. She pointed out the President Monroe candelabra — pairs of them in every room, he'd certainly been keen on candlelight — and a French Empire consul table, presented to the White House by Napoleon's brother Joseph, that had led to a whole Empire theme.

We went up to the second floor, the Kennedys' private living space, and had drinks in a softly lit sitting room with a comfy family feel. Debo Devonshire arrived, she'd been elsewhere that day; we were on a second drink, though, by the time Jack appeared. 'How's the 'heavy cold'?' Debo asked dryly. David whispered to me that Jack had used the excuse of a cold to cut short a

Midwest campaigning trip: he'd had to get back rather urgently. That sounded pretty important and Walter's question to Pierre Salinger clicked in again. I looked at Jack in a sombre dark suit, shuffling his hands; he had bags under his eyes that only added to his charismatic force.

I sat next to him at dinner. Debo was on his right, David on my left; Joe was between Jackie and Sylvia. The lighting was again subdued, only from candles on the table. A waiter served us with shrimps in a dark tomato-red sauce, deliciously sharp and peppery-hot. 'It's fresh horseradish that gives it that special tang,' David said.

Jack turned from Debo as the first course was being cleared and gave me his concentrated attention. 'Good to have you here, great. How's the modelling going? Eileen Ford knows what she's doing, getting you over, with those Nordic looks of yours.' He grinned, full on, full focus, and gave me no time to reply. I hoped I wasn't being as open-mouthed as a goldfish, but he knew how to turn it on. 'I'm interested in the techniques of fashion photography,' Jack said, 'British photographers are way ahead. I saw a spread on Celia Hammond, think it was in *Queen*, or it could have been *Vogue*, and it really pushed the boundaries.' A faint buzz sounded near the window, a transferred telephone-call tone. Jack was instantly on his feet. 'She a friend of yours, Celia Hammond?' he said, still talking as he went to take the call. 'She should come over, too.'

I'd turned and saw him make for a small curved telephone on a corner table. He spoke into the mouthpiece, very abrupt and staccato.

'Yes? Yep. Yep. Okay.' He kept listening, looking intently at the floor. Then he took the telephone behind the curtain where I presumed there was a window seat or place to stand.

'Eileen's a strict headmistress, I hear,' he said, returning after a couple of minutes and pulling in his chair. 'Keeps you under the rod. Early to bed — she doesn't like parties.'

'She tires us out by day,' I said with a grin. 'But American photographers are just as creative, I think. Penn especially. And Avedon certainly pushes boundaries.'

A dark-suited man slipped into the room and spoke to the President. David beside me stiffened, keenly interested; as Ambassador and friend he'd know what was going on.

The telephone buzzed again and Jack rose swiftly. I half-turned, couldn't help being inquisitive, and heard him say before disappearing behind the curtain, 'How big is it?' I felt a pinprick, a spine-tingle of fear as well as curiosity.

At the table we got on with our fried chicken. Joe was being amusing about his schoolmaster bit-part role in the film and Jack soon returned, picking up our conversation again with flirty eyes. 'Aren't you petrified of Diana Vreeland? I met her once and she scared the pants off me, with that mile-long cigarette-holder, blood-red lips and nails.' He was an avalanche of power-fuelled magnetism. I couldn't have escaped its path.

The telephone kept buzzing. Did this always go on at every meal? He was up and down, hardly managing a mouthful between calls, yet seemed able to switch from work to play like a flipped penny. I was in stupefied awe. 'They say Joe's mesmeric on stage,' Jack said, 'you must be very proud. Hey, Joe,' he called over. 'You know *Beyond the Fringe* opens on Broadway this week? It'll hit big. People lap up that sort of satire. It's like caricatures, they love the debunking of authority, especially politicians.'

'They're a class act,' Joe said, 'a bit slapstick, even surrealistic humour at times, but Peter Cook taking off the Prime Minister, that slurring voice, it's genius!'

Another telephone call, another interruption. Slices of squidgy chocolate cake were served. Back beside me once more, Jack stared down at the table. I tried to catch Joe's eye, but he was talking animatedly to Jackie, waving his fork, making her smile.

She'd just taken a mouthful of cake when Jack stood up abruptly and made for the door. A waiter hurriedly opened it for him. It seemed slightly odd and rude, though I recalled reading that Heads of State always leave a room first — perhaps it was simply that. The conversation was rather desultory in his absence; we picked at the gooey cake, Jackie's remained untouched. She soon rose and led the way to the sitting room.

Jack was there, on the telephone — giving orders about appointments the next day. He sat back afterwards, lighting a long cigar, baring his teeth on the first puff, almost as though disliking the taste or the pungent tobacco smell. I thought of Gil, drawing on his cigar and sticking it, still

347

wet from his mouth, into mine. I hurt inside. Would he really come to London to see me?

'Let's have some Sellers,' Jack said, his distinctive voice cutting into the low drone of murmured conversation. 'The *Songs for Swingin' Sellers* album. The 'Lord Badminton's Memoirs' track is a gas — and the *My Fair Lady* in Indian skit cracks me up.'

Jackie went to the turntable, put on the LP and we were soon in stitches. Was I really in the White House, watching JFK lounging about, hooting with laughter? He started recounting a Sellers' take-off of 'Uncle Harold' at a White House dinner, on the Prime Minister's last visit. 'I'm not so sure he found it funny,' Jack chuckled. Then he stood up, said, 'Good night, good night,' with a hand partly raised and strode out of the room.

★ ★ ★

At Washington National airport next morning, waiting to board the shuttle for New York, hordes of people were arriving or leaving, beginning the working week. Whether coming or going, they crowded round the news-stand. Every newspaper's front page bore the word *CRISIS*, big and bold in the headline. I bought the *New York Times*.

There was an atmosphere of crisis in Washington last night as President Kennedy and top Administration Officials were in almost constant conference. In the Caribbean, the Navy and Marine Corps were staging a powerful show of force not far from Cuba . . .

348

I read on. There was a mention of a missile. I thought of Jack saying, 'How big is it?' A Pentagon spokesman was quoted as denying that Cuba was the cause of the crisis. I couldn't take it all in. On the plane the constant rustle of newspapers sounded like a rattlesnake's warning. I sensed people all around me feeling disturbed and threatened.

In Manhattan, walking a few blocks to a studio, the air of tension was unmistakable. And returning to the Ferrones' apartment in the evening I found Walter as grim-faced as I'd ever seen him.

'Pierre Salinger made an announcement at noon today,' he said. 'The President's speaking on television shortly, addressing the nation on 'A subject of the highest national urgency'. It's scheduled for seven o'clock, half an hour's time.'

We didn't speculate. We three, Joan looking older than her years, sat rigid in our seats, waiting and watching the clock. Seven o'clock came. Jack was in his office, the furled Stars and Stripes flag behind him. His voice was calm; he looked out to camera as he found the rhythm and was into his speaking stride. ' . . . The closest surveillance of the Soviet military build-up on the island of Cuba . . . Evidence of offensive missile sites . . . a nuclear strike capability against the Western Hemisphere . . . ' He spoke of enforcing a blockade and said that aggressive conduct allowed to go unchallenged, ultimately led to war. Their goal was not the victory of might, but the vindication of right.

It was a shocking bombshell. I'd only very

briefly mentioned last night's dinner at the White House to Walter and Joan, and told them a little more, about sitting next to Jack and all the calls. I marvelled disbelievingly at his ability to be there at all, to have carried on with a casual supper with friends while taking monumental decisions; surely it would have gone by the board?

'Well, the poor man has to eat,' Joan said, which, on that frightening evening, on the brink of a possible nuclear war, had we three breaking out in laughter.

20

October 1962–May 1963

I woke from a bad dream shaking, feeling the sweat cold and damp on my face. It was about Bella, horrible, ghastly. She was a tiny swaddled bundle, tight-wrapped in a white cotton blanket — airy with holes, the sort the maternity wards used — and being hurled in the air by two men who had glittering eyes and stubbly chins. They were laughing, seeing how high and how far they could throw her, as though playing some heartless ballgame. I was running towards them along a path, screaming hysterically, '*Stop, stop!*' when one of them hurled her so high that she spiralled off over a beautiful silver sea — higher, higher. The pitiful screams of a very small baby were piercing, slicing my heart until they faded to silence and she became the faintest tiny pinprick in the sky.

My pulse calmed. It was only a dream, but I still had an irrational urge to call home, a need to set my mind at rest. With the five-hour time difference it would be lunchtime and Miss Hadley should be home, not gossiping with other nannies in the park.

She sounded guarded, which didn't help my nerves. 'I was in need of a little update,' I said cheerily, 'missing Bella madly. Is she sleeping okay? Are you having better nights?'

'Not so bad, and she's a little angel by day, but I don't like all this they're saying on the wireless, Mrs Bryant, about Cuba and nuclear missiles. My *Daily Express* says the Russians are sending warships, too, with more missiles. And it says — I'm just finding the place . . . *President Kennedy is setting up a blockade with forty warships and twenty thousand marines.* It's a terrible thing. I don't want them starting World War Three.'

Nor did anyone else, I thought. 'We just have to hope and pray, Miss Hadley, that it's all peacefully resolved.'

'The *Express* talks as well about Whitehall being taken by surprise. That's very rude of Mr Kennedy, isn't it, not telling the Prime Minister? I don't approve of that.'

'I'm sure they'll have been in touch.' I smiled at the idea of Miss Hadley as cheerleader for the Prime Minister. 'And the UN is meeting, the wheels are turning. Tell me more about Bella,' I pressed. 'And how you're coping with Frankie. Is he keeping quiet when you need to get her to sleep?'

'I put him in the hall, under his blackout blanket. He's very perverse, throwing birdseed husks out onto the carpet and saying a naughty word. Mr Bryant says that's just letting off steam! Mr Bryant takes him out of the cage a lot; I keep finding little messes . . . '

'I'm sorry about that. But Bella . . . Is she smiling much?'

'Oh yes, lovely smiles — and the way she wraps those tiny fingers of hers round mine!'

'I'm longing to see her. I'm so grateful for

everything, Miss Hadley. Must rush or I'll be late at work. Give her lots of kisses and I'll call again soon.'

I had some toast, packed my tote bag and set off for work feeling doubly tense; my first booking of the day was with Gil, a moody advertisement for a pearl jewellery company.

It went well. He made the work easy and we did good pictures, but in the studio as with everywhere else, a sense of crisis ruled. Gil played Beethoven not pop, and there was little joking around. He still managed to ask on the quiet, 'Any news on the man front?'

'Give us a break! I'm being chased by one, though; I'm on the case.'

In the streets the city went about its working day, drivers leaned on their horns as usual, but there was a palpable feeling of hiatus. Life as we knew it was on hold.

Joe telephoned from Washington. The dance had been cancelled in the circumstances, but a small dinner party was being given for the Jaipurs in its place, so he was still going to the White House. He was staying on till the weekend, he said, seeing a friend, and might try to write an article. Was the friend Jackie? He hadn't asked after me or said anything friendly like wishing I were there. I worried about him in Washington at such a time, while feeling fearful, neglected and jealous.

I'd only just put the phone down when Matt Seeley called. 'Are you all right?' he asked, sounding genuinely concerned.

'I'm fine, but how about you and Pierre with

the world's press on your back?'

'There is that! The decisions on how much to say are so tricky. We can quote Adlai Stevenson at the UN today; he's challenged Zorin, the Soviet Ambassador, about the missiles in Cuba and said he'll 'wait till hell freezes over' for an answer on the Soviet's real intentions. And John Steinbeck's just won the Nobel Prize in Literature; an American winner helps! I can, um, get to the city tomorrow. I'll only have a snatched hour, if that, but can we have dinner? Please say yes.'

'Possibly,' I said, feeling friendly. Did he know Joe was in Washington? 'I should check with the Ferrones first, though. They may have plans.'

'I'll call again, but you must. It could be my only chance to see you. I mean, it's hard to know what's going to happen . . . ' And he knew more than most. My pulse raced.

I decided to involve Joan in whether or not to see Matt. She was no fool, probably sensed things were dodgy with Joe and I didn't want any more secrets. Gil was enough.

'That young man certainly took a shine to you,' she laughed. 'Doggy eyes from the start! I'd go — be nice for you to get out. If Matt actually makes it here, that is; they're in the thick of it, he and Pierre, in Washington. It's dreadful to think of the immense strain they must all be under.'

★ ★ ★

Matt made it. He stared at me in a flattering way, squeezed my arm and suggested we walked.

'I've booked at Le Veau d'Or, on Sixty-first Street,' he said. 'It's just a few blocks.' He kissed me in the elevator, awkwardly and too desperately. I wasn't responsive. 'Don't be cross,' he pleaded. 'It was impossible not to kiss you, seeing you again when I've thought of nothing else.'

'That's a bit hard to believe at a time like this,' I smiled and we set off at a pace.

The restaurant was very French, small and intimate; square tables with white tablecloths as well as red-plush banquette booths. Good cooking smells pervaded with a sort of typical Gallic confidence. 'It's very swish,' I said, as we were shown to one of the booths.

'It's far from that. I worried you'd prefer somewhere more in. And it's a bit empty tonight,' he said, looking round. 'People are glued to their televisions, I expect.'

We ordered celery remoulade and veal escalopes. Matt chose a bottle of red wine that came quickly, as did some crusty French bread. He was beside me on the banquette and seemed to take shortage of time as an excuse for bodily contact, edging near enough to have touching thighs and pressing his calf against mine.

He gave me a look that was half-soulful, half-swaggerish. 'You can't only have ten days left in the city. It's a disaster. How soon can you come back?'

'Not soon. I'm booked up at home and want time with my baby. I'll possibly come in the autumn of next year, even bring her too and stay longer.'

'Next fall? You're not serious! Look,' he

touched my cheek, 'I have a plan. I want you to come to the South of France and meet there — just a little break, a long weekend?'

'I'm married, Matt! It's good of you to take me out while Joe's in Washington . . . '

'Why is he? What's he doing there? Doesn't he want to be with you at this time?'

That got to me. 'He's writing an article,' I muttered.

'I want to be with you very much,' Matt said. 'Is that such a terrible thing?' He hesitated, then couldn't resist adding, 'In the circumstances.'

He held out those three words, the circumstances of Joe, like dangling keys on a ring, offering them as a way in, a pardon, a weaselly excuse to jump into bed with him.

'It is fairly terrible,' I said, softening it, probably too much with my hand on his arm.

We got on with our food, Matt with his body pressed to my side; he murmured lavish compliments. His physical need of me was glaring, quite oppressively so. I was attracted, but with nowhere near the urgent intensity and sense of connection I'd felt with Gil. Casual sex? Would I get too close to Matt if I slept with him? Or would he with me? I thought he was more into making conquests than love matches, but he could prove me wrong.

'I stay at a friend's apartment when I'm here,' he said, as if reading my next thought before it was fully formed. 'He's a fun guy, you must meet him.' Matt picked up my hand, stroking each finger, squeezing them and holding on tight. 'God, it's hell being so up against it tonight. I've got local radio, a press conference . . . ' He called to an elderly waiter for the check then tilted and turned my face to him. 'You will let me see you again? I'd do anything for the chance.'

'Not many of those, I'm afraid. I'd love to see Washington again, and the Ormsby-Gores have said any time, but that's a long way down the line. Joe will be here next week, why not come and have a drink with us if you are, too — come and say hello.'

The waiter was hovering and Matt dealt with the check. 'And the South of France?' he said, lifting his eyes. 'I have a place to stay, you see. A rich old lady in Boston who's my fan has a villa there — well, more of a roadside cottage. It's up in the hills near Saint Paul de Vence. She only goes there for six weeks in the summer and I can use it at other times. I did once, covering the Cannes Film Festival. It's heaven.'

I'd never been to the South of France, but didn't volunteer that. Matt was waiting for a reaction. 'Who knows?' I said. 'Maybe our paths will cross — here, London, even Cannes! We're about to move house, back home, but you could reach us through the Ferrones.'

The waiter brought our coats. Matt helped me into mine, my white Mongolian-lamb-lined leather coat, and we left the restaurant.

It was cold out and he hugged me close. Crossing Lexington Avenue, the wind lashed and whipped itself into a whirlpool round us and I was glad of his protective arm and the snug coat, though it reminded me of Gil. We walked a block and turned down a dark, more sheltered side street, where Matt slowed to a stop in the shadows. He was more cautious about kissing me this time, but I let him and there was no caution about his searching tongue. My coat had easy fastenings, he found his way in, and I could feel every craving contour of his body against mine. I let the sensation flow into me, his hungry passion; it was gratifying and brought desires of my own. He'd have got me into bed probably, but for the constraints of time. I was well aware, though, that they weren't self-imposed. Gil was a bad influence.

I broke away and kept charge of Matt's hands. 'You have to go. I do, too.'

'That's cruel, very heartless, but true,' he conceded, and we hurried on. He held onto my shoulders at the apartment door, staring into my eyes. 'I will come by next week. I'll make it somehow. I have to see you, even if it means a last resort of being civil to Joe.'

Walter and Joan heard the door and came out to the hall like anxious parents. Joan asked if I'd had a fun time, while Walter wanted to know if Matt had had any more news.

I grimaced. 'It's worse, if anything, as far as I can gather. No let-up yet. Matt said the White House is releasing an intelligence report tomorrow, about the missile bases nearing completion, close to full operational capability already.'

Walter looked grave; even his jowls were stilled. 'Oh dear, I'd felt more hopeful today with U Thant at the UN doing his best. Dear, dear, what a world we live in.'

My mind was on Bella. Calling Miss Hadley,

hearing her anxiety, realising how Britain and the rest of the world were holding their breath, made me even more acutely aware of the wretchedness of being so far from home. I'd phoned the Embassy Residence yesterday, needing to talk to Joe, not even bothering to think about his White House dinner the previous night when we could be radiated or blown up any minute. He hadn't returned my call. People were sombrely getting on with life, their minds tight shut; mine had been too, working, seeing Matt, but Walter's gloom had brought a rush of renewed panic. Should I try to book a flight home? Give it two more days? I felt numb, frozen with indecision.

Two days later, a U-2 reconnaissance plane was shot down over Cuba. It felt like a tipping point with the loss of life; the pilot, Major Rudy Anderson, who had a young family and a baby on the way. Walter learned that Khrushchev had toughened his stance, belligerent and defiant in the face of all demands. It was a very black Saturday. I resolved to call Eileen the next day and tell her I needed to get home.

We'd had a flurry of snow on Friday, then Saturday's grimness, but Sunday brought cautious rays of hope. The *Times* headline was encouraging: *CAPITAL IS READY TO LIFT BLOCKADE. KENNEDY ASKS FOR QUICK ACTION TO END TENSION AND PRESS FOR WORLD PEACE.*

We pored over the papers. The Ferrones took me out to lunch; we walked in the park and, returning to the apartment, heard the phone. Joan ran in to answer it. She was listening with a spreading smile as we came in. 'It's Matt,' she

359

said, cupping the mouthpiece. 'Khrushchev's ordered the withdrawal of missiles. Matt's saying we can exhale, at least, if not quite yet spray the walls with champagne. Have a quick word, Susannah. I'm sure he'd like one.'

'More than a word,' he muttered, overhearing. 'God, it's such a relief! I'd been worried enough to make a will, and guys in the office have been writing 'in the event of' letters to their wives . . . '

That really brought home how close we'd been. I returned the phone, touched that he'd taken the trouble to call and feeling quite wobbly with emotion. Walter and Joan hugged each other — and me. Walter even had tears in his eyes.

It was too late to phone home. I slipped away to my room to write down a few thoughts and a letter to my brother, but sitting at the desk the sheet of blue airmail paper became a blur. The world might have teetered and righted itself, but things were no better with Joe.

He had phoned on Friday, finally, yet had done so when he must have known I'd be at work. He'd told Joan he was staying the weekend and would get the shuttle on Monday, be with us by noon. I imagined him being charming to Joan, apologising entertainingly. But he hadn't called again when I'd be in, to explain or say sorry, not once, nor had he asked me to come to Washington.

Joe could hurt me cruelly, which must mean there was still a spark, and most important of all, he was Bella's father. I wasn't sin-free either, far

360

from it now; it was a more level playing-field, although I felt, absurdly, ever so slightly more in the right and virtuous, having done my best to give up Gil. It felt a bit like giving up atheism in an attempt to keep the faith. I didn't hold out much hope for my chances.

On Monday I phoned at lunchtime, between bookings, and spoke to Joan, but Joe hadn't yet arrived. In the afternoon, I worked with Lillian Bassman who was a brilliant if exacting photographer. It was an ad for a fruit juice. A small child was in the picture, too. Inevitably, we overran and I was late away, which meant battling with the evening rush. I pushed through the crowds, laddering a stocking on a woman's shopping basket and fending off a nice-looking man who tried to pick me up.

My good intentions were wearing thin, and arriving back to find Joe lounging in an armchair, legs outstretched, sipping one of Walter's well-shaken martinis, didn't help my mood.

He craned his neck round. 'Hey, it's the worker returned! Hello, the wifey.' He stirred himself and came to give me a peck. On his best behaviour, I thought irritably. 'I was just telling Joan and Walter all about Tuesday's White House dinner,' Joe said, resuming his seat, 'and about to describe Jack's little duty speech to the Jaipurs, which was in his own inimitable style. The Maharanee's newly elected to the Indian Congress, it seems, and — you'll like this, Walter — he called her 'India's answer to Barry Goldwater'! She looked as chuffed as anything, had no problems at all with being compared to a

361

loony right-wing extremist like Goldwater. And I'm sure she knew who he was!

'Bobby appeared after dinner, looking very ragged and hollow-eyed. He and Jack went into a huddle; they sat up at the far end of that long centre-room and they were still there after midnight when we left.'

Walter had chuckled away over Barry Goldwater, but Joan had seemed less amused. I wondered if her eyes were wider open now where Joe was concerned; she knew he hadn't phoned. I was perched very stiffly on the arm of a chair and I thought she'd guess how jealous, sore and neglected I was feeling. 'We gotta go now, Walter dear,' she said, curling a beckoning finger, cosily and bossily his way. 'Forgive us, you two, we're out to dinner, but I guess you've plenty catching up to do. Mary-Lou's left you a scratch meal. Don't feel stuck on it, you go on out, do just as you want.'

Joan smiled at me. 'You look so lovely, Susannah, and with all the strain, and long days in front of the cameras, too.' That was all said for Joe's benefit, she was a brick.

She hustled Walter, bustled about, and they were soon out of the door.

Joe went to refill his glass from the cocktail shaker. 'Drink?' he said, as an afterthought, glancing back.

'Yes, thanks, Campari and soda. How was Washington?' I queried, when he returned with it. I'd sat down opposite and reached out a foot to make contact. 'Have you written anything? You couldn't talk to David Ormsby-Gore much,

362

I suppose; he can hardly have come up for air.'

'No one was talking. I met Pierre Salinger, but he only gave me the press spiel.'

'He and his junior called by the evening I arrived and stayed to supper,' I said, eyeing Joe over my glass. 'They seemed very on the ball, as you'd expect. I liked them.'

'Pierre didn't mention meeting you,' Joe grumbled, with a peevish, disbelieving air.

I ploughed on doggedly. 'What did you do? Who did you see and meet?'

'People were in and out of the Residence. I hung out with Sylvia and her kids, saw a bit of Jackie.' Joe yawned and went to pour himself another drink, switching to vodka.

'Where, at the White House? Did you go again then, after the dinner?'

'God, what an inquisition! Yes, I had lunch with her, helped her cut a face in a huge Halloween pumpkin.' He glared. 'I get on with her, okay? Is that it?'

'Not really. It's been a terrible week. I spoke to Miss Hadley, who was stressed out about Cuba. I worried about you in Washington, needed to hear from you — and I'd been looking forward to the weekend.'

The look on Joe's face, his lightly raised eyebrows said he wasn't so sure about that. It was a cold, supercilious look. 'Were you really?' it implied sardonically. 'Pull the other one.'

I shrank inside. Had I been cooler since Gil? Was I as much to blame? 'I could have come to Washington,' I mumbled. 'You could at least have phoned and suggested it.'

'Could I? And drag you away from your modelling? That always comes first.' God, he could be infuriating, always touching just the nerve to make me feel on the back foot.

'For heaven's sake, you know that's not true — and we're talking about a weekend. I'm hardly working then.' But there was that germ of truth, that raw nerve. I felt small.

Joe rolled his eyes. 'Here we go again, nag, nag! Look, you're my wife; we live together. But you go off working in New York and I have a weekend in Washington — on my own. That's how it is in the big wide world. You need to wise up a bit, old girl.'

'Oh, I've done that, don't you worry,' I bit back, fuming. 'I'm wised up just fine.'

It was no good being goaded, not going to solve a thing. 'Let's forget it,' I muttered, calming down. 'And we should eat — I'm starving. Probably the relief of not being radiated to a cinder last week. It had really seemed we were all done for.'

Joe fixed himself another vodka while I went to the kitchen. Mary-Lou had put ready some soup and a pie. I turned on the oven and warmed the soup, stirring it slowly, thinking about Joe and Jackie — even Joe and Sylvia. He was so wittily amusing and appealing when he wanted to be, certainly with First Ladies and Ambassadors' wives; they'd enjoy having him around. Walter had said Jackie didn't go in for female friends, that the only woman she truly trusted and liked was her sister, Lee. Perhaps Joe was a sort of girlfriend to Jackie and filled a gap for her. He

364

could act any role, after all.

'Supper's up,' I called. Joe wandered in with a full glass. How many was that? He hitched up at the kitchen counter and peered at the thick deep-red mush in his soup bowl. 'Beetroot,' I said. 'I don't know what's in the pie.' It turned out to be chicken and mushroom, very tasty; we had it with a heated-up baked potato. I made a pot of coffee and made an effort as well. 'How about going to the Village to hear some jazz?'

Joe stared. It wasn't what he'd expected. 'Where? How do we know who's playing?'

'Eric Dolphy's live at the Gaslight Café this month. Pity Thelonius Monk isn't at the Five Spot as he's recording, but you love alto-sax, Joe, and Dolphy's one of the greats.'

It was a mini-breakthrough, thanks to Gil. Joe was up for going, curious, too. I'd managed to surprise him and pushed it a bit, saying Bob Dylan played at the Gaslight and had even done an album there recently. I wondered, knowing I was secretly longing to, whether we'd happen on Gil. No good thinking that way, I was trying to mend my marriage.

Joe loved the whole scene, clicking his fingers, eating up the music for hours. No Gil, the smoke-filled Gaslight had been quiet that night, but after Eric Dolphy's sultry, moody, beautiful playing, Joe was in the mood and squashed into one of the cots to make love to me. 'How come you're suddenly so up in jazz and the Village clubs?' he'd asked, still huddled close, given the size of the bed, and showing a little jealous interest at last.

'Music's a big deal in the studios,' I said. 'I work a lot with a jazz freak as well.'

We went to other Village hangouts over the next few nights; Joe was wired up, sexed up. New York did that to people. I didn't ask about his daytimes, feeling he needed that space; it was a fragile togetherness at best.

★ ★ ★

Matt came for drinks two days before I left. He'd called and invited himself, much to Joan's amusement. I sensed her absorbing the body language when he arrived and shook hands with Joe. Walter came out into the hall looking intrigued as well, and pressed cocktails on us. 'My best martinis coming up,' he said, going ahead to fulfil the task.

Joan took Joe's arm. 'You know us Yanks and our martinis,' she laughed. 'You have just what you want, Joe!' They carried on into the sitting room, while Matt held back; he stared hard then gripped my arm and kissed my mouth with fierce controlling passion.

I broke away panting, feeling surging adrenaline as I frantically wiped my mouth and smoothed my hair. 'How have you been?' I asked loudly, trying to avoid suspicion about what was holding us up. 'We so appreciated that call last week — goodness, what a relief! Now you must come and have a drink.' Walter looked over curiously as we appeared.

'How's Pierre, Matt?' he asked, holding out a martini and a Campari and soda for me. 'Don't

366

let on to him, but I haven't got very far yet with Jackie's little request.'

'I won't,' Matt promised, taking the glass. 'But I'd say that's the least of Pierre's worries. Keeping the lid on the press is pretty full-on right now. We're still waiting on confirmation that the missile bases are being dismantled. The Soviets don't exactly enlighten us. Not an easy time if you're Defence Secretary — McNamara said it's like trying to talk to people who've spent all their lives in a cellar.'

'What a gloomy thought,' Joe said. Matt smiled at him agreeably and came to sit beside me on the sofa, the nearest place.

'The British press say Whitehall doesn't entirely trust the photographic evidence,' Joe continued, 'and the PM's in a bate. Is there any real proof — just between us?'

Matt shifted his position, managing to brush my thigh. 'It's sure genuine all right, grainy photographs taken from an Air Force U-2 plane. The CIA has been working on them for days, tucked away — this is certainly not for repeating — in a room over a downtown Ford car-dealer shop with the unknowing used-car salesmen wheeler-dealing below!'

Joe enjoyed that. Secrets and titbits made his world turn. He kept the questions coming and looked quite disappointed when Matt said he must run, much as he'd rather stay.

'Any chance we'll cross paths in Washington?' asked Joe. 'I'm there this weekend, flying home direct from DC.'

'I'll be hard at it in the office,' Matt said, 'but

here's my card. Give me a call when you know how you're placed. Maybe we can meet up for a quick jar.'

Joe handed over a card as well. 'Look us up if ever you're in London, Matt. Susannah's set on moving, but you have my agent's details there — she'll always put you in touch.'

★ ★ ★

It rained the first couple of days I was back home. Bella smiled through it. Miss Hadley needed time off and went to stay with her sister in Corby. She had misgivings written all over her face, relinquishing her charge to my sole care, and checked at least ten times that I had her sister's number. Bella was a peach, however, and slept through till six. I kept quiet about that, though, in case Miss Hadley took it personally.

Joe arrived home direct from Washington, and set about systematically undoing all the good work of our few days together in Manhattan. His mood had plummeted. He had work, a part in a television series — a Lothario-type character, not a role to tax his ingenuity — and a radio play, but after that only voiceovers. His agent told me to keep him sweet, as film parts were in the offing and a new script — but how did you keep a man sweet who drank at least a bottle of vodka a day and was back in Alicia's arms?

I'd cut through Belgravia to avoid a traffic jam, driven down her street and seen his black MGB parked almost outside her door. After that, the urge to keep looking became obsessive; it was like playing Russian roulette, anticipating, tensing-up for the stab of pain, yet if the car wasn't there, feeling a sort of perverse, reverse anti-climax.

I got on with the move to Parson's Green. Joe was no help, but I hadn't expected him to be. He'd mutter glumly about it, through the bars of Frankie's cage. 'Alien territory, this new pad, you old wanker. No good squawking, shut your beak and don't blame me!'

I understood Joe's hurt pride over leaving a rented flat that he'd had some part in, for a house bought with my money. I just wished he didn't have to be so morbidly moody about it.

He was mumbling either to himself or Frankie one Saturday morning while I read a letter from Joan Ferrone. She wrote long rambling screeds, streams of consciousness, gossipy, tangential and fun. I passed on to Joe, who thrived on any Kennedy news, that Ted Kennedy had just been elected as Senator for Massachusetts — Jack's old seat.

'I took to Ted,' Joe said, perking up, 'I met him with Jackie and her sister Lee.'

'Doubt *I* would,' I said. 'He cheated at Harvard for starters, and all that stuff about renting brothels and opening up bordellos on a Latin-American trip is a bit of a turn-off.'

'That's my little bourgeoise hausfrau talking, such a prude!' Not any more, I thought, my mind slipping to Gil spread-eagling me, securing me to a hotel bed with four silk ties.

'Lee said we must come to dinner sometime,' Joe remarked. 'Don't know how often she's in

369

London, though.' It sounded extremely vague and I wondered why Joe had even mentioned it. Lee must have made clear to him that I was invited, too — possibly out of curiosity? She'd been his host at the villa in Italy when I'd been left at home.

Joe would talk to Frankie, but it took news from the States for him to communicate with me. The BBC reported that Fidel Castro had accepted the removal of US weapons from Cuba. That prompted Joe to talk of envying Matt, living in Washington. They'd managed to fit in a drink back in November, it seemed. I thought privately that Joe would soon discover Washington wasn't his bag. Jackie's interest would wane and he'd feel claustrophobic in that enclosed diplomatic world; he was more cut out for the London scene, music, the theatre and the parties of his aristocratic friends.

December brought a rash of those. I saw Joe virtually having it off on the dance floor with a pissed wiry rat of a girl — not Alicia — and the telephone was put down on me at times. The girl, I discovered later, was a duke's daughter. I tried not to imagine what Joe did by day while I was at work. He was in debt. I'd taken menacing calls: 'He pays up or his face won't be a pretty sight, lady. You tell 'im that.' Was Joe into gambling?

The weather was abysmal, freezing smog that seemed to penetrate far deeper than the frosty cold of New York. The high spot of the month was an impresario inviting us to the première of David Lean's *Lawrence of Arabia*. I'd have given a lot for a blast of that dry unrelenting desert heat. It snowed just before Christmas, but steam trains seemed able to handle snowy tracks and we made it to Dorset to be with my parents.

Only just, for the weather forecast was extreme — heavy snows and gale-force blizzards. We had to head back on Boxing Day. I felt sick about leaving, wracked with worry. Dad wasn't a cadaver, he loved chips too much and carried a bit of weight, yet his face had the grey, shadowy limpness of someone drained by a fever. He looked as haggard as if he'd been out all night in the freezing snows. It was overwork. Mum was exhausted, too. I could afford to give them a holiday now if they'd only let me.

January was the coldest month for almost two centuries. The sea froze four miles out to sea from Dunkirk and the BBC news talked of the Straits of Dover freezing. Upstream from London, the skaters took to the Thames and someone drove over it in their car. Milkmen got about on skis, children walked miles to school. Miss Hadley was stalwart, keeping Bella safe and snug with no hint of fluster. I had a new respect for her.

More snow in February, blizzards lasting days, and sport had never been so disrupted: some football replays in the FA Cup had to be rescheduled more than ten times. However, London airport kept going with few cancellations and I was able to get to Paris for the French collections, which always had its moments.

I was still a teenager the first time I'd gone, naïve, new to modelling and Paris, too. The *Sunday Times* had booked me, working with

Terry Donovan on a spread for their new colour supplement. Yves St Laurent's Trapeze line was the big story that season; I thought the clothes looked like children's stick drawings of their mummies, but all those chic blasé fashion editors were in a spin, drooling over the look. I knew nothing.

Terry was pissed out of his mind. The couture houses only released the collection clothes for photography after ten o'clock at night; the buyers came first, and since newspapers and magazines fought over who had first go after that, it could be two in the morning before a photographer could take a shot. Terry must have been lining up the bottles. He'd laid in plenty more as well and it was a mad session. We only had one night, given the paper's deadline, and how he took such a spread of zany brilliant pictures, God knows.

At five in the morning we rolled back to the cranky offbeat hotel where we all stayed; the rooms were poky, crammed to suffocating with enormous pieces of dark gloomy furniture, and the antiquated lift was minute. It wasn't built for a gang like ours, hefty Terry, his assistant, two models and the paper's fashion editor . . .

The lift gave a wheezing sigh and gave up the ghost; it sank several feet below ground.

We giggled drunkenly, leaned on the alarm and eventually two cursing, sweating garlic-reeking electricians turned up; they got the door open so we could be pulled up through the space, except for Terry who was just too big. But with its lesser weight the lift suddenly jerked itself up to ground level and he amiably sauntered out.

The hotel's manager, a madame whose scorpion tongue could inflict a thousand lashes, added £50 to each of our bills. I'd just started modelling and was broke; I'd had to live on bread and mustard, always on the tables in cafés, and watch others eat steak.

★ ★ ★

I set off this year, older and wiser, booked by French *Vogue*, but still staying in a hotel with other English photographers and models. Returning at 4 a.m. on the second night, the hotel reception was a bear-pit, people close to fisticuffs, insisting they'd booked rooms, being told there were none. The night porter shrugged, the hotel was full.

Pete, a photographer I'd worked with and quite liked, sidled up to me. 'You've got a room and a kind heart, Susannah, can I sleep on your floor?'

'No, sorry, that's a bad idea,' I said tiredly. 'I couldn't possibly trust you.'

'On my honour — only the floor.' I could have done without it, but it was too late to argue and he had very pleading eyes.

I was just drifting off when my lumpy bed complained loudly. 'Shit,' Pete muttered, 'didn't want to wake you, but it's very hard . . . ' Somehow I didn't think he meant the floor. 'We'd both sleep better,' he whispered, 'if I just slipped in quietly, just a little bodily warmth . . . '

Was he in league with Gil?

* * *

On 6 March, excited weathermen told us it was the first day that year with no frost. The temperature soared to a heady 62 degrees and the snows melted in a flash — we'd had sixty consecutive days of the stuff. I felt like a hamster unballing from hibernation and trying to remember what sunshine and warmth were about.

People practically danced along the pavements, faces wreathed in smiles. Bella's was too. She was six months old now, teething and greedy, but we forgave her anything for those smiles. Spring changed the shape and feel of life; everything burst forth. Photographers blossomed creatively. I worked with Cecil Beaton at his sublime Wiltshire home, reclining on a chaise longue in the conservatory, an elegant jungle of arching exotica, dangling parasols to match the dresses. The pictures were for *Queen* magazine. I did pictures with Brian Duffy, whom I adored, and Norman Eales, who always made his models say 'Thursday'; it formed their lips into his trademark pout.

Being around creative people by day was a privilege, but by night I felt despairing and lonely. My relationship with Joe was going down the pan. He loved Bella and would exclaim proudly, 'Clever girl!' when she learned some new trick like rolling over. And if Frankie swore he'd wag a stern finger and say, 'You close your ears to that, young lady!'

He loved all the hot gossip about John Profumo who'd denied having sex with Christine

Keeler, which nobody believed. A new single by The Beatles was a turn-on, celebrities, parties and other women, too, but married life had none of that spice. Evenings in, nights with me, were boring, boring. Joe put on a passable act of Happy Families for Miss Hadley's benefit, but my high hopes after New York were fallen leaves, withering on stony ground. I felt about as wanted and appreciated as a cigarette-butt, vulnerable, neglected and easy prey.

I came home late one fine April evening, after a day on location, to find Bella tucked up and asleep already, which I was sad about, and Miss Hadley having her supper on a tray in her room. She always did, since she had firm ideas about dividing lines.

Joe was in the sitting room, reading the evening paper, glass in hand. He looked up as I came in. 'Pierre Salinger, his underling — what's his name?' he said.

'Do you mean Matt Seeley?'

'That's it.' Joe looked at me in triumph, as if he'd summoned it up himself. 'Forgot for a moment. He's coming over in a week or two and wants to meet up.'

'You'll enjoy that. You liked him, didn't you? Now I'd better get on with supper.'

'Not just me, he's expecting you along, too — he said so. I told him it was best to fix it up with you. And Toby and Alicia want us for dinner at the White Elephant on Thursday. They're taking the Farnley-Huntingtons and some business geezer or other. Swiss, probably manufactures cuckoo clocks.' Joe retreated behind his newspaper, shaking it irritably.

'That might be somewhere to suggest to meet Matt, if he calls,' I said, speaking to Joe's raised paper, 'the bar at the White Elephant.' It was a swank showbizzy sort of club and Joe was a member, unless he'd been turfed out for non-payment of fees.

'Suggest where you bloody well like,' Joe muttered.

'I'd ask him here, but it's so unfinished; I can't wait for the new curtains.'

Joe lowered the newspaper with a look of point-scoring satisfaction. 'That's the wifey — curtains the summit of her horizons.'

★ ★ ★

An evening with Alicia and Toby felt less of an ordeal than previously; I cared increasingly little these days, which was immensely depressing. I cared about looking my competitive best, though, and wore a flouncy low-cut floral dress, deep pinks and yellows, and I loved the way the skirt swung. With high sling-backs and fun earrings, it was a good look.

Matt was next week's problem. He was on my mind, though, as I walked into the White Elephant Club, since I'd just had a call from him — he'd lost none of his keenness and we'd arranged to meet there the following Tuesday. The Club had a long elegant bar made of gleaming mahogany, and the wall behind it was mirrored, so that people sitting at the counter could see into the room. And be seen, of course, which would help curb Matt's advances.

Alicia and Toby and their guests had arrived. Joe and I joined them, and a waiter drew up two more of the Club's navy velvet armchairs. Alicia had pushed up the usual display of cleavage. Was she a touch larger? Pregnant again? Or was it the Empire line, peach chiffon she was wearing? Joe kissed her cheek. He chose the chair facing her and stretched out his legs. I knew he was making contact and playing footsie.

Vanessa Farnley-Huntington, who was an angular girl with frizzy blonde hair, had been talking as we came up; her nostrils flared a bit too frequently and her ruby silk suit did nothing for her skin. She and her husband Perry were just back from Paris, I gathered, as she carried on.

'And darling P was buying me a totally divine evening bag in one of those snooty chic boutiques off the Champs Elysées when that ghastly Binky girl breezed in, Alicia — and you should see what she's done to her hair! It was Jean Seberg meets sucked mango; it hugged the skull and her tint had gone all orange.'

Perry beamed at his wife while Joe told the Swiss gent, Fabio, the best plays to see and Toby ordered another bottle of champagne. Fabio, not a slight man, was wearing a suit with such embarrassingly tight trousers that I couldn't help eyeing his straining crotch, worrying about the harm to his procreative powers.

Joe was suddenly distracted, turning towards the bar. 'Don't look now,' he said, 'but isn't that Richard Burton sitting there all on his own?'

It was one way of stopping Vanessa in her flow; it drew my eyes from Fabio's cluster and caused Alicia's head to spin round. 'How's that for a bit of showbiz spectator sport?' Joe demanded, leaning forward to keep his voice down.

'Burton's face is a bit pitted.' Vanessa cast a superior glance. 'He's not my type.'

'That sounds like meow, meow,' Toby commented dryly, making clear — to me at least — that he could do without Vanessa whether she was Alicia's best mate or not. Toby never revealed much of himself; he merely observed, Sphinx-like, and made money for his faithless wife to spend. But who was I to talk? I wondered if he'd ever chuck Alicia out one day.

'He *is* Miss Elizabeth Taylor's type!' Fabio chortled, giving his trousers extra stress.

We all had to sneak stares, it was impossible not to. Richard Burton was sitting half-sideways on his barstool, his back only partly to the room. I saw him nod at the barman for a refill, glance down towards the restaurant part of the Club, but then I was caught out, still staring when he turned further round and looked directly at me. He beckoned me over — and with everyone in the Club looking on . . .

'Just see what he wants,' I muttered, blushing as pink as the flower petals on my dress, loving the moment all the same, the astounded looks — jealous resentment through amused curiosity to total astonishment — from everyone at our table and others beyond.

I climbed up onto the vacant barstool beside Richard Burton. No one, obviously, had liked to come and sit too close. He gave me an appraising eye and rested his hand on my arm. 'If I had to guess,' he said, 'I'd say you're not having much of a hell of a good time.'

'Well,' I tittered nervously, 'they're more friends of my husband's . . . '

'He's the actor? Couldn't be one of the others.' The barman was waiting. 'Champagne here, Luigi, for the lady, the beautiful lady,' Richard raised an eyebrow, 'who is called . . . ?'

'Susannah. I read you're doing a film called *The V.I.P.s*?' I said, relieved to have seen a mention and have something to talk about. He nodded, watching me, and I sipped the champagne, feeling the telltale heat in my face. 'Perhaps I should re-join — '

'I think we should get out of here, Susannah, and go someplace else.'

'Where? What do you mean?' My heart was pounding, I felt like pressing a hand to it.

'Just a trip round the block — give your husband a surprise. Don't look back.'

'You mean a little drive — somewhere not far? And you'd bring me back soon?'

He laughed, a throaty, sexy laugh, and downed another whisky in one. 'Yes, not far — only up the road.' A thousand thoughts flew in. Elizabeth? Wasn't she around? I could say no. He was staying at the Dorchester, I'd read, which was just up the road . . .

I could see my table in the mirror. Joe was giggling, Alicia responding, Vanessa looking shocked and peeved, Toby enjoying the sport. It would stir them up all right.

'Ready?' Richard touched my arm, amusement in his eyes. I stared back at him, still torn. What the hell! As pick-ups went, it certainly had some class. Gil would approve.

'Yes.' I grinned. 'Just a little spin round the block . . . mustn't be long.'

He took my arm and we left without a backward glance. His car was waiting, engine running, and we spun up Curzon Street — to the Dorchester. 'Elizabeth's having a teeth op,' he said, 'and I hate being alone.' He gave me a lovely time.

★   ★   ★

Joe was asleep when I crept into bed, or pretending to be.

'Nice time last night?' he queried sarcastically, in the morning. 'Vanessa asked how I stood for it and I'm really not sure. I suppose you never considered *my* feelings when you chose to stand me up like that — or the gossip, the harm to your reputation with friends?'

'Isn't that rather bourgeois of you, darling? I thought it was me who's supposed to be the prude.'

Joe almost, but not quite, had the grace to smile.

21

The Jitney ran extra buses to the Hamptons in the holiday season and the 5.55 from 23rd Street fitted very neatly with Daisy's Wednesday afternoons with Warren. She could be back in Southampton in time for supper, just as in her more innocent early days. She never minded the journey — it was time to write her column, read, wind down from the city — but Warren made such a fuss. 'Can't you understand how much of a heel it makes me feel? I want to look after you.' He tried every pleading, black-mailing tactic he could to persuade her to let him send her by limo.

'It's quite enough that you've upped my ticket to Ambassador class,' Daisy argued every time. 'I love that bit of luxury.' Things had a habit of being found out and she didn't want the small matter of transport to be her undoing.

She was enjoying her luxury seat now and wriggled her toes in the Manolo Blahnik sandals Warren had given her that were such sexy heaven, despite the straddling straps looking slightly like an eight-legged tarantula. Daisy cast an eye at her watch. Only ten minutes to go. She sighed and reached for her old flatties in her non-designer-label handbag; she needed to change back and hide the Manolos from Susannah.

Daisy was still in the aftermath glow of her

post-lunch activities, slightly sore and as bewildered as ever at the way sex with Warren continued to be such a turn-on.

She needed her extended lunchtimes with Warren — and any snatched evening quickie when Susannah's old friend Janet, who put Daisy up in the city, was out for the evening. They met at Warren's Fifth Avenue apartment on those times, Daisy clock-watching, worrying slightly about what to say if Janet was back first. An economical half-truth, she decided: her Southampton host had had a small get-together — business contacts — and thought to invite her round.

She wondered at the contrast. Sex with Simon was hard-core, all about the overpowering force of his virility whereas with Warren it was simply the extraordinarily effective tenderness of his touch. True, she always felt sexier in hot weather, but Warren was so attuned to her needs and put them first; with Simon they were an after-thought, if remembered at all.

Warren's presents were a problem — the smallest of beers to a beer magnate, but of a quality that she'd never before been given or able to afford. She knew they had nothing to do with the attraction; she wasn't a sexual fraud, in the business of trying to snare him, yet the gifts gave her a feeling of being bought, which wasn't easy to explain. All she could do was plead with him. 'You mustn't, mustn't. You've showered me with far too much already!'

'It gives me more pleasure than I can say, Daisy darling. You can't deny me that.'

She didn't want to hurt his feelings. He chose presents with great care and sensitivity, like a father intimately familiar with his daughter's more modern tastes and foibles. Beautiful leather belts and bags, cashmere, clothes and accessories that he mistakenly assumed — since he knew how worried she was about Susannah sussing — that Daisy could have bought herself. The exotic underwear was a less paternal choice.

He simply didn't get that Susannah would know the belts were Dolce & Gabbana, the bags Chloé, the cashmere Donna Karan. The hidden presents were piling up; the whole situation was fraught.

The bus was approaching the Southampton stop. Susannah came to pick her up, since Jackson was off on Wednesdays, but she wasn't in sight yet. She went in for fine timing, whereas Daisy was always massively punctual. A text came through. *Two secs!*

It wasn't far to walk anyway and taxis were always lined up. People often shared them from the stop, a little Southampton summer camaraderie that had apparently grown into quite a custom. Daisy climbed down from the Jitney thinking, with a slight jolt, that there were only about two more Wednesdays to go. The job would be finished as far as they were concerned by mid-August. Then it was back to England, time to face Simon again, a pile of bills and a very wobbly future.

Would Susannah keep her on? She had her secretary, Stephanie, in London; all Daisy could hope for was an occasional one-off commission that was large enough to justify an extra pair of hands. So much was in the air. Warren was coming on a bit strong. Daisy remembered his extreme freeze-up, seeing his ex-wife at the restaurant. He showed every sign of having a very possessive nature and she didn't somehow see him waving her off into the sunset, home to England, with a friendly, 'So long!'

Susannah swept up and braked to a stop. 'Good couple of days?' she asked as Daisy climbed in. 'You must be knackered with the heat in the city and all you've been doing.'

That possibly had a little edge, but it wasn't said maliciously. Susannah's warmth was genuine, Daisy knew. She felt as astonished as ever by their friendship. They were different generations, but good together; nothing felt forced. Susannah looked cool, tanned, wearing that witty turquoise tee with a toucan on the front. She'd had a hectic day too, site meetings, window people, marble suppliers, wood-floor people. She hadn't been idling by the pool.

Daisy longed to pour out her heart about Warren, but the sensitivities were just too great. His growing seriousness spelled trouble. Susannah probably saw it as a temporary dalliance with a younger woman and wouldn't take kindly to discovering it was more than that. At best she'd be sad, hurt and fed-up. At worst it could lead to a bare-knuckle fight. Either way, Daisy felt, it would mean a miserable end to their friendship and also, inevitably, her stimulating, satisfying new job.

She shut her mind to it all, and over one of

Martha's delicious light suppers they talked shop and also about the rash of weekend parties on offer: the cocktail parties, Saturday-night dinner with the Stocktons, Art and Maisie, which should be a laugh. Maisie was a riot when she was on form, always the flaunter, out to shock, and she loved to puncture pomposity.

'I have my dinner date with Gerald the auctioneer tomorrow as well,' Daisy said with a grin, relieved that Warren had got it firmly into his head that Gerald was gay. 'I'm looking forward to it, I'd felt quite stood up when he had a sudden important trip to North Carolina the other day.'

Her mobile buzzed and in the uncanny way that often happens, it was Gerald, fixing the time and place. Susannah looked across the table with interest and Daisy said, clicking off from the call, 'Well, it wasn't another brush-off. He's coming at eight and taking me to somewhere called Nick and Toni's in East Hampton that he says is quite 'jolly'.'

'It's about the most in place going,' Susannah said. 'Impossible to get a table there in summer. He must know all the right people.'

An evening with Gerald, Daisy decided, had distinct possibilities. He was certainly younger than Warren, in his fifties probably, and suitably cultured-looking for his grand auction house; he had a good head of thick brown hair and Daisy couldn't forget his impressive nose. She had a sneaking desire to satisfy her curiosity about long noses and kissing. Would this be her chance to find out?

'Is Warren back tomorrow?' she asked, knowing the answer. 'You won't be on your own, Susannah, I hope?' It was almost August; Warren was going to be around a lot more.

'No, he'll be back,' she smiled. 'I expect we'll pop out to some staid trad joint, though — no Nick and Toni's for me! Warren's not one for experimenting with anywhere on-trend, after all. He's an old stick-in-the-mud at heart.'

That was true, Daisy thought. Warren was solidly set in his ways, as conventional as custard pie.

* * *

Gerald arrived at eight on the dot. He brushed Daisy's cheek, a formal little kiss. 'I love your dress,' he said. 'I feel I had quite a hand in that!'

She was in the Carolina Herrera resort dress that Warren had bid for at the Red Tide Benefit's auction — at Susannah's suggestion, which she might now regret. She'd been amused, all the same, about how perfect it was for a date with Gerald.

Susannah came to the door to see them off, and admired Gerald's silver Porsche convertible. 'I've always been a sucker for sleek sporty cars,' she said. The Porsche impressed Daisy no end as well; with this Long Island life she was leading she felt like someone on a crazy credit-card binge. The divorce had left her so strapped. A return to reality — bill-paying in Battersea — was far from a thrilling prospect, yet one that soon had to be faced.

The tall wrought-iron gates were opening, Warren returning. He jumped out and began to come over. Gerald was holding open the passenger-seat door; Daisy climbed in hurriedly, waving at Warren with a backward smile and calling goodbye. She didn't want him slowing them up and embarrassing her with his moony eyes queering her Gerald pitch. Warren stopped in his tracks. He waved back, but looked hurt, taking it as a slight. It was unsettling. Daisy felt disturbed.

'So how did it go, down south in North Carolina?' she asked, once they were through the gates and Gerald was revving down the street.

'Well, the trip became extended, as you'll have gathered,' he said dryly. 'Sorry I mucked you about. One of Wilmington's most venerable worthies had kicked it and her family were selling off some important paintings and French furniture. They feuded on and on about what to auction, the reserve prices, with no thought at all for my time. And Wilmington is the kind of small city where everyone gets in on the act, so other grandees wanted me to see their treasures — some of which were truly grim — but buyers come in all tastes and sizes so I had to take a look.'

'Isn't it hugely satisfying and worth it all when you make a real find?'

'It sure is, and seeing beautiful pieces in situ, too. One house I visited had some rare gems, a perfect French Empire secrétaire and a seventeenth-century longcase clock — only the old lady wanted to hang onto those. She lived in a moated mansion that looked as if it hadn't been touched in a hundred years, even down to the yellowing lace cloth on the hexagonal table where we had tea. She was gracious, with swept-up hair, and we had dainty cucumber sandwiches — but it was the spookiest experience you can imagine.'

'How come?' Daisy asked curiously.

'The house was reached by a path through the garden, and along the banks of the moat — which was stuffed full of alligators watching me! It was a perfect setting for one of your Agatha Christie weekend-house-party murder stories. I've never felt more scared in my life!'

'I long to see the Deep South, but does North Carolina actually qualify?'

'It's a southern plantation state, but not the full Deep South. Wilmington's a port city and was very active in the Civil War, extremely supportive. Not all the state — the struggling farmers in the west were more ambivalent, quite anti-slavery, in fact. Here we are now.' He drew up on the restaurant's gravel parking. 'I hope you like this place. It has a good buzz and gets the celebrities.'

'It's a real treat to come here,' Daisy said, revelling in being out with him, 'I'm having one new experience after another.'

Nick and Toni's had two interior rooms, primitive art on white walls, a centrepiece wood-burning oven covered in mosaic, and an outdoor terrace too, where Gerald had asked to be seated. There wasn't a table to be had; the place was a honeypot for the most social limelight-seeking bees. Daisy liked the coloured lights strung along an overhead awning and the bordering spiky architectural plants.

Their table was to the side, good for celebrity spotting and hearing themselves talk. 'The cocktails are great here,' said Gerald, 'you must try one. I'm going to have a Rosita. It's basically tequila and vermouth, but have a read-through and see what you like.'

'I love the sound of a local berry Rosado, thanks.' Daisy settled back while he gave the order, amazed at who was there. 'I see what you mean about celebrities,' she murmured. 'I mean, isn't that Bill Clinton in that group over there? And Alec Baldwin just beyond — his wife looks very pregnant! I do feel rather the church mouse, very ordinary indeed.'

'You're not. I doubt any one of these people is related to a French countess.'

Daisy stared, bemused and disconcerted. 'How on earth do you know that? And anyway, she's my stepmother — it's only by marriage.'

'Just from a piece in the local rag's diary column. *Society designer Susannah Forbes and Daisy Mitchell, her young assistant, daughter of a French countess, are taking Southampton by storm.* You write a column under your own name too, Daisy; which makes it easy for nosy people like me. But in case you're wondering, I asked you out *before* seeing the piece.' Gerald had an appealing, educated sort of a grin. Daisy felt quite flustered to think of the Beach Club regulars reading about her. Had Warren seen it? She suspected he had, yet wouldn't have wanted to allude to it.

'I've never met anyone with such definitively

green eyes,' Gerald remarked, more curiously than as a come-on, 'and the Herrera dress has green in it. Shall we order?'

Daisy studied the menu. 'Lots of ideas for my column here — red pepper coulis and dustings of porcini. It's so hard to choose — *and* to stop eating these fantastic olives!'

'They cure their own to minimise the salt content. It's a good selling touch.'

Gerald made suggestions: seared tuna, sweet pea ravioli. He was having antelope. He ordered a bottle of Italian white, Vermentino Litorale, and a red Bordeaux to follow.

The white wine came quickly and was deliciously chilled. 'Now we can relax.' He smiled.

He was easy to chat to, not pressurising. Daisy found herself talking about her mother dying, her father busy with his health club and new family, how she hadn't wanted to lean on him over her marital troubles. She even told Gerald her fears about her usefulness to Susannah in the future. 'I'm a real con out here, you see,' she confessed. 'Non-achieving and sewn-up by my ex in the divorce — unlike most females in the Hamptons, I suspect.'

'Hmm,' Gerald said, 'but if I read the signs right, Warren would like to step in.'

Daisy felt her face burn. 'He likes to flirt, sure — and not just with me. Susannah's the main attraction. She's doing a fantastic job on his house — you'll be impressed.'

'It certainly needed a bomb under it, and Warren needed a shake-up. Still, he's bid up for some dull stuff over the years, so I shouldn't complain. But Daisy, you're dodging the business of Warren being hooked. You do like him? He'll be hard to shake off.'

'I've talked far too much about me,' Daisy said, seeing to her relief the waiter coming with their main course. 'Gosh, the ravioli looks phenomenal, what presentation! And your antelope, too.' The waiter smiled and poured the red wine for Gerald to taste.

'Excellent. I'll take care of it, that's fine.' Gerald seemed impatient for them to be alone again.

Daisy felt a little confused. Was he interested and had he been trying to establish where he stood? Did that explain all the talk about Warren, which seemed slightly odd?

'Tell me more about you,' she said, still question-dodging. 'You've told me about your love of travel and Europe, having a pampered East Coast childhood . . . '

'Yes, I was very indulged. My father publishes art books, my mother breeds horses.'

'And your personal life? Warren said you weren't married — have you ever been?'

Gerald refilled their glasses. He sipped his Bordeaux and gave her a gentle smile over the rim.

'Once, a while ago. I extricated myself and it ended fairly amicably — well, just about. No children. It was a mistake, only I hadn't known it at the time.'

'Who does? We could all say the same.'

'No, it's a bit different in my case. You see, I

discovered I was gay.'

He was smiling, but lost in thought for a moment as well, which gave Daisy time to adjust. Had he not known before? To get as far as marrying . . . Her feelings, like one of the House cocktails, had their sharp flavours. Her pride and self-confidence had taken a knock, which wasn't surprising, and she raged internally, unfairly and irrationally, at Warren for being so complacent about her date. And right! But with her mind flitting briefly to her own first marriage and her newfound knowledge, via the boys, that their father had a long-term male partner. She began to be keenly interested too, pleased and touched that Gerald enjoyed her company and had even felt able to talk of his 'discovery'.

'It must have been a great shock for your wife, obviously, but was it hard for you, I mean, quitting the whole hetero way of life?' Daisy queried. 'And peoples' curiosity as well, the looks and undercurrents, that sort of stuff — or did you feel a great sense of release?'

'Oh, the latter. I'd fallen wildly, desperately in love. The trouble is, that can be so painful and difficult, 'no assignment for cowards', as Ovid said. My partner's very young and unsuitable, and I live in fear of losing him; it would kill me. Yet for that reason, conversely, my instinct is to give him space.'

'Like coming to the Hamptons on your own?' Daisy felt fascinated and awed.

'Yes, taking trips to Europe alone as well. It cuts me up, but the coming-togethers are worth anything, indescribably exquisite. And I like the opera, theatre, time with women friends, which is far from his scene. He's a DJ, works nights, funny hours. He goes to disgusting dives, gets pissed and worse, in with druggies, needs rehab, hates himself for it and loves me to pick up the pieces. Those are the beautiful moments.'

Daisy wondered privately if such a misfit relationship had a hope. Was it really worth it? Yet she could see the ecstasy in Gerald's eyes. She jealously longed to feel such love. 'What's his name?' she asked.

'Mark. He's twenty-eight — from the Midwest.'

'I can only imagine that sort of reciprocal love,' Daisy smiled wistfully, 'that kind of certainty. I see a married man in London, can't turn him away, but it's purely physical, two-dimensional — and in fact, he's holding me back. He doesn't care, doesn't love me. I really envy you, Gerald, the completeness of what you have.'

'It'll happen for you,' Gerald said. 'I'd bet on it. And meantime, perhaps I can take you out when I'm in London? I'd love that, my green-eyed French countess's stepdaughter. You have great style, Daisy; don't do yourself down.' He looked at her fondly before turning to summon a waiter. He ordered a lavender white chocolate and pear dessert with two spoons. 'Coffee? Espresso?' He was easy in her company and relaxed.

They drove back, both of them, she felt, in that comforting realm of a fresh new solid-based friendship. Gerald seemed almost like the brother she'd never had, except that he wasn't; he was a male pal, a man who'd been married, a sexual being. It took a little getting used to. 'Did you always know, inside?' she asked. It still felt such a surprising revelation.

'I've wondered about that endlessly, and the fact is, I simply don't know. I suppose I never will.' Gerald pulled up just short of *Great Maples*. 'I won't come in or anything. We might meet over the weekend with all the social goings-on, but if not, thanks for tonight and for listening. It's good to let it out now and then. And we had fun! You're an entrancing girl.'

Gerald put his lips to hers and squeezed her arm. When he was gone, Daisy could still feel the brush of his nose. It felt quite sexy. No need to wonder about that little conundrum any more, she told herself happily, feeling buoyed up and light-hearted. It wouldn't be a precluding factor. She hugged the evening to her. Gerald had given her fresh confidence, and a new sense of contentment, too.

★　★　★

Warren was waiting in the hall, in the shadows; it was hard to gauge his expression. 'I was worried — it's nearly one,' he said plaintively, coming close. 'Susannah said you'd gone to Nick and Toni's, but was the service really that slow on a Thursday? I'm surprised.'

'The place was packed. There wasn't a table to be had, and a Clinton here, a Baldwin there; my head was on permanent swivel.' Daisy laughed.

'But the service was fine; we just chatted on for ages.'

She felt ever so slightly irritated. Warren was intruding into the mood somehow, and she'd had a lot of wine, just wanted to get straight to bed. She smiled grudgingly, only to reel back when he lunged forward and clutched her with force, pulling her into the shadow of the staircase, smothering her in a furious, passionate kiss.

She came up for air panicking, hissing, 'Not here, for fuck's sake!' She flashed a look upwards through the banisters. No sign of Susannah. She let out a breath. 'I'm going up now, Warren, and alone. Promise you won't do that again with . . . others here. It matters to me.'

He was shaking, she realised, looking disturbed and emotionally overwrought. 'I missed you,' he muttered. 'I need to talk to you, Daisy, and if not now, before the end of the weekend. Any time, anywhere we can be private.'

She stared at him, her heart quickening all the more. It was too much pressure and she was longing to get away. 'Maybe we'll have a moment or two at the Beach Club or one of the parties but please, Warren, go easy. There are three of us and I'd really hate any upsets. We're managing fine as we are. Sleep tight,' she murmured lightly, giving him a token peck on his cheek.

Daisy's mellow sleepiness was out of the window; she felt resentfully alert, churning over the implications of Warren prowling around in the hall waiting for her. He'd worked himself up into a frenzy. She feared that he'd decided it was

395

time to come clean and tell Susannah what had been going on. It must surely have got harder for him, unless he was a complete phony, to play the suitor, out with Susannah at a restaurant, alone in the house on their return. Wouldn't Susannah have expected him to cuddle up with her in bed? Martha was off, Daisy out; Susannah must be feeling more than suspicious by now, as sour as an unripe gooseberry, thoroughly pissed off all round.

Yet no resentment showed at breakfast on the terrace.

'Hi, sleep well?' She smiled as Daisy appeared. They'd weaned Warren off the dining room at last and Luisa had set up the table out there. 'Good time with Gerald last night? I'm dying to hear all about it.' Susannah looked rested, bright and fresh in a white top, vivid yellow pants and espadrilles; she had a touch of makeup on too, always did, but at seventy, if you cared, that must be kind of inevitable.

'Lots to tell, but later,' Daisy returned Susannah's smile, trying to imply it was more for her ears than Warren's. 'We were back late and I couldn't sleep, so I feel a fright, a real mess — and you look just the opposite. Doesn't she look glowing, Warren?'

He'd lowered his newspaper when Daisy came out to the terrace, smiled vaguely and raised it again. He did the same now, with a token nod of agreement. Daisy wondered how they'd get through the day.

It was a Friday. She and Susannah had work to do, which helped. An electrician was coming.

Susannah wanted to be sure he knew exactly where to put the floor outlets for lamps, since electrical mistakes were costly. He was late, and waiting for him they wandered in the garden, discussing plant and pot positioning after the reconfiguring of the terrace.

The weather had changed. They'd been caught in a downpour walking from the Beach Club earlier in the week, soaked to the skin, laughing, loving the relief from the humidity. There had been thunderstorms all week, but it was brighter today and the forecast was good.

Daisy asked after Susannah's evening — feeling tense about it, which she hoped didn't show — before embarking on describing her own with Gerald.

'Oh, we just had a quick meal at the café-restaurant on Main Street. I wanted an early night — I need them these days.' That was pretty dismissive. Had she and Warren rowed?

Susannah was warmer, hearing Daisy out about Gerald, and interested.

'It's surprising, isn't it?' she said. 'Not that he's gay, but that he only discovered it so late in life. You'd think he'd have found out earlier, or at least had some sort of clue. Your first husband was only twenty, you said, he'd hardly had time to know his leanings, although a couple of my gay friends have told me they'd known as young as twelve. I suppose falling in love can be such a visceral force, though. I hope Gerald doesn't get too badly hurt — after the ecstasy, the agony, that sort of thing.

So that's that, then,' she gave an ironical smile,

'bang goes one of my small hopes. I'm on the lookout for personable marriageable-age men of means for you, Daisy. Simon isn't for life — or love.'

Daisy went quiet, thinking of how soon she'd be home and the danger of falling into the same old groove. 'Simon's just texted,' she said, 'but only because he's on family hols and bored, I expect. I suggested his kiddos would love a game of Monopoly.'

Susannah smiled. 'Keep your options open. Don't miss out on falling in love.'

'Gerald said the same thing last night, but time's not on my side . . . Ah, here's Jimmy the electrician,' Daisy said with relief, sensing undercurrents in Susannah's advice. Was she telling Daisy to play the field, move on, get Warren out of her hair as well as Simon?

Susannah had her back to the electrician and turning, seeing the sweating lump of human lard slopping across the grass, she muttered, 'Think we were right to check him out.'

★ ★ ★

The weekend parties crowded in and Warren regained his equilibrium, or seemed to. He socialised happily with the moneyed gossiping locals: they were his friends, his kind. The three of them went to the Stocktons' dinner party on Saturday night, where Maisie's outfit didn't disappoint. She was in a flesh-coloured lace corset-dress that pushed up the rising-sun boobs and frothed out in froufrou pink net skirts over seamed black stockings. She looked like a Texan can-can girl. Daisy was feted, asked about her French mother, and it made no difference, patiently explaining about being a stepdaughter. A new gloss of glamour was assured.

Warren slipped her occasional hurt looks of the why-aren't-you-wearing-any-of-my-presents kind, and when Maisie encouraged dancing on the terrace, he asked Daisy to partner him and muttered his whinges in her ear.

'Sorry,' she whispered back. 'I can't. Susannah would know they're from you.'

He still looked injured. Her body responded to the well-judged pressure of his hand on her bare back, his legs pressing, moving with hers, yet he nagged on. 'At least you could have worn the shoes.'

'God, Warren, they're Manolo's — amazing, fabulous. Do you really think Susannah wouldn't know that?' Daisy eased away a little, the sensual moment lost.

* * *

Sunday lunch was at the Beach Club. Others joined them — Warren's neighbours, Elmer and Jan Harvey, and a couple of married roués who chatted up Daisy and Susannah; the roués' wives talked to each other and drank South Siders.

Warren looked across the untidy extended table. 'Come on, Daisy,' he said, catching her eye. 'Come for a hike along the beach. Help me walk off some of this flab.'

'That sounds a bit keen,' Elmer Harvey said.

'You do need to watch the old ticker.'

Warren, who was getting to his feet, looked daggers at Elmer. 'Thanks for that,' he muttered. '*Old boy.*' He came to help Daisy up from her chair. It was a humid day and she had to make an effort to stir herself, which she hoped was apparent to Susannah.

'Less of the hike,' she laughed. 'On a day like this, it's a slow amble for me.'

She kicked off her strappy wedges and left them with Warren's loafers on the steps down from the Clubhouse. The sand was hot under her feet, the breakers thrashing, the ocean, vast and filling the distance. It was always a shock, always gave one a feeling of experiencing it for the first time.

'I couldn't last another minute without seeing you alone. I've been so worked up, Daisy, I had to say it now, not wait till some point in the week that may not pan out. God knows, it's hard enough to be alone with you.'

'Say what, Warren? You've been stressed out and nervy all weekend, that's for sure.'

'I want you to think about marrying me. I love you, I can't bear to look at you and not be able to say so, kiss you and shout it out loud. Don't say a word right now, either way. Mull it over; think it through. You know the obvious downsides, but Daisy darling, I can give you a very good life, no more money worries, the best possible launching for your sons, apartments for them, cars, real security. And for my part I'd trust you not to be marrying me for my money, I know you too well for that. I can't imagine a girl less motivated by gain. And you're kind, sensitive to people's feelings, the way you care about Susannah's . . . '

He'd begun speaking, walking side by side, but slowed and turned to her, taking her hands and fixing her with an achingly painful gaze. Daisy felt softened, touched, the irritation she'd felt with him all weekend melting away in the face of his sincerity.

'I'm glad you don't want me to say a word, but thank you,' she said. 'It's a huge thing, a real bolt from that deep blue ocean out there, and I'm overwhelmed. I'll definitely need time . . . ' She gently extracted her hands and separated from him, looking nervously up and down the beach, which was as near-deserted as ever. 'I'll give you an answer soon, Warren, I promise. Certainly before my flight home.'

Daisy couldn't keep looking at him; the intensity of emotion in his gaze was exhausting. She turned to face towards the Clubhouse, saying, 'Shall we wander back? And,' she hesitated, 'perhaps it would be best not to meet in the city midweek, during this thinking space. It's a very big decision, for both of us, Warren. You need to mull it over too. I'd never, ever hold it against you if, in the cold light of day, you wanted to change your mind.'

22

'Well, Warren, isn't it about time you showed me a little honesty? Perhaps, for a start, you can tell me where things are at with you and Daisy, which I assume is quite far.'

I looked across the sitting room. He was refilling his glass, standing beside the drinks bar with his head bowed. I'd had enough. After his tiredness on Thursday night when Daisy was out with Gerald, after his twitchy, distracted behaviour all weekend and Daisy's impatience with him. And now, after her transformed mood since their walk on the beach, I felt Warren owed me a confession at the least.

I'd heard his footsteps on the landing on Thursday night, heard him slip downstairs, presumably to wait up for Daisy, and I could understand why that had made her cross. She wouldn't have wanted him pouncing while I was just upstairs — which was to her credit on the whole. I could even guess at the reason why her crossness had suddenly dissolved. She'd been gentle with him all evening, ever since our return from the Beach Club.

It was midnight now and Daisy had gone to bed. Warren wasn't going to the city the next day, since it was holiday time. He was spending much of August in Southampton. His shoulders were drooped. He'd been knocking back scotch all evening, which had little to do, I felt, with a Monday lie-in.

'Well?' I repeated, fingernails drumming on the unyielding sofa arm. 'Do I get an answer, or is that too much to ask?'

He looked back at me with a cornered man's pleading gaze. 'Forgive me, Susannah, I'm just collecting myself and my thoughts — and pouring the refill I think I need. Can't I get you a drink, after all? Do have something.'

'A glass of champagne would be nice, inappropriate as that may be — or perhaps not?'

He jerked his head up at that and turned, needing to see my expression, but couldn't keep looking at me for long. He concentrated on the task in hand, pouring several fingers of scotch and freshening the ice in his glass. His shocked reaction to that remark had said it all: I'd guessed right about the beach walk. My blood boiled. Did he think I hadn't had a clue? Had he taken me for a complete fool? Yet in my heart I knew I'd been more than that — a stupid, pathetic, conceited aging woman.

I watched him open the oak cupboard doors under the bar-top and take a bottle of champagne out of the fridge behind. I'd thought I had enough going for me, that Warren was attracted, which he had been — but that was in the absence of a sweet-natured young divorcée nearly half my age, pretty, unspoiled . . . I'd presented him with just that, delivered her right into his home, his lap, for a whole sunny summer. I'd soon cottoned on to male egos and youthful vitality, without seeing, crassly, how much I was losing out. And now the reality, of being humiliatingly walked-over by my client and a younger woman, was sticking somewhere halfway down my throat.

I couldn't hold in the bile. 'Shit, Warren, did you think I was in blissful ignorance of your city love affair? Forget the champagne, just tell me what you need to. I've been humouring you for too long.'

The champagne cork flew off and broke a glass. The fizz frothed down over Warren's hand and splashed his expensively casual linen shirt and shorts. I didn't leap to his aid. He sorted himself out, went to wash his hands and eventually, with a coy, I'm-not-as-bad-as-all-that, go-easy-on-me, rueful look, he came across the room with his scotch and my glass of champagne. 'I think the bottle was trying to tell me something,' he said, sitting down gingerly beside me on the sofa.

'Hmm,' I muttered and took a sip.

Warren spread his hands on his spattered knees and turned to face me with sad, soulful eyes. 'I've just made the most terrible fool of myself, Susannah. I mean, I hardly know the girl — or which way to turn. A couple of lunches in New York . . . I got completely carried away, so flattered she was attracted to me, and then this afternoon . . . '

'You asked a girl thirty years your junior to marry you?'

'Twenty-nine years.' Warren drained his whisky in a gulp. Was his hand shaking slightly? The cubes in the glass kept chinking in a distracting way. 'It's summer madness, Susannah. I didn't know what I was doing and I can't tell you how

404

badly I feel. I couldn't bear to lose our friendship and closeness, our relationship that's given me such immense happiness and pride. The bonding we've done, special times together, our little trips. My admiration for you knows no bounds.'

Did I really have to sit and listen to this crap? I shifted my position impatiently. 'Yes, well,' I said, 'that's all very fine. I assume, obviously, that you love Daisy — isn't that all that matters?'

'She's such a dear sweet girl, it's impossible not to. I am very smitten, I'm afraid. She's not motivated by money, so spontaneous and eager to please, highly-sexed, too . . . '

That wasn't his most sensitive remark, I thought grimly; he'd be biting his lip for sure. It was inadvertent, but showed how much his libido was working overtime.

'Is Daisy's sexiness a slight worry to you?' I asked bitchily, feeling caught on the raw.

He tensed. 'Why? Why should it be? What do you mean?'

'Well, you're in a state of bliss right now — a new, wonderful relationship — but there is the longer term. Suppose Daisy was home seeing her sons and Simon was around? I mean, she's under no illusions about him, but she's never been able to turn him away. Then there'll always be younger men chasing, that's inevitable. But I'm sure you've taken that into consideration in a big-minded way, Warren. You'd be sensibly magnanimous and understanding if she were momentarily attracted, and anyway, it's a worst-case scenario. Daisy wouldn't want to let you down.'

He looked affronted, or affected to be, and exclaimed, very much on the defensive, 'Daisy's not the flirtatious, unfaithful type — not like that at all! She's a sincere, decent girl who'd rise above any temptation. I could trust her with my life, I know.'

'She hasn't turned you down, obviously. I assume she's still thinking it over? Of course, if she's already said yes,' I smiled warmly and held up my glass, 'congratulations are in order and I made the right choice of drink!'

Warren smiled nervously. 'It wasn't an instant no, or she'd have said so then and there. I told her to take plenty of time, give it thought. And I need to as well, after this extraordinary leap of mine into the dark. A breathing space works both ways.'

He gave a long sigh, raising and lowering his shoulders emphatically then carried on.

'If only I could make amends. It wasn't how I planned things between you and me, far from it. You know that. It's just, well, with Daisy it's all kind of suddenly bubbled up.'

That was about the sum of it, I thought sourly.

'I'd give anything to have your forgiveness,' he pleaded, 'and stay friends.'

Warren rose to pour himself a refill and brought the champagne bottle back with him. He took the glass from my hand without asking, but delicately, like a fond husband seeing his wife's eyes droop, and topped it up. I didn't argue, but the glass stayed on the side table where he left it.

He was beside me again, an antiseptic sort of

406

presence, I felt. A faint trace of verbena hung on his skin, some toiletry of sorts, nothing earthy and masculine like smoke or sweat. A florist came to do the flowers twice weekly; the scent of lilies was discernible, but they were in an arrangement that, a little like Warren, lacked a homely, mussed-up touch.

I'd had enough, all I could take. It was time to make a move, go to bed and mope. I had plenty to think about and plan, like advancing my flight and skedaddling home. I didn't want to stick around being a lemon to the lovebirds a moment longer than I needed to. I'd tie up a few ends; Daisy could handle the rest.

She must be in a dreadful twitch about having to face me in the morning. Not easy, since she hadn't been exactly loyal. I wondered if she'd prevaricate and minimise the affair or come completely clean.

Warren put his hand tentatively over mine. 'Thanks for not slapping my face — or telling me I'm a not-seeing-straight old fool, which I am.'

'No, I wouldn't do that; it's your decision, yours and Daisy's. She is indeed a very sweet girl — but she still has to say yes!'

Did I sense a slight reality check? Warren seemed to do a double-take, as though brought up sharp. Had he been leaving that small fact out of account, believing that money and adequate prowess, a sort of gilded prick, was all that was needed? Was he seeing himself as Richard Gere, Daisy as Julia Roberts in the *Pretty Woman* role? But she wasn't a hooker and he was hardly Gere.

I stood up. 'Night, Warren. You'll be glad to have that off your chest, I'm sure, the business of telling me. I'll leave right away, of course, as soon as I've seen to any stray threads of the job, and Daisy will be capably on hand. I'll be very happy for you both if it all works out, and certainly no grudges borne.'

Warren showered me with thanks, apologies and compliments like so much confetti. I couldn't wait to leave him and be upstairs alone. The bedroom was a cool haven, privacy at last, and I collapsed onto the bed to shed a few silent bitter tears.

I hadn't at heart wanted more than a summer flirtation, which in fact I'd had — while magnanimously accepting what I'd thought of as a secondary dalliance with Daisy.

God, it was hard to take. It wasn't as if I'd been in love with Warren, but it was the battering to my pride, the humiliation, shame over my conceit. What really hurt deep down, I had to admit, was the sheer, cruel, galling fact of aging — my lost appeal.

I undressed slowly and went through the drearily held-to routine of cleansing, freshening, creaming up with some expensive gluck in a fancy, heavy pot. It had a vaguely unsatisfactory smell: did they put snail slime in the stuff? Snail facials seemed to be all the rage — at least in Japan. Contact lenses out, flossing, poking around in the gaps between my teeth with little brushes . . .

I thought of my third husband, Edward, father of my sons, struck down by a brain tumour in his sixties. Both of us had been thirty-three when we married; with Edward it was for the first time. Had he lived and we'd grown old together, he'd have accepted my sagging body, teeth implants and arthritic joints, I knew. Love always made allowances. I felt for all the widows and divorcées of a certain age. Men in similar situations found their Daisys.

Charles would help me pick up the pieces. He was a friend for all seasons, but he could be forgiven if his patience was wearing thin. Charles didn't get carried away with Daisy-age girls, he was too wedded to that draughty old Norfolk house of his. He'd probably had one or two of the horsey, hearty huntresses up there in his time — weren't horsey women famously randy? He was a widower, after all — a free soul and might click with one of them soon. They were hardy types, those Norfolk females, who would leap at the chance of Charles and his freezing home.

I lay in bed, miles from sleep, far too hacked-off and brooding. How much did I blame Daisy? Could I still work with her, assuming she didn't marry her beer magnate and ship herself out to the States? Would she be able to resist a personable billionaire? Southampton summers in a redesigned home — to a spec in which she'd had an active hand — an apartment overlooking Central Park, Manolo heels . . . And they'd be the least of it. Warren could give her sons a golden start to adult life, their futures assured. She seemed genuinely to like him, too; she'd responded to him right away.

Would she let go of Simon, even newly

married? I hated myself for giving in to a dreadful attack of bitchiness, the way I'd put that thought into Warren's head, but it had been in his mind already, I knew. Warren was as possessive as he was old, and he'd protested about her virtuous fidelity a bit too keenly by half.

I turned over in bed impatiently; where was the soothing balm for the blistering pain of rejection? The inevitability of what had happened was the depressing thing. Daisy's nubility, Warren's over-excited libido. But if he truly loved her, I tried to persuade myself in a pride-assuaging way, could he really have carried on with me for so long and taken the trips we had? Warren was serious and proper, conventional to the tips of his toes; he seemed less cut out for a double-act than some. He'd enjoyed being with me — a little nervous drinking in Newport, true, but when we'd helicoptered to Martha's Vineyard and also to St Michael's, that cute chic resort in Maryland, he'd been visibly relaxed and contented, as well as in his sexual stride.

There was no way to salvage any pride, no soft landings, no saving graces. By Thursday evening he'd known what he wanted and it wasn't me; contentment in my company was no match for younger physical charms. It did take some swallowing.

Warren's ex-wife, Willa, had been the great love of his life, I believed, from the way he'd talked about her to me. His obsessive need to have every centimetre of his summer home upturned hadn't only been a ruse for a summer

410

flirtation with a design consultant like me. I sensed it had a lot to do with an on-going, all-consuming passion — the smallest reminders of Willa still causing heartache and pain.

Warren was in the grip of a seventy-year-old's infatuation, but was that foundation enough for a quality third marriage? Would comparisons with Willa begin to creep in? How much depth of love did one need for long-term happiness? Perhaps that applied more to Daisy, since it was hard to see Warren as the great all-time love of *her* life: he must surely be less than a grand consuming passion. He had compensating factors, though, in spades and, approaching forty, mustn't she long for more security? It was a tough decision. I cared quite deeply about Daisy. Despite it all, I was truly fond of her.

★ ★ ★

No one was around in the morning. Breakfast was set up on the deck. Martha came out with fruit juice, a dish of fresh fruits, luscious paw-paw with lime, ink-dark blueberries, pine-apple and mango slivers, rich red strawberries for colour. Fresh-baked croissants, the hypnotic smell of the finest Brazilian coffee ... I complimented Martha and said, looking about, 'Surely I'm not the first up?'

'Mr Lindsay's gone sailing with Mr Harvey from next door. I think it was a spur-of-the-moment plan, fixed up just this morning. Mr Lindsay said he wouldn't be back till late, and that we shouldn't expect him for dinner.'

'You don't call him Warren?' I asked lightly, thinking smugly that it was typically male of him, getting out of the heat in the kitchen and making himself scarce.

'He's never actually suggested first names,' Martha replied. 'He's quite formal in his way.' I suspected from her sensitive smile that she had some idea where we were at and felt in sympathy.

'And Daisy?'

'She's gone to the Jitney stop to meet the lady coming to see you about skylight blinds. Jackson's taking the men down to Montauk.'

'In that case,' I said, 'I'd better enjoy this wonderful breakfast while I can.'

Martha knew I liked my coffee in a mug so I could wander about with it, and stepping down into the garden, clasping the mug, I felt renewed. I marvelled at the sunlight slanting through the red maples. It caught the dew, which glistened iridescently. It brought clarity of colour to the pastel roses; it illuminated a patch of dull grey paving, making me decide that the new slabs should be bleached-bone pale. Accepting the job with its interesting Warren possibilities had been an experience, much of it good, but now I was ready for home. I wanted the familiar, my own set-up, and some time in my house in the South of France. I longed for Mediterranean brilliance suddenly, to be in my own skin again, free to do as I chose.

Daisy returned with an over-made-up woman who had sample swatches of blinds slung over her shoulders like onion strings, and a hefty book of glossy photographs under one arm. Doing our business took time; she was talkative. Daisy and I continued to work when she'd left — with no mention made of Warren, not a word.

At twelve-thirty I snapped shut my notebook. 'I've told Martha we'll have a snack lunch at the Beach Club, Daisy, our usual Monday routine, so perhaps we should walk up there now. It'll give you a chance to tell me your decision, if it's made. I'll be going home tomorrow or the next day, leaving you to finish off here. Do you want to change, pick up a bathing suit? Leaving in, say, ten minutes?'

Daisy looked at me strangely. 'Warren's told you then — the bombshell he dropped on me yesterday afternoon? I hadn't realised,' she said, blushing and very flustered. 'I mean, the way you've been so nice and normal all morning, I'd no idea . . . God, how awful! I'd hoped, I suppose, depending which way I made up my mind, that you might never need to know.'

'I'd guessed and tested the theory, and I put Warren on the spot late last night. It was Warren who'd been tired on Thursday, you see, not me. I hope he has his wits about him, out sailing today — he drank a lot of scotch, telling all. You knew he'd be gone till late, didn't you? He had told you?'

'No, but Martha did,' she muttered slightly sullenly, obviously resentful that Warren hadn't even warned her that I knew he'd proposed. 'God, I'm unbelievably sorry about all this, Susannah,' she added passionately, eyes bright with warmth, 'but almost relieved. I've so much wanted to pour it all out to you — even if it

413

meant having to be kicked out on my ear.'

I stared, unsure what I felt. 'Go and get ready then. We can talk more on the way.'

We walked slowly in the heat of the day; a hundred degree high, the weathermen said, still into Fahrenheit. Daisy didn't stop talking.

'I'm entirely to blame, Susannah. It wasn't really Warren's doing, not at the start anyway, which is the point. He'd given me his card, told me if I ever needed help, that sort of stuff, and I'd called him up one day when I hadn't especially needed to. I'd just been feeling a bit lonely in the city, I guess, with time to kill and lunchtimes on my own. It really is all my fault. I'd been stupidly flattered by his flirty little glances,' Daisy drew a breath, blushed again and plunged on, 'and with the summer heat and all the excitement . . . But what sort of an excuse is that, for letting you down so comprehensively? God, I feel so ashamed.'

'I'd already feared you might duck out on me,' I said, 'that you'd feel too lovelorn for Simon to cope. I was certainly wrong there.'

Daisy smiled vaguely, still looking abject and was off again.

'Then it got more serious, you see,' she said. 'Warren started giving me presents. I begged him not to, they embarrassed me, made me feel as cheap as they should have done, and more disloyal than ever. Silver chains, designer bags, you'd have known they were way more than I could ever afford.'

Daisy stopped just short of the Beach Club, dropped down her bag and buried her head in her hands. I waited impatiently for her to look up, feeling I had rather more to cry about than her. I should be the one lifting tearful eyes.

Hers were wetly forlorn as she faced me. 'I can't expect you to forgive me and I'll never forgive myself, ever. After all you'd done for me, taught me, your kindness, the fun times . . . '

'I'd quite like to get on now,' I said curtly, cutting her off. Daisy deserved to stew a bit longer. She'd known what she was doing, she wasn't an ingénue. I wasn't quite ready to draw the line, say all was forgiven and forgotten, and it was blindingly hot, standing on the pavement in the full sun.

We carried on in silence, but by the time we'd arrived and were signed in I was softening. She'd been honest and straight at least, and I couldn't help feeling for her too. While many would die to be in her shoes, choosing to stay or walk away from Warren and his billions was no easy decision.

We bought lobster rolls and glasses of iced tea, which we took to a shady table. Few people were at the Club and I was glad of the Monday quiet. As we sat looking out, I felt drained, listless in the salty humid air. The ocean was misted with a hazy glare, the breakers hypnotic as they relentlessly crashed onto the sand.

Daisy picked at her roll and avoided my eyes. When she glanced up, I broke the silence.

'Have you made up your mind yet?' I asked, though it was pretty clear that she hadn't. 'It must be difficult. Proposals from billionaires have rarity value for a start, and while the pro

415

column's a no-brainer, it's the cons that are harder to flush out.'

'Don't I know it! And then throw in marrying on the rebound . . . ' Daisy laughed, as though feeling a sense of release. She looked lighter and livelier in an instant. 'And that's from Warren's point of view as much as my own,' she said. 'His ex-wife came to the restaurant where we had lunch once, Susannah, and stalked over to our table, pulled up a chair without asking, and set about making trouble. She was a real glamour-puss, the siren type, but terrifically elegant and assured with it; she slotted me into the shop-girl category, I can tell you, with very scratchy claws. I felt mauled to bits. Warren seemed struck dumb, but he soon hit back and put down the harmless old boy she was with, as if he was a comic turn. He matched Willa bitch for bitch, but then afterwards went into a decline. She had quite an effect on him.'

That was interesting intelligence and it bore out what I thought — that Willa was far from out of his system.

Daisy and I had a quick swim, but I needed to get going. With so much to do before leaving, ends to tie up, my professional pride was at stake. I was on a 10 p.m. flight from Kennedy airport the next night.

'A couple of things, Daisy,' I said, as we walked back. 'Those presents, no need to keep them hidden any more. I'd relax and enjoy them, whichever way you decide. I can't see the shame in accepting a few gifts. They weren't the name of the game. And be sure to let me know when

416

you finally make up your mind. Text me or call, won't you? If you're staying on, I wouldn't have to come out in October, you see; I'd promised Warren to fly out to check on progress, but you'd be able to deal with all that. That's the least of it, though. It's your future and I care about you, of course, very much. I'd want to know.'

The tears were streaming down Daisy's face. She was unrestrained, wordy; self-flagellating. I couldn't help feeling gently inclined, understanding and forgiving. Our friendship spanned the generation gap like an elastic band. It could survive a twang or two; I trusted it and knew it would hold fast.

★　★　★

On the plane home I hung onto my sense of calm. Most of the other Club Class passengers were men. I could guess at the ones who played away, for they had a self-satisfied lift to their chins, gave their pink newspapers confident shakes and glanced at the legs of stewardesses, even at mine. The purer characters, men who simply wanted to get home to their wives, worked, looked at their watches and settled to sleep.

I thought back to the sixties, times in the South of France, Manhattan, even Long Island, when I'd behaved, not exactly like Daisy, but slept around a fair bit. I'd been on a trial separation in Manhattan, living there for three months. Still, it was little excuse for going wild. Only Gil, my celebrity pick-up in London, and

417

one other man, a friend passing through New York, had been married, though.

There could have been another if only he'd asked me; I fell for Bobby Kennedy, although much of the attraction was that he didn't make a pass. It was his tousled hair and seriousness that I loved. I remembered him leaving off kicking a ball around with his riotous mob of children to come and talk to me, sit with me on a wooden bench, cogitating and chewing the cud as though we were in a pub garden. It was a golden moment.

I'd seen little more of him. After that, my times in the States were few and far between, but to read of Bobby's violent end, some years later, had been heartrending. My brief warm acquaintanceship came vividly to mind. And recalling the horror of his killing in Los Angeles — that ghastly assassination replay, three shots, no proper security — was to think about single moments, history stopped in its tracks, and imagine what might have been. Bobby securing the nomination, taking on Nixon . . . So many thoughts of the sixties lingered on.

Daisy's worries about remarrying on the rebound also brought back memories. I should have had similar worries, more caution at least, which might have stopped me leaping in again with my second husband, beautiful aristocratic Max — just as Daisy had done with the loathsome-sounding Peter, who'd left her so short of funds. I hoped she wouldn't feel pressured; she was making a lifelong decision.

My decision had been made in the early

sixties. How different things had been then, with chauvinism, casually accepted racism, handed-down prejudices, cigarettes as a way of life . . . It was pre-Women's Lib and bra burning, and male liberty-taking was the norm.

Did modelling and the life I'd lived then make me self-centred? I'm sure it did, but events had kept my feet on the ground. I'd had knocks in my twenties, a little violence, some heartache, but plenty of loving, too. I had been riding the crest of a turbulent, electrifying decade.

23

May 1963–January 1964

'You won't forget the drink with Matt Seeley tonight, Joe? We said seven-thirty at the White Elephant.' Joe was on his way out, due to record a radio play and cursing the early start. 'Try not to be late, love, you're more into Washington than me.'

'Is that meant to be a dig?'

'No, just a fact. You had a drink with Matt there, you've got more to talk about.'

I needed Joe for protection. Matt had been calling from Washington declaring all sorts of undying feelings and I didn't trust myself to keep my distance.

I'd been working hard at my marriage in the months since being back, while Joe kept pulling as hard the other way. I despaired of him. He was drinking tankfuls, vodka all day, quantities of wine, brandy, whisky, and he could be quite frightening when the drink really took hold. He was fine with a party to go to, but his downers were deeper than the Jules Verne depths. I couldn't talk to him; he swatted me away.

It was May, but felt like February and I spent an icy day outdoors, working for Duffy, shower dodging in Hyde Park. I was a frozen block, very glad that we packed up early and I could go home to have a precious hour or two with Bella

420

before meeting Matt.

I changed into a black wool dress, scoop-necked and long-sleeved, not too flaunting of flesh, and was about to go when the phone rang. I almost left it to ring, as it was getting late and was sure to be Joe crying off. He'd thought a drink with Matt and me reeked of boredom, yawn, yawn. I'd picked up that much.

It wasn't Joe, it was my mother and I heard the stress in her voice instantly.

'What's up?' I said, drawing in my breath, feeling fearful.

'Dad's had a heart attack — a small one, I don't want you to be too worried. He just has to rest up for a couple of weeks — and stop eating chips!'

She wasn't up to light asides, close to breaking down, I felt. 'You mustn't worry either, Mum, promise me that? It'll take all your energies simply to keep Dad confined to bed. It would be a bit difficult tomorrow, but I can get out of my Friday's booking and be with you by midday. I'll have Bella with me as Miss Hadley has the weekend off, but you must leave her to me, no picking her up and making more work for yourself. I can arrange to stay next week, too.'

'No, don't do that, it's just lovely if you can come this weekend. It would mean a lot to Dad. And to me too, darling.'

Miss Hadley was beside me. We'd been saying good night, and she'd heard it all. 'I don't need time off,' she said, as I hung up, 'I can come and lend a hand if I wouldn't be in the way. Bella's such a little minx now and your mother will only want to help.'

'You'd be far from in the way,' I said, immensely touched and grateful. 'I'll phone Mum back, if you're really sure, then I must dash.'

Miss Hadley and I had found a rapport. She'd stopped seeing me as flighty, had absorbed that I paid the bills and wasn't just modelling-obsessed. I wondered if she'd taken a call or two from Joe's debtors. He laid on the charm with her, but rather more erratically of late, and with less winsome effect.

I drove on autopilot to Curzon Street, fretting about Dad, praying he'd be a good patient, wind down and have a holiday at last, as well as the enforced rest. I parked my Mini in a tight space outside the Club — too small for Mayfair's Bentleys and Rolls — and hurried in. I was late, distressed, an apology on my lips — frustrated to see, as I feared, that Joe hadn't arrived. Matt was sitting up at the bar, drinking alone just as Richard Burton had been, and must be on his second martini at least.

'Sorry, Matt,' I said breathlessly, 'keeping you waiting like this. Don't be too cross!'

He climbed down from his barstool with a beaming smile, then, taking hold of my shoulders and studying me a minute, he let the smile fade. 'Something's wrong. Tell me. I can see it in your eyes.'

I'd tried to mask the worry and wondered at his perception while explaining about my mother's news. 'It's a small heart attack, no more than a warning call, I'm sure. Dad has a country practice and he never lets up. I'd hoped Joe would be here,' I said, as Matt led the way to one of the tables in the bar with navy armchairs, ensuring the Burton evening stayed vivid in my mind. 'He must have got waylaid, but I'm sure he'll make it soon.'

'I hope not. I hope he's permanently detained. Campari and soda?'

'Good memory! How are you, Matt? It's been six months, which is hard to believe.'

'Six and a half, twenty-seven weeks — I've been marking them off.'

I smiled. 'Tell me what's going on in your life, girls, everything. And how's Pierre?'

'He's fine, as up against it as ever. Who'd be the President's Press Secretary! It's why I've been stuck in Washington, walking up the walls. But why ask about girls? You're the one, Susannah, you must know that by now. I've been out of my mind, desperate to swing getting to London to see you. I've tried every dodge and wheeze over the months, but no dice. God, the frustration . . . ' Edging his armchair closer, Matt covered my hand with his, fingers pressing, curling round my palm. 'I'm passionate about you, so obsessed that it's scary. It carves me up, seeing you in ads everywhere — Jim Beam, Chevrolet. I buy all the magazines, I've got a pile way high.'

It was embarrassing, overdone, and I looked down, avoiding his eyes. Matt knew my mind was on my father; it felt a little insensitive, not the right time. His concern when I came in had been heartening, though, he'd genuinely seemed to care. It was impossible to forget about New York either, how he'd seized me with such passion in the Ferrones' hall, kissing me with Joe only feet away, in the next room.

Matt was fingering my hand, expecting some response. 'Let's talk about anything other than me now,' I said. 'And shall we have a bite to eat here, if you've no other plans? Joe can join us, as and when he shows.' He obviously wasn't going to, that was clear.

I told the barman where to direct Joe and we made our way through to the restaurant. A waiter took us to a discreet back table; the place was so softly lit it was almost in darkness, but Matt was well aware of the news I'd just had and I felt I could relax.

He asked about my childhood and I talked about my brother, my mother giving up a career as a barrister, her wartime struggles — in Malta during the siege, my father away fighting, the desperate shortage of food and me choosing just that time to be born — all the sacrifices made. 'She's always helped with the practice too,' I said. 'She's worn out herself, and now has to cope with the shock of Dad. They've never taken holidays, however much I've tried to persuade them. Maybe when he's a bit better . . . '

Matt surveyed me; his foot was lightly touching mine. With his freckles and short hair, clean-cut all-American look, the sense about him of fast cars and fun, his restraint tonight was a relief and a surprise.

'I've had an idea,' he said, 'and please hear me

424

out. Remember I told you about the rich old lady in Boston who gives me the use of her cottage near Saint Paul de Vence? She won't be there now, or in June. Take your parents. I'd stay in Cannes; you needn't see me at all unless you want to. No strings. The cottage is gloriously peaceful, with fabulous views, no telephone, no distractions — and a great restaurant, the Colombe d'Or, just up the road. If your parents knew it was only costing the fares . . . '

'I don't know, Matt. It's incredibly kind of you, it sounds perfect in every way, but my parents might wonder a little about a guy like you, over from America — certainly not an old family friend — making such an amazing offer out of the blue. You do see it's potentially a little awkward.'

I didn't mention the fact that Mum — Dad, too, now, since Joe's disappearance at the time of Bella's birth — had few illusions about the rocky state of my marriage.

'Can't you say I simply want to help? I can fit in on timing, Pierre owes me.'

'Thanks, Matt, it's wonderful of you. I'll talk to Mum this weekend and see.' I felt terribly torn. 'It would be great,' I added, reaching for Matt's hand. 'I've never been to the South of France, as it happens, but this would be for my parents, their treat.'

'I can't believe they'd mind, though, if I showed you Cannes one afternoon . . . ' He gave me a sideways look.

★ ★ ★

Three weeks later, we landed at Nice airport. Dad looked sickly, Mum, lined and drained. I'd hired a small Renault and drove away nervously on the wrong side of the road, crawling like an elderly Sunday driver with Mum reading out Matt's directions and Dad poring over a huge map. We finally made it to the Villa Laurier-Rose.

I'd been fairly honest with Joe, said that Matt, hearing about Dad, had told of a small villa available near St Paul de Vence. I'd asked Joe to come too, knowing he'd probably be rehearsing in Chichester and saying, truthfully, that the second bedroom at the house was extremely small. Joe wasn't interested anyway. The opening of the new Chichester Theatre the previous year had been a success and he was pleased to be acting there again. He'd half-apologised, in his terms anyway, for not showing at the Club that evening, saying he'd had a better offer during the day. 'I'm sure you did,' I'd muttered sarcastically, while not forgetting my own mad moments, my rush of blood, the last time we were there.

Matt was watching out for us, sitting on a stone wall, luxuriating in the warmth of a sunny day. The temperature was in the seventies. He greeted us, tactfully avoiding kissing me.

It was early afternoon. We'd eaten on the plane and I urged Dad to hurry to bed and rest. 'You're here to take it easy, remember, that's the whole point.'

'Fuss, fuss!' He was clearly exhausted, though, sinking down gratefully onto a cushioned bench against the wall of the veranda where we'd just come in. He stared ahead, his attention held, looking enraptured. 'I've never seen a more stupendous view. It's magical!'

'Your bedroom has the same outlook,' Matt said, 'with more sea. And a bathroom.'

That got Dad climbing the single flight, still marvelling, but finally stretching out on the bed. 'This bolster pillow thing is more comfortable than it looks,' he said.

The other bedroom was little more than an alcove off the living room, but there was a downstairs loo. Matt showed us the kitchen, the basic provisions he'd brought. He explained about the hot water, rubbish collection, quirks of the keys — and then made us some tea.

The covered veranda where he took the tray had a sizable refectory table and ladder-back rush chairs, comfy basket armchairs, a cushioned bench along the wall. I could see we'd eat every meal there. The garden was terraced to cope with the terrain, tended, yet given its head; roses and peonies mingled with cottage flowers, plants tumbled over the retaining drystone walls. 'There's a small swimming pool that you can't see from here,' Matt said, 'and a patio with sun chairs and stuff. Come, take a look.'

'I'll stay here, I think,' my mother said. 'I'll pop upstairs soon to see how Dad is doing.'

Matt beamed at her. 'Should I perhaps run Susannah up to the village, show her the shops, the boulangerie, that sort of thing? Would you and Henry be okay for a while?'

'Happy as sand boys,' Mum assured him. 'Off you go and explore, love,' she said to me, 'and no need to hurry back.'

She rose and picked up the tea tray, only to smile helplessly when Matt was quick to take it from her. I worried about what she was thinking, whether she was disapproving at heart. She must know that young men like Matt didn't hang around being altruistic. He didn't give off an aura of innocence — there was nothing of the saint about him. Still, Mum seemed happy for me — or maybe she was just too concerned and preoccupied. I should be too. I felt guilty, anxious, and said a small prayer for Dad.

'Those are grapefruit and mandarin trees,' Matt said, as we walked down the garden. I was glad he didn't take my hand. 'And the pink oleander hedges give the villa its name. Just past that old olive tree is the best place for the view.'

I stood looking out over a panorama of villages, church steeples and sleepy countryside with the sea in the distance, gleaming like polished silver; a haze softened the hills that framed and encircled the bay. It was the still of the afternoon, calming. Perfect peace.

'I could stand here till the leaves have fallen from the trees, drinking this in.'

'But I think we should go to the village.' Matt lightly stroked my bare arm, giving me tingles. 'And perhaps after that have a swim? Then I must get back to my hotel.'

'I should be paying for that!' I exclaimed, shocked not to have thought of it before.

'Pierre's picking up the tab — well, the government is. I'll scout about a bit while I'm here.'

We set off up the winding road to St Paul de

Vence. I hadn't had a holiday since that unique, unbelievable time in California with the Romanoffs and Sinatra, though tensions with Joe had cast a shadow even then. It was nearly two years ago now.

'They like it all right, don't they?' Matt turned with a grin. 'It's working out?'

'It's heaven — everything is.'

He left the car by the roadside and we walked the last bit to the village, strolling into its medieval heart, down narrow cobbled lanes, cool and dark in shadow, illuminated where openings gave way to the incredible view. We watched a game of pétanque going on under huge plane trees in front of the Café de la Place; leathery old men in brown trousers intent on their play. A church bell was chiming, competing with the metallic clink when the heavy balls made contact — to satisfied Gallic grunts.

'Yves Montand plays here with the locals,' Matt said, 'or brings his celebrity friends. He and Simone Signoret were married here, having met at La Colombe d'Or. You must have dinner there, if only to see the paintings — Chagall, Braque, Matisse, the Picassos — they litter the walls.'

'I'll suggest it to Mum and Dad. Would you come too, but definitely on me?'

Matt rested his arm on my shoulder and fondled my neck under my hair. 'I'm sure this isn't allowed,' he said, without removing his hand, 'if I'm to stop you imagining ulterior motives. It's just, in this very romantic setting . . .'

That was all very well, yet his offer of the

cottage, possibly not quite as genuinely spontaneous as I'd imagined, was a wonderful boon and Matt was persuasive. It wasn't easy, at this stage of knowing him, to resist. 'Time I did some shopping,' I said, 'and we started back.'

'One kiss,' he said in the car. 'And am I going to be allowed to show you Cannes? A turn round Antibes, Cap-Ferrat, Juan-les-Pins — of course asking your parents along, too.'

'In the hope that they don't come?' But he was closing in, muzzling me.

We had a swim and Matt stayed for a drink when he mentioned Cannes and sightseeing. My parents loved the idea of a drive, but said they weren't up to exploring in towns. 'Say we pottered to somewhere like Antibes, had a light lunch and I dropped you back here for a nap?' Matt suggested, which went down well. 'I could whizz Susannah on into Cannes perhaps then for a quick mooch at the boutiques.' Neatly done, I thought.

★ ★ ★

I didn't window-shop in Cannes. I caved in, gave in. It was inevitable — it could have happened in New York. Matt parked off the Croisette and we meandered; I soaked up the beauty of it all, admiring too, the splendid Belle Epoque façade of the Carlton Hotel.

'It's where I'm staying,' Matt said. 'Come and have a Knickerbocker Glory, or its French equivalent, on the terrace. It's worth seeing.'

The terrace looked out through tall palms to

the beguiling Bay and the Croisette. We had a clear view, a table right by the solid, elegant balustrade; we gorged on exotic ice-cream sundaes and I said how very glamorous and swish it all was.

'The interior's even more so,' Matt said. 'You should see my room.'

'Which you'd like me to?' I raised an eyebrow, but I wanted him now. I worried how casual an affair would be, not Gil's ideal blueprint, but with Joe's remoteness I felt starved of a sense of connection. It was good to feel lusted after and adored.

Matt leaned forward, resting an elbow on the balustrade. 'It's extraordinary, the human condition,' he said. 'I've survived without resorting to throwing stones at your bedroom window, without touching you all today. But right now . . . ' He caught a waiter's eye, motioned for the chit.

Matt's lovemaking was frenzied, quick and explosive, passionate and very voluble. I thought of people having siestas in next-door rooms. He buried his head in my neck as he climbed down, panting and heaving, saying he felt dreadful about it. 'I wanted to make it last, to take you on the journey . . . ' He kissed my fingers. 'Can we call it a taster? Don't talk about going, give me a moment or so.'

'An hour, two hours, three?' I turned to smile as he feigned shock at the slur on his manhood before falling into a deep sleep. I lay beside him in a contented daze.

I thought about Joe. With no phone at the cottage I'd rung from Nice on arrival and again

431

yesterday from the post office in Vence, to ask after Bella. Joe hadn't left a number where he could be reached in Chichester as he'd promised. I was angry. Miss Hadley needed to be able to call.

I was sad to feel so little guilt; was I so hardened and brash, so removed from the days of feeling love and devotion, a simple belief that our marriage was for life? Joe had affairs and the bottle; I had affairs too, now, and my work. But there was Bella.

I made a decision lying beside Matt. Now, while Bella was so little, was the time for a trial separation. I could go to New York, find an apartment; see if Miss Hadley was willing to come. I'd put it to Joe when we were home. How he'd react, I had no idea.

I slipped out of a bed that felt impersonal and transitory in the way of hotels and went to the bathroom to wash. 'My God, where have you gone?' Matt called out. He appeared at the door of the sumptuous bathroom looking dishevelled, freckled and nakedly keen; he dropped down on his knees, parted my legs and began doing what he'd said he'd wanted to, taking me on the journey rather beautifully.

I was back at the Villa Laurier-Rose by seven and doubted that my parents would imagine how I'd spent the afternoon. I mentioned exploring, idling over a Knickerbocker Glory, and left it there. I'd told Matt my time was with them now, that I'd see him on our last night, at dinner at the Colombe d'Or.

I took Mum and Dad to the village and to see

432

the starkly simple chapel in Vence, designed by Matisse as a thank you to the nuns who'd nursed him back to health. I prayed that Dad's own health would hold; he had a little colour and looked refreshed.

On our last evening Mum, overwhelmed by the beauty, the food, the art, simply couldn't thank Matt enough. Her happiness was a joy. She'd wanted to eat early to see that Dad had a decent night's sleep before the flight and insisted they went back to the house first, by taxi so that we could linger over our wine. Matt immediately booked a room. He was lucky to get one.

★ ★ ★

Joe slept through Bella's breakfast-time, all the banged spoons, demanding wails and kerfuffle. I looked in on him before leaving and he turned over in bed and squinted open an eye. 'You off? Isn't it your birthday today, the wifey? Want to go to the Trat tonight?'

I was impressed he'd remembered. 'Sounds good. Thanks, darling, I'd love to.'

I'd been back from France three weeks. Terraced hillsides in the South of France seemed light years away. Joe had been in Chichester much of the time and was only home now for three days. He'd returned Sunday, gone out Monday, 'seeing friends' and crept into bed at about four. I hadn't had a chance to talk about separation.

A birthday supper, people-spotting at Trattoria Terrazza, was hardly the time, but Joe was due

433

back in Chichester next day. He half-turned to squint at me again, looking sunken-eyed and sickly green. 'God, my head! It'll take a few hairs of the dog, egg-nogs, Fernet Branca or whatever, but I'll be the life and soul on the wifey's night out, you'll see.'

But Joe wasn't on form at the restaurant, still looking lousy. He picked up with a few glasses of vino, though, and banter with the cheery waiters in their Neapolitan fishermen's jerseys; the Trat was his sort of 'in' place. Mario had given us a table in Enzo Apicella's Positano room too, where it all happened. David Bailey and Jean Shrimpton were there, David Niven and Terence Stamp — whom I knew slightly and whose looks turned me on no end. I waited till Joe was on a second bottle and our fritto misto and pollo sorpresa had been served with panache, then took a breath.

'This mightn't seem the time or place, but I want to talk seriously about our future.' Joe rolled his eyes. 'I think we need a break from each other, a friendly trial separation. You've been very hard to live with, Joe, you've been violent at times and I worry what the drink is doing to you. If I just went away for three months . . .'

'It might help.' He yawned, which wasn't over-encouraging. 'I know, I know,' he said. 'You want me to run round Hyde Park, lick the booze and get a job as a bank clerk.'

'Not that last, but the rest sounds good. What do you think?'

'I think you want to swan off to New York and make pots of lolly.'

'Yes and no. I want us to be together, Joe, here, there, anywhere, but with you as a more loving, less sodden husband. Swanning off wouldn't come into it then.'

Joe shrugged. 'So go, if that's how the mood takes you. Maybe it's not such a bad wheeze. I'll try to shape up and sort myself out a bit in the allotted time.'

'Oh, Joe, would you really?' My eyes were moist. I blinked hard, feeling a rush of love and hope. 'It means me taking Bella, of course, and Miss Hadley if she'll agree; renting an apartment too, since we obviously couldn't stay with the Ferrones.'

Joe stared. He hadn't factored that in. 'No. Forget it, just forget it.' He downed his wine.

'Think how much you actually see her, love,' I pleaded, 'not even once a week. She's still a baby, it really is the best time. She won't remember when she's three, four, five . . . '

Joe fidgeted and turned away, attracted a waiter and ordered more wine. Facing me again he looked sullen and almost ready to cry. He gave me a cold stare. 'I'd want to come to see her. Is that allowed?' The wine arrived, presented with a waiterly flourish, and we both beamed. 'Well, here's to separation and the wifey's birthday,' Joe said, only slightly sardonically, when we were alone again. 'Sorry about no present and all that . . . '

I was smiling, crying, tears dripping noiselessly, while Joe drank quantities, rubbernecked, and called hi to a friend.

* * *

I rented a mid-town apartment on East 48th Street from a rich Greek living in London, who fancied me a bit and was prepared to let me have it cheap. 'It's only free till mid-January,' he said, 'so you're neatly filling a gap.'

Miss Hadley, after initial sniffy dubiousness, was quite excited about going. 'Fancy me,' she said. 'I never expected to see New York in my lifetime. My sister's very jealous.'

'You won't know anyone at first,' I warned, 'and it's a fair distance from Central Park.'

'I like to walk. Will we buy the pram out there?' It was a reminder of all I had to do.

* * *

We settled into the apartment, glad of the friendly doorman and good living space, which was soon covered with toys. Miss Hadley was delighted when a second-hand shop yielded a British Silver Cross pram. It helped to make up for her disgust at the grime, the people pushing past without apology, the total strangers who, conversely, struck up a conversation. She loved Bloomingdale's, couldn't believe how fast people talked, and was fascinated by the drugstore and deli scene. She and the doorman, Herman, passed a lot of the time of day together, with much cooing over Bella on his part.

I plunged into work. Eileen Ford had it all lined up, bookings, go-sees; I needn't have worried. I worked with Penn on a Johnson &

Johnson baby ad. Penn had booked twenty babies, and the minute one cried, he'd call out calmly, 'Next baby, please.' He was immune to the bedlam in the outer office, screaming infants and twenty mothers who all wanted their darlings to star.

I called Gil and felt the old fluttering ache deep inside. His voice did it, the loving inflections, the layer of feeling behind the arsing around and casual-sex chat. He was extremely keen to do mother and baby pictures. 'Come with Bella, this Friday evening, and bring her minder along. Then when we're done you can put 'em in a cab and stay on a while.'

'What for, Gil?' I smiled down the phone.

'The teacher's turn. Or do I have to stand in line?'

I wrote a long letter to Joe, begging him to think about treatment. I'd given him another small loan before leaving and knew he'd had a much larger one from an impresario fan. How he had got into so much debt was a mystery to me. Gaming clubs? Was that where he went to, so late at night?

I called Matt and left a message with his office, giving the apartment telephone number, but he hadn't rung in two days. I was surprised.

He was full of apologies when he did. 'Great to hear you! I was out of town. I can't get to New York for a bit — you coming to Washington any time?'

'The Ormsby-Gores have asked me, but not till next month. Are you here sooner?'

'Possibly — I'll call.'

I got the message; he was winding me down. It had been all about the chase and winning through. That had been my first thought, meeting him, yet having begun to believe that he genuinely cared, my own feelings had grown stronger. It was desperately hard to take. My heart was thudding, I felt really let down and upset.

'Sounds like you're pretty busy, Matt,' I said, cooling my tone. 'Thanks again about the cottage, my parents had a blissful rest.'

It hurt a lot. Like hell he'd been out of town — his office had said he was in conference with the Press Secretary. Matt clearly didn't go in for serious relationships, not with me at least. His outpouring of passion in New York, devouring kisses, beautiful declarations on transatlantic calls, the 'spontaneous' offer of the cottage in France — it had all been to one end: to lay me and chalk up another scalp. He'd probably made a bet with his mate who had the apartment in New York.

The hurt went further than pride. I'd been longing to see him, having fallen for him in the end and gone happily to bed with him in Cannes. He'd invested a lot of effort, broken me in like a horse and made me docile, but one more for his stable and nothing more. And the pleasure he'd given my parents? Whatever the opportunistic motives, he'd done some good and a kindness there, I had to hand him that. I wondered if he'd ever call; I felt physically in need of him and hated myself abjectly for it.

Janet, my model friend, told me to give him the finger. 'You're separated, Susannah. You can

438

get stuck in, join the creeps at their game. You're on the Pill, aren't you?'

'Yep, came out with a three months' supply,' I said, thinking back to Gil's wry amusement that I'd got as far as a bed in his loft with no protection. The Pill hadn't been available then, it was a Dutch cap or relying on the man.

I went a bit wild in Manhattan, trying to dull the hurt of Matt. It wasn't Janet's influence, more a souring inside, disillusion, despair at my failure to find love and trust. Men made advances non-stop. Most were married, but never let on, and I felt desperately disenchanted. Gil was a married man, true, and a flagrant womaniser, yet he was probably the most honest man I knew.

The husband of a fashion editor at *Vogue* chased me as persistently as Matt; he'd be in his car outside a studio, say he was waiting for his wife, but had time to give me a lift. I'd accepted at first, though soon wised up. I was in agonies one day when his wife picked up my little red address book that I'd inadvertently left by the studio phone. She stared so long and hard at a page that I knew she'd seen her husband's number, innocently written in once, when they'd invited me out to Long Island for a lunch party. Her pensive gaze was hard to bear. She left the book open at the page, but couldn't mention it without admitting to snooping. I was surprised that she ever booked me again.

I had a whacky affair with another photographer, a gorgeous six-foot-something hunk called Dale. His thatch of hair was a triumph, blond as straw from the bottle of peroxide he frequently tipped over it, and with an impressive layer of dark roots. He wasn't married, he said, and his apartment had the bare boards and lack of furniture to back that up, but who knew? I'd lost all ability to trust.

Dale took me away on a couple of working trips and his enthusiasm was catching. 'Ace!' he'd say, scrunching me into his side, pointing out a handsome crescent in Boston where I'd been to with Gil. 'Ace architecture, just ace, the symmetry, the *elegance*!' I adored him. 'You've turned up the volume on my life,' he said once, 'way high!'

He had colourful turns of phrase. 'Never squat with your spurs on,' was his take on watching your back, and he'd stand in his boxers in front of the television and jab at some hapless politician. 'He's the kinda creep who can cry out of one eye.'

Bert Stern featured in my life, too. He was into pot and more adult fixes, but I was for the foothills and didn't go there. He photographed me for *Vogue* covers. We did one with large, sunny flower heads pinned to a strapless bra, and my bare midriff held his eye. It was how we got to know each other.

Friends from London passed through. Ludo Kennedy, the writer and broadcaster, was one. He'd heard from Joe that I was in New York, called me and we went to see Tom Courtenay in *The Loneliness of the Long Distance Runner*. Afterwards we ate at his hotel, discussed the gritty film, Courtenay's genius, and talked far into the night.

We had a new Prime Minister and I said, curious, 'I miss not seeing the British press with Alec Douglas Home taking over. I know you're a Liberal, but what do you think?'

'He was a good Foreign Secretary, at least. Of course, all bets had been on Rab Butler. It was a surprise.'

'Cecil Beaton was funny about that when I worked with him before coming here,' I said. 'He really didn't fancy Mr Butler. 'Just imagine that dull, plain, bulbous face on our television screens every night,' he said with a wicked eye. He does love a little bitch!'

I asked Ludo about a shocking report on the news earlier in the evening — Adlai Stevenson, the UN Ambassador, being booed, spat at and hit with a stick in Dallas.

'It's Kennedy's focus on civil rights,' Ludo said, 'and his hints over pulling out of Vietnam. The extremists and Southern racists can't handle it. They're in revolt.'

'It's dreadful. I read about all these radical groups — there's even one called the National Indignation Convention trying to get the entire Texas Democratic Party to defect to the Republicans. And to think Jack's going campaigning there next month.'

'He needs to, though; he can't win in sixty-four if he loses Texas, especially if he dumps Johnson from the ticket as he wants to. There's the rest of the South as well.'

'I'm off to Washington tomorrow,' I said, reluctantly parting from Ludo, 'having a weekend with the Ormsby-Gores. I don't suppose there'll be much talk of this, but you've helped me to feel more primed. Thanks. I really must go, but it's been great.'

★ ★ ★

I caught the five o'clock shuttle to Washington, which put Matt powerfully in mind. He'd called, but only to say that he couldn't make the supper party with the Ferrones. I hadn't even known he'd been asked. Joan must have wanted it to be a small surprise. I'd written to her about my father, so she knew quite a bit.

Having thought about Matt the whole way on the plane, I discovered he was asked to lunch next day — Sylvia Ormsby-Gore doing a Joan Ferrone.

It was hard to handle, a struggle sitting next to him, chatting politely — especially when over the coffee he suggested a spin in his car. I didn't do well, saying with a panicky heart that I'd love that, completely failing to act with any suitable dignity.

But going to bed with Matt that Saturday afternoon ended up being good for me. It was flat, mechanical, meaningless. I felt unloving, unclean, and knew it was closure, an upper and downer in my life and nothing more. 'So long, Matt,' I said, as he drove me zippily back to the Residence. 'It's been nice knowing you.'

'I wanted to ask after your father,' he said, absorbing the finality of my words and not quite ready, it seemed, to let go of a not-so-bad occasional lay. 'How's he doing?'

'Medium-ly. I'll always be grateful for those few days in France.'

Dad had occasional angina chest pains, but he was being sensible and Mum wanted me to carry on as normal and see through the separation time. I was going along with that while saying a quiet prayer now and then.

Over drinks that evening, David Ormsby-Gore told me he was going to see Bobby Kennedy next day and we were all invited, children as well. 'Ours wouldn't be noticed anyway, in that ear-splitting madhouse. We could bring them and leave them there!'

Bobby and Ethel Kennedy lived at Hickory Hill which, like the White House, was large, white and handsomely proportioned. It had silver-grey shutters and immaculate front lawns where a tall flagpole proudly fluttered its Stars and Stripes flag. There were no Secret Servicemen to be seen as we trooped up to the front door. A maid hoovering in the hall let us in and David led the way purposefully through the house and out to the garden. He knew the form.

It was a boiling day, well into the 80s, and everyone was outdoors, back from church and letting off steam. Children were everywhere, racing and wrestling, rolling down the vast sloping lawns; a small boy was sailing up wildly high on a rickety rope swing. The branch it hung from was creaking ominously, but nobody seemed bothered. An older boy careered about in a Hot-Red Go-Kart, upsetting a horse in an adjacent field. Bobby was out in the garden too, wearing a yellow sweatshirt and pink trousers, leaning forward in a deckchair and talking on a telephone brought out from the house on an extended lead. He was concentrating intently and seemed undistracted by the noise.

Ethel appeared, followed by a maid carrying a tray of drinks, just as the black Labrador by Bobby's side shot off after a squirrel. There was a near collision, yet even that seemed to pass the master of the house by. He absently patted the panting dog on its return, putting his hand over the mouthpiece then, but only to yell out, I wasn't sure at whom, 'Get him, get him!' He indicated to David to pull up another deckchair and carried on with his call.

When David and Bobby, the British Ambassador and the President's brother, had finished their murmured chat they rounded everyone up for a game of touch football. I was in a fog of incomprehension, being manhandled, childhandled, yelled at to run, to watch out, but exhilarated and enjoying it like mad. When a child shrieked triumphantly, 'Gotcha!' and I was out, Bobby came to sit with me on a bench.

I fell in love instantly. He talked about Neil Simon's *Barefoot in the Park*, just opened on Broadway. 'It'll be a smash hit. People love all that witty schmaltzy humour and happy-endings.' He heaved a sigh. 'I don't think it'll be one of those in South Africa this week, with the Nelson Mandela trial; they stifle any breath of free speech out there, let alone political dissent.'

'Unlike America, where no one holds back,' I said, thinking of the UN Ambassador's treatment in Dallas and the piece in the newspapers

444

about crude anti-Kennedy *Wanted for Treason* pamphlets being scattered round town the next day. 'It must give you particular headaches of security at times,' I ventured, with a cautious smile.

'Yes, sure, and some places are worse than others, but that's politics — campaigning and facing your critics!' Bobby smiled in return and ruffled his unruly hair, reducing me to an ever more adoring pool. 'You have to take the flak.'

We talked on and it was a wrench when the time came to leave. My heart had been fluttering like the flag on Bobby and Ethel's front lawn.

★ ★ ★

I was in Lillian Bassman's studio when the President was shot. Sitting in a bath in a strapless bathing suit, a head and shoulders photograph, a cosmetics ad; the futile incongruity of that got to me. Lillian had the radio on and we'd caught the first bulletin, United Press saying that three shots had been fired and the wounds could be fatal. We listened, stunned, as more details began to filter through. Lillian, who was visibly moved, motioned me out of the bath.

'I think we'll call it a day,' she said. 'I can't carry on. Everyone can go home.'

The account executive had left by the time I was dressed. I stood by the radio, tensed for news, needing to keep listening, to hear that Jack would live. It was terrible, frighteningly extra-dimensional too, having talked and laughed with him and seen his private face. 'Sorry, I should go,' I said, embarrassed at hanging around. 'I just . . . ' I waved the air with a helpless hand, unable to explain.

'You don't need to,' Lillian said, 'but it'll be on television soon, I expect. Do you have a set where you're staying? You may prefer to watch than listen here.'

It made sense to get back to 48th Street, to Bella and Miss Hadley, and leave Lillian to her privacy. I admired her all the more, seeing her emotion, and left the studio fortified by her dignity. I wasn't anxious for a taxi driver's take on the shooting and walked the ten blocks down Third Avenue to the apartment. A curious hush had descended, as though a heavy snowstorm had blanketed the city, muffling the traffic and muting the horns. Few people were about; sparse huddles had formed round news-stands, although no news-sheets could surely have arrived. One stand had a radio on behind the counter, but it was hard to catch anything and I walked on.

Miss Hadley had the television tuned to CBS, and as I came in Walter Cronkite was saying, stumbling over his words, 'Two priests who were with Kennedy say, apparently, that he is dead from his bullet wounds.' Cronkite stressed that the President's death wasn't officially confirmed, but from his tone there was little doubt. It was 2.30 p.m. New York time, an hour since the first bulletin.

Cronkite talked about fearful concerns of demonstrations similar to the attack on Adlai Stevenson. When a paper was placed before him, the official news, he had to take off his glasses to blink away the emotion.

'Awful, awful,' Miss Hadley muttered. Bella was sleeping longer than usual, almost as though with an unconscious sense that it was helpful, and we watched in a daze. Miss Hadley sensitively didn't intrude. She took Bella out for a walk eventually, telling me to stay by the screen, that I'd known him and must want to be alone.

I thought of Jackie, spattered with blood and brain, crying out, 'Oh no!' I thought of Bobby Kennedy in Washington, how close he'd been to his brother. I thought of the unendurable pain. I imagined the news spreading ever more widely like spilt ink, and the differing reactions around the world.

Lyndon Johnson was sworn in as President aboard Air Force One at Love Field in Dallas in stifling conditions, we were later told. Twenty-seven people had had to squeeze into the plane's small stateroom with the air conditioning shut down for a speedy take-off.

At six that evening the new President and Jackie touched down in Washington. Bobby boarded the plane to escort Jackie off and when she and Bobby appeared they descended from the plane holding hands. She was still in her blood and matter-stained pink Chanel suit. Her legs, too, were still smeared with the shocking stains of her husband's blood.

★   ★   ★

I'd thought of the Ferrones at the time, how close Walter had been to Jackie, and wondered if

447

he'd been in touch. I'd commiserated, but hadn't probed. Shortly before I was due to go home, though, when Joan and I were having a farewell omelette supper together, she began to talk about Jackie. Joan was always one for going into detail.

'Walter spoke to her just after Jack's death,' she recalled. 'Jackie had refused to change out of that pink suit, you know? 'I wanted them to see what they'd done to Jack,' she said — and she'd also refused to leave without Jack's body on board the plane. It caused a terrible rumpus apparently, as it was against the wishes of the Dallas Medical Examiner; he'd insisted an autopsy was required and had been furious.

'She sure has guts, that girl!' Joan burst out. 'She told us how proud of the children she'd felt at the funeral — and on the very day of poor little John's third birthday, can you believe?' Joan paused, overcome, and wiped away a tear. 'President Johnson was kind, it seems, despite the tricky relations between them, calling, telling Jackie to stay at the White House as long as she wanted. Even saying she should come right on over, have a good cry and he'd 'put his arms around her'. She told us all about it.'

Joan, in her emotional mood, asked about Joe and the separation, what I felt about going home and whether I'd seen much of Matt Seeley. That was a fishing question; she felt involved, eager to know where we were at.

'Matt's for a good time, not for anything serious,' I said, glad to feel a vacuum where black heartache had been. 'It's as well really.' Joan squeezed my hand, she understood. 'I've had one

448

or two dates, though' — only a small understatement — 'one with an English guy, passing through. Max Thorsby, he's called. He's very beautiful and aristocratic, attentive without pushing it. He's one of these impecunious younger sons of a lord, his father's the Earl of Wickham.' I smiled at Joan's open-mouthed interest, but didn't want her making a meal of it and I was keen to talk about Joe. He'd been in touch after a long silence and made me feel quietly hopeful.

'Joe says he's getting on top of things, Joan. I do hope so. It would make everything possible again if only he'd just settle into some sort of vague routine. I know regular life is a bit much to expect!'

Joan looked down at her manicured nails and back at me with a long face. 'Now this is your Manhattan Mom talking, Susannah dearest. Don't expect honey and apple pie when you get home. In my experience, people are what they are. Joe needs his kicks and I'd say he always will; I'd hate you to be too let down. I just want my girl to be happy.'

'Oh, Joany!' I burst into tears. She came round the table and gave me a long hug and cuddle, smoothing back my hair. She and Walter would miss me so very much, she said.

I told her how dreadfully I'd miss them, too.

* * *

Landing home, early morning on 13 January 1964, the temperature hadn't squeaked above freezing. It had snowed the day before, not

449

much, but Miss Hadley and I, both worn out from the journey, felt chilled through. Joe had promised to come to meet us. He was excited, he'd said, at the thought of seeing Bella.

He wasn't there. We waited and waited. I phoned home. No answer — he'd probably overslept, early mornings weren't his strong suit. Eventually, after an hour, we gave up and took a taxi. I had a bleak sinking feeling, hope snatched away like a cap in a blast of cold wind.

Joe wasn't at home. Most of his clothes were gone, Frankie's cage, too. The house was quite clean, which pleased Miss Hadley who looked desperately fatigued, older than her undisclosed years. I ordered her to bed and talked baby talk to Bella who was toddling about exploring. I needed her distracted, though, and gave her a Laughing Cow cheese triangle to nibble on while I read the two notes I'd found.

One, under a bowl on the kitchen table, was from Palmira, my warm-hearted Spanish help. Her writing was uneven and spidery, crawling over a scrap of lined paper.

Hallo Mrs Susann. I clean house. I take Franky at home. He Lonely. Mr Joe — he go. I come Tuday. I see you? My Spanish wouldn't have been half as good.

The other note, on the hall table, was written on Basildon blue paper, not Joe's fancy engraved stuff.

Guess you're home now, wifey, if you're reading this. I'm taking a break, a three-week holiday. It seemed like a good idea, as I

450

*haven't been feeling that great. Frankie will
need a good clean-up, the old squawker, and
some chatting-up, as he's been on his own
quite a bit. I may not come back properly,
but will want to see Bella, of course. Not
sure what I'll do: move to the country, near
the sea: bucket and spade — or possibly go
to California: Hollywood and the movies. I'll
send a PC. Joe.'*

A tear plopped onto the paper. I sniffed and
folded the note over and over, tucked it away
carefully in the zip pocket of my handbag. Was it
for the best? I thought of the wretched hour at
the airport, Bella grizzling, with a stab of anger.
He could have let us know. Was Joe ill? Was I
being unfair? A sense of weary shame overtook
me, deep sadness at the utter failure of my life,
shame at the past wild three months.

Bella was at the stair gate and I chased after
her. 'Upstairs we go, angel,' I said. 'Let's get you
changed first, then we'll wrap up warm and go
out for some food for lunch.'

★ ★ ★

I called Joe's agent, who said he'd gone to the
Bahamas — an invitation to stay with friends,
she thought. January work was slow.

A month later I heard his key turning in the
door. He'd come to see Bella, and looking at
him, his tan, I felt any so-called illness was on
hold. And when the glamorous invitations dried
up? My anger was momentary. I knew Joe's

451

moods, knew his depression would always dog him and return. Could I have helped more, done more? It was too late now, Joe had chosen to go it alone.

He played with Bella and asked suspiciously after Frankie. 'Palmira took him home when you'd gone, and her husband, Fernando, wants to keep him now. He's teaching Frankie Spanish! I said I'd have to ask you first.'

Joe shrugged, losing interest.

'I think I must file for divorce, Joe.' He stared at me hard, with cold, hurt eyes. Then he shrugged again and turned away.

The divorce was misery. I had to tell my solicitor about Gil; Joe had to go to a hotel with a woman and be seen by a chambermaid. It was a farce, but it was the law.

★ ★ ★

Dad had another heart attack, there was no treatment and it was unbearable news. He was advised that if he stayed in bed, stopped smoking and ate fat-free foods he could have a few more months, maybe six. My life was crumbling, tumbling. I drove up and down to Dorset. I wanted my father to live. It was heartbreaking and I clung to Mum.

I worked, but had lost every scrap of confidence and felt bruised, scarred and bleeding. I was a free woman by July, yet it left me with a sense of empty nothingness; I felt vulnerable, all too aware, with Bella to support, that modelling was ephemeral and would

452

inevitably give me up in time.

By September, beautiful blond Max Thorsby was in my life, repairing my battered morale, surprising me with lavish gifts, making me feel he was proud of me and pleased to show me off to his friends. They lived in vast houses and ran family estates; Max dealt in antiques and lived in a rambling, slightly gloomy flat in Kensington.

By November we were married. I'd rented out my house and moved in with him a month before. Miss Hadley, who loved babies, had gone — after a fond parting — to be nanny to a newborn boy. Bella was going to a smart little morning playgroup and we'd moved smoothly on to au pairs.

My father was managing, saying he felt fine, so Max and I honeymooned in Portugal for a few days. Max popped out from the hotel one evening; he'd bumped into an old mate, he said, and was going for a jar. He was back at six in the morning. On our honeymoon? Was it hopeless naïvety to have yearned for marital perfection?

A month into our marriage I knew he had lovers, lots and lots of them. Max loved me, too. He never put me down, never stopped spoiling me, and I had the joy of Bella — but I wasn't built to be one of a crowd. What was going to happen? Would I be able to stay the course?

It was hard to stare facts in the face. Rushing into marrying again hadn't been the wisest of moves. My life at twenty-four was stricken, poised for loss and sadness, and it wasn't turning out, for a second time, to be the marital bed of roses of my dreams.

24

Daisy was having dinner with Warren at the Meadow Club and feeling bereft. Susannah had left that evening, and the pangs Daisy had felt, watching Jackson turn the car out of the gates, taking Susannah to the airport, were still with her. She'd stayed on the steps long after the gates had closed.

Susannah had postponed leaving for a couple of days, doing all she could to ensure that the construction work went ahead smoothly and was finished on time. It was important to her, Daisy was in awe of her professionalism, *and* that she'd faced staying on, being so fantastic and normal. Warren had taken off for the city, understandably, which had been a relief to all. They'd got on with the job, she and Susannah, even had some fun and laughs as ever, and been able to make light of what had happened.

Warren had returned in time to say goodbye — he hadn't ducked that — and he'd gently encouraged Daisy to come away from the steps, ushering her indoors. He'd remarked on how stressful and awkward it had been, although Susannah had been very good about it all, hadn't she — on the whole.

What the hell had he meant by 'on the whole'? She'd been phenomenal. Daisy thought of him consulting his watch, saying he'd booked for eight o'clock at the Meadow Club since it was

454

lobster night, and how she'd said lovely, she'd be glad of the hour or so till then as well, as she needed to get sorted. She'd hurried off to her room and cried her eyes out.

Daisy smiled over the table at Warren now, feeling a little better. She knew the form at the Club as they'd been here once before on a Thursday night, the three of them. The lobsters were jumbo-sized and everyone wore ridiculous but necessary white paper bibs. Daisy also knew she was acting a little distantly, casting round the dining room, which was large and routinely appointed, brightly lit, far from romantically atmospheric. A tennis club, however exclusive, wasn't a natural for evenings à deux. Her smile felt a little fixed and she hoped Warren would think she was obsessing about his proposal, the decision she was about to take, not still brooding miserably about Susannah.

It was awful, missing her with such pangs, feeling so defenceless and alone. What made it worse was how dignified Susannah had been. No shrill bitching, no slammed doors — but who knew what had been going on inside? Susannah had come out to Long Island, interested, expectant; she'd only taken the commission because the seeds of an attraction had been sown.

'You okay, darling?' Warren reached for Daisy's hand. 'This is a precious evening, a special occasion, our first night alone together.'

'Not quite alone. It's packed tonight, *tous* Southampton is here — well, the key players, at least,' she added, feeling a bit mean and trying to

455

be more diplomatic. 'And from the sound of things, they made an early start at the bar.' She was glad of the people and noise, in fact, grateful to be able to postpone facing Warren emotionally head on.

People were looking their way. It was hard to believe the word was out about Susannah leaving, but Daisy remembered how Warren had once said that the car only had to turn out of the drive for gossip to spread. She wondered at him, bringing her to the Meadow Club. He must have expected, even wanted to cause curiosity; he was giving her adoring glances in full view, loving being seen together, very happy to share her. Daisy found it embarrassing. She went back to absent smiles and distant gazes round the room.

Lobster night seemed to attract a pretty geriatric crowd. Apart from a few juniors — pampered conventionals who looked too laundered and picked-up-after — and a table of young-middle-aged, the mums with great legs she saw at the Beach Club — the majority of diners were oldsters. They were the Club's mainstays, Warren's mates, and openly staring. They were sure to come by any minute to say hi, and sniff the scent of the gossip.

'Can I ask a favour?' Daisy said, dreading Warren making any painful nudge-nudge, watch-this-space remarks. 'If people come over, you won't, um, say anything?'

He looked surprised, as if the idea that anyone would come over hadn't entered his mind or, which seemed more likely, he'd been planning to say, grinning and just as she feared, that he had

456

Daisy all to himself now.

'Not if you don't want me to, darling, but people will draw their own conclusions, you must see that?' Warren looked chuffed at the thought, though quite sweetly so.

'Perhaps you could simply say that Susannah's had to go home for whatever reason, and I've stayed on to see to a few loose ends? That leaves an aura of mystery,' she suggested guilefully, 'about where we're at.'

Warren gave her a sexy eye. 'I like where we're at,' he said, 'very much.'

Daisy couldn't easily suggest that it was far more face-saving and pride-saving, should she turn him down, if nobody had known much in the first place. She also realised, dismally, that in any event he could give whatever reason he liked — gold-digger flirt, frigid cockteaser, anything. Men could always manage to persuade themselves that black was white . . . and who'd think she wasn't after his money anyway?

Was she? It was undeniably a factor. Yet she liked Warren; he even quite excited her at times. She wasn't shutting her mind to all the longer-term ramifications of marrying him, his advancing old age: the need for thinking time was vital. She hoped Warren would understand and give her space.

She looked past him and her heart sank. Shit, shit, his neighbours, Elmer and Jan Harvey, were coming over. Didn't they see enough of him already? Elmer was tottering, red and blotchy in the face, leaning into his wife, and he was a monotonous droning old creep on a good day.

Daisy assumed another rigid smile that she hoped wouldn't fade too fast.

'What you doin', out on the town with this lovely lady then, old shport? Where the booful Susannah got to? She given you a free pass?' Elmer leered at Daisy and leaned, teetering, to speak to her. 'You watch out, m'dear, couldn't trust this one as far as you could throw 'im.' He held onto his wife, sodden with drink, wobbling like a pillar in an earthquake. Jan was steadying him, looking both prim and wearily indulgent. She was a drab, grey woman, not face-lifted, her natural self, but without the personality to turn that to advantage.

'We've shipped Susannah home,' Warren said cheerfully. 'Her side of things was over. The house is being pulled apart next month, but after Labor Day, so it shouldn't inconvenience you guys any too much.' The Harveys would probably be back in Manhattan by then anyway. 'So I am indeed 'out with this lovely lady'!' Warren gave Elmer an infuriating, yuk-making wink. Daisy felt angry; it was cheap, that wink, unnecessary. And he'd omitted to say that she was just staying on to tie up a few ends. Warren would be pushed to be as jerkish as Elmer, but he'd just had a jolly good stab at it.

Elmer still had his lobster bib on, which was some compensation; he looked like the village idiot in a panto and Daisy had an urge to boo him off stage. He'd shaken free of Jan's wifely hold, but then over-balanced and reached to cling onto Daisy's chair-back, breathing heavily. He was very drunk.

The Harveys were friends of Warren's, as well as neighbours; they met up at the Beach Club and were always in each other's houses. Daisy had made plenty of polite chitchat over the weeks; smiled, suffered the tedium, endured Elmer's pomposity, kept schtum through his preposterous reactionary views, and now she felt on the butt-end of his banality. He must have inherited his money. He was acumen-lite, a bonehead buffoon.

'My good lady wife here . . . ' Elmer shifted his weight, losing the thread as Jan took a firm hold of his elbow.

'Is trying to get you back to your table, old boy,' Warren finished, grinning. 'If you can make it. And I can see our food coming now.'

Elmer craned round, stiff-necked. 'You got the prettiest waitress of this Caribbean lot too, typical that. Cocksure bugger, aren't yah?' Jan got him away.

'The waitresses were all Russian last year,' Warren said, once the girl who had a sunny smile had delivered their fearsome lobsters and departed. 'It's summer work, they live here in dorms.'

'Do I have to wear a bib?' Daisy said, as Warren put his on with a sorry-about-this wry smile.

'Best to, the butter spatters everywhere. And that's the auction dress, isn't it? Pretty. We'll go shopping tomorrow, buy up Carolina Herrera's entire stock!'

He tackled the cardinal-red beast on his plate, cracking claws, looking up now and then with as sunny a smile as the waitress. He'd enjoyed humouring Elmer, enjoyed being at the Meadow Club where he came back to every year. Daisy felt he could have asked her where she'd like to go, even if she wanted to eat out at all, since he'd seen how upset she'd been, saying goodbye to Susannah. It was Martha's night off, yet Daisy loved to cook. It would have relaxed her, and allowed her to surprise him with a culinary star turn. But it was a bit much to expect Warren to have thought of that, she could see.

'Elmer's certainly had a skinful. He won't be up for much tonight!'

'No, I shouldn't think so.' Daisy gave a little giggle, finding it hard to imagine Elmer up for anything much, even on the most sober of nights.

She retreated again, recalling the restaurant Nick and Toni's where she'd gone with Gerald, the auctioneer. It had class food and the place had rocked — no shortage of atmosphere there. Surely Warren could venture beyond Southampton now and then? Dear Gerald with his nose, she would always have a soft spot for him.

He'd found love. As had her own twins' father who'd turned up so unexpectedly from New Zealand with his male lover. That visit had been two surprises in one. Gerald's was a more risk-all relationship, but both had been a case of falling in love with dramatic force. Even Peter, Daisy's second husband, had a new squeeze, according to Simon — a girl with a rich daddy. Daisy felt bitter; it would be quite something if Peter ever made a love-match. He was incapable of genuine, deep feelings, a man with not a jot of love in his soul.

And Warren? He had feelings, he wasn't just a dry old stick, stuck in his golden rut. It was slowly dawning on her that as well as wanting to be seen with her — he a seventy year old, proudly out with a moderately good-looker half his age who wasn't a tart — his choice of the Meadow Club had been as much from a sense of emotional insecurity.

He was treading cautiously, not entirely sure of her, nor probably of his own true feelings. His libido was doing okay now, but what about further down the line? What about when he was as droopy as old Elmer? Did he wonder how much he'd be able to trust her at the Zimmer stage of life — if not before? How much could she trust herself? Suppose she was home to see the boys, would she ever be able to resist seeing Simon as well? Warren was possessive; she could even imagine him resorting to employing a private detective. He'd want to keep tabs on her.

She felt his hand close over hers across the table. 'There's a lot of thinking going on behind those lovely green eyes of yours,' he said. 'Want to share anything? You haven't eaten much, either.'

Daisy looked down at her lobster. 'He's a very big chap, this one. Do you want my claws?' Warren smiled and patted his still lean stomach, shaking his head. 'There is one thing,' Daisy held his eyes. 'I'm worrying a bit about bedrooms,' she confessed, whimsically aware it was half-true. 'I mean, no problem tonight with Martha away seeing her poor son, but I'd be a little sensitive, moving into your room otherwise. Susannah's only just gone, and I need time alone, a bit of private space with such a lot to think through. Giving up my life in England . . . and the boys have another year at university, they'll need me around a while yet. You need to be truly sure as well, Warren love, to think through all the facets of your life and whether I'd really fit in. Shall we, just for the moment, keep separate rooms, ostensibly at least?'

'I couldn't understand more.' Warren squeezed her hand. Did he look ever so slightly relieved? Though any upheaval like sharing a room would be the last thing on his mind if it were a real *coup de foudre*. But it wasn't that. Weren't they past love at first sight anyway, both of them too old? Weren't they more of an age and time of life to rationalize and think about practicalities? Daisy stifled a heavy sigh. She wanted love in her life.

Warren smiled up at the waitress, arriving to clear the plates. 'What desserts have we?'

'Gooey choccy gateau, ices, all the usual,' she said cheerily. 'Any takers?'

'I'm done, couldn't manage another thing,' Daisy said, longing to go.

Warren wanted fruit salad; he worked hard at staying slim.

'Did Elmer inherit his money?' she asked curiously, out of private amusement, yet immediately feeling cross with herself as she realized it made her sound money-obsessed. 'I just can't imagine him as a demon tiger in business, one of the giants.'

'Oh, you're quite wrong there. He didn't

inherit, he grew a vastly successful pharmaceutical company after some genius thinking that turned up a new drug.'

Daisy looked, and felt, suitably impressed. It was salutary. Bad for her confidence, though. She needed to believe in the soundness of her judgement — never more so than now.

$$\star \quad \star \quad \star$$

Daisy slept in Warren's room with Martha not back till noon the next day. She knew the room's staid, masculine décor, its exact dimensions, Willa's effeminate bedroom leading off, every centimetre of the house. She and Susannah had been measuring up for weeks.

She hadn't slept with Warren before, only fucked. He'd asked her to marry him without having seen her early-morning face. Fifty years ago when living together was a rare event it wouldn't have been so surprising. Nowadays he could have asked her to move in with him, seen how they got on. She decided Warren was just very old-fashioned.

The sex wasn't the best, certainly not for her. Warren was excessively passionate, panting out declarations of his love and the wonder of her, but she wasn't responsive, unable to relax, not in an orgasmic frame of mind. The exertion took it out of him as well. He had to recover and was breathless for ages. 'Whew,' he said, turning to her finally, putting his arm round her and pulling her close. 'What are you doing to me! Come and snuggle up.'

463

Daisy rested her head on his hairless chest with just the hint of a sense of giving him his money's worth. 'Did you mind Willa sleeping in the other room?' she asked, mildly curious, massaging his thigh. 'Did she visit you or was it the other way round?'

'It was only early on that I got anywhere near her. Willa was soon pretty disinterested, sour, bitchy, slagging me off in public so there was no question of any visiting! She complained I snored too,' Warren said with plaintive hurt, 'which I don't think I do.'

'Tell you in the morning! You know double doors are going in when the work starts, to make it effectively one room again — you okay with that?'

'I guess.' But he sounded a little dubious.

'Better get some sleep now,' Daisy said, easing out of his hold and settling on her side. She turned back. 'But just one thing, shopping tomorrow: I don't want you buying me loads of amazing presents, certainly not Carolina dresses — not now, not when I'm still thinking things through. Suppose I decided that I couldn't transplant, couldn't make you truly happy . . . I'd feel simply dreadful about it if you'd been wildly extravagant. It would put me in an agonizing spot. You do see?'

Daisy looked at him anxiously, slightly wishing she didn't have to be so virtuous. She'd never been shopping with a man who could buy a jet plane and throw in a designer's entire stock. What would be the joy, though, in wearing an eye-poppingly expensive summer frock, only to

464

sit listening to Elmer Harvey sounding off about dog shit or calling Obama a Communist who wasn't born in the USA.

Warren leaned up to kiss her. 'We're having none of that, we're going shopping. Think of the pleasure it'll give me. And I've never been called extravagant before! When you're rich, people expect you to pick up the tab as a matter of course; no one ever considers repaying hospitality. They think there's no need. They never bother, and they forget all about manners and generosity.'

Daisy wondered about that. People with little money had their pride. And in her extremely brief experience, on the strength of a summer on Long Island, she reckoned the very rich competed over who could be seen to spend the most. Their wealth was a badge of belonging and superiority, a form of gilt-edged snobbery.

Warren was up and dressed when she woke. He sat on the edge of the bed and kissed her forehead. 'You looked so lovely, sleeping. Did I snore?' It really seemed to bug him.

'Only when you were on your back — and not much then,' she said, though she hadn't a clue, hadn't heard a thing. But she wasn't having him think he was faultless.

★ ★ ★

They shopped in Southampton. Warren didn't go as overboard as promised, so Daisy was almost disappointed, but she still returned with two new designer dresses and some stylish jewellery. Strolling up Main Street in her Manolos, her Chloé handbag slung over her arm, wearing one of the arresting necklaces they'd just bought, Daisy was aware of people giving her interested looks. It felt good, she could get used to this . . .

Warren made no secret of how much he enjoyed being seen out with her; he had his arm round her, a broad smile on his face. She absorbed the way he naturally expected and accepted the fawning fuss that shop managers and owners made of him. It didn't bother him; it was routine.

He took her to Sag Harbor in the afternoon. Great for early sundowners, he said — but she had a cup of tea. When they were home, he pottered next door, smirking and saying Elmer must be ready for a reviver or three. Daisy said, if he didn't mind, she'd stay put; she was excited to try on her new clothes and needed to call the boys, see how they were doing. Warren was prompted to ask after them and he showed a new, keener and more solicitous interest. Daisy was happy to talk about them. They'd been playing a lot of tennis, staying with friends whose parents lived in the country; her father had given his grandsons some holiday work too, which had been timely, as they'd been on the scrounge, fresh out of the readies. And now, she said, since the boys had jointly managed to wheedle a bursary out of the university, they were off to Siena for a few days, on a culture kick. They were hardly feeling neglected — there was no question of her being missed.

With Warren out of the house she went to her bedroom and called her sons, who were partying at home to judge from the noises off. God help the state the house would be in. She nagged them about watering her tiny back jungle. She knew the dramatic difference very regular watering made to London gardens: shrubs and climbers shot up with rainforest speed. She was longing to be able to afford a computerised hose system. It would be needed all the more if she were going to branch out and try to build up a new career.

She felt homesick.

The doorbell rang. Martha had returned and went to see to it. Daisy heard Jan Harvey's voice and cursed quietly as she dutifully went to say hi. God, the thought of living with regular, if not daily, visits from Jan . . . She could imagine how soon she'd be making excuses and ruthlessly turning her away.

'I decided to leave them to it,' Jan said, beaming. 'Warren and Elmer love their naughty boys' talks and I thought we could have a nice little gossip.'

'Of course, come and have a drink,' Daisy said, feeling put-upon, intensely fed-up and resistant, and in the wrong pair of shoes, playing host. 'But I'm not up in what's going on,' she forced a smile, 'not at all.'

Listening to Jan's aimless witters she thought feverishly about how to cut short the visit and chipped in at the first chance. 'Um, I'm frightfully sorry, Jan, but I really need to speak to my sons, give them some instructions, and it's midnight back home, you see. Forgive me, but I should do it now. It's been lovely to chat, sweet of you to call.'

Jan seemed immune to the possibility of a brush-off. 'I must just tell you,' she murmured, hushed and confiding, rising reluctantly from her chair, 'that I had a call from Willa this morning. Very curious she was — news does get around!'

It was all she'd come about. Daisy couldn't wait to get her out of the door. Tears were close, but she was too angry to cry. If even Willa could know that quickly ... Warren had been bragging, embellishing, he'd made sure that the world and particularly his ex-wife knew his game. Daisy's pleas and sensitivities had stood for nothing. Where was the love in that? It seemed the final straw, cementing her decision. But hadn't she really known it in her heart all along? Known the very moment Warren popped the question — a rushed, ill-thought-through proposal, if ever there was one, awkward, lacking that quality of hardly needing to be said — that she wouldn't feel able to accept him? Daisy sighed. She'd had a few wobbles, but could never have gone through with it. She wasn't cut out for riches, could never be the third Mrs Warren Lindsay whose financial future was assured.

She texted Susannah. *Decision made! Haven't, as yet, told Warren — that's the tricky bit — and still have to do those last few chase-up calls you wanted before heading home.* It was spelling it out, telling Susannah before doing the deed with Warren, but Daisy needed to: she needed Susannah to shore her up. It would be so easy to

468

weaken and backtrack, decide to bag Warren while the going was good, but it would be another mistake, one she'd regret — more than careless, a disaster.

Would Susannah call? It was her first day home and eleven at night; she'd have gone to bed early, she'd had a tiring overnight flight. And even if she did call, would it be before Warren was back? He'd be keenly curious if he heard her on the phone, not shy to put his ear to the door. Daisy's heart was thudding like a dog's thumping tail, her fists so tightly clenched that her nails — newly and expensively manicured at Warren's insistence that morning while he read a newspaper in the coffee shop — were digging painfully into her palms.

She rose from the edge of the bed, leaving her mobile on the bedside table for watched-pot reasons, and went to the window. Her room looked out over the garden and she couldn't see Warren returning, walking round from next door; it was quite a little constitutional for him, considering the length of the Harveys' drive.

Her mobile shrilled. Daisy spun round and slipped on an Aubusson rug, nearly going crashing as she grabbed the phone. 'Well done,' Susannah said. 'I had great faith, knew you'd get it right. Stay on a few days, finish those last chores and take your time; let Warren down gradually, preparing him all the while — that's my advice for what it's worth. But you'll play all that side of it by instinct, I'm sure.'

'What can I say! You're wonderful, Susannah, I can't thank you enough — even calling when it's so late for you. Nothing's been harder, though. Just as I've felt a lead weight lifting off my heart, just as I've thought of Warren on his Zimmer frame, crotchety and popping pills, some temptation or other rears its head and I slide backwards. I needed so badly to be told it was right. I can't believe you've called and we're talking! But why aren't you asleep anyway? You must be wiped out.'

'I slept this afternoon; I gave into it. The jetlag business gets harder as you get older. It's good to be home, even to April weather.'

'Can I come and see you when I'm back? Could you put up with a visit? Or have you had more than enough of me, given the trouble I've caused?'

'Love you to come. But there's another thing you need to think about, Daisy. That decision you've just taken was good, but it's not all.'

'What do you mean?' Daisy drew in her breath. Susannah's tone had been admonishing, like a mother advising a plump teenager against another sausage — not with a sort of hopeful, cheerful lilt to it like the promise of a productive talk over future careers.

'Simon,' Susannah said. 'Give him up, he's a no-good shit. If ever there was a moment, this is it. He'll hold you back, use you and drag you down. It's time, Daisy. You need to leave space for that Mr Right to walk into your life. It's the only way.'

Daisy was staying silent too long, she knew — and Warren was back, she could hear Martha greeting him, doing the unwitting kindness of

470

alerting her to his return. From Susannah's reaction, Daisy felt, her judgement could be on the mend, however patchy it had been over Elmer and his elusive acumen. But was it?

'I'll have to sleep on the Simon situation,' she said lightly, 'if I'm not going to funk it. One decision a day!'

Did she have the guts to walk away from Simon, she thought, as she ended the call. He'd make it impossibly hard. Also, it wasn't a decision she could take long distance: she had to see if she could still say no when he appeared on her doorstep, when she was put to the test. It was easy to say fine now, but really, however much long, hard thinking she did, only time would tell.

25

'It's good to hear you, Susannah — and that British ringtone! I thought Mr Warren had kidnapped you forever.'

'Are you out somewhere, Charles? Is this a bad time? Sorry to call on the mobile, but the landline wasn't answering and no voicemail. Quite contrary of you, that.'

'People like you can reach me and it saves a long list of tedious calls.'

'People like me? Do you have a stable of lady friends?'

'I wouldn't put you in that category. I was thinking more of family, I'm a bit bogged down with mine right now, in Herefordshire, helping out Rose, my eldest, and here for a week or so yet, I fear. She knew I'd finished the book and she's got problems. I had to come.'

'Isn't Rose the one who farms? Not serious problems, I hope?'

'Not desperately. Her mother-in-law, who's a boozer, has had a bad fall, and Rose's father-in-law is half-blind, so she's helping with the driving and meals. Only problem, the in-laws live in Scotland and I've been hauled in to help out here on the farm while Rose is away; I feed the hens, cats, dogs — who snarl at my Ollie very inhospitably — and mind my sixteen-year-old grand-daughter too, who's hanging loose in the holidays while her father's out rounding up sheep. When did you get back? I wasn't expecting you till mid-August — if at all.'

'Come on, Charles! You knew I was doing up a house for the client, not myself. Warren Lindsay's fine, very friendly, but it was a summer commission, nothing more. And anyway, Daisy was younger.' It helped, knowing her decision, and that was all the honesty Charles was going to get.

'I got in this morning,' I said, 'but slept all afternoon, which is why I'm badgering you now, saying hello at midnight. The job went well. Daisy's fun and works hard; she's stayed on a few days to wind things up' — in more ways than one, I thought — 'but will be home in a week. I'm going to suggest setting up together; she can do all the sloggy stuff and I can put my feet up now and then.'

'You don't need to work. But you're being very big-hearted towards Daisy. I'm impressed.'

Little did he know quite how good to her I was being, but all my wrathful frustration was directed at myself.

'If you're going to carry on, though,' Charles continued, 'it's definitely no bad thing to have her along. I might get more of a look-in too, and I'd like that.'

'Working, which I enjoy, and seeing you aren't mutually exclusive. And anyway, you're up there communing with your house, you can't push it all onto me. When do you leave Rose's? When do we meet? Will you detour to London on your way back up North?'

'East, Norfolk is east. Soon, I hope. She's

473

trying to sort something out for the in-laws. Still, what's another week or two after all these fallow Warren months? I'm in waiting mode. Patiently hanging fire while you fraternized with your Lord of the Long Island.'

'You were finishing a book! You do try it on. Glad you have, by the way — congrats! It's been a long time coming. So if I'm not going to see you for a while I may take off to my house in the South of France. August's not the best, but it's a haven of quiet once I'm there, even so close to Mougins. Cypresses, pines, olives, you'd like it. You have dog-walkers in your life, don't you? You go away; you go to China. Perhaps you'll make it as far as France one of these days. I wouldn't mind getting more of a look-in either.'

'You'll see a fair bit of me soon; I'm working on it. Two weeks? I'll come to the flat?'

'Sounds good. And Charles . . . have you missed me?'

That wasn't cool, said with too much feeling, showing the vulnerability I was fighting, which wasn't part of the deal. We kept it to light banter, Charles and I, it was how we'd lasted so long. All through his wife, who'd led him a dance before popping off, my run of husbands; we'd had some sex in the in-between times, it was a very solid friendship.

'Daily,' Charles said cheerfully. 'I've missed you daily.'

'It's late, I'm keeping you up,' I said briskly, keen to sound back on top. 'I'm sure the cock crows inconsiderately early down on the farm. Remember the Austrian Ambassador, years ago, when we were trying to leave a party? 'You Englishmen are all the same, early to bed and up with zee cock!''

'And you should try to get some sleep after that flight,' Charles said. 'Talk soon.'

I was stupidly close to tears. I'd felt in need of a fond, supportive reunion; it had been a morale-bashing last few days. And two whole weeks — would the mood be as good then as in the first flush of a homecoming? Charles didn't need a clinging oldie, he wanted someone to laugh with, someone positive, a strong-willed entertaining friend.

He saw me in that light now. He'd wanted me to move in with him. He'd pressed the delights of a freezing house in Norfolk — possibly knowing it wasn't for me. True, I could have insulated it and put in a fancy new boiler, but in a way the charm of a house like that was that it hadn't been hacked about with predictable interior designer zeal.

England's east coast was crumbling, falling into the sea, being pushed westward. I didn't want to face the tail end of howling gales whistling over from the Siberian Steppes every time I put my nose out of the door. I wasn't hardy, I wanted convenience stores, my snooty little cat and the London theatre.

I let out a dribble of a tear, couldn't help it, sniffed and climbed into bed. I was aching all over, desperately tired yet restless and awake.

Hadn't I used Charles over the years? I'd always taken him for granted. Charles would cheer me up, Charles would fill in the gaps. I'd been flitting around the sophisticated hotspots, soaking up any appreciation going, obsessed with my career all over again. He understood me, though, and had always seemed to put up with my selfishness and flaws. He hadn't teased me when I'd owned up about Daisy, which a lesser man couldn't have resisted doing. But Charles had that quality. He seldom let his own feelings show, which made it harder to be sensitive to them. The signs of touchy jealousy he'd shown over my summer flirt with Warren were rare.

I wasn't entirely sure what I was so upset about. After all, I'd see Charles before long. Stephanie, my saint of a secretary, had fattened up Posh, my skinny little puss, filled the flat with flowers and kept all the paperwork in order. Everything was hunky-dory and tickety-boo. I had my children and grandchildren to see, a pile of invitations from September onwards, and the prospect of an unwinding week in my own home in the South of France.

Bella was coming with Rory and the girls, my twelve and fifteen-year-old granddaughters, for the second half of the month. It was ideal, a few days on my own and a little time with the family. Strange to think that Bella was nine years older than Daisy — strange, and rather daunting. Not a thought for the wrong end of the day.

* * *

At Nice airport I queued with the August holidaymakers to pick up the hire car. Arriving there never failed to stir potent and moving

476

thoughts of my parents. It was fifty years since the first time, coming with them to the South of France, my father recovering from a heart attack, Matt chasing. I treasured the memory of the happiness those few days gave my parents and queued for the car with a large lump in my throat.

An argument had broken out at the counter, a red-faced father shouting his head off. He'd paid in England, they needn't think they could try that on . . . He elbowed his sighing wife out of the way like a rude man at a theatre bar, while the grumbles behind him grew louder. 'For God's sake, it's only the insurance,' someone yelled. 'Just get on with it!'

We hadn't queued fifty years ago. I'd driven straight off, very cautiously, to St Paul de Vence.

Those few days at the cottage on the hillside, the sunshine, luminous light, distant steeples and silver seas, had brought a quality of peace to what little was left of Dad's life, images for him to hold onto and store away in his soul. He'd lived for a year and a half more, surviving another heart attack, and died at the age of fifty-two, six weeks after I'd married Max. He'd known Bella but not the grandsons to come, Josh and Al. He hadn't known that I'd failed a second time, nor that I'd found true happiness in my third marriage, with Edward.

My mother's dignity at the time of Dad's dying had moved me almost as much as his loss, seeing her sitting stiffly, looking into a private distance, managing to stave off a collapse. She'd had no one with her when he'd had a massive final attack — not the doctor, not me. I couldn't have made it in time and my brother was abroad; she'd had to cope alone. When I arrived and held her hand, she'd said I looked golden, a light in the dark.

We'd grieved, Mum and I, leaned on each other, and then our worlds gradually moved on. Mine had been full, a kaleidoscope of high excitements, troubled lows; hers had been one long struggle, scrimping, teaching, carving out a life with a few local friends. Being there for me.

Now, she was no longer there to turn to, to call daily, to shop for and help with the indignities of old age — to be by her side, mumbling my love for her as she slipped away. It had been a year after Edward had died — more numbing pain, the loss of a mother I loved completely. It was the kind of pain that dulls, but never goes away — it becomes embedded too deep. Clive, my fourth husband, had been gentle elderly support in our short time together, before he too was another loss to grieve.

I reached the head of the queue, collected my car and drove to the house where Michel, the ancient weathered gardener, and his tiny wrinkled wife, were on greeting parade. The garden was thriving in the dry heat: crinum lilies, lime-green fennel, tall spiky cardoons swaying lightly, whose deep blue-mauve thistle-heads, Michel assured me, were edible. A more delicate flavour than their cousin, the artichoke, he said, just pricklier; the French grew them in vegetable patches and wrapped the heads in brown paper.

It was an eighteenth-century stone farmhouse

that Clive had bought years previously. We'd had a happy month there, a sixth of our short marriage, before he'd died and left me all that he owned. I hoped, in another life, he'd forgive me for turning the interior upside down and putting in a feast of mod cons.

Neighbours called. I drank with them and also alone, sipping chilled rosé on the terrace. The evenings were pink-gold: they seemed to have absorbed the daytime brilliance to slant out in concentrated, softer form, long pleats of light across the garden. The heavy scent of pines and cypresses surrounded me in this scene of Mediterranean serenity, distant Alps and the sea. I thought backwards. Of Matt, wondering what had happened to him, whether he'd married, stayed married. Had his elderly Bostonian fan left him the cottage in St Paul de Vence? Was he there now, in his seventies, drinking and reminiscing? The Ferrones had soon lost touch with him. They were long gone, sadly, my mothering Manhattan Mom and kind Walter with his wobbly jowls.

As was Sinatra and poor, defenceless Marilyn Monroe, worshipped by the world and lost to it before she was forty. Jack Kennedy and Bobby, Martin Luther King, all cruelly wiped out in their prime. They'd staked a claim on history at least, and taken steps along the rocky path to progress. We owed them much.

Gil had died recently as well. I'd seen a feature on him in a New York newspaper supplement a year or two back that had paid homage with a spread of his work. I was in two of the

479

photographs, one with Bella, soft-focus, heads touching. The blurb talked of the soft intimacy captured. I had that picture: it was fading fast, framed and hanging over a filing cabinet. Another lump in my throat, a grieving ache, long ago as it was.

Joe had died over a decade ago now, in California. He'd had so many hang-ups, not least his constant need for kicks and the highlife, and his corrosive envy — especially of fellow actors like Peter O'Toole and Terence Stamp, who'd succeeded big-time in films. There was no greater boozer than Peter, yet he'd achieved stardom, while the drink had stunted Joe's life and career. Still, he'd remarried and straddled his crises; he'd got by.

After five days of perfect peace, Bella, Rory and the girls arrived. The house was soon jumping, with noise and giggles, loud CDs, cooking smells, wet towels and slippery foot-prints on tiled floors. We ate out sometimes and I suggested going early to La Colombe d'Or one evening, walking in the medieval village while it was still light.

I hadn't been back for nearly fifty years. The memories were so poignant, but now I felt able to cope. Any shame over Matt had faded to nothingness.

The road up from the coast seemed wider and the land, the sleepy countryside, was a built-up mass of villas, enclaves — a different world. I couldn't even make out the cottage. The fortress village was unchanged, despite the teeming tourists squeezing up the steep stone alleyways.

There was serious art to be had, though; not all the shops were draped in tat. And La Colombe d'Or was as exquisite as I remembered — with its curtaining ivy and nestling Léger mural on the terrace where we ate — the age and beauty of the place. The food was perhaps more consciously gourmet, the paintings — Picasso, Utrillo, Duffy, Miró, Matisse — still all there, part of the furniture, the history. I'd stayed away too long.

★ ★ ★

I flew home after a few precious days with the family, aware that grandmothers could smother, and sons-in-law needed holiday privacy. I wondered about Charles. He'd sent witty texts, mainly about the teenager and the straw-behind-ear boyfriends whom he'd had to shoo away like the hens poking their heads in at the kitchen door. He'd called too, and while not being distant or cool, he'd still left me with a sense of remoteness, as if he had things on his mind, elsewhere thoughts. It was unsettling.

With my new electronic passport, I was away from Heathrow in no time. In the taxi, I turned on my phone and saw that I had an unknown voicemail message.

Susannah dearest, it's Warren. I'm here, staying at Claridges, briefly. I need to talk to you, to see you. I'd heard from your PA that you were due to return from France today. Are you back yet — can I call by? Please say yes — or tell me when is a good time.

481

What on earth had got into Warren?

Daisy was in London, back over a week now. She'd phoned from the States and said the deed was done and that telling Warren hadn't been quite the agony she'd feared. I was intrigued, impatient to hear more. She'd texted me in France, too; apologies for disturbing my holiday, but she was sooo bursting to give me the full lowdown. Could she perhaps come round when I was back home? I knew she had her future on her mind.

I'd have liked to see Daisy before Warren, to be primed and properly filled in, but he'd seemed a bit desperate in that whiny voicemail. Perhaps it was only fair to see him quickly while he was here. He'd implied coming over specially, yet knowing Warren he was sure to be combining it with some business interest; he mapped his life that way. It was a tantalising twist, a call from Warren — the last thing I'd expected. The summer saga not yet quite put to bed, it seemed.

Home by eight o'clock, I unpacked and settled in before phoning Warren. I couldn't face him coming round that night. Charles might even appear.

Warren answered instantly. 'Hello, hello?' He sounded very staccato and on edge.

'I found your voicemail,' I said. 'It was quite a surprise. What's brought you over?'

'You, Susannah. I need to talk, and thought the only thing to do was to take action and grab a plane. Can I take you to dinner?' He sounded really worked up, but too bad. He could wait a few hours; he'd given me enough aggro. I'd felt virtuous even answering his call.

'I'm a bit whacked tonight, Warren, just got in. Let's make it tomorrow.'

'Even just a drink? I'm going spare, alone in the hotel. It's full of tourists in sneakers.'

'Sorry, Warren, not tonight. why don't you give Jimmy Rose a call? I'm sure he'd love a catch-up. You could tell him that, having met me at his drinks party — what is it, nearly three years ago now — I've been out all summer doing your Southampton house. Jimmy's around, busy writing a political exposé, which should scatter a few pigeons over here.'

Warren seemed happier, given something to do and with a time fixed to come by next day. It was mid-week in the middle of August, not a lot happening. Lunch at one of the outdoor cafés in nearby Duke of York Square might be an idea if the weather held. I wanted to keep the meeting local — and short.

I called Daisy in the morning with the news of Warren's odd, unexpected hop-over. 'He's probably come all the way to London to cry on my shoulder about you and ask if he should get in touch. It's a bit of a liberty! I take it you don't want me to pass anything on, and that you're not having second thoughts? He's at Claridges, if you are.'

'God, no. No way! But I'm sure it's not about me anyway. I must tell you — I've held off with Simon so far, stopped him coming round. And he's in Cornwall this week.'

'We'd better have that chat you want soon then, so I can keep stiffening your resolve. No sagging backbones allowed. He'll be more trouble when he's through with family holidays and back at work again, and we can't have him camping on your doorstep, wearing you down. How's Friday morning?'

'It'd be fantastic. I'm terrifically grateful. And perhaps we can share notes about Warren,' she added shyly — as well she might.

* * *

Walking into the living room of my penthouse flat, Warren looked round carefully, cautiously, like someone who has seen too many spy-thrillers. He needed the familiar, to know the parameters of a room, where the doors were. I could imagine him always double-checking the exits on a plane, front and back. The room, the whole flat, was sunny and splendid — hardly a penthouse to him, of course, being only five floors up — but it was new territory.

Warren's eyes had made their circuit. They were back on me now and he seemed unsure whether to smile, even. He was unusually tense.

'Champagne?' I had a bottle of Bollinger in my hands.

'Mineral water, if you don't mind. I'm on a new regime — no alcohol before six. It's hard to stick to, but I hate to gain weight — it's bad for longevity!' His smile was a relief, he was sounding like an American abroad. He gazed out of the window. 'So much green space. London's full of surprises.'

'That's Burton Court,' I said, 'cricket and

tennis and stuff. It's great having it there.'

Warren followed me to the drinks table, standing oppressively close as I poured Perrier over a glassful of ice. I had the same without ice. I handed him his and went with mine to an armchair. He came to the one beside it, leaned over the table between us and held my eyes. I could smell the faint residue of a perfumed soap on his hands.

'I had to come, had to see you. I'd made such an unbelievably dreadful fool of myself over Daisy.' He kept up his gaze. 'I mean, asking her to marry me! I'd felt nothing for her, no more than a typical urge, that stupid sexual itch men have to learn to control.' I raised an eyebrow, wondering when that would be. 'I was blinded, Susannah. I had floaters in my eyes, faulty vision. It was male hubris, kidding myself that I could mould her to my lifestyle. I mean, she'd be decorative, a sweet docile young wife at my side, but not a real mate.'

I felt a need to defend Daisy. The whole point of her was her spark; Simon could subdue it, of course, but only with brute force.

'I'd hardly call Daisy docile!' I said. 'Aren't you rather doing her down?' I stood up, feeling slightly bored. I'd made a fool of myself, too — and didn't need reminding of it. All this was a waste of time: there was nothing more to be said.

'How about a spot of lunch?' I went on. 'It was generous of you to come to explain, but it was only a near-mistake, after all, not one you actually made, or so I gather. I'd put it all behind you now, since I assume none of your friends knew and nobody's any the wiser.' I suspected that Warren had dropped a few broad hints, but he'd cover his back, he could say what he liked about Daisy. And would do, I was sure.

'Do you mind a short walk to one of the local cafés?' I suggested. 'They have outside tables and I thought perhaps a light salad lunch — good for your new regime. I mustn't be too long. Stephanie's just gone on holiday, now that I'm back, and I need to be at my desk.'

Warren looked strangely panicked. I wondered why. He was in a dark suit, a safe, striped tie; dressed for a city meeting, but obviously not in a rush. He'd probably had a business breakfast.

'Susannah,' he leaned forward again, 'I can't talk privately over a café table and I must say what I need to, what I've come to say — even if it makes you justifiably angry. There's no easy way to put this, but it's just that, well, you see . . . ' he drew a breath. 'The full misery of what I've been living with is that I asked the wrong woman.'

He bowed his head. Looking up coyly he said, 'I knew instantly. I felt sick as a dog, out on the ocean with Elmer next day, and it had nothing to do with the swell. I was lousy company for Daisy, the evening you left as well. I took her to the Meadow Club and sat in a stew of gloom, wondering what the hell to do . . . '

It did indeed make me angry. I wasn't in the business of being anyone's second choice, certainly not Warren's. I wasn't that desperate, even at my grand old age. It was a load of baloney anyway. If he'd known that quickly, he'd

486

have done something about it, not left it to Daisy to see her personal light.

Warren studied his neatly clipped nails; he had them manicured weekly. He looked up. 'Would you, Susannah dearest, consider coming out for a couple more weeks — to relax, not to work, of course; no pressure, just as a good friend? It'll be Labor Day in Southampton. Everyone's around, I know they'd all want to see you . . . '

He was newly into pregnant pauses. His eyes were limpid like a pleading child's, begging to be allowed out. He'd broken the back of his homework, presented his *mea culpa* face, made a tentative start at reparation and now wanted the girl next door to come out to play mummies and daddies. Warren was pretty transparent, as I well knew after a couple of months of a non-admitted-to ménage. I felt determined to cling onto a bit of dignity and not let fly; no stroppy, loss-of-face bitching. I'd leave that to his ex-wife.

'That's no go, I'm afraid, Warren. There's no chance of my coming over, not least because of Stephanie's holiday. And while you may have decided you fell the wrong way, that's hardly going to inspire me with any great confidence. It doesn't mean you'd have felt it a right decision if you'd fallen the other way in the first place! You're set in your ways and lifestyle, too, and by the same token, understandably at our age, so am I in mine.

'My life's here in London. We're not in love, after all — which is not to say we're too old, nor that there isn't a fulfilling relationship out there waiting to happen. Yet from one who's made

487

many mistakes in her time, I'd advise you to hold your horses.'

Warren was looking more and more hunted and I eased up a bit. 'I appreciate all you've said, and taking the trouble to make this trip, though perhaps you've managed to combine it with a little business?' He flushed, always so easy to read. 'Anyway, I've got an off-the-wall suggestion for you, if you'd like. Let's go for a bite and I'll try it out on you.'

He took my hand and squeezed it as we started out round Burton Court. 'Friends?'

'Of course. Oh, and how was last night with Jimmy, by the way? All good there?'

Jimmy had called me that morning to thank me warmly; he'd managed to get Warren to buy up quantities of his wine company's top-notch stock.

'Very convivial,' Warren said. 'He's invited himself out to *Great Maples* next summer — to see the transformation, he said, the fruits of Susannah's stay. Tell me this suggestion of yours, though. Don't keep me hanging fire.'

I'd kept up a brisk pace to Duke of York Square and made for the Saatchi Art Gallery's outdoor café. 'It's to do with Willa,' I said, as we sat down at a table. 'She's not out of your system yet, Warren. Anyone else in your life is by way of a passing affair.'

His mouth hung open. He shut it hurriedly, self-consciously, his eyes darting about. He never let go of appearances; 'convention' was his middle name. No one was looking; only shoppers gossiping, a young couple flirting, a bearded loner

488

fixing people with hopeful gazes. An artist? Willing everyone to go into the Gallery and admire his paintings?

Warren was more in control now — wary and on the defensive. 'I don't know what you mean by that, Susannah.' He impatiently waved away a tall thin girl offering bread rolls.

'Hear me out,' I said. 'Keep an open mind. Daisy told me about Willa coming up in a restaurant, you see, and the crumbly old bore she was with. She hasn't found her match, Warren, obviously, and I'm sure she'd be more amenable to an overture from you than you'd think. She wouldn't take you so much for granted, second time round either, having had her bluff called and seen your tough, don't-cross-me-or-else side. You were bitter, sure, but I'd thought when we met that you protested it a little over-much. It seemed more a case of bruised pride — on both sides — than being simply bored and out of love.'

'Wouldn't *your* pride have been bruised, if you'd been constantly belittled and put down?' Warren demanded. He looked insulted, deeply injured and all the more on the defensive.

'But you still care, be honest with yourself. And *you*'d be in command this time round, Warren, and able to call the shots. You can give her a lifestyle she loves . . . I think she'd bite.'

'But the house!' he exclaimed, hit by the thought. 'All your work, the plans, the orders in train; everything would have to be stopped — and the cancellation fees involved! I mean, just imagine!' True to form he was instantly into

489

financial practicalities while not dismissing an approach to Willa out of hand.

'Why cancel the conversion? Go ahead with it, do the work. Don't tell her. Willa needn't see the house till Christmas or next summer anyway. You could say you did it for her as a surprise! She'd see you were far from in a decorative rut, which you've said she complained about, and if she likes to be the centre of attention, allow in the magazines to do features. They'd want to, there'd be a lot of interest.

'Give it some thought,' I said. 'Examine your feelings, and if you do decide to ask her out and see how it goes, take it slowly, won't you? Plan your strategy like a business deal.'

Warren's mouth was open again, he'd forgotten about appearances. He was thinking hard, staring at me as if I was completely off with the fairies — yet probably, I suspected, weighing up the risk-to-gain ratio even as his head was in spinning confusion.

'Are your children and grandchildren home from Europe yet?' I enquired, and he gave an absent nod. 'Why not have them out for Labor Day weekend?' I suggested, mindful of his need for company. 'The work isn't due to start till the Wednesday afterwards. Now can you catch that waitress's eye, do you think? I really mustn't be long.'

★   ★   ★

Daisy breezed in, looking fit for the front row of a fashion show, confident and classy, smelling

490

deliciously of some soft rich decadent perfume. Balenciaga? Warren bounty?

'It's fabulous to see you,' she said, 'and of you to let me come.'

Her arms were dropping off with all the carriers and panniers she was carrying; she'd brought enough home cooking to stock a farmer's market. More of her fresh baked bread, which smelled intoxicating, sexy little cupcakes with a nipple-like glazed raspberry on top, a tub of her scrumptious marmalade ice cream. Tomato chutney, red Thai curry . . .

'I make the curry with chicken thighs,' she said, as we went into the kitchen with it all. 'It's quite tasty. I just thought perhaps you could use a few bits with Stephanie away. Hello, Posh! Doesn't she look well? Silly little puss cat, aren't you?' Daisy bent to muss her fur affectionately. Posh lapped up the fuss, which she seldom did; she was Siamese, it must be the Thai curry.

'You've gone quite mad,' I said. 'There's enough food here for a week! And the smell of that bread . . . Well, let's look at you then. That's some necklace. Great with the shirt; you do get it together, Daisy. The handbag's not so dusty either.'

'Warren insisted on buying up half Southampton. I'd told him not to before I'd made up my mind, how embarrassed about it I felt all round. He was just showing off, wanting to remind me how rich he was. He shopped for himself, too.'

Daisy was trying to tread sensitively while only underlining how conclusively I'd been Second-hand Rose. It blew Warren's cover over being a misery at the Meadow Club; he'd hardly been that, strutting up Southampton's Main Street with the bouncy young Daisy on his arm. I was past caring, all the more fascinated to hear it from her side.

'We've got plenty to talk about,' I said. 'There's a proposition I want to put to you and notes to share about Warren. I'm dying to hear all! Let's have coffee and some of that irresistible bread.'

I ground the beans, which along with the fresh-baked aroma and Daisy's scent produced an orgy of delectable smells. And finding some damson conserve in the back of the cupboard we got stuck in, feet up at the telly end of the kitchen, gorging ourselves silly.

'You look terrific,' Daisy said, in her typically gushy way. 'So rested. The sun's blonded your hair and I adore your stripy trousers, they're so cool. Um, did you see Warren yet? I just wondered what brought him over?'

'It wasn't actually you, Daisy. He started by pouring out the apologies then got round to asking me back out to Long Island — to hold his hand! I resisted telling him what a filthy cheek he had and suggested he was still hooked on his ex-wife, the toughie cow, dangling the idea of him taking up with her again. He was in shock, horror at the thought, but didn't rule it out. He's gone off now, to do profit and loss columns on Willa!' I grinned. 'So tell me how you managed to extricate yourself and turn away your billionaire.'

'It was surprisingly easy,' Daisy said. 'Elmer

Harvey helped, coming staggering up to our dinner table, drunk as a raisin in rum. All the nods and winks when I'd asked him not to, Warren's bragging and swagger as though I were the victim of a takeover; it was too much. It crystallized my decision. And as the week wore on, Warren genuinely seemed to see for himself that he'd been a bit carried away with the imagined pleasures of a dolly bird at his side. He'd muttered about lawyers and premarital contracts too, which hardened my resolve. I'd rather kiss goodbye to all the billions in America than marry on contractual terms. I encouraged him in downside thinking as best I could. Little things like reminding him without actually saying so, how set in his ways he was, that his bedroom wouldn't look quite the same, no more staid orderliness in his life; girls spread themselves, they had a lot of *stuff*.

'He was still so infuriatingly pleased with himself, though, and . . . ' Daisy hesitated, tailing off with a slow-rising blush.

'And? You can't stop there.'

She was in it, stuck, no backtracking, whatever it was, and looked distinctly sheepish.

'Well, this gets a bit personal, Susannah, but you see, I tried on a wheeze . . . He was way out of puff after going at it on the first night, so I decided to have a bit of fun and try to make him see that he wasn't quite the testosterone-tops boyo he thought himself. Men are so sensitive in that area and I reckoned he was twitchy anyway, worrying about being able to keep me in the sexual manner to which I was accustomed. He

493

wouldn't want me to have a second helping elsewhere. So I set about putting him through his paces. I did have a little wobble at one stage — a momentary panic vision of, well, coitus permanently interruptus, if you get what I mean. It does happen! I've read about it.'

I had to smile — although I couldn't help feeling a pang of sympathy for poor Warren, as exhausted, by the sound of it, as a mating male lion keeping at it for days on end. 'It's a new slant on getting his comeuppance,' I said. 'Quite fitting really.'

Daisy giggled. 'Anyway, when I told Warren that, sad and wretched as it was, I knew in my bones my true home was in London, he quickly assured me that he quite understood. He even patted his chest, saying perhaps it was for the best. He had to have a mind to his health these days, the old ticker and all that — the worry of getting old before his time.'

It explained the new longevity regime. The phone had been ringing and we needed to get going. 'More coffee, Daisy? Want to hear my proposition now?'

'Yes, please. I've been a bit shy to ask. It's made me keep wittering on, I'm afraid.'

'I wondered if you'd like to set up together? Partners. I'd bring in the business and you'd do most of the work. I'd like to start doing a little less now. It would be a chance to build up your skills, but it would be full on, not much time for cooking!'

'Never in my wildest dreams . . . ' Daisy was off into a sea of superlatives, eyes shining like the evening star; her enthusiasm was a joy.

'It's hard work, it takes dedication, slog and perseverance — no running home to put on the corset for Simon.'

'No,' she said, 'but I'll be out of the house all day, so he can sit on the doorstep and whistle for it. I feel stronger, Susannah, properly over the beastly divorce now. I had a call from Gerald, the auctioneer, as well, which was cheering. He's coming over in September, wants to take me to the opera, and has a friend he wants me to meet.'

'And there's always my forty-year-old son, Josh, whom I'm dying to see married! We'll get together and sort all the work details very soon, Daisy, but right now I need to hit the phone. And my friend Charles is turning up later, so I want to titivate myself up a bit. Your food cornucopia couldn't come in handier. He can have one of those sexy little cupcakes with his tea.'

26

Charles came out of the lift wheeling a suitcase and carrying a Tesco cardboard holder with six bottles of wine. He usually brought me bundles of home-grown veg with clods of rich Norfolk earth stuck fast, but he'd driven straight from his daughter's farm in Herefordshire and hadn't, it seemed, dug up half her vegetable patch before coming. That was the trouble with garden produce, however same-day fresh, all the scrubbing clean and washing away of little living horrors on lettuces. It was more than a supermarket's life was worth, to leave a grub or mini-snail clinging on, which was compensation of a sort for loss of taste and mass-market uniformity — just about.

'I'd have brought you a tray of eggs as well,' Charles said, kissing me cursorily as I went with him into the kitchen where he took the wine, 'but I called in on my sister in Clapham to park old Ollie while I'm here and she swiped them. They were hand picked-up by me first thing, but probably a bit chicken-shitty for a townie like you.'

'How can you do that to me! I have an absolute passion for new-laid eggs and you could have washed them and shown me you cared. Why didn't you bring Ollie here anyway? I love dogs and Ollie's such a slow old thing now, he'd be no trouble at all.'

'Posh wouldn't have thought so, a hick canine invading her palace. I mean, if you call a cat a ridiculous name like that, she has to live up to it.'

'Cats can adapt. There's the whole of Burton Court too, for walking him — strict rules, but dogs are allowed. I've got my nice shiny electronic pass card and hardly ever use it.'

'Well, you haven't had much time to lately, have you, out summering with Mr Warren?'

I glared at Charles. 'Am I ever going to hear the end of him? And you've done that silly name business to death, too; you're a grown man, for God's sake. He's called Warren Lindsay, Mr Lindsay, whose Lippy Lager went viral with its lips bottle top.'

Charles was looking round the kitchen, hardly giving me his rapt attention; he'd put his six-bottle carrier on the island and seemed to want to tidy it away. 'There's room in the fridge for a couple of the Montrachet, which I love, thanks, and for the red too, Gruaud-Larose, no less. It could go on the racks in my new temperature-controlled wine cabin. I'm making tea, okay? And we've got cupcakes, courtesy of Daisy.'

'How was the meeting with her? Cute little chaps, aren't they, her cakes — one saucy bite.' He polished one off, in two bites, and licked his fingers.

'I suggested setting up together and she was rhapsodic about the idea, euphoric. And so she should be. I'm giving her a great break, but it suits me too — it's the right time. She works hard, just needs a little guidance and won't need much of that for long. So I'll be a lady of more leisure soon, free to go and idle my time in France.'

Charles didn't say, as I'd hoped, that there was always Norfolk. I wouldn't have minded a few spells up there, spring, summer and autumn preferably. 'I'm going next door with this tea,' I said a bit more coolly, picking up the tray.

He took it from me, looking over it with a soft smile. 'You look delicious. Honey gold, how I think of you. And I put that healthy glow down to the South of France entirely — which is my last word on the subject of your American.'

I winced, but it had been sweetly put.

Charles seemed tired, more mentally than showing any particular sign of physical stress. He seldom did. Some men — and women — took on the mantle of their age, stooping needlessly, thinking themselves into slowing up, discussing retirement, their ailments and creakiness with a certain pride. They enjoyed saying how out of date and past it they were; they took autumn to their hearts. Not Charles — he didn't do stooping. People didn't look at him and wonder, is he in his seventies, eighties? He held their attention, made them laugh and respond. He was an initiative-taker, a doer; he even pottered in a positive way, sharing thoughts and making interested observations.

His hair was silver-grey, what was left of it, a bohemian length, curling onto his collar, until he'd absentmindedly allowed some terrible local hairdresser to give it an appallingly vicious cut. His face was more folded than lined; nut-brown eyes, bushy eyebrows that were still dark, and his lips hadn't yet disappeared into his gums. He had a Herefordshire tan to mask any tiredness; I did enjoy him.

'You must be weary,' I said, 'after that long drive and squitty egg-collecting at dawn.' I handed him his tea. 'Dash of milk? Is all well with Rose now, everything sorted?'

'Yep, sure.' He hadn't dismissed the mention of tiredness. I hoped he was okay.

Charles was in the armchair that Warren had sat in a couple of days ago, but he wasn't leaning over the table to me with pleading eyes, wanting his hand held. He was preoccupied, annoyingly deep into some excluding private thought. 'How long have I got you for?' I asked, which made him start and remember I was there.

'I need to talk to you about that actually,' he said, snapping back and giving me his full concentration, 'perhaps over dinner. What's your mood? Chelsea Italian? Somewhere like Wilton's where it's easy to talk? Gastro pub? Just name your place.'

'How about staying home? Who needs the West End — and everywhere round here is just as loud and noisy on a Friday night. It's a gorgeous evening, we could wander up the King's Road and get something for supper. M & S and Waitrose are on my doorstep . . . they have good fish and meat. Daisy brought me some red Thai curry, but it would kill those delicious wines, be a crime to turn them up for Asian beer.' Charles was looking irritatingly indulgent. 'Daisy was bounteous this morning,' I said, 'even threw in a tub of her homemade marmalade ice cream. We could get some raspberries and blueberries to have as well — my locals have it all.'

'The locals up east do, too,' Charles grinned. 'I've been ordering online . . . '

He had another of Daisy's little cakes, another cup of tea, took his case to my bedroom and came back jerking his head bedroomwards. 'Would you rather I put it in the spare? Mustn't make assumptions.'

I stood up and draped my arms round his neck. 'You can give me a kiss and not say the unnecessary. We should go if you're up for this shopping jaunt. It's six o'clock.'

Charles took the tea tray through to the kitchen and I followed, watching as he put the cups in the dishwasher, typically leaving the teapot and the rest. 'Daisy would be thrilled to know you had three of her cupcakes,' I said. 'She thrills easily, though.'

We walked alongside Burton Court, up Smith Street and into the King's Road. Charles was in grimy cream chinos and a blue check shirt; he hadn't cleaned up yet from his long day. He held hands, threading his fingers through mine. His hands were roughened — it was from country living, long-ago days of backpacking and espousing of causes. Then came journalism; marriage, children, a hefty spell in the civil service. Writing biographies was a more recent development. Charles knew a lot of people and a lot of what went on.

Along the King's Road shoppers and office workers struggled to get home, in tired huddles round bus stops. The traffic was nose to tail, the drivers of cars drumming their fingers on the wheel, keen to be off to the country, impatient to be out of town. Charles let go of my hand as groups of Sloaney girls with bare midriffs and puppy-fat thighs pushed past, tourists too, and soigné old ladies dipping their heads like birds. Charles, I felt, must be pining for pure air and a springy lawn under his feet.

We bought crab and fillet steak, well-washed new potatoes, packaged field mushrooms and squeaky-clean baby leeks. I was glad to get in again; it hadn't been quite the balmy evening meander I'd envisaged. Perhaps not such a great idea, London's charms were easily missed on a busy Friday at the end of the working day.

Charles deposited the carrier and stretched, long and lazily, before opening a bottle of the red wine, tasting it, tasting me and leading me by the hand to bed.

'It's been too long,' he said, turning onto his side to face me and stroking my stomach with the back of his hand. 'I've hated the summer, every single day of it. You see, I wasn't at all sure you'd come back. It knocked me, thinking about how it would be, how I'd feel and what it would mean. When one knows someone quite as well as I know you, it becomes unthinkable that you wouldn't be there.'

'Ye of little faith,' I said, feeling a contented completeness, however heavy with guilt. 'Didn't you have a little summer moment or two,' I asked, turning to smile, voicing the thought, 'in the past months?'

'It crossed my mind, but the urge wasn't there

501

— and a dreadful dearth of temptation. No, I put all my energies into finishing the book and a few thises and thats.'

'Such as?'

'Tell you over supper. It's getting late and I should have a shower.'

'You need to, you've been smelling like a wet dog. Was Ollie rolling in hen dung?'

I had a pampering scented soak, dressed in Izabella printed palazzo pants and a silk top, only to go into the kitchen and cover them up with an apron while making mayonnaise. Charles was ahead of me, pouring glasses of Montrachet.

'Staying home was a great idea,' he said. 'Do we have candles, or is that overdoing it?' He nuzzled my ear, slipped a hand under the loose top. 'You weren't smelling of dog or even cat food, and now you're filling the whole kitchen with Chanel, I'm feeling quite light-headed.'

'The candles are second drawer down and there's an array of holders in the walk-in cupboard to choose from. Shall we stay in here? The lights are on dimmers and you can talk to me while I cook the steaks.'

Charles went to put on a CD, Bill Withers, and we sipped our wine in the sitting room with the evening light slanting in, eating too many cashew nuts. 'We'll get fat,' I said, palming another handful.

'You could do with putting on some weight.'

'Can't you say I'm skinny and scraggy if you think it? It's so maddening that. Anyway not every-one agrees: some people write me up as svelte.'

'Then 'some people' must be right.'

'Stoppit! I'll have a complex now, and want the lights out in bed.'

'You're past having complexes, too old for all that.'

'I'm not too old to be sensitive or have complexes, and I resent that — and if you knew me half as well as you say you do, you'd know that already.'

'Can we eat now, in the interests of building you up?'

*   *   *

The table was at the living end of the kitchen, very small, a round, white modern design. Charles had found glass candle-holders, fat white candles, and brought in a bunch of sweet peas from the sitting room. 'Those are out of son Al's North London garden,' I said, coming with the crab and a bowl of mayonnaise. 'He's discovered soil — he'll be bringing me earthy veg soon, like you. You're not opening the other Montrachet? We'll be blotto.'

'It's Friday night. And it's had more time to get properly cold. I was thinking, on the way here,' Charles said, 'slogging down the motorway, about when we first met and what I'd felt. Can you remember where it was, anything at all about it? I'd be impressed — we were at different stages of life.'

'I can remember exactly.' I said, having in fact been very aware of Charles at the time. 'It was soon after I'd married Max, on a weekend at Mondstowe. It was actually only days before my father died. That house was such a vast unforgiving old place; Max had a great childhood there, but even tiptoeing around made the most frightful clatter on the flags and stone stairs. It was quite a family reunion, that weekend, as I recall. Both Max's brothers were there, along with their girlfriends and friends.'

'Yep, I was one of the friends. Not the best of company, since you ruined that weekend. I couldn't take my eyes off you and you were newly married to your effete antique-dealer whom I instantly loathed. I developed a good line in dry cynicism . . .'

' . . . which you've never really lost?' I finished for him. 'Come off it, Charles, I'm not having any of this. You'd had a sumptuous brunette on your arm. I take it she didn't last? She'd looked Brazilian or Italian or something, but sounded very Home Counties. Which of Max's brothers did you know?'

'The elder, Humphrey. I still see him on and off. He keeps going — outlived Max, is still running the estate. We were at school together, we go back that far.'

'You were at school with everyone.'

'Big school.'

'I remember thinking, that weekend,' I said, 'that you were very straight up and must be in the Army. We weren't next to each other at any meal and you never sought me out so I couldn't ask.'

'Can you really recall that much? Have another glass of Montrachet, it seems to work wonders.'

504

I was rather amazed myself, but Charles was the catalyst and it was all coming back. Memories of the years with Edward were always with me, but everything before — save for Bella and a few harrowing dramas with Joe — was more soft-focus, curled at the edges, only coming clearly to mind with a prompt. Now Charles had handed me the sepia photograph album, open at that page.

'I'd have liked to ask about the Army, see if I was right. You could have come to chat that weekend! Remember old Ronnie Wickham, Max's crusty father? He was the most blatant womanizer going, pounced on every girl his sons brought near the place. I'm sure the one you came with was no exception.' I could see her now, displaying her wares, her cleavage elevated to magnetic effect.

'Anyway, Max once told me about a joke trap a gang of their friends had decided to set for his father. A famous redhead model, I won't say who, had bet that he'd come knocking on her door, the old grabber, and said if they hid after lights out behind the heavy curtains in her room, where, with the thick castle walls, there was a window-seat and space to crouch, they'd have their proof. Sure enough, old Ronnie came tap-tapping on the door and crept in, advancing on her in his striped pyjamas — only for some drunk fool to start giggling hysterically, and then they'd all tumbled out, bringing the curtain rail down with them. The redhead was never allowed back, but she'd won her bet.'

'I had heard it before,' Charles grinned, God,

he could be maddening. He'd eaten every morsel of the crab, always had a great appetite and had developed quite a little paunch of late. It was there to stay, I thought; hard to see him sticking to a 'longevity regime' like Warren.

I rose to clear the plates and Charles came over for the red wine. He stuck around while I saw to the veg and steaks, watching me. Not my cooking — he was looking at me, my face in profile, though not for any good reason, I felt, other than being companionable.

'Max could never forgive Humphrey for being born first,' I said, still focused back forty years. 'He had a real chip about the unfairness of primogeniture.'

'I remember he was always short of the readies,' Charles said, 'and trying to touch his big bro for a loan.'

'Yes, it was a problem. Whenever Max made a good sale, a set of Coalport porcelain, some rare tapestry or other, he'd blow it all, buying me furs in the days when people did that, sapphire earrings, treating everyone in sight, trying to double it up on a horse. He was over-generous and loved splashing out, along with a Kennedy-style interest in girls.'

We took the food to the table. Charles tackled his steak, but he wanted to talk — he had that look in his eye. 'You know, the weekend at Mondstowe wasn't the first time I'd seen you,' he said, catching me by surprise. 'I'd got a bit obsessed with you the year before, although only from afar. I hadn't really seen you close up and in your full glory till we met at Mondstowe

— and by then you were in your married bliss.'

'The way Max carried on that weekend I hadn't been feeling entirely blissful. But you've got me all curious. Where and when did you see me? I'm dying to know.'

'It was in New York, in my journalist days when I was on the *Dispatch*. The paper didn't go in for much foreign stuff, not many by-lines, but I wasn't complaining, being based in Washington, and in and out of Manhattan. I saw you in the 21 Club. I was interviewing the New York Mayor, Robert Wagner, over a jammy expense-account dinner, and you were there in a party with Ari Onassis. Wagner had his back to your table, but I had a hard time of it, with you in my sights, trying to ask him salient questions, scribble shorthand and keep looking. Ari Onassis was being full on, making a play for you, and when he stuck his cigar down your throat, laughing, telling you to suck on it, I presume, I'd wanted to get up and punch him all the way to Greece. I had to come a bit clean with Wagner after that, and try to explain why I'd been black-faced and spitting venom right past his ear.'

'My old lover, Gil, stuck his cigar in my mouth once too,' I said, 'but that was an intimacy thing, different, and I'd minded it with Ari.' The thought led me to Matt. 'I don't suppose by any chance, if you were based in Washington — not that you'd probably remember — you came across a guy called Matt Seeley? He was on Pierre Salinger's team.'

'Nope, didn't know him. Another of your

507

lovers — a new one to me?'

'Only very briefly, and not my finest hour; he dropped me and I hadn't seen it coming.'

'Seeley rings a faint bell. I had a friend in Pierre's office and can remember his shock when a key player was killed in a car crash. I think the name was Seeley.'

'Yes, Matt Seeley was Pierre's number two. That's sad, awful; he did love fast cars.' I had a vivid flash of Matt on his knees in his Cannes' hotel bathroom, the heady moment, his expert tongue. It wasn't a fitting image, but memory was indiscriminate, neither conforming nor decorous. I sighed to think of Matt's short life, and felt humble.

'Out of mild curiosity,' I said, bringing my mind back, 'why haven't you ever mentioned seeing me with Ari before?'

'One or other of us was always married, and between times you seemed to think of me as a friend. It was about revealing my feelings, too — something I've never been good at.'

'That's certainly true. Now, how about some cheese? I brought back a Pont l'Evêque from France; it's pretty pongy.' Charles looked delighted. He was such a foodie — I longed to get him to Mougins. Perhaps there'd be a chance of it in the next few weeks. 'I asked how long you can stay. At least through the weekend, I hope.'

'I've been waiting to talk about that. You see, there's a bit of a problem over it.'

I tensed, drawing in my stomach with a sinking sense of dread. Surely Charles wasn't going to say he'd found Mrs Horsey Right and this was a swan-song sweet parting? It would be my just deserts. I'd done it to him in the past, but he couldn't spring it just like that, surely? It would be too cruel. My heart felt at one remove, out in the cold.

'Go on then,' I said, managing a stiff smile.

'I'm a bit stuck for somewhere to stay for a while. You see, I've sold my house.'

I gaped at him. 'Is this for real? You're not serious? Are you moving into somebody else's rambling old frost-box then?'

He smiled. 'No, not that. I just wondered if I could bed down here for a week or two and discuss a few possibilities. My other two kids are holidaying, and staying at my sister's isn't really on.'

'I don't believe this, Charles. You *can't* have sold your house! It was your grandfather's before you — your great love. It had real meaning, and you treasure all that family stuff.'

'Don't talk to me about stuff! I took a mountain of it to Herefordshire, more to my sister's. The other kids won't touch it, they're into white walls and post-minimalism.'

'But why, Charles? I don't understand. You loved that house, every gap under the door, every cobweb, every stained basin and leaking tap.'

'You were never going to come to live there — some of the time maybe, but you're not a natural discusser of mole dispensing and turnip rot. Mothballs work best for moles, I've discovered, by the way, kinder than traps and fumigation. Anyway, when you went off to America and I felt you slipping away again, I knew absolutely how much I didn't want that. I'd felt it before, when you married Edward; that had caused my own marriage, which had been a bit on the rebound anyway because of Max, to go more pear-shaped. So you see, selling the house was in fact an easy decision, I saw how very selfish I'd been, naturally expecting you to come to me . . . '

'And if I hadn't come back, wouldn't you have wished you hadn't sold it?'

Charles rubbed his foot against mine and gave me a sly look. 'Well, it's a lot of upkeep and poor old Ollie's half-blind these days . . . '

'You mean all this lovey talk is codswallop, a load of crap! You're just not getting any younger and finding it all a bit much — and blaming the poor dog! Perhaps we'd better get down to business. You can stay as long as you want — I'd even like it, even after that last little dig — but what about these 'few possibilities' you said you wanted to discuss?'

'Too many for tonight.'

'But like? Come on, give me a taster.'

'Well, there are plenty of permutations. We could set up together, that's top of the list, or have separate pads and visit. If we went for my first option, of course, we'd have a whole new set of decisions to take. Whether you'd want to stay here, or have a similar penthouse, for example, which wouldn't be ideal for me. I'd have to put my name down for an allotment. You could, of course, keep on this flat as an office and *pied à terre*, and we could look for a well-insulated house in the pampered south. Is that enough to keep you going?'

'Just about.'

'I'll give you one more.'

'Oh yes?'

'We could get married.'

'Sorry, no go with that one. I couldn't possibly have a fifth husband. Four's bad enough, five's in the realms of farce. Couldn't we be partners? It's simpler for our children at this stage of life, I think. And I'd get quite a kick out of saying, when people like Ginny and Maynard Wilson invited me to one of their mind-numbingly conventional dinners, that there was my partner now, too. I wouldn't be just a spare, fill-in female any more.'

'That's to suppose I'd want to go to a Wilsons' dinner in the first place,' Charles said. 'And why should you either, when they're such a yawn?'

'To show you off, to laugh about it with you afterwards, to get new business, especially now I've taken Daisy on. It was at the last Wilsons' dinner that I met her, actually. I was between Daisy and a dreadful city caricature called Godfrey Croft. And don't you think a little give and take is called for over invitations, especially from one who's just admitted to male selfishness?'

I'd gone for the ripe smelly cheese; it was reeking between us. Charles leaned over it and held my face. 'You're never going to let me forget that, you're storing it up for credit.' He leaned further across to kiss me, undeterred by the cheese. 'Partner is it, then?' He raised an eyebrow. 'Our children are married, they've seen sense.'

511

'All credit to them. You should have asked me earlier, you missed your chance. I just wish Josh would get married or he'll miss his, too. You know it was the night of the Wilsons' dinner that Warren Lindsay offered me the Long Island commission, and on the very evening of meeting Daisy. Timing is all.'

It hit me then that I had a tricky little conundrum, having promised to go back in October to finish the *Great Maples* job. I had to be professional; it had to be right. There'd be no need to see Warren if I went for the inside of a week, but it was his house; he could turn up any time, and would, I imagined, if he wanted to talk about progress with Willa — or lack of it. Charles, though, wouldn't be over-keen on the idea either way.

I told him the problem while he dug into the cheese, explaining that it had to be me; Daisy wouldn't want to go anyway, I was sure.

'Well, I'm coming too,' Charles said. 'You can tell Mr Lindsay that you've taken me on as a partner, part of the team, and I need to see the work. Perhaps we can have a few days in France before then and a few in New York afterwards, when you've done what you need. Coffee? I'll make it. Then bed. I'm exhausted!'

I smiled to myself, imagining Charles trying out his dry wit on Warren, showing a phony professional interest in décor; they might even become friends. 'How did you manage to sell your house so quickly?' I asked. 'It's not an easy market — or an easy house.'

'With great good luck,' Charles said. 'A young

American blonde, newly married to an English academic, Cambridge-based, came to see it. Quite a girl, she was, usefully rich, and she saw its point, rather remarkably. She was onto her mobile instantly.

''Murray, hon, this is just the *Greatest* with a capital G! You gotta get right on over here, like now, right this minute',' Charles mimicked, in a squeaky, girly American accent. ''You'll love it! It's got shutters and a darling folly, you can hunt 'n' shoot and all that, and I can have a Labrador puppy and take long walks on the beach — and you'll *adore* the garden . . . ' 'So the deal and the deed were done.'

* * *

Charles's luck with his sale was nothing to mine with him. He'd parted with his great love — his secondary love, so it now seemed, since he'd finally revealed some feelings — and I knew at last what I meant to him and he to me. Loving was different from being in love. It was a constant, someone to lean on, which is what we all need — the words of the Bill Withers song on the CD that Charles had played earlier in the evening.

A thought flashed in. I remembered Warren once talking about both of us being in New York at the same time. 'And to think we could have met then,' he'd said. 'What a missed opportunity!' It applied much more poignantly and pertinently to Charles.

I held his eyes. 'Suppose you'd made contact

when you first saw me with Ari all those years ago, Charles — come over, made some excuse and found a way through. You were a journalist, I'm sure you could have cracked it. How would it have been? Saved a lot of time, do you think, or would we have come unstuck?'

'I'd tried to follow through. I dug around the next day, found out all about you, and discovered you were married. It seemed pretty final. I was in my twenties and shy, believe it or not — not a womanizer like Max, ready to chance my arm. And as to how it would have been,' Charles said, 'you'd had plenty of life to get out of your system, let's face it. Better, I think, that we did things upside down, friends first, albeit for all our best years, then lovers, then an old unmarried Derby and Joan. Although,' he added cheerfully, 'I hardly see this as our twilight time, more the start of a new dawn.'

'Trite, but I'm glad you said that. I'd like to think there was a bit of juice in us yet with all we want to see and do.'

I'd had many questions in my head in my twenties. What would happen? Would my future flower beautifully? Or shrivel and end in a whimper? Now, with Charles at my side, it seemed what time I had left was going to be rich and full. I couldn't wait to get on with it.

Acknowledgements

My warmest thanks are due to the many friends who have answered questions and listened patiently while I've reminisced at length about the sixties, and it's been a delight to share memories with Sheran Hornby, Gloria Romanoff and Eileen Ford. Particular thanks, too, to Dorothy Wolfe, whose friendship and supportive help over the years has been invaluable I have leaned on two other friends most especially, over this book, and owe them the greatest debt of gratitude: John Sullivan, without whose support and forensic interest I would have lost much of my nerve, and Eileen Powers, whose colourful inside knowledge of the Hamptons and Long Island has been such a joy. Two wonderful sounding boards.

Huge thanks too, to New York interior designer, Jennifer Powers, and Angelica Kavouni of Cosmetic Solutions in London, both geniuses in their respective fields, for their expert advice so freely given. I would like to thank Charles Villiers for generously bidding at a fundraising event to name a character in this book. He chose the name of a distinguished, but unsung ancestor of his, Charles Palmer, whose fictional recreation I sincerely hope doesn't let the side down.

Heartfelt thanks, as ever, to my editor, Suzanne Baboneau, to whom I owe so much, not least for her warm encouragement and unfailingly all-seeing eye, and my magnificent agent,

Michael Sissons, without whose sagacity and guiding hand I would be adrift. A special thank you, too, to Fiona Petheram at PFD and the terrific team at Simon & Schuster for all their support.

The patience of my family leaves me in awe. I love you all; I am lost in gratitude. You make everything possible.

We do hope that you have enjoyed reading this large print book.

Did you know that all of our titles are available for purchase?

We publish a wide range of high quality large print books including:
Romances, Mysteries, Classics
General Fiction
Non Fiction and Westerns

Special interest titles available in large print are:
The Little Oxford Dictionary
Music Book
Song Book
Hymn Book
Service Book

Also available from us courtesy of Oxford University Press:
Young Readers' Dictionary
(large print edition)
Young Readers' Thesaurus
(large print edition)

For further information or a free brochure, please contact us at:
Ulverscroft Large Print Books Ltd.,
The Green, Bradgate Road, Anstey,
Leicester, LE7 7FU, England.
Tel: (00 44) 0116 236 4325
Fax: (00 44) 0116 234 0205

THE TWO OF US

Andy Jones

Fisher is fizzing with the euphoria of new love — laughing too loud, kissing more enthusiastically than is polite in public. How he met Ivy is academic; you don't ask how the rain began, you simply appreciate the rainbow. The two of them have been an item for less than three weeks — and they just know they are meant to be together. The fact that they know little else about each other is a minor detail ... But over the coming months, in which their lives will change forever, Fisher and Ivy discover that falling in love is one thing, while staying there is an entirely different story ...